J.D. MOYER

THE SKY WOMAN

This is a **FLAME TREE PRESS** book

FLAME TREE PRESS
6 Melbray Mews, London, SW6 3NS, UK
flametreepress.com

Distribution and warehouse:
Baker & Taylor Publisher Services (BTPS)
30 Amberwood Parkway, Ashland, OH 44805
btpubservices.com

Publisher's Note: This is a work of fiction. Names, characters, places, and
incidents are a product of the author's imagination. Locales and public names
are sometimes used for atmospheric purposes. Any resemblance to actual
people, living or dead, or to businesses, companies, events, institutions, or
locales is completely coincidental.

Thanks to the Flame Tree Press team, including:
Taylor Bentley, Frances Bodiam, Federica Ciaravella, Don D'Auria,
Chris Herbert, Matteo Middlemiss, Josie Mitchell, Mike Spender,
Cat Taylor, Maria Tissot, Nick Wells, Gillian Whitaker.

The cover is created by Flame Tree Studio with
thanks to Nik Keevil and Shutterstock.com.
The font families used are Avenir and Bembo.

Flame Tree Press is an imprint of Flame Tree Publishing Ltd
flametreepublishing.com

A copy of the CIP data for this book is available from the British Library
and the Library of Congress.

HB ISBN: 978-1-78758-043-5
PB ISBN: 978-1-78758-041-1
ebook ISBN: 978-1-78758-044-2
Also available in FLAME TREE AUDIO

Printed in the US at Bookmasters, Ashland, Ohio

J.D. MOYER

THE SKY WOMAN

FLAME TREE PRESS
London & New York

For Kia

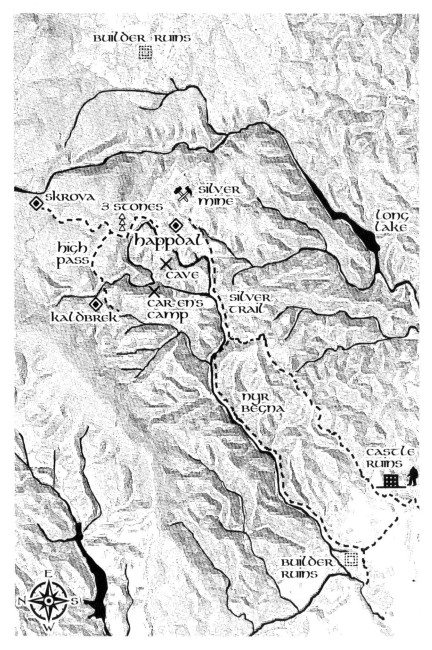

The village of Happdal and the surrounding Five Valleys area

··· Trail — Water

PART ONE
THE GAST

CHAPTER ONE

Trond struck the thin steel rod with his hammer. Each precise blow sent up a fine spray of sparks. Slowly he flattened and shaped the rod into a narrow leaf: an arrowhead. He pretended not to see Elke, his mother, watching him from across the anvil.

A piece of charcoal ricocheted off his forehead. Trond lowered his hammer and sighed.

"Respect your elders, you ungrateful fool!" bellowed Jense. The older smith readied another piece of coal. Trond raised his hands in surrender and gave his attention to his mother.

"I'm making leaf-points for the Burning. Whatever it is you need, can it wait?"

Elke shook her head. Her pale blue eyes rarely blinked. "We need bodkins. Can you make me five by midday?" The bodkins, long needles for piercing and sewing leather, could be made from the same narrow rods Trond was already using. This was not lost on Elke; as usual, she had timed her request well.

"I have twenty more leaves to make before dusk," Trond grumbled. "Urd will need time to make them into arrows."

"Make the bodkins first," Elke said. "Time enough to finish your work." She reached across the anvil and pinched his bearded cheek. "The Red Brother guides your hand. And Jense will help you. Right, Jense?" She turned her gaze to the older smith. Jense did not look up from his work, but grunted in assent. Elke strode to the door and left the smithy as if all were settled.

Trond shook his head. "The day of Bjorn's Burning, and my mother is worried about bodkins."

"Your mother worries for all of us," Jense said. The older smith always defended Elke in her absence, though in her presence he was standoffish. Trond did not understand their relationship, so he simply accepted it. Easier to let some mysteries go unsolved.

Elke had gotten it into her mind that each man and woman in Happdal should be equipped with boiled leather armor, a spear, and a dirk. The steel bodkins were needed for sewing the tough cowhides into armor. Elke was convinced Haakon and his raiders would descend upon Happdal any day. Trond had given up arguing with his mother. It was easier to just work day and night at the forge, growing the village armory to immense proportions.

Trond finished the arrowhead – not his best – and quenched it in a bucket of ice-melt, unleashing a plume of steam. Though the winter snow had mostly thawed, there were still icicles to be gathered in the shadier sections of the riverbank. He listened for the high ping of cracking steel, but heard nothing. This was more of a danger with larger pieces – spearheads and swords – but every silent quench was a good one.

Haakon was a real threat, and his mother was right to insist they fortify their defenses. But the real problem was a shortage of fighting men. He wished Bjorn was not Afflicted, and could help in the defense of Happdal. His uncle had been a formidable warrior before falling ill.

A young woman's voice rang out over the clanging of Jense's hammer. His sister, Katja. "Brother! I hear you are tasked to make bodkins this fine morning." He could barely see her through the steam of the quench. Trond ignored his sister's taunt and grabbed a thin heated rod from the furnace. Katja did not relent. "Maidens will sing of your greatness at the forge, the huge beast of a man who made the sharpest sewing needles in all the Five Valleys!"

Holding the cold end of the rod, Trond placed the glowing tip on the anvil and prepared to strike it. "And will bards write epic poems about Katja Elkesdóttir, the smith's little sister, and her laziness?" He struck the rod with his hammer, hoping the racket would silence her. Trond Ariksson had two siblings. Katja was the youngest – not quite a woman. While everyone in the village was expected to contribute to the *prif* of the village, Katja worked less than most. She got by with charm and beauty. And she was the jarl's daughter. Only Elke dared scold her.

Katja stuck her tongue out at Trond and sidled up to Jense, who lowered his hammer. "Jense, how is my blade coming along? Will it be ready for tonight?" She slipped past his anvil and gave the huge man a tight bear hug. Jense blushed deeply and lowered his eyes.

"Not for a week."

Jense adored Katja, and Trond's sister was taking advantage. She had convinced the elder smith to forge her a godsteel blade. Usually Trond and Jense worked with mudsteel, raw ore quickly melted in the big charcoal oven. Mudsteel was soft and easy to work; after hours of pounding most of the impurities could be driven out with brute force, each spray of sparks purifying the metal. Mudsteel worked well for plows, hammerheads, hinges, kitchen knives, dirks, arrowheads, spearheads, and most every other item produced by the two smiths. But for longer blades, swords and greatswords, mudsteel was not ideal. Even if the ingot was pounded and folded for hours to drive out the impurities, mudsteel was brittle and stiff.

"Make haste!" taunted Katja. "*Haakon* is coming." His sister did not take their mother seriously.

"Out!" Trond bellowed. "Leave, or make yourself useful."

Katja wrapped one of her long braids around Jense's face, lending him a blond mustache. The older smith grumbled and gently batted Katja away. She stumbled back, collided with a heavy wooden beam, and exhaled sharply, clutching her midsection.

"Sorry...I'm sorry!" Jense rushed to Katja and patted her back gingerly. Trond's sister coughed until she regained her breath and color, then grabbed Jense's beard and pulled herself upright.

"Will you never learn your own strength? You nearly broke my back!"

"Forgive me."

Katja released Jense's beard and slapped him on the arm. "No apologies. Just finish my blade. And you, brother – finish those bodkins!" She staggered to the door, coughing. Trond bit his lip until she was gone.

"Forgive me," he teased, wiggling his fingers in the air. Jense scowled and went back to his hammering. It was obvious that the older smith and his sister were fond of each other, but Jense refused to admit it. Trond shrugged and went back to work.

In many ways Trond and Jense were a matching pair. Jense was nearly twice his age (Trond was one and twenty), but both men had dark blond hair, thick red beards, and limbs as massive as oak branches. Trond had been strong for as long as he could recall. When he was little, his father Arik had given him full sacks of grain to carry, or buckets of ice water, while his younger and smaller brother, Esper, carried only a stick, or a hatchet, or nothing at all. "You are built for it, Trond," his father had said. "It's your destiny to heave and ho, like the Red Brother and his hammer. Might as well get used to it."

Trond *was* used to it, after a seven-year apprenticeship with Jense. Now he was a full smith, his back as broad and powerful as his mentor's. His beard was shorter, but his shoulders and forearms were thick and dense with muscle. No man was stronger than Trond. Not Jense, not his father, not even bloodthirsty Haakon.

Using a small hammer, Trond pounded the end of the heated rod until it was as thin as a reed. He clipped it, shaped a sharp point, and used a thin spike to make a tiny hole for the thread on the flat end. Working quickly, he repeated the process four times.

"Deliver those yourself!" yelled Jense from across the forge. "You sweat like a pig – spare me your stench for a few moments. I'll send the leaves to Urd for fletching."

Trond grinned and picked up the still-warm bodkins. He was a full smith and free to do as he pleased, but Jense would never break the habit of giving him orders. "I'll leave you to your own sweet smell, old man!" he yelled back, slamming the massive oaken door on his way out.

The bright light and cold spring air had a bracing effect. Trond stood on the small porch until his eyes adjusted. Nearby, four bellows boys fought with sticks and makeshift shields, while a fifth dutifully manned the bellows handles that fed life into the big furnace inside. A small overhang protected the bellows station from the elements; lately they pumped day and night without pause. When the boy on the bellows tired (Trond was fairly sure the blond tyke's name was Grundar), another would take over.

The other four boys played a fighting game: Haakon's raiders against the brave defenders of Happdal. A pair of dairymaids passed by, yoked side by side, sharing the burden of three brimming milk buckets. One waved to Trond with her free hand. Trond waved back. Her name was Lissa, or was it Kirsten? She blew Trond a kiss and the other maid laughed. He quickly turned away to hide his blush.

Trond grabbed the shoulder of one of the warring boys, buckling the lad's knees. "Take these bodkins to Elke, and I'll let you swing a real sword tonight." The boy looked up with wide eyes. "Quick!" The bellows boy dropped his stick and ran off, leaving only one defender of Happdal. Trond picked up the branch and brandished it at the remaining children. "I am *Haakon*," he bellowed, "and I will flay you alive!" The boys screamed gleefully and sprinted away, spraying flecks of mud back into Trond's face. The blond boy, Grundar, still pumping the bellows handles, scowled at him.

"Do not worry, they will come back. Enjoy the work! Grow those twig arms of yours."

Trond brushed the mud off his beard and headed up the road. Chickens scattered in his path. Trond remembered winters in his childhood when nearly all the animals – even the working ones – had been eaten in the snow months. His father, Arik, had told him stories of horses – proud animals that could be ridden as mounts – but these beasts had all been made into stew long before Trond's time. This most recent winter had been as cold as any, but the jarl had made sure every larder was well-stocked before first snow. Happdal had plenty to eat, and they would feast tonight at Bjorn's Burning.

Trond knocked on the door of a small stone building. A

bent crone opened the door and waved him in. "Is he awake?" Trond asked.

"Yes. You can go in," said Ilsa. The old woman, nearly sixty, was the mother of one of Arik's cousins. Trond's great-aunt was a healer, and a caretaker for the Afflicted.

Trond nodded and bent to pass through a narrow, short hallway. The sickhouse was cramped and hot, and already Trond longed to be outside. He knocked on another door.

"Farbror, may I visit?" He heard a muffled groan, which he took as assent, and entered. The tiny room smelled of herbs and disease.

Bjorn, pale and thin, smiled at him. "My heart rejoices, son-of-my-brother. My night of glory draws near."

"Your Burning will be a great one. This morning I made twenty leaf-points to pierce your flesh, and I will make more before sundown."

"You honor me. But do not let them loose the arrows until you smell me cook!"

Trond laughed. "Rest your mind, Farbror. You are stronger Afflicted than most men in the prime of health. You will not raise a fist until your flesh smells like roasted pig."

"Perhaps you should cut out my tongue, to make sure." Trond's grin faded. Was his uncle serious? Bjorn's eyes unfocused, and he was silent for some time. Finally he looked at Trond imploringly. "Why are we Afflicted? I hope you are spared."

Roughly one in three men, and one in five women, sickened in early adulthood. Trond's father, Arik, was a few years older than Bjorn, and still hale; he would likely be spared. Jense was nearly forty and in the prime of health; he would live to be a graybeard as well. The Afflicted weakened, could not hold down food, and gradually wasted away. The men were Burned to return to the sky, the women Buried to return to the earth.

"I know not, Farbror."

Bjorn's eyes widened. His pale flesh became paler still. He reached out and weakly gripped Trond's hand.

"Nefi, I saw the gast last night."

"You dreamed, Farbror."

Bjorn shook his head with surprising vigor. "I did not dream it. I saw the gast. He wore the body of Henning, and that body had not aged a day. Except for his hair, which was white as snow."

Henning was Elke's grandfather – her morfar – and Trond's great-grandfather. According to village lore, Henning had wielded twin godsteel swords, and was fast enough to cut a man in three before his foe could raise a weapon. The legend told that the gast, an evil forest sprite, had razed Henning's mind and stolen his body. Trond suspected that Henning had merely wandered off with a pretty maiden from one of the Five Valleys, leaving behind a hen-pecking wife and a house full of noisy children.

"A fever dream. The gast is a tale to frighten children."

"The gast is no tale," said Bjorn fiercely. "He steals the best from Happdal every three generations. He took Henning, he took Per Anders. He might take *you*, son-of-my-brother. The gast would look fondly on your brutish frame, and want to wear it as a prize."

"Why would he, if the flesh of my great-grandfather is still young, as you say?"

Bjorn shook his head. "The gast has always stolen from us, and he will not stop. Have Esper watch your back with his night eyes, and keep your pommel warm." Bjorn closed his eyes and released Trond's hand. "I need drink, then rest. I must gather my strength for tonight."

"Do you want spirits? I have a flask."

"No. Only water. Fetch Ilsa."

Trond found Ilsa and passed on Bjorn's request. She nodded and squeezed Trond's arm before shuffling down the hall.

Back in the cramped foyer, he found his father waiting. Trond was a head taller than the village jarl and half again his weight, but Arik carried himself with calm authority. Most men deferred to him naturally. The rest were cut down by Arik's quick tongue.

"How is he?" Arik asked.

"Strong and stubborn, as always," said Trond. "But his mind

is half-gone from fever. He spoke of the gast."

"The forest sprite? I have not heard such talk for many winters."

"He spoke of Elke's grandfather. And of Per Anders."

As boys, Trond and Per Anders had often climbed the High Pass, leaving the valley and exploring the outskirts of the Blood Forest. Sometimes Per Anders had explored alone for days at a time, leaving with a knapsack full of dried meat and returning thin and dirty, full of outlandish tales. But Per Anders had not returned from his last expedition. Seven years had passed – most believed him dead.

"Bjorn rests now," Trond said. "I have more leaves to make. I will see you at the Burning." He gripped forearms with his father and left the sickhouse.

Outside, the streets were clear, but the village was no quieter. Most took their midday meal on their porches, shouting at each other throughout. It was good that the mood was cheerful on the day of Bjorn's Burning, but Trond's own mood was sour. Bjorn's feverish rants had clouded his mind.

He walked to the end of the road, passing hand-plowed fields ready for planting oats and rye. Next was the apiary – a patch of rocky ground dotted with spruce boxes. He watched the bees go to and fro, collecting spring pollen from nearby oak, beech, birch, and pussy willows. Spring honey had a more intense flavor than the flowery summer honey. Ilsa preferred the former for her tonics.

The road opened into a large clearing ringed by stately oaks and tall beeches. A few men put the finishing touches on the scaffold. Children stacked firewood beneath the raised pyre. Long tables and benches were already arranged for the feast.

He hoped Bjorn would find strength and courage tonight, and not regret keeping his tongue.

CHAPTER TWO

More than anything, Car-En longed for a hot shower. The bioskin regulated her body temperature – at least according to her m'eye biostats – but she *felt* chilled, constantly. The sensors also told her she was running a caloric deficit (no wonder she felt cold), but she was sick of the dense, dry nutrient bars. Yesterday, with the hood of her mirror cloak pulled all the way up, she had pilfered a warm loaf of bread from a roadside food cart, and eaten half of it in one sitting. Despite scraping a tooth on a piece of baked-in grit, she'd enjoyed the meal immensely. Adrian wouldn't approve (if he knew), but she'd turned off her advisor's patch for that little escapade. Besides, minor thievery didn't constitute Intervention. It wasn't right, but neither was it altering the course of Happdal history.

Despite the chill, it was all worth it. She felt more alive, doing her first fieldwork on Earth, than she ever had studying or working on the ringstation. Life on the *Stanford* was good, but this was a different world, fascinating and vast and dangerous. The cold and the hunger she could brush off. The only real downside to her field research was the loneliness. She missed Lydia especially. But she had chosen this, to focus on her work, to keep her patches off. It had taken a few days to adjust, hearing her own thoughts so loudly and her friends' voices not at all. But she was progressing in her work, and even though it was a silly notion, it felt as if she was doing what she was *meant* to do.

Car-En crouched behind a thick beech tree and watched the men build the wooden structure. The villagers were preparing for a large gathering or celebration. It would involve fire – obvious from the growing stacks of firewood. There was an archery component as well; earlier a man had shot arrows into a target affixed to the upper part of the structure. So, some kind of fire-arrow ritual, maybe related to the pseudo-Viking identity the people of Happdal seemed to have adopted – despite living more than three hundred kilometers south of where any real Vikings had ever lived.

Nobody knew much about the New Iron Age. Some of Car-En's colleagues preferred the term Late Remnant Age, as there was no evidence of any current mining operations. The Remnant Age proper, two hundred years of scavenging culture and technological descent, had fizzled out over a century earlier. Only a few archaic hunter-gatherer groups, hidden deep in the world's densest jungles, had ridden out the rise and fall of civilization entirely (even now continuing on with their old ways, as if nothing had ever happened).

With the attrition and eventual disappearance of the Survivalist tribes, ringstation anthropologists had assumed that all technologically adapted human lines had gone extinct. That is, until five years earlier, when Penelope Townes had spotted some anomalous activity in a north-western sector of Eurasia. Townes had documented wooden structures, smoke and steam clouds, small plowed fields, and a dozen more indicators of a 'neolithic or higher' level of technology. Further research had turned up three similar communities in the immediate vicinity, as well as tantalizing evidence of two other isolated agricultural settlements in the Mediterranean region.

For years, the ringstation anthropologists observed from their high vantage point. The idea of field research, once rejected for safety and contamination concerns, gained support over time. The right precautions could be taken, and the wealth of knowledge to be gained from up-close observations was too great to pass up. After eighteen months of meticulous planning and training, Car-En Ganzorig was part of the first wave of field researchers. She was the *only* researcher assigned to this area. It had been hard to find volunteers within the department, and many had dropped out during the rigorous training program. But she had stuck it out, always envisioning what it would be like to set foot on the planet where her ancestors had evolved for millions of years.

And now she was here, and the experience was every bit as exhilarating as she had imagined. But she often wondered as to the ultimate *purpose* of the research. Was it merely academic? Or were there practical considerations as well? Ultimately, she supposed, that was up to the Repop Council.

A branch cracked behind her. Car-En turned slowly (the mirror cloak worked better with slow movements) and scanned the area. A man – one of the villagers – was peering in her direction. He was about forty meters away. She froze, issuing a subvocal command to her cloak to match the ambient temperature. Some of the villagers carried wildstrains that enhanced their vision in various ways – including infrared thermal vision.

After a full minute the man looked away and continued walking toward the road. If he stayed on course he would pass no closer than twenty meters. So far, none of the villagers had seen her. The *Stanford*'s Over Council had agreed to a strict Non-Interventionism policy for at least two years. The decision had faced rancorous dissent from several camps, including a few radicals on the Repop Council who were in favor of immediate contact. But more conservative voices had won out. Her orders were to remain completely invisible to the people of Happdal, to avoid interference of any kind.

The villager was young, tall, and slender, with long brown hair that fell to his shoulders. He carried a short, recurved bow, and two dead rabbits hung from his belt. He looked familiar; Car-En had observed him before. She requested facial recognition from her m'eye.

Esper, brother of Trond, son of Arik and Elke. But his genetic analysis was missing; she'd yet to collect a sample.

She liked the look of his face. He had intelligent eyes. Could you really tell if someone was intelligent from their eyes? It was probably a cognitive illusion. If you *liked* a person, you were more likely to perceive them as intelligent. But she decided to believe it anyway, for the moment. Esper had high cheekbones, a long but not overly big nose, and pale blue *intelligent* eyes.

She would have to collect a biosample.

Esper reached the road and greeted a tall, broad man. That

one she recognized right off. It was Trond, Esper's brother. She didn't need to consult her m'eye to remember his stats; Trond was one of the first villagers she had secretly bioanalyzed (using hairs from his beard, collected during a night visit to the smithy). He had a fascinating genome, including myostatin suppression and growth factor wildstrains. The man was built like an ox on steroids. In addition, he had an incredibly robust immune system, and was likely a fast healer. He was also resistant to radiation (as was Car-En, as were all space dwellers; radiation resistance was part of the Standard Edits).

The radiation resistance was interesting and, for Trond, useful. Background levels were abnormally high in and around Happdal. She had gathered that a large number of the villagers sickened and died in middle age, most likely from radiation-induced leukemia or gastrointestinal cancers. Many of the adults had cataracts, indicative of high radiation exposure. Adrian was still trying to pinpoint the source, but the isotope signatures (mostly U-233) were consistent with nuclear power plants used in the late twenty-first century. Her hounds had turned up nothing; the nearest reactors from that era had all been safely decommissioned.

The brothers gripped forearms, a greeting ritual Car-En had previously observed. A minuscule directional microphone adhered to her ear oriented itself in the direction she was looking, feeding the stream to her cochlear implant. Her translator module had nearly mastered the local dialect, a devolved mishmash rooted in various European languages of the Corporate Age. After a few seconds of processing and noise cancellation, the conversation came into focus.

"...eat one of those raw." Trond pointed at the rabbits hanging from Esper's belt. "Instead of a midday meal I've been running errands for Mother. Soon she'll have even the infants wearing boiled leather and carrying knives."

"She'd rather be too cautious than reckless. She fears the Rat," said Esper.

"Haakon? Maybe you and I should make a trip to his valley and return with his head. He's not so tough. I remember wrestling him as a boy during Summer Trade. He was a dirty fighter – a biter. And he had a strong grip. But he was small, and easy to outmaneuver." The bigger man vigorously pantomimed a wrestling match, securing his imaginary foe in a crushing headlock.

"Every man is small compared to you, brother. And how will you remove his head with Trondfist? A hammer does not cut."

"Good point. Perhaps if you hold him down, I can take it off with my tongs."

Esper smiled. "Mother would be pleased. But not Arik."

Trond nodded. "Father is a man of peace. But if we brought Elke the head of Haakon, there would be joy in our house. When Mother is happy, so is Father."

Esper grinned, patting his brother's huge shoulder. "Go back to work. And get some sustenance in you. Perhaps that dairymaid Lissa will let you take a draught from her bucket – I've heard she's fond of you. Maybe you'll work up the courage to kiss her tonight, at the Burning."

"Lissa? Who told you that?"

"Our sister. Who else? She loves gossip as much as swordplay."

Trond laughed and ambled down the road toward the village. Esper lingered, watching the children stack firewood. When he looked in Car-En's direction, carefully scanning the trees, she checked the temperature of her cloak in her m'eye. It was still concealing her body heat.

Quickly, before she could react, Esper drew and nocked an arrow, pulled back the string, and loosed. The arrow thudded deep into a beech trunk a meter to her left. Had he seen her? She startled, but managed to override her body's desire to flee. Her heart pounded against her ribcage.

Esper continued to scan the area with predatory intensity. She was too close; somehow he could sense her presence. She made a mental note to maintain a minimum distance of eighty meters. It might be too far for her microphone to pick up conversations, but she didn't want to be the first academic field casualty in three hundred years. These people were dangerous.

Esper re-slung his bow and headed back toward the village,

leaving the arrow stuck in the tree trunk. She watched him closely, wondering if he would look over his shoulder, but he didn't.

Car-En opened a small med-kit strapped to her thigh and removed a biosampler. With some difficulty (her hands were trembling) she swabbed the notch of the arrow where Esper had touched it with his bare hand. It was a long shot; she was just as likely to get rabbit DNA, or even Trond's. She snapped the sampler closed and it began its analysis automatically. Worth a try.

Keeping her hood up, Car-En started the hike back to her camp, about two kilometers west of Happdal. She crossed the river on a fallen tree, hoping to obscure her tracks. Even after walking for twenty minutes, her heart was still pounding. Her hands and feet were frigid. She considered a small sedative dose from her pharma implant. No, it was better to just tolerate the effects of the adrenaline. Maybe she should *learn* to be scared. Mild sedatives were useful to suppress an adrenergic response before public speaking, or on a hot date. But nearly getting impaled by an arrow? That's what fight or flight was *for*. The thought made her grin, then laugh. The sound of her own voice startled her. She stopped in her tracks. Slowly, she turned in a complete circle, patching in the stream from her ear-mike. She heard birds, insects, and small fauna rustling in the brush. But nothing big, as far as she could tell. Nothing human.

She had hidden her camp almost too well. She wandered in the general vicinity for a few minutes, briefly considering pinging her backpack. She resisted the impulse. She'd been living in the rough for weeks; she should be able to find her own camp without cheating. Calming herself, she looked for the landmarks she had noted earlier: a gray snag, a copse of slender silver birch trees. Her camp was right where she had left it, concealed by a dense thicket of young saplings. As she approached, her backpack de-camouflaged. She pinged her dart rifle, hidden nearby in the brush. Still there, as were her numerous clips of sedative, explosive, and screecher darts. She had overpacked in terms of ammunition, at first intending to hunt. So far she had only eaten nutrient bars and a few handfuls of wild berries (after carefully identifying them in the flora database). And the stolen bread, which she felt guilty about. Maybe she should confess the indiscretion to Adrian, clear her conscience.

Car-En pulled the tent from the backpack and commanded it to unfold, but it stuck halfway, resuming its process only after a sharp tug. Finally the single-occupant tube self-assembled, masking itself to match the green saplings and brown earth. She told her pack to stay camouflaged until instructed otherwise, covering it with some fallen branches for good measure. She crawled into the tent. It didn't do much for warmth – that was the job of the bioskin and her own metabolic implants – but the fabric kept the bugs out. Most importantly, it felt like she was *inside*, at least for the moment.

Something was sticking in her side. She unclasped the sheathed carbonlattice knife from her belt and placed it within reach. It was so light – she'd forgotten about it entirely. Like much of her gear, she hadn't used it at all. Adrian had advised her to look at all the equipment she planned to bring, then leave one item in three behind. She had ignored him and brought everything. Maybe the blade would come in handy.

She closed her eyes, setting an alarm for ninety minutes with her m'eye. One REM cycle and she would awaken refreshed. Trond and Esper's conversation had confirmed her guess that the village celebration was happening tonight. She wanted to observe. Maybe she would even patch in Adrian.

She lay on the cold ground for twenty minutes, struggling to keep her eyes closed. Even with the ear-mike turned off, the unfamiliar forest noises distracted her. She told the tent to increase its opacity. The compact tube darkened.

Finally, she slept.

Her bioskin woke her with an electric tingling on her left side. The proximity sensors. Two days ago, after setting up camp, she'd released two handfuls of what looked very much like black flies. She'd thrown the insect-drones into the air, instructing them to patrol a two-hundred-meter radius. Each one was equipped with a tiny array of sensors, as well as simple evasion algorithms to prevent the local birds from getting indigestion.

The swarm metaprogram was set to ignore all small and non-threatening fauna. But she'd been awakened with some insistence. Something big, and possibly dangerous, was out there: most likely a boar, or possibly a lynx. Or maybe something not in the database.

The visual telemetry was coming into focus, feeding to her m'eye.

Not a boar or a hunting cat, but a man, carrying a sword, creeping toward her. One hundred fifty meters away, closing rapidly.

She whispered a command to her tent: "Unseal." She grabbed her cloak, slithered out, and stood. The electric tingling of her bioskin reoriented and increased in intensity. She squinted in the direction of the threat but could only see a hundred meters or so in the dim light. She switched to heat vision. Still nothing. Her ear-mike was picking up only ambience, even at maximum sensitivity: a thundering breeze and roaring insects. She switched off audio and focused on the images coming in from the swarm.

The low-res stream showed a man with long white hair striding through the trees. In his left hand he held a long, narrow blade. He stopped for a moment, sniffing the air, then redoubled his pace.

What to do? Her heart was racing again. Could this man actually *know* she was there, from such a distance? For a moment, her mind went blank. When she forced herself to think, all she could summon was a vivid image of her own decapitation.

Think, Car-En!

The rifle?

Shooting a villager, even just with sedatives, would not advance the cause of her field research. They'd never let her off the *Stanford* again. She'd have to leave the weapon hidden and hope for the best.

She put on her cloak, activated the climbing spikes on her boots, and modulated the surface of the bioskin to provide more grip. Slowly and deliberately (she couldn't afford a bad fall), she scaled a sturdy birch tree. Perching on a high, slender branch, she pulled up her hood, wrapped her cloak around her legs as best she could, and commanded it to conceal her heat signature. Breathing shallowly, she waited.

Seconds later, she heard his approach. He strode into the camp as if he owned it, immediately zeroing in on her tent. From her perch, she could barely see it in the dusk light, camouflaged as it was.

He drew back his sword and violently slashed at the tube-tent. The silk-like fabric yielded but did not tear. Despite her panicked feeling (or possibly because of it), Car-En had to stifle a laugh. Synthetic silks were practically indestructible.

The man sheathed his sword in one of the long scabbards slung across his back. Car-En now saw there were *two* crossed scabbards: a pair of matching swords. The white-haired man crouched and peered into the open tent. He reached in.

Dammit. Her blade.

Sure enough, his hand emerged holding the carbonlattice knife. He hefted it incredulously, sniffed it. He drew the blade from its sheath and gently tested the edge against his finger. The material was a complex matrix of carbon, silicon, zinc, and titanium, optimized to provide hardness, lightness, and a persistent razor-sharp edge. The man sheathed the weapon and tucked it into his own belt. Car-En winced. *There goes non-contamination. New Iron Age, welcome to twenty-eighth-century materials science.*

He paced a perimeter around her tent. Her pack and rifle were both hidden, but not carefully. If he found and took those, she'd be out of air. What exactly would she do in that case? She'd have to hike back to the mule station, over one hundred fifty kilometers, a journey that had taken weeks on the way in. Subsisting on what, exactly? Wild berries wouldn't cut it, and she couldn't hunt without her rifle. Maybe she could learn to set snares? Or fish?

She'd be *really* out of air. She'd have to call in a rescue party. Mortifying.

The man wasn't digging around in the brush; that was good. He approached her tree. Not good. She tried to stay calm, but her heart refused to co-operate. She ignored the pounding in her chest and concentrated on not hyperventilating. Fainting would be a poor choice.

The man sniffed and looked up. He was looking *right at her.* From his perspective she might look like a gray blob. The mirror cloak worked better in daylight, where it could mimic its background and provide a kind of moving camouflage. In this light, the best it could do was to conceal detail.

His white hair had a silvery sheen. His skin was smooth, and extremely pale, like some kind of subterranean creature. There was something wrong with his face; just beneath his skin she could see a web-like pattern of black threads. Car-En had seen many kinds of body modification among ringstation citizens, both cosmetic and functional, but the veiny threads resembled none of them.

He reached up and leapt, trying to grasp the lowest climbable branch: about four meters up. He jumped shockingly high, but failed to reach it. Next he tried to climb the trunk itself, but his hard leather boots found no traction on the smooth white bark. Pausing in his efforts, he stared up at her, silently, hands hanging loosely at his sides. Using all her powers of concentration, she remained completely still, holding her breath.

Finally, he loped off in the same direction he had come. She watched him on her m'eye, via the dispersed swarm, until he left the security perimeter.

She exhaled and inhaled deeply. That had been much too close. To her surprise, she began to sob uncontrollably. She clutched the trunk of the birch for support, trying to calm down. Each time she got ahold of herself, another wave of emotion overwhelmed her, and she continued to blubber. She considered using a short-term mood stabilizer from her implant, but once again resisted the urge to medicate. She was experiencing a normal emotional response to an extreme incident. Eventually her sobs decreased in intensity and frequency.

Once again, she forced her mind to work. *One step at a time.* What was the next rational action to take? The swarm of sensor drones had given her a false sense of security; in reality, she was completely exposed. She needed new security protocols.

And she needed to get out of this tree and relocate her camp, *right now*. The man might return with an axe, or climbing gear, or a bow. He didn't strike her as the type to be reasoned with. He seemed determined, and malevolent. Perhaps that was an unfair assumption, but she didn't care. She could *die* down here. She wasn't ready to run back to the mule station just yet, but she had to make safety a higher priority.

Keeping the swarm stream open, she climbed down the tree, told her tent to compact itself, and readied her pack. All her gear was optimized for lightness, but the full pack still weighed twenty kilos (down from thirty, at the start of her adventure, when she had stepped off the Orbital Earth Transport Shuttle and for the very first time set foot on her ancestral planet). She directed the swarm to expand the perimeter to five hundred meters (at a lower altitude, to preserve some coverage density), and to stay centered on her at all times. She uncovered the rifle, loaded it with a clip of sedative darts, and repacked the remaining ammunition. Finally, she scanned the ground and picked up a small piece of silvery nutrient bar wrapper. Contamination had already occurred, but she wasn't going to add to the problem. Also, it wasn't nice to litter.

She hefted the pack onto her shoulders, picked up the rifle, took a deep breath, and began to walk.

CHAPTER THREE

As a sign of respect, Trond and Jense (the two strongest men in the village) carried Bjorn on an open litter supported by thick poles. In truth, Bjorn was so frail and light that two children could have lifted him. But Bjorn seemed happy to be carried by his nephew and his good friend.

"Slow down, you fools," said Bjorn cheerfully. "Let me enjoy the night. Are you in such a hurry to see me off? Let me look upon the people of Happdal one last time."

The entire population of the village, several hundred people, lined the road to the clearing. They waved their torches and cheered for Bjorn.

"You are beloved," yelled Trond, twisting his neck so that his uncle could better hear.

Arik, walking next to the litter, grasped his brother's forearm. The jarl's face was stony. Not a word had passed his lips.

"Why so glum, Father?" asked Trond. "A Burning is a happy night." Arik stared ahead as if Trond had not spoken.

"Let your father be somber, Trond," said Bjorn. "He will miss my wise counsel, and he feels the burden of the world on his shoulders."

"I will miss *you*, my brother," said Arik, breaking his silence. "Why must a Burning be happy? What is so happy about sickness and death?"

Bjorn laughed, which turned into a coughing fit. He recovered and spoke in a strong voice. "It is good to choose your own death. Today, we steal from Disease and give to Glory."

Arik grunted. Esper, who had been walking on the other side of Bjorn, darted off into the crowd.

"Where is he going?" asked Jense.

"To have a piss, I think," said Trond, looking for his brother. "His bladder is the size of an acorn."

Through the crowd, Trond caught a glimpse of Esper in the shadows. His brother was kneeling next to a tree, examining the ground. Esper could see just as well at night as during the day. If there was anything to be seen, he would see it. The crowd surged forward and Trond lost sight of his kin.

"Attention," commanded Jense. "We will not dignify your uncle if we drop him like a coal-sack."

"When was the last time I dropped anything, old man?" shouted Trond over his shoulder. "Check that all your toes are there before accusing *me* of clumsiness." Jense had all his toes, but several were crushed and deformed from hammer drops in his youth.

"Back then our boots were soft leather...before your mother learned to harden the toes. Without boiled leather your own toes would not be so pretty."

Trond grinned. He and Jense had had the same conversation many times. But in spite of the jesting and Bjorn's buoyant mood, he felt uneasy. His uncle would die tonight. Yes, he would die with dignity, he would be spared the humiliation of rotting in a bed, but still he would be gone.

Esper, now holding an arrow, fell back in stride with the litter. "Where did that come from?" asked Trond. The arrow had a simple tapered point, the kind Esper preferred for hunting small game. But Esper was not carrying his bow or quiver.

"I pulled it from a tree. I shot it earlier today."

"Target practice?" asked Jense. "I would think you might choose a smaller target. You may practice against the side of the smithy, if you aim has worsened so much."

"Thank you, Jense. I am touched by your concern for my eyesight. But my aim is still true. I shot the arrow to startle game."

"What game?" asked Arik. Trond had not realized his father had been following the conversation.

"Hard to say. A spirit, perhaps."

"The gast," said Bjorn, quietly, from his litter. Only Trond heard him.

"In any case, whatever it was, the arrow was still there. Perhaps it was just a grouse."

"You left it as a test?" asked Trond, confused. Esper only smiled in response (a bit smugly, Trond thought).

They reached the scaffolding. Esper, being the lightest, helped Bjorn ascend the ladder and stand on the platform above the pyre, while Trond stood below and watched. The makeshift structure looked strong enough to support his own considerable weight, but he could not be sure. Atop the platform, Esper helped Bjorn seat himself on a sturdy wooden chair (one of Bjorn's own, taken from his house). Trond grabbed a passing boy by his collar.

"Get *öl* for Bjorn. The largest stein you can carry." The boy, Jansen's youngest son, nodded and ran off.

Trond heard his name called from some distance. His sister, Katja, held a small boy in one arm and waved at him with the other. The child was not hers; Katja had received many proposals but had not yet chosen a husband. Trond could not make out the boy's face in the flickering torchlight. Likely one of their many cousins. Despite the Affliction, Happdal was growing in size. Trond waved back.

Esper climbed down and stood next to Trond. Together they looked up at their uncle. Bjorn seemed small and lonely on the large platform. "Should we tie him to the chair?" asked Trond.

Esper shook his head. "Bjorn is too stubborn. If we try to bind him, he might stab us."

"With what? His finger?"

"With the longknife strapped to his left calf. You did not notice?"

Trond grunted. No detail was lost on Esper. Jansen's son returned with the *öl*. Trond took it and patted his head. The boy grinned and stared at Trond until shooed off.

"I will take it to him," said Trond. Esper raised an eyebrow.

Trond ignored his brother's doubts and carefully scaled the ladder. It creaked and bent, but held. Atop the platform, he handed the bucket-sized stein to his uncle. "Drink deep – it will be your last."

Bjorn took the stein and took a long draught. "Care for your family, nephew. And for Happdal. They look to you."

"They look to Arik."

"Yes, and to you," insisted Bjorn. "May you live to see our people become as numerous as all the stars and rings in the sky."

The older man wiped the *öl* from his beard, and for a moment Trond saw his uncle as he had been: vital and strong.

Trond bid his uncle goodbye and clambered down the ladder, snapping only a single rung on his way down. Esper glared at him.

"You worry too much, brother. Perhaps your love for me makes me seem bigger than I am. In truth, I step as lightly as a newborn calf."

"A bull, more like."

Trond gripped his brother and hugged him hard. They would all miss Bjorn. The Affliction was a terrible curse, but there was nothing to be done about it. It was time to put sadness aside and celebrate Bjorn's life. Trond's heart was filled with love: love for his uncle, for his brother and sister, for his parents, for all the people of Happdal, even for the mountains and the sky. The Three Brothers had made the world well. Life was sometimes short and often hard, but that made sense to Trond. Men and women killed to live, and in the end everyone died. What was important was to love your family and village while you stood on two feet.

"Release me, you stinking bear!" cried Esper, wriggling out of Trond's grasp.

The musicians played their hide-drums and fifes. For the next hour the *öl* flowed as the people of Happdal climbed the ladder and said their goodbyes to Bjorn. Soon the high platform was littered with wildflowers, tankards, and cakes, all illuminated by the bright half-moon.

Trond wandered to the edge of a sparring circle. Katja was accepting challengers. Older boys wielding wooden swords or sticks slashed at her, sometimes two at a time. She laughed and easily parried their blows, whirling a sharpened stick. When she grew bored with an opponent she poked him hard in the belly or leg with her makeshift spear. One by one, the boys squealed in pain and yielded.

"Are you ready to fight a man holding metal? Or do you only fight boys holding wood?" It was Lars who spoke, a hefty brute a few years older than Trond. Underneath his fat, Lars was strong. Even half-drunk he was as formidable with sword, spear, or axe. "I challenge you to first blood. Though I will spare your pretty face." Lars drew his sword and swung it in a wild arc. Everyone near dove for cover, breaking up the circle. Lars staggered toward Katja. Trond's hand touched the hilt of his own sword, but he restrained himself. Katja could care for herself.

"You would fight me with metal while I hold a stick?" answered Katja.

"You may fight me with whatever you wish. Even with the Red Brother's hammer you could not best me."

Katja gazed at Lars thoughtfully, slowly twirling her sharpened stick. Trond knew his sister disliked Lars. She was in good company; most of Happdal knew Lars to be a brute and a bully.

Lars growled and raised his sword. Fast as a marten, Katja lunged forward and whipped the tip of her spear across his face. Even for a sober man the blow would have been hard to block. Lars grunted, touching his cheek. His eyes widened at the sight of fingers stained red. Trond knew – from many boyhood fights – that Lars had a blunted sense of pain. This resulted in both reckless courage and frequent injury.

"First blood," claimed Katja. "Now I wish we had wagered!"

Lars's face darkened. Drunk and enraged, he charged, swinging his heavy blade wildly.

Katja blocked the first blow easily, and the second. With her third parry, Trond heard the wood crack. The fourth blow broke the wooden spear in half and glanced off his sister's shoulder. A slightly different angle would have cleaved her skull in two.

Trond pushed through the crowd, pulling his sword from its scabbard. "Stop this!" he yelled. The combatants ignored him. Katja kicked Lars in the belly, then struck him across the face with the broken shaft. She ducked a wild swing, and from a crouching position shot out her leg toward Lars's knee. Her heel connected with a crunch. He buckled. She finished the fight with a sharp uppercut to his chin. Lars crumpled to the ground.

Katja glared at Trond. "I do not need your protection," she snarled, and stomped off.

Esper patted his shoulder. "You learn slowly, dear brother. Katja loves us, but she will never graciously accept our help. She is too proud."

The crowd dispersed, leaving Lars flat on his back on the trampled dirt. Trond watched for a moment, making sure his chest still rose and fell. "The sight of her own blood might do her good," said Trond, sheathing his blade. "She walks the Earth as if immortal." Esper nodded. There was nothing else to say; both men had long ago given up trying to control their little sister. They could only try to protect her, and risk her disdain.

The music changed, for the Lighting, then stopped. The crowd gathered round the pyre. The archers formed a half-circle twenty paces back. With a nod from Arik, a small boy lit the kindling. Quickly the flames rose. All of Happdal fell silent.

Bjorn stood, holding the back of his chair for support. Orange flames flicked around the edges of the platform. Black smoke seeped up through the cracks. Bjorn pushed the chair aside and rose to his full height. Standing high above them all, obscured by smoke, Trond's uncle looked more god than man.

"All sing for Bjorn!" cried Arik, and they sang the Burning song. It started slow and mournful, but became more joyous as the children and women sang the higher notes of the harmony. Trond sang the same low notes as Arik, while Esper sang the middle line in his clear tenor.

Bjorn did not raise his hand until the platform was largely obscured by thick black smoke. When he did, the archers let loose, and a dozen arrows sank into his frail body. Bjorn fell. Flames engulfed the platform.

Minutes later, as the flames subsided, the music resumed, as did the flow of öl. The people of Happdal continued their feast. Several roasted goats and a whole pig were pulled from the coals, and the sliced meat was served in sourdough trenchers. Trond ate until his belt was tight, and drank öl and mead until the earth tilted beneath his feet. Many crept off in the darkness to find their beds, but Trond sat near the embers of the pyre, sharing stories of Bjorn with his father and his brother and the other men of Happdal. When there was nothing left to say, they sat in silence, staring at the heap of blackened wood and bone.

Just before the sun came up, Elke came to Trond. "Where is Katja?" asked his mother.

CHAPTER FOUR

Car-En crouched in the dark behind a giant beech, fully cloaked, watching the villagers prepare for the ceremony. She zoomed in with her m'eye on the tables laden with food: wheels of cheese, thick loaves of bread, pots of mead. Even in infrared black and white, the food looked delicious.

For additional surveillance, she'd dispatched part of the swarm to observe from the center of the clearing. Splitting the swarm in two – to both observe the ritual and maintain her security perimeter – was less secure, but she didn't want to miss a thing.

She tried to open a patch to Adrian. She wanted her advisor to be there, watching through her eyes; this had all the makings of an important event. She'd record it, but she wanted his help *now*, to advise her and guide her focus. This could be the most significant episode of her field research. She didn't want to mess it up.

No sign of the white-haired man. He was probably a scout or a spy from another village. The most recent observations from the *Stanford* indicated at least three settlements in the general region (a series of valleys in the midst of a large mountain range).

She tried Adrian again, via her m'eye. Some models were implanted into the optic nerve, but hers was external, an interactive display embedded into her films. By focusing her vision on icons within the display – some of which blossomed into menu trees – she could contact the *Stanford*, issue commands to her own implants and bioskin, control the swarm, ping her gear, navigate, dispatch hounds, and much more. The processing and communications unit was a thin, flexible strip secured in the bioskin fabric covering her left thigh. In addition to the optic interface, bioskin sensors near her larynx picked up subvocal commands to her gear.

The patch went through. Adrian's face, semi-transparent, came into view. "Where've you been?" asked Car-En.

"Apologies," said Adrian. "Things are heating up with the election. How's it going down there?"

"A bit of a scare this afternoon, actually. Someone chased me up a tree."

"Were you detected?"

"I don't know. Well, yes, probably. I had my cloak on, but he was looking right at me."

Adrian scowled. He might have asked, *Are you all right?* instead of going right to contamination. But that was Adrian: business first.

"It's important that you don't interact with the villagers at this stage. If you do, we'll have to terminate your project." *Her* project? Wasn't it *their* project?

"I'm not going to. I'm staying hidden. I'm hidden right now. The villagers are about to start some sort of ceremony or celebration."

"Villagers," Adrian muttered, sounding distracted. They had debated, within the department, how to refer to the recently discovered denizens of Earth. *Earthlings* was accurate, but not specific enough. Ringstation citizens were Earthlings too, after all, as were the members of the few surviving hunter-gatherer tribes that persisted deep in the jungles of South America and Southeast Asia. Car-En had argued for *natives*, an ironic, archaic reference to the era of colonialism, but nobody else thought it was funny. They had settled on *villagers*, though nobody really liked the term.

A swarm alert lit up her m'eye. "You should stick around and watch the ceremony," she said. "I'll keep the patch open." She deactivated her vocal output. Adrian, on the *Stanford*, would still be able to see what she saw and hear what she heard. She suppressed the data interface from her m'eye, which was standard practice. Adrian had his own m'eye, and overlaid fields were confusing. Impulsively, she also suppressed the telemetry from the swarm. If Adrian wasn't that interested, she wouldn't share more than was necessary.

She checked the alert from the swarm sensors. Her heart jumped as an image of the white-haired man came into focus. He was on the other side of the clearing. Like her, he was hiding in the trees. In addition to the two swords crossed on his back, he wore her carbonlattice blade on his belt. She watched him for a few minutes. As far as she could tell, he was watching the ceremony preparations, just as she was. She instructed the swarm to alert her if he moved more than two meters.

The torch-ringed clearing was quickly filling up with people. To one side, long tables were stacked high with loaves of bread, roasted meats, and kegs of *öl*. The smell of the food made Car-En's mouth water, and she wondered briefly if her cloak could conceal another theft. She quickly scolded herself out of the idea. She was a scientist, not a thief. Also, Adrian could be watching. He seemed ready – even *eager* – to kill the project. Early on, he'd been one of her most enthusiastic supporters. Officially he was a collaborator, as well as her chief advisor. Should she succeed (whatever that meant – she still wasn't sure), both of their careers would benefit. But his career didn't *need* to benefit; he was already the preeminent anthropologist on the *Stanford*, if not the entire Ringstation Coalition. Lately, his attentions had moved toward politics; he was running for a seat on the Repop Council.

In any case, she wasn't going to give him any ammunition by stealing a pork chop, no matter how good they smelled. And she wasn't going to let him know about the white-haired man, at least not until she figured out who he was. *A silent man with two swords chased me up a tree and stole my carbonlattice knife.* Embarrassing, to say the least, and maybe enough to end her field research and bring her home.

Another alert from her m'eye: the biosampler kit had finished its analysis from Esper's arrow. She brought up the results. *Sample size insufficient.* The sample had included a few skin cells, but not enough DNA to sequence. The mysteries of Esper's genome would have to wait.

What she had discovered so far from genomic analysis of the Happdal villagers was fascinating. Ethnically, they were just as diverse as ringstation citizens, with almost every sample showing heritage from multiple continents. But for the most part they skewed Northern European, and that was how they looked as well. On the *Stanford*, Car-En was used to seeing a plethora of skin tones and facial types, most of them ethnically mixed, many with light brown skin like herself: the full spectrum of human ancestry. The Happdal villagers, on the other hand, all *looked* Caucasian, without exception, though genetic analysis revealed small traces of Asian, Middle-Eastern, and North African ancestry.

Another point of interest: Car-En had so far identified nineteen wildstrains of what had once been commercially trademarked genetic enhancements from the Corporate Age. She had isolated artificial genes related to superhuman strength, rapid healing, pain resistance, high visual acuity, night vision, fast reflexes, enhanced immunity, photographic memory, and accelerated learning. Not all of the wildstrains were expressing, but they were definitely there.

Ringstation citizens had their own style of genetic manipulation, significantly less ambitious than the Übermensch experimentations of the Late Corporate Age. These days most rare disease traits were absent from the gene pool, having been selected out on an embryonic level over the generations. Most couples chose to just procreate naturally; it was simply less hassle than creating a bunch of sex-cell combinations and then having to choose, or building an embryo from scratch. There were screenings, but it was the rare embryo that was terminated for genetic reasons. In terms of human potential, the frequency of 'genius' genes in various categories (mathematical or musical aptitude, learning and memory, athletic ability, extreme sensitivity/empathy) was already so high that any given offspring was bound to get at least a couple. And one was enough, really. Early experiments in maximizing human genetic potential had shown that being too ambitious was counterproductive. Too many 'genius' genes often produced a complicated, neurotic person who amounted to nothing much at all.

The noise level rose. A parade or procession was entering the clearing. Car-En sent part of the swarm toward the commotion to get a bird's-eye view. Trond and Jense, the two towering smiths, were carrying a frail, middle-aged man on a crudely made stretcher. When they reached the clearing, Esper helped the older man ascend the scaffolding. The guest of honor. As far as Car-En knew, Arik (Trond's father) was the village chieftain; nobody else in the village held any particular rank. Maybe it was the older man's birthday.

An alert: the white-haired man was moving. She selected an infrared feed from the insect-drone nearest to him, watched as he crept along the tree line. He moved about ten meters, crouched behind an old beech, and stayed there. Spying from his own vantage point.

Musicians took up their instruments. For the next hour the people of Happdal sang, drank, and feasted. Car-En monitored the white-haired man on the opposite side of the clearing, but he didn't move. The villagers brought food, drink, and gifts to the older man on the platform, spoke with him at length. As the level of drunkenness increased, several fights broke out. Most were playful in nature, competitive jousts more than actual combat, but one in particular attracted a crowd and much yelling. Car-En had a poor view of the commotion. She sent a few drones above the fray to get a better angle.

A young blond woman was fending off a huge, drunken man. He swung at her with a heavy steel blade; she parried his blows with a makeshift staff. The stick broke, the girl yelled in pain as the sword connected with her shoulder. Car-En recognized her: Katja, Trond and Esper's younger sister.

Katja, more angry than injured, incapacitated her opponent with a series of quick, deft attacks. She stormed off, leaving her vanquished foe unconscious. The crowd dissipated, leaving the loser lying in the dirt, flat on his back. Car-En watched the man for a full two minutes. His temperature remained stable. Unconscious, but alive.

Her m'eye interrupted her observations; the white-haired man was on the move again. She tracked him, via the drones, as he crept along the circumference of the clearing. Once again he stopped and watched. Was he watching someone in particular? She surveyed his field of vision with a few of her drones, looking for anyone familiar. She saw Katja, sitting at one of the long tables, eating a piece of meat with her hands. Juices from the roasted flesh ran down her chin. As far as Car-En could tell, Katja was eating alone.

The music stopped. Villagers gathered around the wooden structure in anticipation. Her m'eye registered the heat before she saw the fire. Her stomach turned. The man on the scaffolding....

She pinged Adrian. "Are you getting this?"

"I've been watching the whole time."

"They're going to burn him alive. Should I...." She didn't finish the question, and Adrian said nothing in the ensuing silence. "He's sick," she finished lamely.

"It had occurred to me this might be a euthanasia ritual."

The flames rose. The villagers were singing. The emotional tenor of the song was inconsistent, vacillating between mournful and celebratory. At times the men and women sang in unison, in other sections their parts diverged into haunting harmonies.

"You could have mentioned that," she said.

"I wasn't sure. You know, I've been looking at your genetic analysis. I have a theory as to the cultural origins of this group. It's just speculation at this point – I'll need you to gather more data."

She couldn't concentrate on Adrian's voice. The man was standing up on the platform, surrounded by orange and yellow flames. The pain – it must be unbearable. Yet he seemed calm. Suddenly his hand shot up – a signal. Seconds later, a hail of arrows pierced his body, felling him.

Something shifted inside of Car-En. She didn't know the man on the platform, but he was obviously beloved by those she *did* know: Esper, Trond, Katja, their father Arik. At least she *felt* as if she knew them, in a unilateral sort of way. They might not be friends, but they were more than subjects. She cared for these people.

"Did you...." said Car-En weakly. Adrian had stopped talking, at least. Of course he had seen. She sat down heavily, turning off the feed. She would complete a detailed report later, after she'd had a chance to reflect. Adrian might complain about being cut off, but she needed a moment. She was still recording everything. He could watch later. It wasn't as if he needed to see everything in real time. Why would he, considering it was against his philosophy to Intervene?

All she could see from her seated position was a thick plume of black smoke rising from the burning platform. She smelled roasted meat, but now she couldn't be sure of the source. Her appetite was gone.

Once again, the white-haired spy was moving. He was entering the clearing.

Most of the villagers were clustered around the remains of the platform, now a smoking inferno. The white-haired man was making a beeline toward the food tables. She almost laughed. Was his plan simply to steal food, as she'd been tempted to?

She had a direct line of sight; she could now see him without the assistance of the drones. He crept past the food tables. Katja stood nearby, her arms folded across her chest, watching the blaze from afar. The white-haired man sneaked up behind her.

Without thinking, Car-En cried out. "Watch out!" Katja looked in her direction, not seeing her (she was still fully cloaked), and not understanding her either (her translator was input-only, and did nothing to modify her voice).

The white-haired man pressed his palm against the side of Katja's neck. The girl turned, grabbed his wrist, and stared at him defiantly. Seconds later, she slumped into his arms. In one powerful motion the man slung Katja's limp body over his shoulders, like a hunting kill, and strode swiftly toward the tree line.

Car-En followed them from what she hoped was a safe distance, instructing the swarm to do the same. She kept the pair just in sight, relying on the drones to direct her when she lost visual contact. Several times the drone count in her m'eye ticked down; she was losing a few to mechanical failure (or maybe something was taking them out) but she still had enough for the job. The white-haired man walked quickly; Car-En was soon perspiring from exertion. The bioskin absorbed and recycled the moisture for the most part, but the sweat felt cool on her forehead.

They were heading south, higher into the mountains. From her m'eye she dispatched a hound to gather information on the surrounding area. Seconds later, after accessing the databases on the *Stanford*, the hound reported back. The mountain range had been called the Harz during Late Inhabitation, within an area known as New Saxony. Before the era of nation states, inhabitants had included Iron Age Germanic tribes; before that a number of neolithic pottery cultures; earlier still various Neanderthal culture groups had called the area home. The hound was predictably thorough, offering to display a long-view inhabitation chart. She brought up the chart in her m'eye.[1]

It was notable that the hound had tentatively classified the Happdal group as Phase 1 Repop. She wondered who in the anthropology department had made that classification. Definitely not Adrian. His vision for Repop (which was clearly articulated in his election platform) was orderly, slow, highly organized, and definitely did not include a raggedy bunch of neo-Vikings most likely descended from tribes of Germanic Survivalists (harboring unknown wildstrains and who-knows-what unclassified mutations).

She cleared the anthropological timeline – interesting, but not relevant – and asked for a detailed topographical map. She'd slowed down, and the white-haired man – a bright blue dot on her display – was now about five hundred meters ahead, veering west.

Car-En forced her pace. Gradually, the thick brown beech trees gave way to more sparsely spaced silver birch. The white bark shone in the early twilight; it was nearly dawn. She entered a wide clearing filled with high grass and fragrant lavender; the pale purple flowers took on an indigo cast in the dim light. She hadn't slept since her brief nap at her camp, but felt wide awake.

She crossed the clearing cautiously, though the display indicated they were still far ahead, out of visual range. What was she doing, tracking this man? It wasn't Intervention, at least not yet, but certainly Adrian wouldn't approve. Compulsively, she double-checked her feeds to the *Stanford*. They were still deactivated.

A warning from her bioskin: background radiation levels had ticked upward. Whatever the source of Happdal's radiation poisoning, she was getting closer to it. With her genetic resistance and limited exposure, she was still in the safe zone, but the thought of the steady, cumulative damage made her uneasy.

At the far end of the clearing she reached a dirt trail running east–west. She followed it west, tracking the blue dot in her display. She kept her distance, staying at least one hundred meters back. The challenge was to keep up. The white-haired man, despite his heavy load, was increasing his pace. Car-En bit her lip and walked faster, ignoring the discomfort of the pack straps cutting into her shoulders. Even the rifle, constructed of ultralight materials and weighing less than two kilos, felt heavy in her hands. She was losing ground. Unless she used a stim she wouldn't have the strength to catch up.

The blue dot on her display stopped, about one hundred fifty meters ahead. She brought up a visual from the swarm drones. The white-haired man was sitting, his back against a tree. Katja lay supine nearby, absolutely still. Her body was still giving off heat and there were no visible injuries. Car-En was relieved to see that the blond warrior was still fully clothed; whatever the white-haired man's interest in her, it didn't appear to be sexual. At least not yet. Kidnapping for ransom, maybe?

She commandeered a single drone and sent it closer to Katja, trying to get a close visual on her neck where the white-haired man had touched her. Contact poison? She dispatched a hound to search for compounds that might be extracted from nearby fauna or flora, poisons that could quickly induce unconsciousness. Almost instantaneously the hound returned a negative result.

The drone display blacked out. *Crap.* She switched to a composite 3D display from other nearby insect-drones. The white-haired man was holding a closed fist near his face, peering at a narrow crack between his fingers. She switched back to the single drone feed. A single gray-blue eye stared back at her.

She killed the drone, switched back to the overhead view, and watched the man slowly open his fist to reveal what she hoped looked like a dead horsefly. He inspected the small insectile machine, lifting it up by a single wing and sniffing it. The drones were fabricated from a chitinous material; they were synthetic but appeared organic. But she couldn't account for odor; she had never thought to smell one.

The man closed his fist, crushing the drone, and shook his hand clean.

Car-En stopped in her tracks, fending off a wave of fatigue. What was she getting herself into? She should contact Adrian and ask for advice. Even as the thought occurred to her, she knew she wouldn't follow through. Already she had gone too far. Explaining her predicament at this point would bring her field research to a quick and decisive end.

She pulled her long hood forward, turning off the m'eye displays entirely. She wanted to rely on her physical senses, and there was now enough light to see without infrared enhancement. As she neared the spot where she had last seen the white-haired man, she slowed her pace, stepping more carefully. With her cloaking maximized, she would appear merely as a ripple of light moving through the trees. Moving slowly, she noticed the early morning sounds of the forest: singing birds and, in the distance, running water.

She stopped when she saw them, thirty meters ahead. The man was crouching over Katja, his face close to hers, silently retching. His white hair hung down over her face, partially obscuring Car-En's view. As far as she could tell, he was dry-heaving. Katja still appeared to be unconscious.

Car-En crept closer, fascinated. A string of dark blood dripped from the white-haired man's mouth onto the girl's pale cheek. His abdomen contracted violently. He gripped her jaw and pulled her mouth open. A small, black, oblong object emerged from his mouth and fell into hers. He slammed her jaw shut and massaged her throat, forcing the object down her gullet. Katja convulsed, choking.

Terrified, Car-En leveled the rifle, then immediately lowered it. The sedative might take too long to kick in. She had to force herself out of her paralysis, to do *something*. That, or regret doing nothing for the rest of her life. *Move now, think later.* She dropped the rifle and launched herself from her hiding place in a flat-out sprint. She closed the gap in seconds, greeting the white-haired man, who was sitting back on his haunches, with a flying kick to the face. His head snapped back and he collapsed.

She landed, stumbled briefly, and recovered into a low fighting stance. She wasn't a martial arts expert, but she'd taken the mandatory self-defense classes required for fieldwork, and a few beyond that. She was ready to fight.

But the white-haired man lay motionless on his side, eyes closed, apparently out cold. She had already won.

Gingerly, she placed the ball of her foot against his shoulder and rolled the man onto his back. His chin was smeared with blood. A smear of dirt on his forehead marked where her foot had connected. The dark, vein-like web she had noticed earlier stood out beneath his pale, translucent skin.

Katja, after a brief coughing fit, once again lay motionless. Keeping the white-haired man in her field of vision, Car-En knelt next to the girl, feeling her neck for a pulse. Slow, but steady. A little color had returned to her cheeks.

Car-En looked back at the white-haired man, switching to heat vision. His temperature was dropping steadily, with no visible respiration. Dying, if not already dead. She didn't care. She hated him.

She stood and slowly retraced her steps along the trail, trying to think. First things first: she instructed her implant to administer a mild sedative; her hands were trembling violently from the adrenaline coursing through her system. She sat on a fallen tree trunk, taking in her surroundings. The east–west trail through the wilderness looked well-used. She wondered by whom.

In her m'eye, she reviewed the fight in slow motion. The white-haired man had been sitting upright *before* she'd attacked. In the recording, blood dripped down his chin, his eyes looked unfocused. He hadn't seen her coming, even as she'd barreled through the brush like a wild boar.

She watched her foot connect with his forehead. A solid hit, but it hadn't knocked him out. *He'd already been unconscious.*

The black egg-thing – what the hell was that? And what was she going to do now?

She hadn't thought it through; she'd just reacted. She'd been sure the white-haired man had been trying to *kill* Katja. That hadn't been the case. The young woman was unconscious but very much alive.

Her implant sedative was kicking in, maybe a little too fast. She was deeply exhausted, coming down hard. She could give herself a stim, but she desperately needed rest. And she *should* rest; the immediate danger was gone. While she could still think clearly, she instructed the swarm to maintain a tight perimeter, to wake her if anything entered the safety zone. She didn't trust the m'eye display to wake her; she gave her kit permission to wake her chemically if necessary. Struggling to stay conscious, she shrugged off her pack and lay down next to Katja. Using her cloak as a blanket, she covered both of them, pressing close. The girl smelled like smoke and sweat. The ground was mossy and spongy, slowly heating in the morning sun. For the first time in weeks, Car-En felt warm.

★   ★   ★

The girl was gone when Car-En woke. She sat up slowly, squinting in the bright daylight. She was stiff and sore. Her foot ached from where she had kicked the white-haired man. His lifeless body still lay there, a few meters away. His twin swords, including the scabbards and belts, were gone.

Stupidly, she now realised, she had told the swarm to wake her if anyone *entered* the perimeter. She hadn't given any instructions for if someone *left*. From the swarm's recordings she saw that the girl had taken the trail east, away from Happdal, and had a two-hour head start.

Her m'eye blinked with alerts. Adrian had been trying to get hold of her for several hours – he was still trying. She opened an audio-only patch.

"Where are you?" he asked crossly – and unnecessarily. He knew exactly where she was; she wasn't masking her coordinates.

"There was an abduction. I followed the kidnapper." She didn't have the energy to lie. Adrian would find out everything anyway. He always did.

The patch was silent for a long time. She checked the indicator to make sure it was still open.

"You Intervened," he said, finally.

"I didn't think about it. It was the right thing to do." She was surprised to hear how strong her voice sounded. She was angry.

Another long pause. "Please send me a full report within two hours. And forward all recordings from the last forty-eight hours."

"I'm okay," she said. "There was…a fight."

"Good." He cleared his throat. He wouldn't ask her any more questions. He didn't trust her; he would need to see for himself. "Please don't leave anything out. We'll review your case immediately." He closed the patch.

So, he would take it to Academic Conduct. Her fieldwork was over.

She stood, woozily, and approached the body of the white-haired man. The black lines under his skin had faded. His skin looked old and leathery, no longer smooth and translucent. She knelt and examined the corpse, looking for anything of interest, but especially hoping to find her carbonlattice knife. It, too, was gone. Katja had left him with only his clothes and boots.

Where was her rifle? She'd dropped it in the brush, before her valiant charge. If the girl had taken it, Car-En would have no means of defending herself. With a sense of rising panic, she ran to the spot where she had dropped the weapon.

It was still there, fully loaded with sedative darts. Car-En retraced her steps, and checked her pack. It hadn't been tampered with, as far as she could tell. The girl must have been confused, waking up next to such a strange-looking person as Car-En (with her brown skin and weird cloak), but she had chosen not to harm her or rob her. Car-En felt strangely grateful. It seemed like an act of kindness, and it had been a long time since another human being had been kind to her. She sat down heavily and sighed.

So, she thought, this Earth adventure was nearly over. The most exciting time in her life was concluding, prematurely. Would they send a crew to extract her? Or would she be expected to trek back to the mule station? She would prefer the walk – more time on Earth. She wasn't ready to resume her life on the *Stanford*. She missed her friends – especially Lydia – but she wasn't ready to see any of them.

Leaving the withering body of the white-haired man behind, she left the path and walked into the woods, heading north-west. The indicator on her m'eye pointed to a set of coordinates marked 'OETS' (Orbital Earth Transport Shuttle): the mule station, over one hundred fifty kilometers away. She told her swarm to follow.

Footnote 1. Known human inhabitation of the Harz mountain region

Human subspecies: Homo erectus
700Kb–350Kb   Lower Paleolithic hunter-gatherer groups, Acheulean tools

Human subspecies: Homo heidelbergensis
350Kb–250Kb   Lower Paleolithic spear hunters, ancestor of Neanderthal

Human subspecies: Homo neanderthalensis *('Neanderthal')*
250Kb–130Kb   Mousterian culture (Middle Paleolithic, megafauna hunters)
130Kb–115Kb   Emergence of Keilmesser (bi-facial stone knife), Eemian
                     interglacial warm period
100Kb–50000b   Post-Eemian/global cooling, climactic adaptation, start of
                     Weichsel glaciation
50000–35000b   Aschersleben culture (composite material tools/birch
                     pitch adhesive)

Human subspecies: Homo sapiens sapiens *(Eurasiatic 'Cro-Magnon'*
[Neanderthal hybridization/subsumption])
40000b–26000b   Aurignacian (Upper Paleolithic, megafauna hunter-gatherers,
                     stone blades, cave art)
26000b–21000b   Gravettian (Upper Paleolithic, small flint tools, Venus figurines,
                     Last Glacial Maximum)
21000b–15000b   Solutrean (Upper Paleolithic, articulated flint and bone tools)

15000b–09000b	Magdalenian (late Upper Paleolithic, bone microliths, receding ice sheets/Tardiglacial)
09000b–05000b	Maglemosian culture (Mesolithic, start of Holocene – interglacial warm period)
05500b–04500b	Western Linear Pottery culture (early Neolithic, early agriculture)
04500b–04300b	Rössen culture (mid-Neolithic, farming and husbandry)
04300b–20800b	Funnelbeaker culture (late Neolithic, farming and husbandry)
02800b–02500b	Corded Ware/Battle Axe culture (late Neolithic/Copper Age)
02500b–01200b	Bell-Beaker culture (late Copper Age/early Bronze Age pastoralists)
01200b–00800b	Urnfield culture (late Bronze Age, cremation burials, swords, chariots)
00800b–00600b	Hallstatt/Wessenstedt culture (early Iron Age, trade with Greece)
00600b–00100b	Jastorf culture/Nienburg group (pre-Roman Iron Age, cremation burial)
00100b–00200	Cherusci tribe (Roman Iron Age)
00200–00800	Saxons (Roman Iron Age/Early Middle Ages)
00843–01500	East Francia/Kingdom of Germany (Holy Roman Empire, Middle Ages)
01500–01800	Kingdom of Germany (Renaissance, Reformation, 'Little Ice Age')
01815–01860	German Confederation

Human subspecies: Homo sapiens populensis *(urban population explosion, genetic integration and diversification)*

01862–01918	German Empire (ending in World War I, early Industrial Age)
01919–01933	Weimar Republic (Industrial Age, start of Anthropocene)
01934–01945	Nazi Germany (ending in World War II, Industrial Age)
01946–01989	West Germany (mass media, early Corporate Age)
01990–02072	Unified Germany (Corporate Age, global population peak, rapid climate change)

Human subspecies: Homo sapiens melior *(genome editing and design)*

02073–02210	Northern European Confederation (Corporate Age, Phase 1 Depop, peak warming)
02211–02386	Unified Europe (Revival, Phase 2 Depop, ringstations)
02387–02450	New Saxony (Campi Flegrei, Regionalism, end of global trade, Phase 3 Depop)

02451—02634   Germanic Survivalist tribes (Remnant Age, Phase 4 Depop, continued global cooling)

Human subspecies: (none detected)

02635—02721   Post-Inhabitation, end of Holocene interglacial/return to Quaternary glaciation

Human subspecies: Homo sapiens? *(yet to be classified)*

02722—present   New Iron Age, Phase 1 Repop?, New Glacial Maximum

CHAPTER FIVE

Trond dreamed that a fox was lying on his face, making it difficult to breathe. He awoke to Esper's hand covering his mouth. He knocked his brother's hand away and sat up, ready to curse. Esper's finger was pressed against his lips.

The brothers shared the loft, with Trond taking the east side, Esper the west. Arik and Elke slept downstairs near the hearth. Their mother was a light sleeper.

"Katja has not returned," whispered Esper.

Trond was parched and his head ached. He took a long draught of cold water from an earthenware jug he kept near his bed. "She will be back by morning. Go back to sleep."

Esper shook his head. "A boy told me he saw her taken."

Trond pressed the heels of his palms into his eyes. Too much öl. "Who? Who told you and who took her?"

"Jansen's boy – the one missing a finger. He said a tall man with white hair took her."

Bjorn had spoken of the gast. A tale to scare children. He remembered, in his groggy state, that his uncle was dead. It seemed impossible; they had conversed only hours earlier.

"Come with me," said Esper. It was too dark to see his brother's expression, but Esper sounded worried.

"Elke will not like it if we both leave."

"Our mother can defend Happdal on her own, wielding only a wooden spoon, if need be."

What Esper said was true. Elke was fierce, and she could fight, but men feared her because she was clever and ruthless.

"Very well," Trond said. He rose and dressed quietly, strapping his sword to his belt, as well as a hatchet and a dirk for good measure. He glanced at the immense warhammer hanging on the wall, supported by a pair of iron spikes. He would leave Trondfist here. Nor would he bring his shield, a sturdy circle of oak. They were off to fetch his sister from her latest misadventure, not marching into battle. He hastily stuffed a few more items into his pouch: a tinderbox, a jar of herbal ointment for cuts and scratches, a small bag of rock salt, and a candle. Esper stood waiting, bow in hand, a sack slung over his shoulder.

"I have food. Some, anyway – we can hunt if we need to. And wool blankets, should we need to sleep in the rough."

Trond suppressed the urge to ask Esper how long he thought they would be gone. They would return when they found Katja. Probably she was curled up with a boy somewhere, he told himself, but again he thought of Bjorn's story. His uncle had insisted he had seen the gast, and that the sprite had looked like Henning, Arik's fierce, long-missing grandfather. It was as if Henning had not aged, Bjorn had said. A body thief.

The brothers crept down the ladder (Esper silently, Trond creakily), and made their way to the door. In the dark, Trond could just barely make out the form of his mother blocking their way. Elke had not bothered to light a candle. She could see in the dark as well as Esper.

Esper spoke first. "Katja is missing. We are off to find her." His brother sounded resolute, a feeling that Trond did not share.

"No. She will find her own way back. Your sister needs no protector."

"This time is different," said Esper.

Elke said nothing, but did not move from her door-blocking position.

Trond surprised himself by gently moving his mother aside and opening the door. She did not resist (there was no point in resisting Trond physically), but Trond was glad he could not see her face in the darkness.

"You leave us defenseless," said his mother. There was real fear in her voice. "Haakon is coming."

"We will be back soon, Mother."

Esper followed him into the road. Elke watched from the doorway as they walked away.

"What was that?" asked Esper, when they were far enough away. "You *moved* our mother, like a child."

"We are doomed," Trond said. "We might as well live out our days as forest wanderers."

Esper laughed. "She will forgive us, in a year or two."

They returned to the moonlit clearing, where the remains of the pyre still smoldered. A few of the village dogs gnawed on the remnants of the feast. Trond shouted and the mutts trotted off, prized morsels clutched in their jaws.

"This is where Jansen's boy said he saw her," said Esper, pointing to a spot near the long wooden tables. He crouched and examined the ground. To Trond's eye there was only well-trampled dirt, but he knew better than to doubt his brother's sight. Esper moved to the edge of the clearing, examining the meadow grasses and wildflowers. "Look here. A boot mark – deep. Someone carrying a heavy load."

Esper continued into the woods, pausing frequently to look at the ground, or to inspect a trampled bit of vegetation. Trond followed slowly, twenty paces back, letting his brother do the work. Unlike Esper, Trond could not see well in the dark. The stars, rings, and half-moon gave him enough light to see his feet in front of him, but not enough to track their quarry (though even in full daylight, Esper was the superior tracker). There were only two things Trond could do better than his little brother: forge steel, and lift heavy things. A short list indeed. He was only a little jealous; mostly he felt pride and admiration toward his younger sibling. The skinny whelp who had tagged along, practically his shadow for so many years, had grown into his own. Esper was a man now, wise and skillful.

They were heading south, through the beech wood they both knew well. Happdal lay in the center of a large, flat valley, surrounded by mountains on all sides. They hiked uphill for the night's remaining twilight hours. By the time they came to the Blue Meadow, night had yielded to day. The lavender was in full bloom. The sickly sweet smell made Trond's nose itch. Esper had already crossed the meadow and was beckoning to Trond.

"Help me. Can you see which way they went?"

Esper stood on the Silver Trail, which ran east–west. To the east lay the silver mine, beyond that the ruins of an ancient Builder town. To the west the trail led to the river, following it south-west to the foothills and eventually to the decayed remains of another Builder settlement. Though Trond had never seen it, he had heard there was a stone fortress at the end of the western way, built during an even earlier age. The Builders, for all their brilliance, had rarely used stone as a building material; few of their structures remained standing. Builder ruins were vast, but the buildings themselves had succumbed to rain and roots. Only the odd rusted frame stood higher than a man. Still, there were treasures and oddities to be found among the rubble.

Esper had picked up the trail again, and was heading west. Trond yawned and followed. His stomach rumbled; he had not eaten since last night's feast. He imagined Katja sitting at the table by the hearth, eating hot porridge and crispy bacon, laughing at her foolish brothers. Arik would be laughing with her. Even their mother might forget her worries and crack a smile at the thought of her foolish sons. Perhaps she would even forgive Trond for moving her like a doll.

"Brother," Trond cried out, "can we stop for breakfast?" Esper shook his head and kept walking, not bothering to look back. "Surely Katja is home by now," Trond continued. "Should we go back and check?"

Esper kept walking, ignoring him. Trond hurried to catch up. They walked in silence, side by side, and Trond's hunger pangs faded. Dappled sunlight played on the trail, reflecting off the white bark of the slender birch trees. It was good to be in the woods; lately he had seen little but the top of his anvil and the blackened walls of the smithy.

"Did you know, not so long ago, we were all one great family?" Esper asked, out of the blue. "All the villages of the Five Valleys."

Trond grunted. He had heard such tales, but believed them no more than stories of body-thieving sprites.

"Even Haakon," continued Esper, aware of his brother's

skepticism, but pressing on nonetheless. "He is but another cousin, no more than five generations removed."

"Haakon is not my blood," said Trond, matter-of-factly. He tolerated Esper's speculations on such matters – and his brother had no shortage of speculations on all manner of things – but he refused to agree to such a ridiculous idea. A vile animal like Haakon was not their kin.

"Do you think the song of the Ice Trail is just a tale?" Esper challenged. "It is the history of our people. We came south together, and settled in the Five Valleys. The high mountains have snow, like our ancient homeland, but the loam of the valleys is rich and fertile, and free of frost for most of the year."

"Why would the Three Brothers cover our ancient homeland in ice, like the song says? It makes no sense. Our people have *always* lived in the Five Valleys." Even as Trond spoke the words he felt unsure. Esper's point of view made little sense, and most in Happdal would agree with Trond, but out here there was no one to back him up. "There are *old* buildings in Happdal," continued Trond, raising his voice, "very old ones. The smithy. The longhouse. Nobody even knows how many generations ago they were built."

Trond turned to his brother for a response, and discovered he had been talking to himself. Esper was crouched down, examining something, ten paces back.

"What have you got?" asked Trond, retracing his steps.

"Just a dead fly. The light caught it in a certain way.... I thought it might be a coin, or a piece of glass. An odd bug, though. Look for yourself."

Trond held out his hand. Esper delicately dropped the dead insect into his outstretched palm. "It does look strange," Trond said. "As big as a cow-fly, but it looks more like a house-fly. *Shiny.*"

"The carapace gleams," said Esper, peering into Trond's palm. "One moment it looks black, the next like a brilliant rainbow."

"Heavy," Trond said, dropping and lifting his palm to better gauge the weight.

"Let me see it again," said Esper. Trond gave it back. Esper examined the fly for some time longer, then tucked it away in a pocket. "Are you ready for some food?" Trond grunted in assent.

Esper had raided Elke's pantry well. They broke their fast on dense rye bread, thick yellow butter, hard cheese, and crisp apples. With such provisions their rescue mission seemed more like a picnic. Perhaps Esper had the same thought; he ate quickly and soon pressed for them to move on. Trond wrapped up the food reluctantly, not quite sated. They each took a swig of water and set out.

Not long after, Trond heard the sound of running water. The Silver Trail joined the Nyr Begna, following along the rocky south bank. Trond was ready to make water himself. He stopped in his tracks and undid his trousers while his brother walked ahead. It was good to piss in the woods, where the air smelled clean, away from the pungent odors of the village. Why did he not spend more time walking these trails? For seven years he had thought of nothing but gaining the title of smith, of shedding the *apprentice* that preceded it. Now everyone acknowledged him as Jense's equal. Some even preferred his workmanship. But what of it? He spent all his days in the smithy, seeing the same sights, smelling the same smells, making the same tools. Lately, urged on by Elke, he had forged many knives and spearheads, and even a few godsteel swords. While Jense's swords were still superior, Trond knew the Four Secrets of godsteel and could forge a fine blade. All in all, Trond felt proud to be a smith; he enjoyed both work and title. But it was good to be outdoors, pissing on a young sapling.

His brother called out from ahead. Trond shook himself dry, retied his trousers, and jogged to catch up. Esper knelt amidst a copse of beech trees. Next to his brother lay a body, lifeless and supine. The dead man had long, white hair. His skin was pale and withered, his mouth and chin encrusted with blood. Esper waved his hand, shooing away the flies.

"Do you recognize him?" Trond asked.

"No," said Esper, "but he dresses as we do. Look at his boots. Were they not made by Gustav?" Trond looked closely, and nodded. His own boots were made by the Happdal cobbler.

"Do not touch him. He looks diseased, or poisoned," advised Trond. "It looks as if a spider has woven a web inside his face, beneath his skin."

Esper gingerly lifted the body without touching the skin directly, heeding Trond's advice. There were no wounds on the man's back. The only blood came from his mouth, and a little from his nose. Esper stood and paced slowly, eyes on the ground. Trond sat on a rock and waited, knowing he could not match his brother's vision, nor outthink him.

"Help me, you lazy oaf," Esper complained.

"I was not born with the eyes of an eagle."

"Help anyway."

Trond obeyed his younger sibling and searched the area. The winter frost had melted; the ground beneath the beech trees was moist and mossy. Trond noticed a torn patch of moss. Looking more closely, he found a clear set of tracks heading north-west. Just as he turned to alert Esper, his brother called out.

"Trond, look here! Does this not belong to Katja?" Esper was holding his hand up, his fingers pinched together. It seemed as if his brother was holding...absolutely nothing. "Come closer!" commanded Esper. Trond did so, and saw that his brother held a single long flaxen hair. It was the same as many hairs Trond had seen in the family home: on the floor, on chairs, even in his morning porridge. He knew his sister's hair better than he knew his own.

Esper seemed elated, but Trond felt an icy chill in his chest and arms, and shivered. Two minutes ago, he had truly believed his sister was in no danger. She was safe at home, her stomach full of hot porridge and bacon, sleeping off the previous night's adventure. But now his happy vision was smashed. Katja had been here. Perhaps she had seen the death of the man who lay on the ground. Perhaps she had killed him. *Where was she now?*

Trond showed Esper his own discovery, the tracks heading north-west. He then returned to the white-haired man and stood over the corpse, staring down. Bjorn had spoken of the gast (or what he *thought* was the gast, in any case). He had said the apparition's hair was as white as snow. Could this dead man possibly be Trond's great-grandfather Henning? Trond had never met the man, and possessed few memories even of his grandparents. Arik's parents had died young, both Afflicted, Buried and Burned. Elke's father had died in a raid when Trond was a little boy (killing three men even *after* being impaled on a spear, so the story went). That left Elke's mother, Mette, who he remembered well. The old crone was sometimes kind, baking sweet rolls for Trond and Esper. Other times, for no reason at all, she would fly into a rage and hurl rocks at the boys. The old woman had a terrifyingly good aim, right up to the day she went to fetch water one cool autumn evening, and was found frozen stiff in the woods the next morn.

Mormor Mette was Henning's youngest daughter, and the tales of his great-grandfather had come from her. A fearsome warrior, Henning had fought with two godsteel longswords: Biter and Taker. Henning could kill a man so fast that his opponent would continue fighting and boasting for some time, until a severed body part fell to the ground, reminding the man that he had already been killed. One day Henning simply wandered off, never to return, leaving his wife, children, animals, and a fine house behind. Over the years there were sightings. A boy had seen Henning striding through the woods, as if to an important destination. A man had spotted him from across the Long Lake, to the south, sitting on a rock and fishing. After many years, all those who knew Henning by face grew old and died. So did, eventually, all reports of seeing or hearing the man in the wild.

And what of the gast? Trond had grown up with the same tales as every Happdal child. If you were wicked, the gast would take you away to his cave. He would use you as a slave, or possibly cook and eat you, especially if you were a bit fat. The gast also stole from the villagers: clothing and tools, and sometimes animals. Some left sacrifices of food and drink, and swore they were taken. Trond did not doubt this. As a boy, he had enjoyed a few of the offerings himself, once getting sick after swilling an entire pot of mead.

"Brother, look here!" Esper interrupted his dark reverie. "Another set of tracks. These are Katja's.... See the heel of her boot? She took the trail south-west, along the river. She could still be on the Silver Trail. It continues all the way to the stone fort on the ridge, and beyond that to the Builder ruins."

Trond gripped his brother's shoulder and looked him in the eye. They would find Katja, together, no matter how long it took. He tried to speak but could find no words. Esper seemed to understand, and smiled. "Do not worry, our sister lives. She might be hurt, confused and walking in the wrong direction, but she is made of tough stuff. We will find her and bring her home."

Trond nodded, returning the smile and releasing his brother from his vise-like grip. He did not feel as confident as Esper. In the pit of his stomach, there was a sickening knot of fear and worry. But stronger than that was the resolve in his heart. His parents would have to wait, to defend their village without the help of their sons if need be. Their task was to find Katja and bring her home, and that's what they would do.

"What of the other tracks? Who might they belong to?" Trond had no idea, but there was no shame in asking. His brother's intellect was superior; Esper might already have an idea. "Perhaps just an animal?" Trond had thought he had seen the outline of a small foot, but he was no expert tracker.

"No. A woman, I think," said Esper. "The tracks are just as fresh. But that riddle will have to wait. Perhaps Katja will give us the answer when we find her."

Trond nodded. He took one last look at the corpse of the white-haired man. He imagined his sister kicking the man in the face, downing him with a single mighty blow. In Trond's mind, blood sprayed from the man's mouth; he cried out and fell to the ground. The thought made Trond grin, and the knot in his stomach loosened a bit. Trond strode down the trail along the south bank of the Nyr Begna at a fast pace. Esper followed close behind.

CHAPTER SIX

The smithy was silent as Elke approached, no clang of hammer on steel. Still, Elke knew that Jense was there even before she opened the heavy oaken door. She could smell him. Jense was not particularly pungent – the smith scrubbed the sweat and soot from his massive body every evening – but Elke had the nose of a wolf. She could identify each and every villager by scent alone. Every person and every beast had their own distinct odor, and once Elke had smelled it – even once – she would remember that unique scent forever. While everyone knew of her eaglesight, she kept the knowledge of her keen nose to herself. It was more useful that way. The time Arik had strayed, she had known immediately, and with whom. She had paid a visit to Harald the cheesemaker's buxom daughter, and that had been the end of it. She had not even needed to threaten the poor girl. The wench had paled at the sight of Elke, then fled to the barn to hide among the cows. Arik came home earlier than usual that night, befuddled. She had welcomed him back to their bed without a word.

It took her eyes a moment to adjust to the dim light. Jense sat on a stool, polishing a long, slender blade. "For Katja?" she asked. He nodded, but kept his eyes fixed on his work. Elke's pulse quickened at the sight of his bare arms and shoulders, powerful muscles rippling beneath his skin. Briefly, she imagined his hands on her body, gripping her roughly. She suppressed the thought. There was work to be done, and Jense would help her.

"Has she returned?" he asked, still not meeting her gaze.

"No. The boys have gone to find her. And that is a problem. We need them here when Haakon comes."

"*If* Haakon comes," he corrected, finally glancing up. He dropped the cloth and held up the blade. It was a narrow, wicked-looking weapon, longer than a traditional sword. He had not yet fashioned a hilt or guard, but the tang looked long enough to grip with two hands. Jense was wrong about Haakon, but she would not waste her breath arguing.

"You will find the boys and bring them back," she said, using a tone reserved for the end of conversations. She knew Jense would protest, but eventually he would do as she asked. She might as well let him know what she wanted up front.

He laughed. "You think I can still grab Trond by the scruff of his neck and bend him to my will? Have you seen your son lately? My days of being the strongest man in the Five Valleys are over."

"He will obey you still. Old habits die hard."

Jense shook his head. "No. Trond is my equal now. I might ask him to return, but he will do as he sees fit."

For an instant Elke's will faltered. She thought of Trond moving her aside like a paper doll. But she steeled herself. "Go and ask them. You only need to convince one. Where one goes, the other will follow. And then, continue on to find Katja, and bring her home as well." This was the killing blow, and they both knew it. Jense loved both mother and daughter.

Jense sighed. Elke stepped close, taking one of his giant hands in her own. Finally, he met her gaze and held it. He did not completely trust her, but nor could he resist her. She saw frustration in his eyes, then, briefly, anger.

"Fine, woman, I will fetch your sons. And your daughter. Now leave my smithy so I can finish my work – the work *you* assigned me. Five spearheads by day's end, or had you forgotten? You know what they will say of Jense? That he did Elke's bidding. When I am dead and burned, that will be my legacy. He worked for Elke, until his back curved and his fingers bent like claws. Not one day did she let him rest."

He griped, but there was no malice in his tone. She stood on her tiptoes to kiss his bearded cheek. For the moment, her passion had subsided. Jense was loyal, and she valued that as much as anything. She left the smithy without another word.

★　★　★

Elke had gotten an early start. Even after two hours of hiking, the sun had not yet reached its zenith. She climbed the High Pass, a narrow switchback trail ascending the ragged slope that protected Happdal's western side. From there she descended into the steep valley that housed the south-flowing Upper Begna, then climbed the trail until she reached the top of the high ridge that formed the western part of the narrow, cramped valley sheltering the village of Kaldbrek.

Haakon was jarl of Kaldbrek. For years, Kaldbrek and Happdal had lived as sister hamlets, trading goods, joining sons and daughters in marriage. At Summer Trade, the people of Kaldbrek had brought fine pottery, wool clothing and blankets, fresh mutton, iron ore, sturdy axes and tools, fish from their lake (dried and smoked), and ancient artifacts collected from the Builder ruins to the north. Happdal folk had traded their surplus food (milk and cheese, oats and rye), some of Jense's fine blades, pure godsteel ingots, silver jewelry, and their own found artifacts from the sprawling ruins to the east of the mountains.

It had been seven years since the last Summer Trade, and Elke regretted every scrap of steel that had made its way from Jense's forge to the Kaldbrek armory. What cruel irony, if Jense were to be slain by a blade of his own making. With this thought she redoubled her pace up the narrow trail. Soon she would crest the tree line.

Haakon had been a small, mean boy, who had grown into a strong, cruel man. He had slain his own cousin to become jarl. Fear kept him in power. Ending Summer Trade had been only the beginning; Haakon had twice raided Happdal. The first time, Haakon and his men robbed both the armory and the granary, killing a man and wounding two others. Arik had chosen not to retaliate, pointing out that the people of Kaldbrek were friends of Happdal; it would do no good to steal from them. "Then kill Haakon," she had pleaded. "The people of Kaldbrek will thank you for ridding them of a tyrant." Arik had refused. There had been a year's respite, then another raid. This time they came in the dead of night, silently. Haakon and his brutes murdered old Hinrik and raped his three daughters, tearing the youngest so brutally that she later died. The savages desecrated the longhouse, pissing and shitting on the floor, then lit the sacred building on fire. The men of Happdal, led by Arik and Bjorn, finally chased them away.

Hinrik's surviving daughters took herbs to end the cruelseed growing inside of them, and demanded vengeance. Arik begged Elke's forgiveness – he had been wrong to turn the other cheek – he was ready to march the next day. This time, she held him back. It was possible that Haakon had grown too strong. What if the raid was a trap, a provocation meant to trigger a hasty, poorly planned response? Kaldbrek would be well-prepared for retaliation after such a brazen attack. Let *us* be ready next time they come, she said. We will prepare for them, and serve them a feast they will never forget. A feast of steel and blood.

Walking south along the ridge, she could see the rock outcropping that was her destination. A slab of stone had fallen on a boulder, creating a natural shelter. She saw a thin wisp of smoke curling around the stone roof, and cursed. She had told the boy that he was never to light a fire. But Karl was willful.

He was awake, and looked exhausted. That was good; at least he had not slept through his task. Karl gave her a guilty look as he threw dirt on the glowing embers.

"I was cold. Even with the furs you gave me." His voice always surprised her. It had already dropped, though this would only be his thirteenth summer. He was tall for his age but still lanky. He might never fill out. Hinrik had been lean until the day of his slaughter.

"Your excuses will do you no good if Haakon sees your smoke and comes to slit your throat. He would do so merrily. Or have you forgotten what he did to your father and your sisters?" Karl looked away, and Elke regretted her words. There was no need to be so harsh. The boy had enough rage without her stoking it. Better to let his anger simmer until it was time to act.

She gently touched his shoulder. His father slaughtered, his mother Buried long ago, Karl had only his sisters, and they had little time for him. He was a bit lost, like all the children she took in. She gave them work, and purpose, and love. They drank it up like berry juice.

"What did you see?" she asked.

"Forge fires, and men sparring."

"The same, then." She crossed the open cave, pausing at the Builder artifact. The long spyglass was mounted on an elegant wooden frame. Esper's work. Her sons had found the spyglass in the ruins, lovingly stored in a wooden case, stashed away on the upper floor of an ancient stone house. The stone structure, one of the few that still stood among the sprawling ruins to the east, had protected the case from the worst of the elements. The metal hinges and lock had long since rusted away, but the wood had survived. They had opened it, blown off the dissolved remains of the cloth lining, and found the spyglass in near-pristine condition. It was a hand-built artifact, made of polished wood, bronze, and glass, using none of the cheap, short-lived materials that the Builders had so often preferred. The glass had warped slightly over the years, but still the thing worked. Hidden behind the rocks, Elke and Karl (and her other boys) could observe the goings-on at Kaldbrek. When Haakon marched, they would know. And hopefully they would be ready.

"If they march, what do you do?" she quizzed the boy.

"Light the signal fire, then run and tell you."

"Good. Here, eat something." She opened her pouch and handed him a block of cheese and a large piece of oily dried fish. He grabbed the food, tore off a piece of fish with his teeth, and mumbled a word of thanks. The salty meal would make him thirsty; she handed over her waterskin as well.

"You may go, after you eat. Tell Jesper to meet me here at sundown, then get some rest." Karl nodded, still chewing. After several more bites he took a drink of water and paused, staring at the spyglass.

"What will we do, when they come?" he asked.

It was good that he said *when*, not *if*. Unlike Jense, the boy understood Haakon. The brute of Kaldbrek had taken their lack of retaliation as a sign of weakness. He would come again, to rape, plunder, and kill, as sure as the sun would rise.

"We will give him a taste of the Red Brother's wrath, and the Black Brother's justice. He will beg for the Brown Brother's mercy, but he will not have it." Karl grinned. She had told him nothing, of course, but the answer seemed to satisfy him.

"Did you bring any bread?" he asked, his mouth already full of cheese.

CHAPTER SEVEN

Car-En's eyes were fixed on the ground as she made her way through the beech wood undergrowth. Adrian hadn't yet contacted her. She wished he would, if only to replace her dread with some sense of closure. She was ready to mourn the end of her field research; she had resigned herself to this inevitable conclusion. But the call had not yet come. She was in limbo. So she trudged along, heading north-west toward the faraway mule station, feeling sorry for herself.

A wolf howled in the distance. It was getting late in the day and the large trees blocked much of the afternoon light. She had descended into some valley; the twisted beech grew thick here, along with a few ancient, gnarled oaks. For some reason the closed canopy made her feel safe. Maybe it reminded her of home, of being inside.

Out of habit, she checked the swarm. There'd been some attrition; the swarm had shrunk by twenty per cent. Rewinding the data-feeds, she had learned that dragonflies were the culprits. The swarm bots' evasive algorithms were sufficient to avoid birds, but were no match for the hunting dexterity of *Insecta* suborder *Anisoptera*. It was a type of insect she was familiar with; there were dragonflies on the *Stanford* as well. Many other insects had not been invited aboard, including mosquitoes, ticks, lice, and cockroaches.

She came across an old trail and followed it due north. It was overgrown, but the packed earth was more traversable than the spongy debris that covered most of the forest floor. There was a rock formation up ahead: some large boulders stacked on the left side of the trail, leaning against a hillock. An alert from her m'eye indicated a radiation spike, a level higher than any she had yet to encounter. Even with her bioskin and her genetic resistance, the algorithm was recommending a maximum four-hour exposure. What was the source?

The boulders concealed a cave entrance. A muddy trail sloped down into the dark. She could just make out the rotted remains of wooden steps carved from logs. She switched to infrared vision and boosted the light levels, but it wasn't much help. The tunnel descended into deep blackness.

It would be stupid and rash to explore this dark pit. Her research was as good as over, and she could easily injure herself in a dark, slippery cave. A sprained ankle would make the long walk to the mule station slow and painful; a broken bone might leave her stranded and helpless. It was probably just an old mine.

However, even as she had these thoughts, she knew that her curiosity would win out. There was a chance that this hole led to the source of the radiation that was sickening the Happdal villagers. What if she could find it? What if the radiation could be contained? Could she persuade the Over Council to change their Non-Interventionism policy? Even if she couldn't, the policy was temporary, to be reviewed in two years. The data would still have value if she could collect it.

She switched on the narrow-beam torch attached to her rifle, dialing the intensity down to a dim five hundred lumens. Best to conserve energy; there wasn't enough light leaking through the forest canopy to recharge the device. Not this late in the day.

She told the swarm to patrol the vicinity of the entrance, then cautiously descended into the dark cavern. The dim light of the torch beam, combined with her enhanced vision, allowed her to see about twenty meters ahead. The tunnel turned right, sloping farther down.

Soon she was walking on stone instead of dirt. The temperature dropped sharply. Her bioskin tried to compensate, but still she shivered; it was hard to stay warm when running a caloric deficit. She didn't have a way to weigh herself, but she guessed she was about ten kilos lighter than when she had started her field research. On the ringstation, she'd stayed in shape, but had always been a little thick around the middle. Not fat, just smooth, with no visible abdominal muscles. Now the bioskin felt loose around her abdomen, and her body became more angular with each passing week. At first she'd been happy with her new shape, looking forward to showing off her slender form to Lydia and her other friends. But now she was just gaunt, tired, and malnourished. Her rations wouldn't last. Despite her misgivings, she needed to kill something and eat it. Her rifle would make the killing part easy enough, and she'd checked the archives on the *Stanford*; there were a number of antique guides to the grisly business of gutting, skinning, cooking, and preserving wild meats. But while her body needed the food, she wasn't sure she could stomach the task. Maybe she could ration out her energy bars and supplement with wild berries and edible roots.

Her m'eye flashed a warning; she'd lost contact with the *Stanford*. The signal couldn't penetrate solid stone. Adrian, with his bad news from Academic Conduct, would have to wait.

The descending passage had a natural, irregular feel. Any markings from picks or drills had been smoothed over by the water dripping over the cool stone. Several times she stepped over icy rivulets carving their way across her path. She checked the radiation levels – still rising. The passage opened to reveal an immense cavern, punctuated by stalactites dripping onto stalagmites, some of them joining to form icy pillars. Continuing forward, she lost sight of the walls, surrounded by tapering white columns of calcium salts, shining in the light of her torch. The beam cut across the mineral towers, creating a dance of shadows. Or had something actually moved, deeper in the cavern? Startled, she stopped, pointing the rifle and light at the ground. She stared into the darkness, listening, but heard only slow, reverberant drips of water.

She tried to summon a few drones from the swarm. No response – she was too deep underground. Briefly, she considered going back. This was a foolish mission. But she'd come this far, and she was curious. She raised her rifle and continued onward, placing her feet carefully on the slippery stone.

The cavern narrowed; she could see the walls again. They pressed in farther until she found herself in a funnel-like tube.

The passage turned again, to the right, descending sharply. She stepped on some loose pebbles, slipped, fell, hit her hip on a sharp rock, and tumbled down a rocky slope. She cried out when she landed. Her voice echoed as if inside a vast cathedral.

She was on her hands and knees. Having dropped her rifle, she could see nothing at all. Beneath her hands were cold, smooth pebbles. Water seeped through the permeable skin of her gloves. Shakily, she stood. Her left hip hurt badly. She gingerly touched the wound. The bioskin had torn, and the exposed skin felt damp. In the darkness, she couldn't tell if it was blood or water, but an icy chill was spreading down her leg where the bioskin was no longer protecting her. She ran a quick diagnostic on her kit. Luckily, the thin, flexible strip strapped to her left thigh, packed with computing and communications technology, appeared undamaged. She ignored the frantic alerts from her m'eye regarding her own physiological status. She could guess their contents well enough: elevated heart rate, spiking cortisol, physical injury, core temperature precipitously falling. She didn't need her m'eye to tell her she was cold, terrified, and alone.

Car-En turned in a slow circle. She spotted the dim light of the torch, partially buried in gravel, halfway up the slope. Wincing in pain, she slowly climbed the hill. Retrieving the rifle, she slid back down on her butt, not willing to risk another fall. Back on level ground, she detached the torch from the rifle barrel and pointed the light at her hip. It was a shallow cut, only about five centimeters long, but it was still bleeding. Beneath the smeared blood the surrounding flesh was already starting to discolor. She would have an ugly bruise. It must have been a razor-sharp rock; the bioskin material didn't tear easily. Without it, she would surely be looking at a gaping wound down to the bone.

She extracted the first aid kit from her pack and smeared a disinfecting gel over the cut. Within seconds the gel stiffened and became opaque, forming a flexible bandage. Luckily the cut wasn't deep enough to require sutures. It was the bruising and muscle damage she was worried about; she still had a great deal of walking to do. And the cold added to her worries; she was starting to shiver. Reluctantly, she signaled her implant to release a brown adipose stimulant. Minutes later she was comfortably warm, but her body had only so much fat left to burn. Now that her suit was torn, her food situation was more desperate than ever.

She dialed up the torch and expanded the focus from a narrow beam into a bright cone of light, then gasped at what she saw. The strip of wet pebbles formed a narrow beach; ahead of her stretched a vast underground lake, black and calm. She shone the light above; she could barely make out the outlines of the rocky ceiling, which must be at least sixty meters above. The cavern was immense.

She reattached the torch to the rifle, dialing back the intensity to conserve energy. Slowly, she advanced up the beach, the pebbles crunching beneath her boots. Her hip still hurt but the gel's numbing agent attenuated the pain. She ascended a gentle slope. Now she was walking on rough, larger rocks. Looking down, she saw rubble, the crumbled remains of a large concrete slab. Twenty meters ahead she could make out the decaying outlines of what might have been a live-work area. Rusted cot frames lay next to moldy residue from fiberboard partitions. Not far away, a few rotted timbers were all that was left of a long communal dining table. Farther on, she found the collapsed remains of a large kitchen, compost toilets, and a greenhouse once fueled by artificial light.

From her history lessons, she knew this was a Survivalist camp from the Remnant Age. To see it in the flesh was both fascinating and creepy. From the looks of it, a few dozen people had lived in this cave, hidden away, protecting their scarce scavenged resources from other tribes. This sad existence was the dying breath of Earth-based civilization (already weakened by population decline and natural disasters). Leading up to the Remnant Age, global commerce and industrial-scale production had collapsed, leaving civilization's stragglers to scavenge what they could from fallen cities, cobbling together the rest. Early Survivalist tribes had been well-stocked and industrious, but without formal education, and without a global network providing access to the world's accumulated knowledge, expertise deteriorated with each generation. Machines were poorly maintained. Fuel ran out, as did ammunition. Technology devolved. The last of the Survivalists, savage and illiterate, had killed each other off with rusted machetes and antique crossbows.

Car-En stumbled on a chunk of rubble, almost going down. She had to be more careful; she couldn't afford another fall. Past the greenhouse, she found the remains of a laboratory or workshop area. This group had been well-organized and, from the looks of it, creative. The torch beam gave her glimpses of what had once been work benches, bins of parts, half-assembled projects, even what might have once been a computing tablet. Maybe this tribe was early Remnant Age, from the late twenty-fourth century, before things had gotten really bad. Certainly they'd generated electricity; they'd managed to grow food underground.

What had happened here? She'd yet to see any human remains. The settlement had been abandoned.

Beyond the workshop, the rest of the concrete slab continued for as far as she could see. Carefully she picked her way across the field of rubble. Ahead, she saw a squat, roughly constructed stone tower. She could hear a brook trickling in the distance. Even before she checked the ambient radiation levels, the scenario became clear. She stopped in her tracks.

The reading confirmed her suspicions. These Survivalists had been industrious indeed, constructing their own miniature nuclear reactor, housed in a stone tower, cooled by a natural stream (which fed into the lake below). The reactor had provided all the electricity they'd needed to grow food underground, to stay warm, to power their scavenged and constructed devices. The reactor had probably fueled their lifestyle for a number of generations.

She imagined the sequence of events as it might have played out. The engineering genius who had built the reactor had passed away. The survivors painstakingly followed the instructions for maintaining the device. Until they didn't. Something bad had happened – a breakdown or a radiation leak – and a mass exodus had followed. The isotope signatures pointed to a thorium reactor, one of the 'safe' types of reactors that should not have been capable of a core meltdown. But something had gone wrong. At least they had known enough to get out.

Now, over two hundred years later, waste from this miniature power station was contaminating the underground lake, seeping into the groundwater that fed Happdal's wells.

Bad luck. That's what was killing the villagers. The radiation levels weren't that high, nor of the most lethal variety. If only Happdal had been founded one valley over....

But if they were willing to *relocate* their village, the people of Happdal could stop dying young.

Car-En shivered. Using the torch, she examined the remains of the pipes and cables that connected the decrepit reactor to the infrastructure ruins of the camp. She tried to imagine people working here, maybe even children running around, playing in the nearby lake. Even populated and well-lit, this place must have been dreary. Though was it so different from the *Stanford*? For most of her life she had lived in an artificial ecosystem, protected from the harsh outside environment. But the ringstation had trees, and natural sunlight streaming in from the mirrored hub. Most importantly, ringstation citizens still had a sense of *progress*, pushing forward the horizons of science, invention, and the human spirit. On Earth, progress had died sometime during the Corporate Age; the Survivalist tribes of the Remnant Age had devolved into a grim sustenance existence ruled by fear and superstition.

Having seen enough, she turned and picked her way back across the dark field of rubble. Alone, there was nothing she could do to contain the radiation. Surely the right team of engineers and decontamination specialists from the *Stanford* could deal with it, but that would constitute Intervention. Without a political sea change, there was nothing to be done. At least she had discovered the nature of the problem. She would include the details in her final report. Maybe in two years' time the policy would be revised and a team could be sent.

Because of what she had done, trying to rescue Katja, she would surely be censured by Academic Conduct. But that wouldn't invalidate her research. She'd collected a huge amount of valuable data, a trove of information that would benefit anthropologists and archeologists on all the ringstations. It might be a long time before she was allowed to do more field research, but it wasn't as if her career was over. Her colleagues would still want to talk to her, to learn from her, to hear firsthand what it was like to walk on Earth.

She returned through the giant cavern with the stalactite/stalagmite pillars, feeling tired but buoyant. Her hip ached, but she could still walk. Her m'eye informed her there was no incipient infection; the wound was clean. Whatever penalty Academic Conduct meted out, she would accept without complaint, move on with her life. In some ways it would be a huge relief to be back home. She could *eat*, for one thing, and sleep in a real bed. As she walked, her mind cycled through various comfort and recreation fantasies; a hot shower, a spa session in the low-grav inner rings, catching up on the latest shows and music, drinking wine and gossiping with Lydia. It would be good to relax, to not be so *alert* all the time.

As she neared the surface and regained connectivity, several messages from Adrian queued up. The first was audio-only. Her body tensed as the recording of his low, sonorous voice transmitted through her cochlear implant.

"I've discussed your situation with Academic Conduct. They're...deliberating. We'll know something soon." It was hard to tell from his tone where he stood. What would be a good outcome, from Adrian's point of view? Did he want her to continue her research on Earth or not? After a pause, her advisor continued. "Look, I've been thinking about the Happdal villagers. From the genographics and other data you've sent us, we're starting to get a clearer migration picture. This group definitely migrated from Northern Europe, probably moving south with the glacial line. They were nomadic for a number of generations, which may explain why they escaped detection for so long. They weren't building anything that would have been visible from space – no structures, no fields, no large fires. They eventually resettled, probably about a hundred years ago, in a more temperate region, but by that time we'd classified Earth as post-Inhabitation and weren't really looking. Until Townes."

Ahead, Car-En saw a dim patch of gray light that might be the cave opening. She increased her pace.

Adrian's message continued. "But all that is beside the point. What I've been thinking about are their cultural traditions. These villagers have retained preindustrial metalworking, woodworking, and glassmaking techniques that were all but lost during the Corporate Age. Such crafts might have been practiced by hobbyists and eccentrics, but were far outside of the mainstream. So I don't think we're dealing with the descendants of a Survivalist tribe. At least not a normal one." The last line gave Car-En pause for thought. Did the profile of a 'normal' Survivalist tribe include a nuclear reactor?

"So here's my idea: the Happdal villagers are descended from a Scandinavian traditionalist group, maybe a 'medieval Viking town' of sorts. There was probably a tourism aspect, but the inhabitants actually lived without electricity or industrial tools. They practiced traditional metalworking, leather-curing, glassblowing, cheese-making, various modes of fish preservation, and perhaps even spoke an ancient dialect – maybe Old Norse or something similar. During Depop and the decline of global commerce, this group thrived. Economic collapse didn't matter to them. While other Survivalist tribes were running out of canned food and ammunition, these people were forging swords and growing their own food. The others might have been stronger at first, but their traditional skills gave them an edge. After Campi Flegrei, they migrated, probably with animals and carts in tow, to escape the advancing ice fields. And here we find them today, in the Harz mountains." Adrian paused for breath. "Pure speculation, of course. But that's my hypothesis."

The message ended without any sign-off. Car-En advanced to the next.

"Why are you still offline?" Adrian sounded irritated, perhaps even a little hurt. "I'd like to discuss my hypothesis with you. Also, I heard back from Academic Conduct. Contact me as soon as you can."

Car-En emerged from the cave. It was the middle of the night; light from the three-quarters moon filtered through the canopy. It was enough to see by, so she switched off the torch. She found a flat spot and unpacked her tent, instructing it to assemble and mask. Shivering, she crawled in, pulling her rifle and pack in next to her. "Standard night security," she muttered to the swarm, rummaging in her pack for a nutrient bar. Only five left. Tomorrow she would hunt and gather, and learn whatever she needed to learn to make herself a decent meal in the wild. She unwrapped the bar and bit off a dry chunk. Even with frequent sips of water it was hard to swallow. Despite her underweight condition, she had no appetite. After choking down a few bites, she called Adrian. He answered immediately.

"Where have you been?" he snapped.

"Exploring a cave. I found the remains of a Survivalist camp. They built a reactor. It must be the source of the radiation pollution. Of the water supply. Happdal's." She was having trouble putting a clear sentence together. She needed to sleep.

"Hmm. Interesting. But you can't go offline for that long. I was worried."

Touching. She was touched. She wondered if it was true, that he had worried.

"I spoke with Academic Conduct. They've issued an official warning, but you're free to continue your research. For now." The same neutral tone. Was he happy for her or not? And how did *she* feel? There would be no comfortable bed, no wine, no Lydia.

"Good," she said, because she couldn't think of anything else to say. "I'm really tired. I'll call you in the morning, okay?"

"Fine," he said, and disconnected.

Her hip ached. After some tossing and turning, she discovered that if she lay on her right side, with her left knee pulled slightly up, the pain was bearable. As she drifted off to sleep, a plan formed in her mind. It made her laugh. What if she actually did it? It was the right thing to do. She was a good person, and good people did the right thing.

CHAPTER EIGHT

The path looked vaguely familiar. After a hundred paces, Katja remembered its name; she was on the Silver Trail. The Nyr Begna was to her right – she was heading west, the same direction as the water. She'd once walked to the end of the Silver Trail to explore the ancient castle ruins. Her brothers had told her about the place but never let her tag along on their adventures. So she went alone. She had seen giants, and told them, but they had laughed at her.

Her throat hurt, as did her shoulder. She had a headache. *Everything* ached. Why was she here? She considered stopping, even turning around. "Keep going," said a voice in her head. A familiar voice, though not her own.

She had been eating a piece of meat at Bjorn's Burning. She had won a fight, besting Lars. With a stick! She laughed aloud. It had been night, now it was high noon. Where had the time gone? Why was she walking west on the Silver Trail? As she contemplated these questions, her vision dimmed and narrowed. She could still hear the river to her right. Also the distant hammering of a woodpecker. Was she still walking? She could no longer feel her legs.

Katja looked up at the stars. She lay on the damp forest floor, no blanket to cover her, yet she felt warm. Heat radiated from her core to her extremities, all the way to her toes and fingertips. Her entire body itched, but it was a deep itch, *beneath* her skin, that she could not scratch. Her headache had subsided, as had the pain in her shoulder. Her throat still hurt, but overall she felt better. Warm, and tingling with energy.

Why was she lying on the ground in the middle of the night? Did it matter? Who was she to question? She felt alive and strong. Nothing would ever hurt her again. It occurred to her that she would never die.

She relaxed and took in the beauty of the clear night sky. There were so *many* stars, and a few rings as well. The stars moved, as did some of the rings, but a few of the southern rings held their position through the night. What were they? "People live there. Tens of thousands of them," said a voice in her head. It was a different voice than before. What a ridiculous thought. She drifted off.

She awoke to bright sunlight shining through her eyelids, coloring the membranes a deep orange. She sat up, squinting. She was seated in a strange reclining chair, fabric stretched over a flimsy frame. As her eyes adjusted, she saw a broad wooden deck beneath her, and an artificial rectangular pool just ahead. Her hardened-leather armor and dirk had been taken. In their place she wore a white linen gown. It was full-length, and comfortable, but the material was light and thin – she felt exposed. Her feet were bare.

Katja stood, taking in her surroundings. Past the large pool were several smaller pools, one of them steaming hot. The water gave off a sulfurous smell. Beyond the pools were some squat buildings that vaguely reminded her of Builder ruins.

A tall man approached, climbing a winding stone trail. The large flagstones were set among neatly landscaped flowers and ferns. He ascended a short flight of wooden stairs and came across the deck, smiling.

Katja glanced around for a weapon. There was nothing to grab, not even a rock or a stick. Trying not to be too obvious, she shifted her right foot back into a fighting stance, rolling the shoulder that had been bludgeoned by Lars's sword. She vaguely noticed that the pain was now entirely gone.

"Relax," the man said. He was tall and striking, with long, ashen-blond hair and gray-blue eyes. She knew him, but could not say from where. "I am a friend, and family too. You will want to hear what I have to say."

"Close enough," she said, extending a hand in warning. If it came to it, she would defend herself with her fists (the gown not ideal for throwing kicks). "I know my family well, and you are not one of them."

"But do you know the faces of your ancestors? Your grandmother, Mette…do you remember your mormor's face?" He stood, hands on hips, in a confident stance. A flimsy, short-sleeved shirt revealed lean, muscular arms.

"I remember a wrinkled old crone who was fond of throwing things," said Katja.

He laughed. "Yes, that sounds like my Mette. She was my youngest, and fiercest."

"Your youngest what?"

"Daughter. And child. I am Henning, morfar of Elke. I am your mother's grandfather."

Katja frowned. "Your skin is smooth and your back is unbent. You age very well, or you lie poorly."

He smiled slyly. "Have you considered that you might be in another world? Asgard, perhaps? A world where you could converse with the gods, and the dead?"

"Are you dead?" she asked.

He nodded. "In Midgard, yes. But only recently. And I only know because you arrived. I was the most recent, until today. I felt sad, when I first saw you, because I knew that my body had finally perished. But also happy, because it has been so long since I spoke with someone new. And family, no less!" He seemed genuinely happy to see her.

"How do you know who I am?" she asked.

"We have spoken before. When you were walking, before you crossed over."

Without taking her eyes off the man, Katja took a few steps toward the edge of the deck. The pool area had been constructed atop a hillock, surrounded by light forest. At the bottom of the slope there were half a dozen small houses, connected by stone trails. Scattered among the trees were flowerbeds, stone statuettes, decorative fountains, and a meandering brook crossed by several arched wooden bridges.

"Asgard, I think not. Álfheimr, perhaps, the land of the elves."

The man laughed. "Yes! This place has needed a name for eons. We shall call it Álfheimr. Will you come with me?" Without waiting for an answer, he turned and walked away.

Not sure what else to do, she followed, ten paces back. He skipped down the stairs and continued down the hillside trail.

"How do I get back?" she asked. "I need to go home. My family will worry, and they will not rest until they find me. Especially my brothers."

"Hmm," he said, but did not answer her question. Well, she would find her own way back, if necessary. She did not believe she was in another world, and she did not believe this man was her great-grandfather. But for now she would follow him; her curiosity was piqued.

"There are six of us, including you and Raekae," said the man over his shoulder. "He was the first, and he controls the host." The trail narrowed at the bottom of the slope. The air was cooler here, in the shade of the trees. They passed by towering tree ferns and spiky succulents. "Of the remaining four, one is a hermit – she rejects the group entirely. And Raekae visits only rarely. So since I arrived, I've had only two others for company."

They came to a small, neatly built house, not much more than a hut with windows, with a door painted bright red. Katja tried to peer through the glass as they approached. The interior was dark; all she could see was the edge of a table and a blue ceramic pitcher. The man who called himself Henning knocked on the red door. She heard a muffled "Enter!" from within.

Inside, as her eyes adjusted, she saw two men seated at the table near the window. One was broad and bearded, perhaps Jense's age, and similar in appearance to the Happdal smith. Thinking of Jense, she felt a pang of loneliness. The other man was slender, and wore a device on his head, circles of glass suspended in wire. Behind the glass circles his blue eyes appeared unnaturally large. The smaller man stood and extended his hand.

"Franz Schultz. A pleasure to make your acquaintance." She gripped his forearm firmly. He withdrew his arm, wincing. The bearded man laughed.

"Someday you will learn to make a proper greeting, Franz." The bigger man stood and gripped her forearm. "My name is Stian. And you are the most beautiful sight I have seen in nearly a century."

Katja pulled her arm away. She wished she had more to wear than a flimsy white gown. "Mind your manners, blacksmith," said Henning. "Respect our new host."

"I meant no disrespect," said Stian, "but what I said is true. I have had only *this* to look at" – he gestured at Franz, and then at Henning – "and *that*, for many, many years. The sight of your face makes my heart sing. You may smack me in the head, or poke out my eyes."

"No need," said Katja, "because I will not be staying."

Franz, the smaller man, nodded sadly. "That's what I said too, when I first arrived. I spent years looking for a way out. There was no one to guide me, when I came. The first host had already gone into seclusion. I caught a glimpse of her now and then, like a ghost. After a few years Raekae explained the situation to me. I didn't believe him at first."

"Are you thirsty?" Stian asked. He took a clean glass from a nearby shelf and filled it with water from the blue ceramic pitcher. He offered her the glass, returning her glare with a friendly smile. The big man seemed harmless enough. She took the drink and sipped; the water was cool and sweet.

"You will find that your body is different here," said Henning. "You will feel thirst, and hunger, but if you go without water and food, your bodily urges will fade away." He turned to Stian. "Katja has found a name for our little world. Álfheimr!" Stian laughed uproariously. Franz looked confused.

"Indeed, this place is magical," said the big bearded man. "Once I cut off my own finger, to see what would happen. By the next morning it had grown back."

Franz offered her a chair and sat back down himself. "Do you have questions for us?"

"Questions for three crazy men living in a hut? No, I have no questions. This place is your home, not mine." She planted her bare foot on the chair and shoved it away. "I will take my leave now. Goodbye to you all." Franz's eyes widened. Stian grunted.

Henning stepped aside to let her pass. "We will be here when you return," he said. "It is the only house with a red door. The house with the yellow door is your own. You will find your belongings there, and clothes that fit you."

Katja left the hut, slamming the door behind her. She looked down at her bare feet. It would be nice to have her boots back. She could see several houses from where she stood, but the only visible door was green. She wandered along the stone path, ferns brushing against her gown, and turned left at a fork. She examined herself as she walked, and found herself uninjured. In fact, her body was in a pristine state. There was not a single bruise or scratch or smudge of dirt on her skin. She touched her scalp, seeking out the familiar contours of a scar she had received during a childhood game of catch-the-hatchet with Trond. Her fingers touched only silken hair and smooth skin.

She saw a hut up ahead – the back wall had a single small window. The path curved around to the front of the tiny house, revealing a small garden: pink and white roses and a miniature tree bearing orange fruit. The front door was painted yellow. She knocked, waited a few seconds, and hearing no response, tried the handle.

The inside of the hut consisted of a single room. Toward the back, near the window, was a squat black iron stove. A cord of firewood was neatly stacked nearby. On top of the stove was a large covered iron pot, emitting steam and a mouthwatering smell. She lifted the lid and peered inside – a meat and vegetable stew. Who had cooked it?

A ladder led up to a loft bed. Below that was a finely crafted chest of drawers, where she found her clothes, clean and pressed, and other shirts and trousers that looked as if they would fit her. In the bottom drawer she found her leather boots, cleaned and polished to a high sheen, and her long steel dirk. She tested the edge with a fingertip. Someone had sharpened the steel. It was a mudsteel blade, made and gifted to her by Trond long ago. A little heavy, and not balanced for throwing, but familiar and reliable. Still, she longed for the godsteel sword Jense was making her. That would be a truly fine weapon. She had a name for it ready.

She dressed, donned her boots, and tucked the dirk into her belt. She found a wooden bowl and spoon on a high shelf and filled the former from the iron pot. She had no idea how far she was from Happdal; she might as well eat while she had the chance. The stew was delicious, filled with tender chunks of lamb, sweet onions, carrots, and forest herbs. She ate a second bowl. After so much food she expected to feel sleepy, but instead she felt alert and refreshed. Perhaps she should explore this place a little longer before heading home. Where was the hermit that Henning had mentioned, and what did she have to say for herself? And who was this Raekae fellow? She already had a good story to share, but there were many unanswered questions. Esper and Trond would give her no end of grief if she told them of this mysterious place but neglected to explore it. Her brothers would mock her, as they had when she fled home, excited and scared, after seeing the giants in the castle ruins.

Leaving the hut, she stood in the garden for a moment, inhaling the bouquet of the roses. A sweet smell, but she did not trust it. Esper and Trond could come back and explore this place for themselves. It was time to leave, *now*, to return home before her mother worried herself into an early grave. And before this place seduced her with its easy comforts, or the men took her as a prisoner.

The sun was high in the sky – early afternoon. She checked the moss on some nearby trees and walked in what she guessed was a northerly direction. She vaguely remembered walking on the Silver Trail, with the river to her right. To the north of the Nyr Begna were steep mountains, but there were no mountains in sight. So she was most likely south of the river. If she could find the Nyr Begna, she could make her way home easily enough.

She left the landscaped area and continued into the forest. She recognized the gnarled, sprawling oaks, but there were many trees and plants she did not know. Perhaps she was *far* to the south. In that case she might first reach the Long Lake, or the South River. That would be a longer trek home, but she could still find her way. She looked behind her. The huts and gardens were already out of sight. She listened for running water but heard only birds. She had not taken a drink since Stian had offered her water from the pitcher, and there had been no wineskin among the various supplies in the hut with the yellow door. Thirst could become a problem, if she had far to travel. She remembered what Henning had said about hunger and thirst, and wondered if it was true. How could it be? A person could not live for long without water – a few days at most. The stew had been well-salted, and she began to feel thirsty.

She pressed on, walking for an hour or two. The ground was mostly level, but always the trees blocked her view. There were no towering spruce or thick-trunked beech here, only the broad oaks, and spindly, leafy trees that would not offer a high vantage point. She reviewed her plan to continue north and could find no flaw with it. Soon enough she would reach either the South River, the Long Lake, or the Silver Trail. But where were the mountains? Still walking, she closed her eyes and tried to recall details from before she awoke near the sulfurous pools. She had been heading west on the Silver Trail, with the river on her right. The sound of a woodpecker. Sleeping under the stars. A voice in her head, telling her that thousands of people lived in the shining rings above. A familiar voice, not unkindly. A face came to mind. Big blue eyes behind circles of glass. Franz, the small man in the hut.

Katja stopped and opened her eyes. There was something ahead, through the trees. She broke into a jog and soon came to a hill, with a structure on top. She scaled the hill quickly and carelessly, sending bits of rock and dirt cascading down behind her.

She smelled her destination before she saw it. Sulfur. Her heart sank. She clambered onto the wooden deck and regarded the pools with dismay. The long, low chair was still there. Across the deck, Henning sat on the stairs, facing away from her.

She spat onto the deck. "What trick is this? Is there no escape from this place?" Henning turned and gazed at her, his expression grave. "Well? You had better give me some answers." She gripped the hilt of her dirk. "I am in no mood for riddles, or tales of Álfheimr."

He leapt up, quickly closing the distance between them. She pulled the dirk from its sheath and held it ready. "There is no way out, as far as I know," he said, ignoring her blade. "But you can ask Raekae for yourself. I do not know if he made this place, but he is the one in charge. He controls the host."

"What is the 'host'?" she asked.

"Who. *Who* is the host. *You* are. Your body. Your real flesh and blood." Henning slowly reached for her free hand. Though she did not trust him, she did not pull away. She felt safe holding steel, while he was unarmed. He held her hand and gently touched her palm with his fingers. "Not this. *This* is an illusion."

He snatched away her dirk and slashed it across her palm. Never had she seen a man move so fast. She jerked her hand away and jumped back. Henning stood still as a statue, watching her. The gash filled with blood. She closed her fist. A rivulet of blood dripped onto the wooden deck. Her palm throbbed, but the pain was bearable.

"Tomorrow the wound will be gone. Your hand will be as good as new. Maybe then you will believe me when I tell you where you are, and what has happened to you."

CHAPTER NINE

Trond and Esper camped in a glade just off the Silver Trail. Except for the distant howling of wolves, a lone owl, and the crackling embers of the campfire, the forest was quiet. Still, Trond slept poorly. For much of the night he stared up at the stars and rings, thinking of his sister and listening to his brother softly snoring. Finally, at twilight, he fell into a deep slumber, but was soon awakened by the sound of Esper making breakfast. "Must you be so loud?" he complained.

"Since when do you greet frying pork with complaints, brother? Your mood must be foul indeed."

Trond's stomach was still knotted with worry; he picked at his food with no appetite. Esper cheerfully wolfed down the remains of Trond's meal after finishing his own.

They continued west along the Silver Trail. Trond, feeling weary, followed a few paces behind Esper. He wondered if it was possible to catch a bit of sleep while walking, and tried, during a straight section of the trail, to close his eyes and let his feet find their own way. This experiment ended when he collided with his brother.

Esper skidded to the ground. "You oaf!" he cried, standing and dusting off his knees.

Trond blinked and slapped his own cheeks, trying to wake up. "Why did you stop? It was your own fault."

Esper pointed to a rock in the center of the trail, twenty paces ahead.

"You stopped because of a rock?"

"Not a rock. A hand."

Trond squinted and lurched forward, but Esper grabbed his sleeve and held him back. "Go carefully." Esper nocked an arrow and crept forward cautiously. Trond drew his sword and moved parallel to his brother, on the other side of the trail.

It was, in fact, a hand: a giant one, the skin gray and dirty, fingers curled inward, nails long, sharp, and crusted with filth. A good section of the forearm was attached, severed clean by sharp steel.

"Where is the rest of it, I wonder," said Esper, kneeling and examining the big hand.

"And who wielded the sword?" Trond said, hoping that it was his sister who had done it.

Esper poked at the hand with his dirk. "A clean cut. Could one of your blades have done this?"

Trond nodded. "Perhaps. Certainly one of Jense's." Truthfully, Trond doubted that a sword of his own making could cut so clean. The heavy forearm bones were not even cracked or shattered, but sliced clean through.

Esper looked up at him thoughtfully. "Do you remember Katja's story? About the giants?" Trond had forgotten it, but now it came back. Katja had gone off on her own, far down the Silver Trail. She did not return for three days, and on each day Arik gave the brothers a taste of his birch lash. It was their responsibility to look after Katja, even if she rejected their assistance. Katja finally returned, with a tale to tell. She had seen giants living in the ruins of an ancient castle. Trond and Esper, still smarting from Arik's blows, had been in no mood to hear her fantasy.

"I thought she was making it up. To make us jealous," Trond said.

"I thought the same," confessed Esper. They stared at the monstrous mitt. Esper pointed at the ground nearby. "Look, signs of a fight. This mark here – that could be from Katja's boot. And over here – a trail of blood."

Trond saw a few droplets of blood, but soon he lost the trail and simply followed his brother. After a hundred paces, Esper veered to the right. Soon they stood on the rocky south bank. Trond took a drink of water while Esper inspected an outcropping extending into the wide, shallow river.

"This rock is stained with blood. Perhaps the creature washed the wound here." Enlivened, Esper resumed his search, but after a short while gave up, discouraged. "I saw both blood and tracks up to this point, but there is nothing else. The trail goes no farther."

"Do not give up," said Trond. "Perhaps he walked in the shallows for a time, to cool his giant feet. We should search farther up the bank."

They found nothing more. Defeated, they returned to the trail and continued west.

"Do you remember how far it is to the ruins?" Trond asked.

"We only slept one night, arriving the next day. We must be getting close."

The woods thickened. Some of the oaks reached across the trail, closing the canopy above. The loamy, uneven earth slowed their pace. At first the shade was refreshing, but eventually Trond flagged. His restless night was catching up with him, and he fell behind. Seeing Esper pull ahead angered him; Trond redoubled his pace and overtook his brother. Esper chuckled as Trond passed. "No race, brother. The first to find our sister will be the first to receive her scorn and ingratitude. She will insist she did not need our help."

Trond ignored his brother and pressed ahead, putting ten paces between them. Green leaves and twigs crunched beneath his feet.

"Stop!" cried Esper from behind. Trond pressed forward. Let Esper stop and nurse his tired feet. Trond would take a nap up ahead, and let his younger brother catch up.

Trond's foot caught on a root. At the same moment, he glimpsed a quick movement in the brush. Perhaps a snake. Something yanked on his leg, ferociously hard. The world inverted and the ground rushed away. Trond writhed in the air. He was high up, caught in a snare, hanging by his ankle. He looked for his brother, expecting to see Esper laughing.

Esper looked up at him, eyes wide and mouth agape. Then his brother's gaze shifted, his expression changing from surprise to horror. Then with dismay, Trond watched his brother turn and flee.

CHAPTER TEN

In bright midday light, cloak camouflage deactivated, Car-En limped down into the broad valley that was home to Happdal. The time for concealment and subterfuge had passed; she was going to openly Intervene.

She'd deactivated her feed to the *Stanford*. Her m'eye was still recording, but there was no reason to let Adrian in on her plan. He would find out eventually, and try to stop her, but at least she would have a head start.

At first she drew only stares and wide-open mouths. She imagined how she must look to them: strange clothes, brown skin, emaciated and injured. At least she was not obviously threatening. She'd hidden her rifle and pack away in the woods. The villagers might not identify the rifle as a weapon, but it wasn't worth the risk.

A pair of bucket-carrying dairymaids backed away, sloshing creamy milk onto the dirt. A pack of boys stared and pointed, then sprinted off. An old man, sitting on a stump and smoking a pipe, watched her impassively. She smiled and nodded in greeting.

"My name is Car-En. I am a visitor. I wish to speak with Arik, or Elke." She spoke in Orbital English, but the names would be clear enough. Her m'eye prompted her with a display of the words she had just spoken, translated into a rough approximation of the Happdal dialect. Over the last few months her kit had mostly deciphered the local language: roughly one part Old Norse, one part Corporate Age Norwegian, and a smattering of words not found in the *Stanford*'s linguistic databases.

The old man drew on his pipe and blew a smoky cloud. Closer, she saw that he was not that old; under his wiry white beard his bronze skin was smooth. "You're not from Kaldbrek, are you?" he asked. Her cochlear implant provided a translation.

She shook her head. "Not from the valleys at all?" He raised an eyebrow. "From the south, past the Long Lake?"

She was from the sky, she thought. She wanted to tell the truth, but how much would he accept? She compromised. "I'm from very far away. From the north-west." True enough; she had hiked south-east from the mule station to reach the village.

The man shifted his eyes, glancing behind her. She turned to see a thickset man approaching, sword drawn. It was Lars – the brute who had challenged Katja the night she was kidnapped. His face was a wreck: a long, inflamed scratch on one cheek, bloodshot eyes, his left eye socket bruised blue and yellow. Car-En showed her palms. "Peace," she said. She repeated the word in the local dialect. "*Grið*."

"She wants to see Arik," said the pipe-smoking man, "or Elke."

"Are you a servant of Haakon?" asked Lars, belligerently. "Perhaps I should remove your head. Go back to Kaldbrek, and tell Haakon we would be delighted to see him. We will prepare a feast. Blood sausage, made from his own drippings."

"Look at her clothes, you fool," said the old man. "She is not from Kaldbrek. And she has no weapon, not even a dirk." Car-En winced, thinking of her carbonlattice blade. How careless she had been to lose it...

"Please let me speak with Arik. It's important." Again she repeated the phrase in their dialect. Lars looked confused, but the older man seemed to understand. He knocked the ash from his pipe with a sharp knock against the stump.

"Come with me," he said. He pocketed the pipe, shook out his legs, and took off up the road at a good pace.

Lars lowered his sword but continued to stare sullenly at Car-En. She followed the old man, keeping her eyes on the town bully until she was a safe distance away.

They came to a large house made from mortared stones and oak timbers. The old man gave a cursory knock on the door but entered without waiting, closing the door behind him. Car-En heard a brief exchange of words from inside, too muffled for her implant to interpret. The door opened again; the old man beckoned her in.

Inside were two girls, no older than fifteen, and a middle-aged woman. The girls were seated at a table chopping vegetables. The woman stirred a giant pot with what looked like an oar. Car-En recognized the woman as Elke, Arik's wife, mother of Trond, Esper, and Katja. The matriarch had the same pale blue eyes as her younger son. Right now those eyes were squinting suspiciously at Car-En. Briefly, Elke's nostrils flared. She issued a clipped command. The girls put down their knives and squeezed past Car-En and out the door, avoiding eye contact.

Car-En held her tongue, waiting for Elke to speak. Elke nodded for Car-En to sit, but remained standing herself. The old man pulled out a chair and settled in.

"You are injured," said Elke. After a beat, listening to the translation, Car-En nodded, and touched her hip. Elke walked around the table and stood behind Car-En's chair. Softly, Elke ran her fingers along Car-En's shoulder, examining the texture of the bioskin material.

"*Silki?*" Elke asked. Silk, the words were nearly the same.

Car-En nodded. Close enough. There were enough things to explain without getting into the details of the intelligent synthetic polymer fabric that functioned as lightweight armor, homeostatic responsive insulation, alarm notification, moisture recycling, and hygienic maintenance system.

Elke took a seat across from her. Her tanned face was beautiful, marked only by worry lines. In her youth she must have been stunning. "What do you want?" Elke asked. Not *Who are you?* or *Where are you from?* Right to the point.

I want to help you. That was the truth, wasn't it? She'd volunteered for the field position hoping to secure her professional reputation as a post-Inhabitation expert. But at some point her priorities had shifted. She'd lost objectivity regarding Happdal's fate. She *knew* these people, even if they did not know her.

Looking into Elke's eyes, seeing her suspicion, she knew the matriarch would not accept this answer. In this case, the direct and simple truth was not the best strategy. If she was going to help the people of Happdal, she would have to deceive them. Her mind raced. Why hadn't she thought this through?

Naively, she'd marched into Happdal with only a Plan A: confess everything. But revealing the whole truth now seemed like a terrible idea. The truth was too complicated, overwhelming, and ultimately implausible.

"Your people have to move," she blurted out. "The entire village, you need to relocate." She painstakingly repeated herself in the Happdal dialect.

Elke's eyes narrowed. "Why?"

"The…earth. It is making your people sick. The well water is not safe to drink. You need to move. Or get your water from somewhere else, perhaps far upstream. Maybe you could build an aqueduct."

Her m'eye had provided a translation for 'aqueduct' but Elke didn't seem to understand. She repeated the word and looked to the old man, who shrugged.

"Farrel says you are from the north-west. What town?"

"The *Stanford*," answered Car-En. No Plan B.

"How do you know this? About the Afflicted?" Farrel asked. Elke gave him a sharp look but said nothing. Was she afraid of revealing any sign of weakness to Car-En?

"I saw the Burning ceremony," said Car-En. "And I see that there are very few old people here." Her translated speech was halting and awkward, but they seemed to understand her.

"You have been watching us," said Elke. "A spy."

Car-En nodded. "I have been watching you. But my intentions are good. I am an emissary."

"You say our water is foul," said Farrel, "but I drink it every day. I am as healthy as a goat. The water is clean." He did seem to be in fine health. The lucky owner of radiation-resistant genetics, no doubt.

"It doesn't make everyone sick," said Car-En, lamely. "Some are immune to the effects." She sensed that the last part of the translation was worthless, but she was having trouble dumbing it down. There were so many basic scientific concepts that were outside of their experience. Yet they were metallurgists, not completely ignorant of chemistry. Could she explain radiation to them? Chromosomal damage?

"The punishment for spying is flaying," said Elke, grimly. "We peel back your skin, slice open your guts, and let the crows feast on your innards. While you watch." The speech was clearly meant to intimidate Car-En, which it did. She guessed that Elke was *probably* bluffing, but a trickle of sweat ran down her back. The bioskin, which would have usually absorbed the perspiration, was not as form-fitting as it had been weeks earlier. Hoping for some reassurance, Car-En glanced at Farrel. He met her gaze with stony indifference.

"I mean you no harm," Car-En said. "It is the...belief...of my people that we should help when we can. I found a cave – I can show it to you – I saw with my own eyes what is polluting the water."

Elke picked up one of the knives left behind by the girls. She pointed it at Car-En. "My people, too, believe in kindness and mercy. So you may leave now, with your life. Show your face again and we will kill you."

Car-En rose from her chair. There had to be a way to get through. With the point of the knife, Elke gestured toward the entrance. Car-En walked to the door and slowly opened it, her mind racing. In the doorway, she turned to face Elke.

"I saw your daughter. With the long blond braids. South-east of here, half a day's march. She was alive and well when I last saw her."

In a moment, Elke was on her, grabbing her arm, pointing the tip of the blade at Car-En's throat. "Is that what this is about? You are a kidnapper, a ransomer?"

"No! I merely saw her. I don't know where she is. I just want to help you!" She shouted in Orbital English, not bothering to translate. Elke let go and stepped back, but did not lower the knife.

Car-En fled. Stubborn old woman. She walked as quickly as she could, in the direction she'd come, but the cut on her hip throbbed with each step. The dirt road was pocked with muddy holes and wheel ruts.

"Wait!" yelled Elke from the doorway. "Did you see my sons? Trond and Esper? One is tall and broad, the other lean."

Car-En turned and shook her head. She could see Esper's handsome face in her mind, so easy to recall. The same pale blue eyes as his mother, but kinder.

"Find my children, any or all of them, and you will be welcome in Happdal."

Car-En nodded. Elke stared at her, perhaps with less hostility. Maybe, underneath her anger, she was also curious. Car-En turned and trudged up the road.

What in the hell had she gotten herself into?

CHAPTER ELEVEN

From what had Esper fled? Trond heaved and twisted in the air, upside down, trying to get a look at whatever it was that had terrified his brother. He glimpsed an immense figure lumbering toward him, but then continued to spin, losing sight of his captor. Looking east, back toward Happdal, there was no sight of Esper. Had his brother deserted him entirely?

Trond took stock of his situation. He hung by his ankle, high above the ground, but one leg and both arms were free. His scabbard dangled near his face. With some difficulty he grabbed the hilt of his sword. He would cut himself down and take his chances with the fall.

Spinning farther around, he set eyes on his foe. The manlike creature was half again as tall as Trond and twice as wide, limbs thick with muscle and fat. Its face was grotesque: oversized jaw, drastic underbite, protruding eyes, bulging forehead, a mostly bald pate draped with a few greasy wisps of black hair. Below the neck, the creature was no prettier. Its hairy feet were bare, it was naked from the waist up, and a large belly hung over its hide pants. It carried a thick branch, hardened and blackened by fire, in its right hand. The brute's left arm ended in a stump, wrapped in dirty, blood-soaked strips of hide.

So, Katja had not been telling tales after all. She had indeed seen giants. Trond made a mental note to apologize to his sister, should he be so lucky as to see her again. With a quick prayer to the Red Brother, he awkwardly drew his sword.

Trond hacked at the snare. The crudely woven plant fibers yielded easily to the sharpened steel. For a moment he was weightless, but then the snare caught again. He swung in the breeze. His blade had not passed all the way through the bundle of vines. It was difficult to land a strong blow from his inverted position.

As Trond pulled back to swing again, the giant's maul crashed into his shoulder. His sword flew out of his hand and stuck in the dirt below. The giant roared and struck again, smashing Trond's face with the charred end of the club. As his vision darkened, Trond heard a whistling sound, a quick thud, and a guttural cry of pain. Could it be the sound of an arrow biting through hide and into giant flesh? His last thought was one of gratitude toward his brother, who perhaps had not deserted him after all.

★   ★   ★

Trond's shoulder throbbed painfully. He was naked and trussed with dried vines, lying in the dirt. A stone wall obstructed his vision. Behind him he could hear and feel a crackling bonfire.

With some difficultly, he rolled over. He was tied to something, a long, straight branch, but the branch itself was not secured to anything. The bonfire was framed by sturdy supports for a roasting spit. Crumbling stone walls surrounded the area on all sides. He recognized the castle ruins he had explored long ago with Esper. Looking up, he could see the stars and gibbous moon shining brightly – a splendid view under better circumstances. Trond strained against his bonds but succeeded only in intensifying his pain.

A bulky form shambled from the darkness. It was not the same creature as before. This one was smaller (though still much larger than Trond), and female. Her large, pendulous breasts were smeared with dirt. A ragged animal hide was wrapped around her waist. She carried something heavy, a pail, and before Trond could brace himself she splashed him with icy water.

"Curse you, you immense hag!" shouted Trond from the ground. "May the Red Brother smash your head with his hammer! May you fall in your own fire and roast alive! And save some of that water to wash your own filthy flesh!"

The great hag ignored him and shambled off. Well, at least he was cleaner now, and wide awake. Where in the Red Brother's name was Esper? He shivered. The front of his body was warm but the back was freezing, each gust of breeze like icicles against his wet, naked skin. He clenched his jaw to silence his chattering teeth.

A few minutes later the giantess returned, this time carrying a cracked ceramic pot. She dipped two fingers inside, scraped out a large glob of brown, filthy grease, and generously smeared the fat on Trond's thighs. Trond writhed against his bonds and cursed. His insults fell on deaf ears; his cook and captor methodically prepared him for the roast. She spared no inch of his flesh from the rancid animal fat (he *hoped* it was animal fat, and not the drippings of some poor villager). As she roughly smeared the foul-smelling grease on his cock and balls, Trond was horrified to find himself partially aroused. "Curse you! Off of me! Off!" The giantess finished her preparations by sprinkling his body with a handful of coarse gray salt. She stood back, sniffing the air, and with a final self-satisfied grunt, wandered off.

"Esper! Brother!" he yelled. "If you can hear me, I could use some help! I'm sorry for passing you on the trail, earlier today." Then more quietly, to himself, "I wish I had not."

Now, dimly, he could see three forms on the far side of the fire. The big dirty she-beast, the one-handed brute who had clubbed him, and a smaller, man-sized form. Had they captured Esper as well? No, the third creature was much wider than his slight brother. It was coming around the fire, staring at him hungrily: a child-giant, buck-toothed and drooling, with matted black hair, and the same bulging eyes as its father. It spoke in a low, guttural voice.

"What was that?" asked Trond. He had little hope of talking his way out of captivity, but it would not hurt to try. What did the huge child have to say for itself?

The same guttural sound, but this time the creature came close. It tapped Trond's greasy leg and made a questioning noise. The father grunted in assent.

Ah, the choice bits. The young one wanted a thighbone. Trond tried to spit at the creature's face but managed only to wet his own cheek. The child-thing laughed and kicked his ribs.

The parents joined their offspring, flanking Trond at either end. They squatted, each grabbing an end of the spit (the father, closer to Trond's head, using his one remaining hand). With a few guttural words, maybe a three-count, they hoisted him into the air. As they carried him toward the fire, Trond noticed a gaping arrow wound in the big one's belly. Perhaps the iron leaf was still lodged in the creature's guts. Try to digest *that*, thought Trond as they placed the spit on the frame. He swung facedown over the flames. He felt an instant of intense heat, then pure, searing pain. *So this is what it feels like.* Trond was having his Burning a bit early. Instead of screaming, Trond decided to laugh. Life had been good! He squeezed his eyes shut, inhaled the stench of his own burning beard, and cackled like a madman.

CHAPTER TWELVE

After retrieving her hidden rifle and pack, Car-En hiked back to her old camp. It was the closest thing she had to *home*. Now she was high in a birch tree, fully cloaked, rifle at the ready, waiting for something edible to come along. She was desperate to eat something besides nutrient bars (of which there were only three left) and wild berries (the black ones were sweet and edible, but the red ones, despite registering as non-toxic in the biosampler, had given her stomach cramps and a bad case of the shits).

She hadn't seen any game yet, but it was something to do while she waited for the drones. She'd sent out the majority of the swarm to search for Trond, Esper, and Katja. She didn't have enough to cover a wide area, but if any of them were within five kilometers the drones would soon tell her.

Elke had clearly stated her terms. She would try to find the woman's children. She was going to *help* the people of Happdal, despite Elke's suspicion and resistance. Katja's condition worried her. She'd continuously replayed the sequence of the white-haired man transferring the black, oblong-shaped object into Katja's mouth. She'd even image-searched for a match on the black egg-thing in the *Stanford*'s databases, but nothing relevant had come up. Whatever it was, it hadn't killed the young woman, at least not immediately. That much of what she'd told Elke was true; Katja had been whole the last time Car-En had seen her.

A nearby drone – one of the rearguard – directed her attention to a tree, fifteen meters to her left. Car-En turned, zoomed in with her m'eye, and spotted a red squirrel, bushy-tailed and elfin-eared. It was the third one she'd seen within the hour. She relaxed her grip on the rifle. She'd told herself she wouldn't bother with the squirrels because of their diminutive size. Skinning the creatures would be too much work for a few morsels of meat. But really, who was she kidding? She could never kill something so adorable.

She'd never killed an animal, either accidentally or purposefully. There were fishponds on the *Stanford*, and a few rustic farms with chickens and goats and sheep that were used for historical education and children's petting zoos. But the meat they ate was vat-grown, isolated muscle tissue grown and exercised in nutrient broth solutions, not connected to any sort of brain or consciousness. Not once had she eaten the actual flesh of a once-living, breathing, *feeling* animal. At first the idea had nauseated her, but the hungrier she got, the less revulsive the notion became. Now, she relished the thought of bringing down a hairy, grunting wild boar with a sedative dart, slitting its throat, gutting and skinning it, roasting and eating it. The last part of the daydream made her mouth water.

Her m'eye blinked – Adrian was trying to contact her. She ignored the alert and deactivated the connection to the *Stanford* entirely. She hadn't yet decided what to say to Adrian. Yes, she was Intervening. Or attempting to, if she could get through to Elke. Maybe she should have insisted on seeing Arik, the village chieftain, instead. Farrel had probably taken her to Elke either because Arik was busy, or possibly because he thought Elke was level-headed and would not freak out at the sight of a brown-skinned woman in a silver suit. In any case, Car-En had not gotten very far in her Intervention attempt. If she was going to come clean with Adrian about what she was trying to do, she at least wanted to make some progress first.

Another alert flashed in her m'eye, this one from a drone 4.8 kilometers east by south. A possible match for Esper, the younger brother. It wasn't much to go on, just a moving silhouette. Car-En instructed the drones to follow from a safe distance. She'd lost more of the swarm to dragonflies and mechanical wear and tear; the drones were down to half their original number. She wished she'd brought more of the insectile robots.

She slung the rifle over her shoulder and gingerly climbed down the tree. The wound on her hip was healing clean, but it still hurt, and her malnourished state made her prone to dizziness. She unmasked her pack, shouldered it, and began a slow trudge in an easterly direction.

After an hour of walking, the drones confirmed it was Esper she was tracking. He was about one kilometer away, sitting on a fallen tree trunk, sharpening the end of a long stick. Though his long brown hair partially covered his face, Car-En still recognized him. He looked up and made direct eye contact. Car-En's heart skipped a beat. But of course he couldn't see her; he was looking at a fly on a tree. *Examining* the fly, suspiciously. This one had sharp vision, if he could see an insect from ten meters. Or maybe he was just looking at the tree? After a few seconds he returned to his whittling. Heart still pounding, Car-En picked up her pace. She wondered where Trond and Katja might be. The drones were still searching but so far had found no sign of Esper's siblings.

Closing the distance, she tried to come up with a strategy. She didn't want to repeat the experience with Elke, tripping over her own words and making a mess of things. What would be the best way to approach Esper? What did she know about him? He was looking for his sister. He seemed to get along with his brother. She wished she had managed to obtain a viable biosample; it would be helpful to have a few genetic insights into his personality. Really, she knew very little about this young man. He was *handsome*, that much she was sure of. She grinned. She was getting loopy from hunger.

She stepped on a fallen branch, breaking it. Watching via the drones, she saw Esper stand, drop his spear-in-progress, and retrieve his bow. Within seconds he had an arrow nocked and was advancing toward her. She was about to become prey.

"*Frændi!*" she yelled. She was learning a little of the Happdal dialect, especially the words that were similar to English. "I mean you no harm!" She slung her rifle over her shoulder, threw back her hood, decamouflaged her cloak, and waved her hands in the air.

Esper kept the arrow nocked but didn't draw. He moved through the trees almost silently. Without the drones he would have easily surprised her, shooting her dead if he'd wished.

"*Frændi!*" she shouted again. They were close enough that he should hear her.

He came into view, looking taller and stronger than she remembered. It was only next to Trond that Esper looked small; in fact he was just under two meters tall, and broad-shouldered. His ash-blond beard, though sparser than his brother's, had grown since she'd seen him last. His face was smudged with dirt and his eyes looked wild and sleepless.

He swiftly pulled back his bowstring and released. The arrow swished past her head, sunk into a nearby tree. She could hear the shaft vibrate. "*Haltr,*" he said. *Stop.*

She raised her hands, palms forward. "Elke," she said. Esper would not murder his mother's envoy.

He spoke rapidly in his dialect, and her kit fed the translation into her earbud. "You. You were the one I saw, in the trees near the village, on the day of Burning. Was it you?"

Car-En nodded. She thought she'd gone unseen. He was watching her closely, taking in her clothes, her pack, the rifle.

"You carry Builder things, but new," he said. "Do the Builders still live? Is that what you are?"

"In a way," she answered, after listening to her translator. He was quick. If she told him the complete truth – that human beings lived in the sky – would he be able to absorb and accept it? She made a snap decision. "I come from one of the rings above. We call them ringstations." She repeated the phrase in the Happdal dialect, following the prompts from her m'eye. Unable to find a match for 'ringstations,' her translation module offered 'ring-ships' instead. *Hringr-kjóll.* Would he know what a ship was? It struck her how little she knew of these people, of their culture and knowledge. How much had been lost? It was surprising he had identified her as a 'Builder.' What was their lore concerning the fall of civilization? It occurred to her that she could learn more from a single conversation than she could from months of observations. Perhaps that reason alone could justify her Intervention.

"*Hringr-kjóll,*" he repeated. "The rings are vessels? How many do they carry? How do they stay in the sky?"

"The ringships are home to tens of thousands," she said haltingly, positive she was mangling the Happdal-dialect pronunciation. "Some of the rings orbit Earth, others travel through space. My own home, the *Stanford*, is in synchronous equatorial orbit." She knew that most of what she said was gibberish to him, but he listened intently. "On a clear night, if you look to the south, you can see my home."

"You said my mother's name. What business do you have with Elke? What has she tasked you with?"

"I went to Happdal and spoke with her. I discovered something…something that is affecting…. I know what is making your people sick. I explained this to Elke and told her that you have to move the village. Or find a new source of water."

Esper laughed. "Move the village? You suggested this to my mother?"

"I wasn't able to convince her. Maybe I can explain the situation to you. Perhaps you can persuade her." Car-En knew she sounded overly earnest, and probably too direct, but she sensed that Esper might be more open-minded than his mother.

He glanced over his shoulder, then circled her, keeping his distance. "If you live in the sky, why have you come down? Why are you here?"

At least he was not accusing her directly of being a spy, as Elke had. Though she'd been right – Car-En *was* a spy. But Esper seemed willing to give her the benefit of the doubt.

"To learn about your people. To help you." At least *she* was trying to help, if not Adrian.

"You say you have discovered the cause of the Affliction. Tell me."

"I found a cave," said Car-En. "Deep underground, there is an ancient Builder device, a powerful machine that was once used to produce energy. This machine also produced waste. For many years it has poisoned your water. You can't see or smell the poison, and it doesn't make everyone sick, or kill anyone right away. But over time it causes the illness. The Affliction." The speech took a long time, as Car-En had to repeat each phrase in the Happdal dialect after first saying it in Orbital English.

She had little faith in the translations her m'eye provided for 'machine' and 'device' and 'energy,' but she hoped he was getting the gist of it.

"Do Builders still live in this cave?" he asked.

"No, they left long ago. I think they knew they would be poisoned if they stayed."

"You can show me this place? And this *machine* you speak of?" he asked. Car-En nodded. Esper looked away, considering the situation. Car-En waiting patiently. When he met her gaze again, his jaw was set, his eyes wide. She willed herself to stand still and not look away. "I do, in fact, need help," he finally said. "My brother has been captured by a giant. The brute is too strong for me to fight alone." He pointed at her rifle. "Is that a weapon?"

A giant? "Yes. It can kill, or induce sleep."

"If you help me, I will go to this cave with you, and see what the Builders have made with my own eyes. If I am convinced, we will return to Happdal and make our case to my mother. She is stubborn, but she will hear me out." He took a moment to scan their surroundings. "But first, you will help me find my brother, and also my sister. I swore to the Red Brother I would not return to Happdal until I found Katja." He leaned his bow against a tree and extended his hand. "If you help me, and we succeed, you will forever have an ally." She took his forearm in the way she had seen the villagers greet. His skin was warm, his forearm thick with muscle. "I am Esper," he said.

"Car-En." A lump formed in her throat as she said her own name. She had not introduced herself to anyone in a long time.

"Are you hungry?" he asked. "You look as if you have not eaten for weeks."

"I'm starving."

They returned to the small clearing where Esper had been whittling. He gestured to the fallen tree trunk and they sat. From a cloth sack he removed a block of hard cheese, a half-loaf of dark bread, tiny dried fishes, some kind of jerky, fresh green apples, and a lidded ceramic jar bound closed with twine. "These," he said, holding up the jar, "I have been saving for a special occasion. I hoped to share them with my sister, when we found her. But you are hungry, and maybe I am lucky to find you, so we'll eat them now. Nobody makes better pickles than my mother."

Car-En thanked him, and ate everything he offered. The simple food was overwhelmingly delicious, and once again Car-En had to hold back tears. She had a friend (or at least someone who was not threatening her, or actively trying to kill her), and she was *eating*. "Good?" he asked. She could only nod, mouth full.

While she ate, Esper continued sharpening the sturdy branch and further explained his predicament. "The giant took my brother east, along the Silver Trail. I followed him for a time, but I could not keep up with his long stride. I dared not shoot him with arrows for fear of hitting Trond, whom he carried across his back like a slain deer. I decided to craft a sturdier weapon, then track him to his home. But I don't know what the brute has in store for my brother, so we must hurry." Esper glanced up. "There is still light in the sky. Are you ready?" Car-En nodded, relieved to have someone else take the lead. Acting alone for so long, she had developed decision fatigue. She took a pickled carrot and passed the half-empty jar back to Esper.

They returned to the trail and continued east. Esper carried the spear, using the blunt end as a walking staff, his bow slung over his back. Car-En readied her rifle, still loaded with sedative darts. Esper asked to hold the gun. Would she teach him how to use it? She promised she would show him, later. "Maybe your weapon will be more effective than my arrow, which he pulled from his belly and tossed aside like a splinter. Though he can be injured. We found his hand – severed from his body – before we discovered the rest of him. How he lost it, I have no idea. A steel blade, no doubt, but who was wielding it?"

Car-En was skeptical of this 'giant.' Just a very tall man, perhaps? But who knew what creatures roamed Earth now? If she had learned anything, it was how little the ringstation denizens knew about the current state of their home planet.

As they walked, Esper peppered her with questions. What was her home like? How did she descend from the sky? From what material was her clothing made? She answered as truthfully and as thoroughly as she could. Strange as she must have seemed to him, he took her answers in stride. Just another oddity in an odd world, she supposed. But there was something else to Esper, a natural curiosity and keen intelligence. She wondered, not for the first time, what wildstrains he might be harboring in his genome. She considered asking him directly for a saliva sample. But no, they had only just met.

In turn, she asked about Happdal. What did he know about the history of his own people? He told her about the Ice Trail, the long walk south. Their homeland, which had always been cold, had gotten colder. Summer disappeared entirely, leaving a permanent, barren winter. Nothing could grow in the icy soil. Animals froze to death. Most people refused to leave their ancestral home and eventually starved. But some – Esper's ancestors – came south on the Ice Trail. They settled in these mountains because the place reminded them of home, before the endless winter. Both sun and snow, hills and valleys, fertile land to grow grain, and mountains laced with metal. Everyone in the Five Valleys came from the Northlands, long ago. But now, most considered the Ice Trail a tall tale. They believed that their people *came* from the mountains, that they had *always* lived here. "In a few generations," said Esper, sadly, "the knowledge of our ancestors will be lost."

Car-En nodded quietly. If only he knew how much knowledge had been lost. Should she tell him?

"Our ancestors are one and the same, long ago," she said. "I am descended from the people you call the Builders, and so are you." He looked at her thoughtfully. The idea did not seem to offend him, at least. She continued, "On Earth, most of the Builders died, and most of what they knew was lost. But your ancestors retained more knowledge than most. How to grow food crops. How to work with metals, and make tools and weapons."

He nodded. "That is part of the tale as well. Our people held on to the old ways. That is why we survived. That, and our purity."

"Purity?" she asked.

"Yes. Our strong blood. It was part of Mormor's story."

She wondered if Adrian's 'Scandinavian traditionalist village' hypothesis was missing a critical component: racism. She had a vague notion of a significant overlap between Viking-themed historical enthusiasm and extreme right-wing/neo-Nazi sympathies in Corporate Age Europe. European racism and xenophobia had never gone away after World War II; it had simply expanded from Jews and Roma to include African and Middle-Eastern immigrants. During the Remnant Age, the Survivalist tribes had often segregated along racial lines. Perhaps Esper's ancestors had been no different in that respect. At least Esper himself did not seem bothered by her brown skin.

She had studied her own ethnic composition in great detail; she had ancestors from nearly every continent. Her appearance (light brown skin, large eyes, small, flat nose, compact body) was the result of a wide mix of origins: South Asian (Indian), North Asian (Mongolian), and a variety of European subgroups. She guessed that Esper's lineage was similarly diverse, if heavily weighted toward Northern European. Such was the case with every Happdal villager she had sequenced so far. She'd found ancestral traces from Southern and Eastern Europe, the Middle East, Russia, and every other region that had ever sent emigrants to Northern Europe. Esper's 'strong blood' was nearly as mixed as her own.

Esper was still talking. "...thankfully the Red Brother showed us the way, and we found our home in the mountains. I only wish I could convince the others that the Ice Trail story is real. It's important that we understand our origins."

Understand to an extent, she thought. Perhaps it was better to leave the 'purity' stone unturned. "Who is the Red Brother?" she asked.

He grinned at her ignorance. "A wrathful god. He wields a hammer that can smite any foe. He has two brothers, one brown and one black. The colors of their beards."

The Norse god Thor. But who were the other two, the brown-bearded and black-bearded gods? Were they also white-skinned, and *pure*? Why was she feeling touchy? She reminded herself how little Esper knew of history, of *anything* really. Mentally, she tried to absolve him of any bigotry his ancestors might have harbored. It was just a hypothesis, after all. Even if true, her *own* distant kin had indulged in atrocious behaviors at some point in history (her own genomic analysis listed Genghis Khan as a likely ancestor).

"The Brown Brother is merciful, and believes in forgiveness. Still, he is powerful. He can turn water into wine, and heal the sick. The Black Brother believes in justice above all else. He performs righteous deeds, travels in the night, and can fly to the moon."

Thor, Jesus, and Muhammad. Fascinating. In her m'eye, Car-En tagged what had just been recorded. "Polytheistic theology," she subvocalized. She couldn't wait to discuss this with Adrian. Realistically, after Academic Conduct was done with her, her research on Earth would be over. But somebody, eventually, would learn from the material she was collecting. This knowledge was invaluable.

Dusk fell. The river, and the trail with it, continued west, but Esper, after examining some nearby vegetation, led them south into a thick beech wood. "This brute is easier to track than a boar," he said, as they climbed a steep slope. "We are close to the ruins of an ancient castle – perhaps that is where he makes his home. Long ago, my sister said she saw giants there. We didn't believe her at the time."

Giants, plural. Car-En gripped her rifle more tightly and directed her drones to scout ahead. Her m'eye responded with a DRONES OFFLINE error. Strange. Some local signal interference? She brought up a topographical map of the area; they were roughly fifteen kilometers east-south-east of Happdal, rapidly gaining elevation. She added a landmark layer to the visualization. There were indeed some ruins nearby, less than a kilometer ahead. *Scharzfels Castle, constructed in the eleventh century, an impregnable fortress for half a millennium.*

"Do you smell smoke?" asked Esper. She sniffed, caught a faint whiff of burning wood, and nodded. Esper redoubled his pace. Car-En struggled to keep up. As they climbed the treed ridge she saw stars through gaps in the canopy, and caught a glimpse of the nearly full moon. Finally they crested the ridge, scrambling up a final sheer rock face. Twenty meters ahead was a low stone rampart. Orange and yellow light flickered through cracks in the wall. A bonfire.

They crept forward; Esper with his makeshift spear, Car-En with her rifle held at eye level. From beyond the wall they heard low, coarse voices. "More than one," whispered Esper. "Take care, the brute I saw was swift as well as large."

Car-En advanced cautiously, a few steps behind Esper, trying to keep her breathing slow and even. Oddly, she felt calmer than during her encounter with the strange white-haired man. Maybe she was getting used to living dangerously. Or maybe she just felt safer in the company of Esper.

"*Eins, zwei, drie!*" The deep voices were counting in some Germanic language. The numbers were followed by a peal of loud, wild laughter.

"Trond!" cried Esper, charging forward. Esper cleared the crumbling rampart with a high leap, disappearing from sight. She heard shouts of surprise.

She sprinted to the wall and peered over. Trond was lying on the ground near the fire, naked and bound to a wooden spit, the front of his body scorched raw, his red beard still smoldering with flame. Esper was crouched next to him, clutching his spear tightly. On the other side of the fire were three figures. Two were indeed *giants*, over three meters tall, and immensely wide. The third, a child, was roughly man-sized, with thick, matted black hair. This smaller one roared, revealing a mouthful of large, yellowed teeth, and charged at Esper, jumping over the edge of the fire. Esper met the child-giant head-on, plunging the tip of his spear into its gaping maw. The blow stopped it cold. The beast lurched, clutched at the shaft, and stumbled into the flames. The spear had impaled the back of its throat; it could only emit a gurgling cry, futilely grasping at the shaft with both meaty hands. It collapsed, damping a third of the bonfire with its bulk.

Esper let go of the spear and jumped clear of the flames. Another giant, a lumbering, topless female, cried out in anguish.

She grabbed the child-giant by the ankle and dragged its limp body from the flames. The huge male circled menacingly toward Esper, wielding a massive club. Car-En raised her rifle, aimed center-of-mass, and fired three sedative darts into his chest and abdomen. The giant winced, glanced in her direction, and moved behind the fire, blocking her line of sight. Esper leapt and rolled to the side, dodging a crushing downward strike from the giant's club.

Car-En scrambled over the stone wall and circled around the fire to get a clear shot. Esper crouched in front of his brother, who lay limp and seemingly lifeless, his chest singed raw. The giant raised his club to take another swing, but looked unsteady on his feet. The sedative was kicking in. Car-En fired three more darts in quick succession. One missed, but two thudded into the creature's broad back. He swayed and stumbled, falling to one knee. Car-En fired two more darts, connecting with both. Only two more in the clip, and the remaining ammunition was buried deep in her pack. The brute's head drooped forward. He dropped the club, slumped to one side, and fell with an earth-shaking thud.

The female huddled over her lifeless offspring. She carefully extracted the spear from his throat. A stream of black blood gushed from its maw. She whipped the wooden spear, end-over-end, at Esper, who ducked. The shaft struck the stone wall and snapped in two. The giantess tenderly stroked her child's matted hair, for the moment ignoring the interlopers.

Giving the female giant wide berth, Car-En joined Esper at Trond's side. He was badly burned, but his chest still rose and fell shallowly. Esper drew his dirk, cut the tough vines that bound his brother to the long spit, and gently eased Trond's heavy, limp body into a supine position.

"Can you carry him?" asked Car-En. Esper nodded. "Then let's get out of here." As Esper struggled to lift Trond, Car-En kept an eye on the giantess. Who was she? *What* was she? As soon as Esper had secured his brother in a firefighter's carry, Car-En sprinted to the wall and grabbed the pointy half of the broken spear. "This way," she said, gesturing to the stone ruins of a doorframe.

"His clothes and sword," whispered Esper, "do you see them?"

"Just go!" hissed Car-En. "If she attacks I won't be able to stop her."

They carefully descended a set of ancient stone stairs, then veered north across a grassy hillock. Esper led the way, Trond slung across his shoulders, moving slowly but confidently. Car-En followed, frequently glancing over her shoulder. She activated her thermal vision. The drones were still offline.

"Can you see in the dark?" she asked Esper.

"Yes. Can you?"

"Yes. And I can see great distances as well." There was no reason to be coy about her technological abilities. Sharing knowledge might help them survive.

"Eaglesight. I have that as well, from my mother."

They continued north into a wooded area. "I'll need to rest soon," said Esper. "My brother is heavy."

"A little farther, if you can," she said, looking back. She sorely missed the drones. As they walked she tried to troubleshoot the problem. There was no obvious radio interference. Seeing the long queue of messages from Adrian, a dark thought occurred to her.

They reached a natural clearing among the beech trees, an island of grasses and wildflowers. "Here," she said. Esper gently lowered Trond to the ground, grunting with the effort. She leaned over the hulking blacksmith, examining his muscular body. Next to the giants, Trond had looked small, but up close she realized he must outweigh her by at least a factor of three (maybe four, given her current emaciated state). His arms were wider than her legs, his legs wider than her waist. Unlike the giants, Trond was both strong and lean; he resembled an anatomical model, pure muscle stripped of skin and fat. Unfortunately, he actually *was* missing several layers of skin, especially from his chest and abdomen. Below the waist, his epidermis, though red and raw, was intact (including the skin of his genitals, which, even in proportion to his oversized body, were alarmingly large). His unburned skin was covered in grease or oil, and had a foul, rancid smell. She checked his temperature with thermal vision.

It was several degrees lower than it should be. "Make a fire," she told Esper, "quickly. We need to keep him warm."

"Trond is strong," said Esper. "He'll be fine."

She glared at him. "Please do as I ask. If you want your brother to live through the night, follow my instructions *exactly*."

Esper stared at her, then nodded curtly. "I'll fetch wood."

Car-En removed her pack and retrieved her first aid supplies. She found an antiseptic salve that would relieve pain and accelerate healing. She applied it liberally to Trond's raw burns. The big man flinched and shivered beneath her touch, but his eyes stayed closed. For the best, to stay unconscious for as long as possible. He would be in a world of pain when he came to.

Esper returned with a large bundle of dry branches and built a campfire. She would have preferred to stay dark (there might be more giants, or the mother might come after them), but Trond needed warmth. The night air was cool, he was naked, and his injuries would hinder temperature regulation. Blood pressure and glucose levels were the other things to look out for – that much she remembered from her medical field training.

She retrieved a lightweight reflective emergency blanket from her pack and gingerly wrapped it around Trond. It wasn't big enough to cover him entirely – his ankles and feet stuck out – but it would help. With Esper's assistance she arranged her pack and his carry-sack so that Trond was between their gear and the campfire in a pocket of warmer air. Esper removed his boots and woolen socks, and with some effort got them onto Trond's feet, which were unburned. After a few minutes, Trond stopped shivering.

"I did not mean to sound harsh or uncaring," said Esper. "I love my brother. But he *is* strong. You will see for yourself in the morning." He sat and rubbed his bare feet. "Thank you for caring for him."

She unpacked her medical kit and took Trond's vitals. The results were encouraging. His glucose was within normal range, his inflammatory markers were heightened but not dangerously so, his blood pressure was low but in a safe range, and his body temperature was stable at 36.5°C. "You seem to be right," she conceded to Esper, who was warming his feet by the fire. "Your brother is...strong."

Esper nodded. "He has survived injuries that would have killed lesser men, myself included. Lars once got in a lucky sword thrust while they were sparring. He opened up a vein in Trond's groin. Never have I seen so much blood, or my brother so pale. Lars fled and hid in the woods for three days and three nights. When he dared show his face, Trond was already back to work in the smithy. But Lars was thin and filthy. Not only a coward, but a poor woodsman." Esper stood and stretched. "I am going back, to find his clothes and his sword. Wish me luck, sky dweller."

Car-En looked up, startled. "Are you crazy? That...creature. The mother. She'll crush you if she sees you."

Esper grinned. "She will not see me. Or hear me. Not with bare feet."

Car-En shook her head. "I'll go. Your brother will need a familiar face when he wakes up. My cloak.... Well, see for yourself." Car-En pulled up her hood and subvocalized a command. Her cloak matched the flickering shadows of the campfire. Esper's eyes widened.

"Impressive! Builder magic. I would like to know how that works. Very well – you go. I will warm my toes by the fire and keep my brother company."

"One more thing," said Car-En. She picked up the bloodied point of the broken spear from the rock where she'd carefully balanced it. She'd carried the broken shaft pressed parallel to her rifle. Now, examining it closely, she found a still-moist patch of congealed blood, untouched by dirt or debris. She handed the spear point to Esper, unwrapped a sterile swab-stick from her medical kit, retrieved a glob of blood, and carefully deposited it into the sequencing compartment of her biosampler. The analysis would take a few hours.

Esper watched as she reloaded the rifle with a fresh clip of sedative darts. Was there anything else she could do to prepare? Her adrenaline had worn off and fatigue was setting in – she suspected her thinking was cloudy. She checked her m'eye; the drones were still offline. The queue of messages from Adrian waited, unopened. There would be time for that later. Right now, Trond needed his clothes back.

"Wish me luck, ground dweller," she said to Esper.

"May the Red Brother protect you."

Car-En melted into the dark beech wood.

CHAPTER THIRTEEN

As Henning had promised, Katja's hand healed quickly. The bleeding stopped after five minutes, the pain an hour later. In the evening, alone in her cabin, she stared at her palm in the lantern light, watching her flesh knit itself together.

Henning, after slashing her palm, had offered the dirk back, pommel first. She had grabbed it, and pressed the blade against his throat. If she cut him, he had pointed out, he would not be able to answer her questions until the next day. So she had punched him in the nose, *hard*, and stormed back to her hut without another word.

Now the next day had arrived, and she had questions. Where was she? Who was *Raekae*? And who had snuck into her residence while she had slept to deliver a breakfast of fried eggs, sausages, and hot porridge with currants? She had eaten every bite.

It did not take long to find the hut with the red door. It opened before she had a chance to knock. Stian, the burly one, invited her in with a wave of his hand. The diminutive Franz sat at the small table by the window. Henning leaned against a cupboard, sipping from a steaming mug.

"A drink called coffee," he explained. "Would you like some? Franz has an unlimited supply."

"Where are my spectacles?" said Franz. "Oh, right there. Yes...coffee. The favorite beverage of the Corporate Age, and the Renaissance before that. I'd only read about it – the beans weren't available after Campi Flegrei – so I was delighted to find it here. It tasted nothing like I expected. Honestly I didn't like it at first, but it grew on me."

"Putrid filth," said Stian. He returned to his seat and took a long draught from an immense tankard.

"It's eight in the morning," Franz said.

"So?" responded Stian, taking another gulp. Katja got the impression the same exchange had happened many times before.

"I have come to appreciate coffee as well," Henning said to Katja. "Will you try some? Or would you prefer Belgian *öl*?"

"*Öl* for me," she replied.

Soon all four were seated at the small table. Katja sat next to the bearlike Stian, whose presence she found comforting (perhaps because he reminded her of Jense), and across from Henning, whom she mistrusted. It was true that her hand had healed, but it was reassuring to have a sturdy wooden table between them. Franz and Henning sipped their coffees and looked at her expectantly.

"What?"

"You have questions, don't you?" Franz said. "What do you want to know?"

Katja took a sip of *öl*. It was sweet, with bitter undertones. She glanced at Stian, who stared resolutely into his tankard. Franz blinked his blue eyes behind the glass circles. Henning regarded her calmly, not unkindly. "It is a shock, arriving here," he said. "You are wondering where you are. And why. And how you can return home. We have all been in your boots, so I will save you the trouble.

"So, to begin: *where*. As best I know, we are living inside someone's mind. Raekae's mind. But that is not entirely true, because Raekae does not know everything that goes on. I think he can find out, if he wants, but he cannot directly read our minds. Many things escape his notice. This conversation, for example. He will not know about it unless he decides to later examine this particular time and place. He can do that – see into the past. A kind of magic.

"So we are in Raekae's mind, or in a world of his making. A small world, as you learned yesterday. There are the grounds, with the gardens and the huts and the pools. We are surrounded by woods on all sides. There are a few creeks and streams, and low hills, but no rivers or mountains. Sometimes it rains, but never violent weather or a great storm. I have not once heard thunder here. It is a quiet world."

"Boring," said Stian.

"Yes, boring," Henning agreed. "Yet, remarkably, we stay sane. In fact, we find ourselves in better spirits than we might expect, given our circumstances. We are prisoners, but well-treated prisoners. The books are our salvation."

Franz nodded, and Stian grunted in assent. "Books?" asked Katja. Esper had books. He was obsessed with all Builder things.

"It took me ten years to learn to read," said Stian. "Well, actually only two...the first eight I simply refused to learn."

"How long have you been here?" asked Katja.

"I have not kept track," Stian said.

"He's been here ninety-one years," Franz offered. "I've often wished I could see how I took him down, when I was host."

"It was not you; it was Raekae," protested Stian. "And sneakily, that is how. None of you could take me in a fair fight." Henning raised an eyebrow. "Maybe Henning," Stian conceded, "but only if I had been drinking the night before."

"You have a short memory," said Henning. "Maybe because the last time we fought I left your head rolling in the dirt. About ten years ago, yes?"

"With a soulsword that I forged! Biter. Or was it Taker?"

"Biter, the wolf," Henning said.

"It was I who brought the Five Secrets of godsteel from the Northlands," said Stian, proudly. Katja *knew* the secrets of godsteel. Trond had taught her, after swearing her to secrecy: the Crucible, the Sealed Oven, the Gentle Shaping, and the Flaming Sword. But that was only four. Which one was she forgetting?

Henning returned his attention to Katja. "I have been here the shortest, only fifty-three years. I was thirty-five when I became the host. If I still roamed Midgard, I would now be eighty-eight. An old graybeard." He looked away, wistfully. "I miss Happdal. I miss the smell of fresh milk. And the milkmaids."

"The *öl* is better here," said Stian. "And at least now we have a pretty face to look at."

"True," Henning conceded. He grinned at Katja, his face open and friendly. She reminded herself that just yesterday he had casually sliced open her palm, as if filleting a river trout.

"I do not mean to be impolite," said Stian, "but it is nice to have the company of a woman. We have been only men here for so long."

"Not technically true," said Franz. "The hermit."

"That scary old crone?" Stian said. "May the Brown Brother show us mercy – I hope never to see her again. I would rather drink coffee."

Franz laughed enthusiastically. These men, who had been in close proximity for the better part of a century, had somehow not come to hate each other.

"I've been here one hundred twenty-two years," said Franz. "Of those here at the table, the longest. But the hermit has been here longer." Franz turned to Henning. "You were in the middle of answering Katja's hypothetical questions. I believe the next one was *why*. Why is she here?" Then, to Katja: "You may, of course, ask any question you like."

"I *would* like to know why I am here," she said. She was still deciding if she believed any of it. She tried to remember where she had seen Henning before. For an instant she had a fragment of a memory – a flash of a man with white hair – but when she chased the image it was gone. And Henning's long hair was blond.

"Honestly we don't know why *exactly* Raekae chooses each host," Franz explained. "We've asked him, but all he will say is 'to broaden my experience.' We think it's because each host offers particular advantages that match Raekae's current ambitions. He took me as host when he was building something; he wanted my specialized skills. With Henning here, his motivations might have been martially inclined. With Stian—"

Katja interrupted. "So Raekae is in charge. Can I speak with him?"

The men were silent. Only Henning would meet her eyes. She let the question hang in the air.

Finally Henning spoke. "He is not hidden. We know where to find him. But it is…*difficult*…to go there."

"Difficult how? You said there were no mountains here, nor raging rivers. What could be difficult?"

Franz interjected. "Here, above ground, we're…. How to put

it? Well, *happy*, I guess. There are good days and bad days, but we enjoy our simple lives." Stian nodded. Henning looked at the floor, brow furrowed. "We read books and learn. We discuss things, we play chess. We explore the grounds and the woods, which are constantly changing in small ways. We enjoy the hot pools, and the good food."

"I was going to ask.... Where is the cook? Where are the kitchens?"

"The food just...arrives," said Stian.

Franz adjusted his spectacles and continued. "As I was saying, if we go underground, beyond the library, and even *in* the library to some extent, we grow uneasy. Anxious. If we venture deeper into the corridors, we feel fear. A horrible, *deep* fear, mixed in with dread and hopelessness."

"Extreme dysphoria," said Stian.

"See, he *does* read," Franz said.

"Wait a minute," Katja said. "Underground? How far underground? Is there a way out that way?"

"I don't think so," said Franz. "I mean, we're trapped in Raekae's mind world, so I don't see how there could be. But we've never found the end of it. We've tried to find the deepest level, but each time we break, and rush to the surface. So truthfully we don't know. There are places we've yet to explore."

Stian drained the last of his *öl*. "It is much easier, if you want to talk to Raekae, to just wait for him to visit."

Katja stood, drew her dirk, and plunged the tip into the wooden table. Franz's coffee spilled into his lap, and Stian's empty tankard clattered to the floor. Henning, who was holding his cup, leaned back in his chair and gazed at her expectantly.

"Take me to Raekae. Now!"

Stian bent down to retrieve his tankard, grunting with the effort. "I am sorry, beautiful blond maiden, but I will not accompany you. I will show you the library, but that is as far as I will go."

Franz shook his head. "I apologize as well, but I don't have the stomach to go beyond the library. Maybe in a few years I'll build up the courage again."

"I do not *have* a few years," said Katja. "My brothers must be searching for me as we speak. My mother will be worried sick with Trond and Esper gone. She fears that Haakon will raid the village soon, and she has good reason. I need to speak with Raekae, and I need to convince him to let me leave this place. Who will help me?"

Stian stared at his empty tankard. Franz folded his hands and looked at his feet.

Henning had not looked away for an instant. "I will show you where Raekae lives, great-granddaughter."

Katja yanked her dirk from the wooden table. "Then show me now." She strode to the door and left the hut, hoping that Henning would follow.

CHAPTER FOURTEEN

Car-En knelt behind the low rampart, watching the giantess mourn her offspring. In the warm light of the bonfire embers, stroking her dead child's hair, she seemed more mother than monster.

It took Car-En a full minute to realize that the other giant – the father – was missing. How many darts had she hit him with? At least six. Even considering his size he should still be out cold, unless he possessed some kind of enhanced detoxification physiology. Car-En was curious to see the results of the genetic sequencing. What mix of Corporate Age wildstrains and natural mutations had created these monstrous humans? She assumed they were human. She supposed there were other possibilities, but none seemed likely.

First things first. Car-En switched the rifle to rapidfire, carefully aimed, and sunk three darts into the female giant's broad back. She twisted, staring in Car-En's direction and clawing at her back. A few seconds later she slumped to the ground. Car-En slowly counted to fifty. While the giants didn't seem exceptionally bright, even possum and hyena were known to play dead.

Car-En thermally scanned the area. In one corner, hides and furs were heaped in a rough pile. Keeping one eye on the slumbering mutant, she crept forward and rummaged through the mess. Trond's things were there: his weapons (sword, dirk, and hatchet); a belt pouch containing a small wooden box and a jar of ointment; his clothes (leather boots, thick woolen socks, trousers and a long-sleeved shirt sewn from rough cloth). The giants themselves had few possessions, none worth stealing. Their hides and furs smelled powerfully of urine, a large iron pot was crusted with layers of carbonized food, a small ceramic bowl was filled with filthy grease, a few cleavers and carving knives were dull and rusted. Holding her breath, Car-En slung her rifle over her shoulder, quickly gathered Trond's things, and snuck away.

She returned to the camp slowly. The cut on her hip was still healing, and ached. The extra weight didn't help. Trond's boots and sword were especially heavy. She considered dropping the sword and coming back later to retrieve it. She took a mental inventory. What weapons did they possess? Her own carbonlattice blade was gone. Esper's makeshift spear was shattered. She had her rifle, but the supply of sedative darts – which had just recently seemed superfluously abundant – was nearly exhausted. Esper had his bow, but he might run out of arrows. Each of the brothers had a dirk, but Trond's sword was their only large blade weapon. Better to endure the burn in her biceps and the pain in her left hip, and push through to the campsite.

They'd camped far from the ruins, but seeing the firelight through the trees, Car-En worried it was not far enough. The giants might even be hunting them now. She hoped that Esper was at least awake and alert.

"Welcome back, sky dweller," he whispered, as she stepped into the clearing. She hadn't surprised him. He greeted her not only with a smile, but with a nocked bow.

"How is Trond?" she asked.

"Sleeping peacefully. I've been feeding the fire, keeping him warm as you instructed. Well done – I see you've recovered his belongings." He placed down his bow and took the load from her arms. So close, she smelled his musky, unwashed scent.

Tenderly, Esper pulled his boots from Trond's feet and replaced Trond's own. "A much better fit. And my own feet were getting cold." Esper placed Trond's sword and other possessions by his side. "Ah, Ilsa's ointment," he said, uncorking the small jar. "It will help heal his wounds."

"It looks like somebody tried to eat some," said Car-En, noticing the imprint of a large finger in the salve.

"It would not taste bad. Bitter, from the herbs, but the base is honey. Are you tired? Do you wish to rest? I can keep watch."

Car-En was about to answer no, but the suggestion of sleep had a sedating, hypnotic effect. Her eyelids drooped, her head was suddenly too heavy for her neck. "I'm exhausted."

"Very well, sleep. I will wake you in a few hours."

She considered unpacking her tent, but instead curled up next to Trond. She squeezed in between the pile of gear and his slumbering mass, not even bothering to remove her boots. She lay on her right side, her back to the smith, using her cloak as a blanket, instructing it to keep her warm. Gingerly she touched her left hip. The shallow cut had mostly healed but the surrounding tissue was badly bruised. More worrisome was the tear in the bioskin, which had widened, exposing her bare skin. The intelligent fabric could self-repair to an extent, but this tear was too big. Returning from the ruins, the night air had seeped in, chilling her. Now she was warm under her cloak, but hypothermia was a real threat in her undernourished state. The bioskin's thermoregulation would be rendered useless if the hole got much bigger.

She closed her eyes and waited for unconsciousness, but sleep eluded her. The unopened messages from Adrian blinked in her m'eye. Fine, she would hear what he had to say.

The first message was audio-only, and chatty. Adrian expanded on his migration theory (which felt like old news; she had leapfrogged ahead by conversing directly with Esper). He also suggested that she observe a different village, one just to the west of Happdal beyond a steep ridge. The ringstation telescope feeds were picking up increased signs of activity in that area. Now *that* was interesting. Could the second village be Kaldbrek, the town the pipe-smoking man had mentioned? And the bully, Lars, hadn't he referred to the same place? She played back the encounter in her m'eye. Lars had contemptuously (or maybe fearfully) mentioned someone named Haakon. Who was that?

In the second message Adrian's face appeared, scowling and imperious. "Car-En, if this research project is going to progress, you need to keep your feeds open." Another threat. But if he really wanted to kill the project he could have already done so. He wanted her research to *continue*; he was hungry for more data. "The pardon from Academic Conduct was conditional. The expectation of impeccable future conduct was implied. That includes raw feeds and regular reports to your advisor. That's *me*, in case you'd forgotten. I've received nothing from you since you abruptly signed off over..." – his eyes darted to a display – "...over twenty-two hours ago. I accept that you are fatigued – that's understandable. To be expected, even. Perhaps your judgment is a little clouded. Remember our mission. Remember your pledge, to hide yourself from the villagers, not to Intervene under any circumstances. The pledge we *all* made, even those who disagreed with the ruling."

Adrian paused and took a sip from a lime-green beverage. Probably that disgusting sweet mint concoction he preferred. The monologue had relaxed him; his face bore its normal expression of smug superiority. The message ended.

She had once respected this man, hung on his every word. Now she didn't care what he thought. They lived in different worlds, quite literally. She was on the ground, he was in synchronous orbit high above. He lived in an ultralight torus, constructed of carbonlattice beams and metal foam, insulated with aerogels, protected from high-velocity space debris by a two-meter layer of flexible nickel microlattice, protected from cosmic and solar radiation by ionized plasma held in place by magnetic fields. She lived in the forest, protected by the sky and the trees, and by a handsome archer and a burly blacksmith (though, in some ways, maybe *she* was protecting *them*).

The third, fourth, and fifth messages were short, audio-only imperatives, demanding that she check in immediately. Was she all right? What had happened? He could provide support and guidance, if she would only respond. *Please* respond. He tried to conceal his rage at her impertinence, her outright disobedience. *I am not angry*, he wanted her to hear in his tone, *I want to help you, to guide you*. What he really wanted, Car-En knew, was to manipulate her, to control her like a puppet.

In the sixth message, a full feed, Adrian looked somber and tired. "Car-En," he began. His serious tone, so self-important and grave, made her want to giggle. "It has been thirty-one hours since I last heard from you. Despite the fact that you have withheld all sensory feeds from me, from *this department,* for some time, the telemetry from your kit indicates that not only are you alive and well, but that you are on the move, heading west, *away* from Happdal. I can only imagine what flight of fancy has gotten into you.

"To get your attention, I have deactivated your drones. Since you refuse to share your feeds with me and with this department, I can only assume you are using the technology available to you for your own personal gain, or to deviate significantly from the clearly stated and previously agreed-upon goals of this research mission. You may not be aware that I possess the security clearance to do this, to deactivate your resources remotely.

"I acknowledge and regret that being stripped of your drones may pose a minor security risk, but at this point I am desperate to hear from you. *What* is going on in your mind? Car-En Ganzorig, please talk to me. I am your ally, not your enemy. There are those who disapprove of this research – indeed, of all the ongoing field research. But I am a staunch supporter of your project, of *you* personally. I am not only your advisor, but also your friend. Honestly, I'm worried about you – worried that you've suffered some kind of psychological break. There is also the possibility that you've been kidnapped and are being held against your will, but this seems unlikely – what could prevent you from sending me a silent message? I can only conclude that you are willfully disengaging from me and from the department. That worries me. That's why I have taken the – admittedly drastic – action of deactivating your drones. I hope it gets your attention. Please contact me immediately. All we need is an honest discussion. All will be forgiven. Don't make things worse than they already are. If I don't hear from you…well, I suppose I'll have to take a step that I really do not want to take."

With that, he signed off. There were no more messages.

Fucking bastard.

A *minor* security risk? She could have had her head bashed in by a tree trunk. She could have been cooked and eaten by a bloodthirsty mutant. She *needed* those drones. They were not an *optional* part of her gear.

Adrian was showing his true colors. She had always known and accepted that he was arrogant. Arrogance often came with brilliance (as did forcefulness, and being opinionated). Those traits had been part of what had attracted her to the man, not just as an advisor but as a role model. To be so confident and authoritative, she had imagined that those traits might slowly rub off on her, and that she would gain *respect* as well as seniority within the department. One day Adrian would gracefully step aside. Car-En would be offered a leadership role, Research Director or even Department Head. Her fieldwork on Earth would command admiration bordering on worship. Students would long to hear her stories. *The time she was attacked by giants.*

That was all gone now. She didn't believe Adrian would forgive her. He had no idea what was going on. And why should she tell him? He didn't care about these people as human beings. His only love was for data, and theories, and his own career. Adrian was borderline sociopathic. Maybe that's what it took to rise within an academic department.

She sighed and tried to relax. She knew better than to waste too much time and energy thinking about Adrian. She had made her own choices; she would live with them.

Sleep did not come. Trond's large body exuded warmth, but also noxious smells: burned skin, rancid fat, pungent body odor. He snored loudly. In addition, she was feeling claustrophobic in her bioskin. It wasn't the first time she had experienced the sensation, but the knowledge that Adrian was actively tracking her location enhanced her desire to be rid of the thing.

She couldn't do that, could she? Get rid of the bioskin? Not only did it keep her warm, dry, and relatively clean (absorbing and recycling moisture, gently exfoliating her skin and converting the dead cells into energy), but the embedded kit was her communications center (not only with the *Stanford*, but with her own gear and diagnostic tools, even with her pharma implant when necessary). Her m'eye merely provided the interface; the kit contained the tech and did most of the actual work. But it was also the kit giving up her location and vital signs to Adrian.

Life without the bioskin. Adrian wouldn't be able to track her. And she wouldn't even *know* if he was trying to pester her. And she could get truly *clean*. Months ago, she had removed the skin and gone swimming in the river near Happdal. The ice-cold water had electrified her body. She'd emerged from the river feeling completely clean and fresh. But she hadn't done it since; being naked had made her feel too vulnerable (not because of modesty; not wearing the bioskin left her *technologically* bare, disconnected and helpless). Since then, had self-care routine has consisted of biodegradable sanitary wipes (her supply was running low) and the bioskin's built-in hygienic functionality. Fortunately menstruation wasn't an issue; she had used her implant to suppress her period since the age of fifteen.

But abandoning the bioskin wasn't realistic. She would probably die without it. She wouldn't be able to navigate, or contact the *Stanford*, or find her way back to the mule station. She put the thought out of her mind.

She scooched away from Trond and snuggled up next to her pack. Time to fall asleep, even if by brute force. She instructed her implant to release a moderate dose of soporific into her bloodstream. Her mind immediately began to drift. Forget about Adrian. Forget about everything.

A vivid image appeared in her mind's eye: the giantess extracting the spear from her dead child's throat, dark blood gushing from its mouth. Her eyes snapped open. Despite the soporific, her heart was racing.

She stood. Esper was sitting two meters away, cross-legged, watching the campfire. As she approached him, he stood up to meet her. He started to speak but she silenced him with a finger to his lips.

"Hold me," she said.

He wrapped his lean, powerful arms around her, pulling her close. She inhaled his scent, musky and intoxicating. He held her for a long time without pulling away. Finally he loosened his embrace and stepped back, still lightly holding her arms. For a moment she lost herself in his eyes, pale blue irises surrounded by dark rings. "*Lífs*," he said. *Alive*. She understood the word even before she heard the translation in her implant; she was starting to pick up the dialect. He kissed her, first on the forehead, then gently on the lips when she raised her face. She parted her lips and tentatively touched his tongue with her own. He responded in kind; at least in terms of kissing their cultures were similar. He cupped her neck and kissed her more forcefully. As they kissed, her fatigue melted away, along with her fears, her worries about Adrian and her career, her concern for Esper's village. None of it was important. There was just Esper, his long, lean body and his kind, hypnotic eyes. An electric ripple rose from the base of her spine up to her neck, spreading to her arms and fingers, her tongue, the surface of her skin.

"Wait," she said. She found the small zipper on the left side of her neck and unzipped the bioskin down to her waist. She hesitated for a second, then took it all the way off. She stood completely naked before him, the bioskin tossed to the ground in a rumpled pile.

His brow furrowed. "You need to eat more." But he was already taking off his own clothes.

CHAPTER FIFTEEN

Henning led Katja to a small hut, not much more than a shed. The oaken door was weathered and unpainted. "The library entrance," he said, opening the door and inviting her in.

Inside were a few rickety bookshelves, home to fewer than a dozen leather-bound books. A sun-bleached rocking chair sat near the hut's single window.

Katja frowned. "Even Esper has more books than this. He has recovered at least twenty from the Builder ruins."

"This is nothing," said Henning. "Journals for each of us, though not all of us write in them. Here – this one must be yours." He picked up a slender volume and handed it to her. "If you fill it, another one will appear."

There were letters on the spine; she recognized *K*. She handed it back to Henning, not bothering to open it. "Esper tried to teach me to read, but I had no patience for it."

Henning nodded. "Stian would be pleased to teach you. Any of us would be willing – take your pick. There is plenty of time to learn. Believe me, reading will help keep you sane. And beyond that…it will change you."

"I do not want to change," she said. "I want to go home."

Henning returned the journal to the shelf and knelt on the floor. "Maybe you'll find a way." He grabbed the nearest edge of a throw rug and carefully rolled it up, revealing a trapdoor. "I don't know why the entrance to the library is hidden," he said. "I suppose Raekae gives the old hosts the choice to reveal it to the new host, or not. But Franz showed Stian right away, and they both showed me within days of arriving."

"And by 'arriving,' you mean that your mind came here, while your body remained in the real world?" She did not believe any of it, but she wanted to make sure she understood what Henning and the others believed. That knowledge might prove useful when negotiating with Raekae.

"Yes, exactly."

"And what happened to Stian's body then, when your body became host?" she asked.

"I suppose it rotted away. The same way my own body is dead and decaying, now that you are the host. I have little memory of the exchange – bits come back in flashes. But Raekae explained it all. Ask him yourself." Henning lifted the trapdoor, revealing a narrow stone staircase. "Would you like to go first?"

With one hand on the pommel of her dirk, she started down the stairs, heading toward a warm, steady yellow light below. There was no railing, just stone walls on either side. "Be careful," said Henning. Why, she wondered? If she fell and injured herself, she would heal within a day.

The stairs turned left and the passage widened. Reaching the bottom, Katja looked up and gasped. Before her was a vast room, thrice the size of the Happdal longhouse and five times as tall. Each wall was lined with rows of ornate wooden shelves (at least two dozen from floor to ceiling), and each shelf was packed with books – more than Katja had imagined existed in all the world. There were ladders to reach the higher shelves, and a narrow balcony providing access to the uppermost third. The soft light came from a vast arrangement of hanging crystals, immense glass flowers dripping from the high ceiling.

"The library," said Henning. He pointed to the left side of the room. "History, over there. Some of the books are ancient, handwritten on vellum, centuries old. But most are from the end of the Builder Age. From our own time there are hardly any books at all, perhaps half a dozen." She noticed a quaver in his voice.

"Who wrote them – the books from our age?" she asked. Esper could read, and scratch out characters with a stick of charcoal, but she could not imagine how someone could create an entire book, not without Builder magic.

"There are people beyond the Five Valleys. Raekae is not the only one of his kind. There are other immortals, in other lands.

Somehow, they share knowledge. Raekae told me that other people on Earth – Earth is the planet on which we live – that others have learned things, or relearned them, beyond what we can do in Happdal. But in other areas *we* – you and I and Stian, the people of the Five Valleys who came from the Northlands – are the ones with the secret knowledge. Metalworking and smithing. And cheese-making."

"They are not your people anymore," said Katja. "You are of *this* place now."

Henning's face fell. She felt a hint of remorse but pushed the feeling aside. Even if he was her distant kin, she owed him nothing. And she was still angry; he had cut her. She glanced at her palm. No mark or scar, and no pain when she clenched her hand into a fist. But she still did not trust him.

"To the right, philosophy, and logic, and mathematics, and physics. Over there, biology and chemistry. In the next room" – he pointed to polished wooden double doors carved with elaborate designs – "fiction, which means stories. Novels and plays, epic tales of all kinds."

The words meant nothing to her, but Henning's tone was breezy and cheerful. If her words had injured him, he was trying to hide it.

"Where is Raekae?" she asked.

He looked at her with a strange, wild expression.

"This way," he said, leading her toward the double doors. She followed. For a moment, she was mesmerized by his dark blond hair, which hung loosely, reaching halfway down his back. She felt a strange and inappropriate impulse to braid it. She missed Happdal. She missed braiding Kristin's and Karina's long hair. Hinrik's surviving daughters often spent time at their house, helping Elke cook and then staying for dinner. Katja had no sisters of her own and loved both orphans as if they were kin.

The 'fiction' room was filled with tall shelves, arranged in long, maze-like columns. They took a turn, and another, and soon Katja could no longer see any walls – only books. How large was this room? Which way was north? She had no idea. She would not be able to find her way back without Henning's help. Finally, a book-lined passage came to an end. Henning led them through a plain door into a narrow hallway. The floor was covered with some kind of coarse brown fur, spongy beneath Katja's boots. They passed by several closed doors on either side.

"What is behind these doors?" she asked.

"Collections," said Henning. His eyes were wide, his skin pale.

"Are you unwell?"

"You do not feel it, do you? It's too soon for you. I remember, at first, I was the same way. It is good you are exploring this place now."

Katja opened the nearest door and peered inside. The well-lit room was lined with shelves; each shelf was packed with rows of ceramic cats, in all shapes, sizes, and styles. "Strange," said Katja.

"There are at least two dozen rooms like this. Not only cats. Machines, as well, and all varieties of musical instruments."

Katja closed the door and motioned for Henning to continue. Soon she heard the faint sound of music, a single player executing a complicated tune with many notes, on an instrument she did not recognize. "What is that?" she asked. Henning did not answer, but pointed ahead.

They entered a room, not so large as the library, that seemed designed for comfort. There were many ornate chairs in various styles, and a table laden with food and drink: a cheese plate, bowls of fruit, jugs of wine and water. The wooden floor was polished to a high sheen. In the center of the room a middle-aged man was seated at a large black musical instrument, his fingers moving quickly over white-and-black slats.

"That is Raekae's father," said Henning. "Mostly, he just plays the piano. You can speak with him if you like, but his head is empty." The musician briefly looked up, flashing a smile.

Katja drew her dirk and approached the old man. He ignored her, oblivious to the threat of naked steel. "How old are you?" she asked.

The man stopped playing and looked at her inquisitively, glancing at the knife. "You should be careful with that." His voice was oddly accented but kindly in tone. "Carry it with the

point down. That way, if you fall, you won't stab yourself."
He wore a black jacket over a white shirt, both garments made
of smooth cloth and stitched with precision. Who had made
his clothes?

"Answer my question!" she barked, slashing the knife toward
his face. The motion caught his eye, but he seemed immune
to fear.

"Take care," said Henning. "Raekae loves the old man dearly."

"What did you ask, darling? I've forgotten your question."

"How old are you?" Katja repeated.

"Fifty-two," he answered, and resumed his playing. The
music changed, becoming more melancholy.

She turned to Henning. "Is Raekae a young man?" she asked.
Henning was looking over his shoulder, and took a moment to
notice her question.

"No. Age is relative here. Remember, I am your great-
grandfather." Henning's voice trembled. He was trying to
control himself, but his pallor and sheen betrayed him.

She sheathed her dirk angrily. "Take me to Raekae."

He shook his head.

She touched the pommel of her dirk. "Take me, or I gut the
old man, and tell Raekae you did it!"

"It would not work. He would just replay the scene."

Katja stared him down until he blinked. "Fine." He sniffed
the air. "This way," he said, heading toward a hallway on the
left side of the room. Katja followed. The melancholy music
receded behind them.

The hallway ended in a metal spiral staircase. Henning
hesitated. Katja pushed him roughly, and he began to descend,
gripping the railing tightly. All his bravado and swagger had left
him; what was left was a scared, weak man. He shot her a bitter
look. "This will happen to you as well. You will not own your
emotions so easily. You will feel how Raekae wants you to feel.
You will pay the price if you want to see him."

"Shut up. Take me to him, and then you can flee like
a coward."

The staircase deposited them in the center of a vast circular room with a metal floor. The front half of the curving wall was paneled with giant windows, beyond which Katja could see a moving forested landscape. She gripped the staircase railing, struck with vertigo.

"That's Raekae," said Henning, pointing to a small figure seated among a configuration of metal boxes and lights. Katja nodded and closed her eyes, trying to regain her balance, trying not to vomit. She heard the sound of Henning's boots rapidly ascending the metal staircase.

After a minute, the vertigo subsided. She walked quickly across the room, toward Raekae, averting her eyes from the scenes in the giant windows. Her boot-steps on the metal floor reverberated throughout the chamber.

He was a small man with thinning brown hair, and spectacles similar to those Franz wore. He swiveled in his chair to face her, his hands held up with palms pressed together. "Welcome," he said. "I'm Raekae, though you can call me Rae if you prefer. That's close enough. Please don't touch anything."

She stopped, resting one hand on her pommel. "You have made a mistake in bringing me here. Whatever your plans for me, I will thwart them. I will *fight* you to my dying breath. Your best choice is to let me leave. I just want one thing – to return home." She took a single step forward. "So how do I leave this place?"

Raekae smiled. "This is your home now. I'm using your body, and I'll keep using it until it wears out. Your old life is over. But you'll find you can have a good life here. You can learn more than you ever would in your previous life. And if you're interested, I'll teach you how to build your own world. Recreate your village, if you want. Perhaps Henning and Franz would join you in that project. It would take time to learn the skills, of course – a long time. At least five years. Maybe longer. You're a stubborn one!" He laughed.

"Tell me how to get home. Or I slit your throat and find my own way."

"If you attack me, I'll press this button right here. You'll find yourself back in your hut. Then you'll have to climb all the way back down if you want to continue our conversation. And it will be a little harder next time. I've added some disincentives. I don't mind the occasional visitor, but it's important to be able to think, to have plenty of alone time. I have an open-door policy, but you have to *earn* it."

"You cursed Henning."

"Something like that. Henning and the others are fully virtualized, so I can motivate or demotivate them with a little limbic tweaking. Once they leave the library, the arousal really kicks up. The amygdala in particular. It tends to manifest as fear. You're not vulnerable yet. The tendrils are still mapping your brain. You're still using it – your brain – except for the sensory inputs and motor outputs. Those, I'm using." He gestured toward the giant window panels. "This is what your old eyes are seeing now, in the real world." Katja resisted looking; in her peripheral vision, she saw a blur of green, trees and moss.

Raekae stood and pointed at the vast window display. "See, right now we're about to climb the ridge. On the other side is Kaldbrek. I want to see what Haakon and his goons are up to. I'm afraid they're planning a raid on your old home."

"You know Haakon?" She loosened her dirk in its sheath.

"Not personally. I considered him as a host – he's a fascinating character. But ultimately too volatile. He would try to take over the metamind. That's his nature: he's a conqueror."

"Can you kill him?" she asked.

"I suppose we could. You're good with a sword. You should have seen what we did to the mutant!" Raekae pulled one sleeve over his hand and held the limb up, chortling. Then he half stood in his chair and did a ridiculous imitation of sword-fighting, waving his hands in the air like a fool, thrusting and feinting. He plopped back down in his seat, breathing heavily from his exertions. "Henning's blades are as sharp as ever," he said, between gulps of air. "Biter, the wolf blade, and Taker, with a human soul. Do you know how a soulsword is forged? Did your brother teach you? Trond, the big one?"

It angered her to hear him speak her brother's name. She wanted to spit in his face. "I know how godsteel is forged."

"Yes, but not every godsteel blade is a soulsword. There's some fascinating chemistry that goes on. I'll teach you in a few years, once you get up to speed in the basic sciences. The carbon from.... Well, yes, I should wait. Metallurgy is one of my many interests, as is the metaphorical symbolism of soul-stealing. I am something of a soul stealer myself. You might even say that I'm *literally* a soul stealer. Except that souls aren't real, so that's not quite accurate." He giggled. "But as much as they're real, I steal them."

Katja swiveled slightly and looked up at the windows. It was as if she were inside her own head, looking out from behind her own eyes. 'She' was climbing a hill through a thick beech wood. She could see her own hands reaching out to brush aside branches. Once again her stomach lurched. Breathing slowly through her nose, she suppressed the sensation, forcing her eyes to stay open. Raekae seemed pleased that she was finally looking at the view, and continued to speak. She was no longer listening. She turned so that her dagger side was obscured from Raekae's sight, and slowly inched the dirk from its sheath.

"...looking for the visitor. She was my first choice for a host, you know. Don't take it personally, you're an excellent choice as well! But to have someone from the ringstations join us here, how wonderful that would be. Think how much we could learn! We have three centuries of orbital history to catch up on. Imagine the advances they've made. And we're cut off from it, all of it. As interesting as your people are, I've learned about as much as I can from the lot of you. I want to know what's going on in the rest of the solar system. Perhaps even beyond!"

Katja whipped out the dirk and lunged at his throat. The steel point sunk into the soft flesh of his neck, slipped between tendons, punctured the stiff membranes of his voicebox, and finally stuck in his spine. Raekae's mouth gaped silently. He waved his hands in the air like a helpless newborn babe. Katja wrenched out the blade and watched the blood seep, then gush, from the wound.

With a gurgling cry, Raekae lunged for the button on a panel, the one he had indicated would send her away. But she was ready, and kicked his arm (she was skeptical of magical buttons, but not willing to take any chances). Grabbing his shirt with her free hand, she pulled mightily. The garment ripped, but the force was sufficient to pull him down. His head hit the metal floor with a dull clang. She kicked him in the gut for good measure, but he was already dead.

She sat in the chair, placed the bloody dirk on the machine table in front of her, and examined the array of controls and lights. She would need an ally, someone who understood the Builder machines. Maybe Franz would help. Now that Raekae was dead, perhaps he could come to this place without the sensation of sickening fear.

In the window display, 'she' had stopped moving, and stood among the beech trees in the dusk light. Faintly, she could hear wind in the leaves and the faint chirping of birds. Somehow she was trapped inside her own body. At least now she knew where she was. And she could see and hear the real world. If she could learn to guide her own flesh, then maybe she could make her way back to Happdal.

The others, Henning and Stian and Franz, they were ghosts. But she still had a body. Raekae had merely cut her off from her own senses and limbs. One way or another, she would find her way back, regain control. She had slain the sorcerer – that much was done.

She rubbed her eyes and slapped her cheeks. Why did she feel sleepy? A good fight and the sight of blood usually enlivened her, keeping her up for hours or even through the night. And this was her first real kill, a blessing from the Red Brother. She would lay her head down for just a minute. It was all too much, what had happened to her. Her mind was tired from grappling with these strange puzzles.

*   *   *

She awoke in the loft bed, in her hut. She was naked, the sheets soft and warm against her bare skin. The smell of fresh bread filled the room. She had slept well; she felt rested, and lazy. What strange dreams.

Not dreams. She climbed down the ladder. Her clothes were there, cleaned and neatly folded. Her boots were polished.

Her dirk was missing.

CHAPTER SIXTEEN

Car-En smelled frying bacon. Lurking around Happdal she had smelled bacon many times, but it had been months since she had tasted any. She liked the vat-grown bacon on the *Stanford*, but this smelled meatier and gamier. And probably more delicious. Who could be cooking? Esper was lying next to her. She must still be dreaming.

Esper opened his eyes. She tentatively kissed him on the cheek, snuggling closer. They'd made love three times during the night, but this was the light of day, and she felt shy again. Would she have regrets? She didn't now. Would he? Would Esper want to hide their love from his brother, once Trond awoke?

They were curled up under her cloak and his blanket, both naked. Now fully awake, she could hear sizzling fat. Someone really *was* cooking bacon. She lifted her head and looked around.

"Good morning! I see that you have already met my brother."

Trond had pulled a large flat rock up to the edge of the rekindled campfire. There he sat, holding a long thin stick draped with strips of bacon over the low flames. He had found his trousers and boots, but was still shirtless. In the light of day, his physique was impressive. His chest and shoulders were immense and well-defined; the fibrous striations of each muscle group were clearly visible. The skin on his chest was still red and raw but had noticeably healed over the course of the night. He had burns on his face as well, and a large purple bruise covered most of his left cheek. Still, he looked cheerful, untroubled by his injuries.

Esper sat up and yawned. Car-En grabbed the blanket, pulling it up to her neck. "This is Car-En," said Esper. "She is visiting from the sky, where she lives in a vast floating ship."

"A ship in the sky?" Trond said, raising an eyebrow. "Is she a god?"

"No. Flesh and blood, like us. The Builders did not stop their building here on the ground. They built in the sky as well, and live there still."

Trond furrowed his brow and considered this. "Greetings, Car-En. Are you hungry?"

Using her cloak for privacy, Car-En retrieved her thermal leggings and long-sleeved top from her pack. She wasn't ready to don the bioskin just yet, and stowed it away. Esper dressed as well. They gathered round the fire and ate a breakfast of bacon, stale sourdough, and dried apples. Car-En had never tasted anything better.

"How are you feeling?" she asked Trond. "You were badly burned." Trond looked confused, hearing Orbital English, but he seemed to understand her attempt at translation that followed.

"I awoke with a sore shoulder, a great thirst, and a headache. But I drank a full skin of water and now I feel well. Very well, with a little food in my belly. Though I'm still hungry. Esper, will you kill something for lunch? A deer would be nice. I could do well with a roast leg of deer."

From her limited medical knowledge she knew that Trond had sustained second-degree burns over a good portion of his chest, arms, and parts of his face (the remains of his beard were a sorry sight; most of it had burned off, and his left cheek and jaw were an angry red). A normal course of treatment might include days or even weeks of bed rest, intravenous fluids, antibiotics and steroids, and careful regulation of body temperature, blood pressure, and glucose levels. But Trond had slept off the worst of his injuries with a good night's sleep. She'd seen his wildstrains, but it was one thing to look at genetic markers and quite another to see a badly burned man wake up the next morning, hale and chipper.

"Did you slay the giants?" asked Trond. "The last thing I remember is being rubbed down in rancid grease by that huge horrid hag." He sniffed his own arm. "I still reek of the stuff. I will need to bathe today."

"That reminds me of something," Car-En said. "I'll be back in a minute." She retrieved the biosampler from her pack.

The sequencing was complete; she brought up the results in her m'eye. She was eager to examine them, but first took a few minutes to reorganize her gear. She grabbed the remaining nutrient bars to share with Trond and Esper (she doubted they would like them, but at least she would have something to contribute to breakfast). Her rifle lay next to her pack where she'd left it, with a mostly full clip, safety on. Gear secure, she sat down to examine the genetic analysis of the child-giant.

The results were fascinating. The giants appeared to be descended from subjects of a Corporate Age black-market 'eternal youth' experiment. There were suppressed myostatin genes (similar to Trond's), but also souped-up IGF genes for enhanced growth. Remarkably, there were strains of *shark* DNA interwoven into the sequence, possibly to counteract the cancer risk from long-term growth-factor enhancement, or maybe for other longevity benefits. As far as Car-En could tell, these giants would keep growing for as long as they lived, with no upper size limit. Had that been the original intention, or was it some bizarre side effect of the mutated wildstrain?

There were also genes for enhanced smell. Like bears and other wild omnivores, it was likely the giants could smell food from many kilometers away. That would be an adaptive trait in the current environment.

"Car-En, do you want more bacon?" asked Trond from across the campfire. "Do you mind if I finish it?"

"Go ahead," she said cheerfully. Her own belly was full, an unfamiliar and odd sensation.

Car-En heard the crack of a stick from the beech woods to the south, and rustling leaves. Probably a deer. Maybe Trond would get his lunch request after all. For an instant, she worried that the giants had tracked them to their camp, but dismissed the thought. They were far away from the ruins, nearly three kilometers to the north, and the giants didn't seem particularly bright. She was glad she'd pressed Esper to go the extra distance.

Esper and Trond hadn't yet heard whatever was moving in the woods; Car-En's cochlear implant gave her an advantage. She thought of the drones, and once again cursed Adrian for deactivating them. She'd gotten used to having a near-constant awareness of her safety perimeter. Without the swarm, she felt blind and vulnerable.

Esper was speaking rapidly to Trond, who was chewing a mouthful of bacon and was only half listening. She considered translating Esper's words, but instead kept her attention on the animal in the brush. Whatever it was, it was approaching their camp.

Trond threw the greasy cooking stick into the embers, where the last of the fat sizzled away.

Hungry giants with enhanced olfactory capabilities.

"Esper! Trond! Watch out!" She shouted the warning in Orbital English, but her tone was clear enough. Esper stood and grabbed his bow.

The giants emerged from the beech trees on the south side of the clearing. The female's wild, bloodshot eyes fixed on Esper. She charged, clutching a long, rusty knife in each oversized fist. The male roared and stomped toward Car-En, waving a branch from a dead snag in his single hand.

Car-En froze, terrified and dismayed. Why hadn't they slit the creatures' throats when they'd had the chance? Months ago, on the *Stanford*, such a notion would have seemed savage and cruel. Now it seemed like common sense, a missed opportunity that might now cost them their lives. She'd felt sorry for the giantess, seeing her mourn her dead child. But now the mother's rage might kill them all.

Car-En backed away, trying to draw the male away from Esper and Trond. His bulbous eyes swiveled in their sockets, taking in the situation. He took a great stride forward, raised his club, and smashed it down. The fire-hardened wood struck Car-En's rifle with a sharp crack. She winced. She had underestimated their intelligence.

Esper leapt away, dodging the she-giant's slashing knives. Trond drew his sword and stepped in between his brother and the female. The giantess lurched forward, slashing at the smith's face. Trond parried the blow, breaking a chip of rusted steel from her decrepit blade. Trond drew back and struck the creature's weakened longknife again with his steel sword, shattering it.

"Ha!" yelled Trond. "Take that! You wanted to taste my flesh, but you will taste my steel instead!" He lunged forward and thrust the tip of his sword into her meaty thigh. The giantess screamed in pain and rage.

Car-En caught a blur of movement to her left. Was there a third giant? She had no idea how many lived in those ruins; perhaps there was an entire tribe. She kept her eyes fixed on the one-handed male. He approached her slowly. While the female fought recklessly, this one seemed cautious. Was there a hint of fear in those bulging eyes? Somehow he'd lost a hand. The stump was wrapped in a dirty, bloodstained cloth. Even from where she stood she could smell the fetid stench of gangrenous flesh.

The giant blinked, perhaps deciding that Car-En was not a threat. Unfortunately, she agreed with his assessment; she was unarmed, and her limited martial training would be useless against an opponent twice her height and ten times her weight. He snarled, raised his club, and charged.

A figure leapt between them, a blur of blond hair and flashing steel. There was a sickening sound, the crunch of metal slicing through flesh and bone. The giant's severed head hit the dirt with a thud. Car-En stumbled back as the headless body collapsed, shaking the ground.

Katja strode around the edge of the fire. She wielded a bloody longsword. A second sword was strapped across her back. Her eyes were cold and empty, with no trace of joy at seeing her brothers.

"Katja!" yelled Trond.

"Sister!" Esper cried.

Confused, the giantess wheeled around to face the new foe. Katja's blade sliced across her cheek. In the same smooth motion, Katja whipped back the blade and thrust it forward in a deep lunge. The point of the long blade plunged through the giantess's left eye and into her brain. Her corpse toppled. Katja wrenched the blade out and stood before them in a relaxed stance, breathing evenly.

"Katja," said Esper softly, "are you all right?" The young woman looked paler and thinner than Car-En remembered, but not unwell. She thought of the black egg that Katja had ingested before the white-haired man had died. What had passed from his body into hers?

"Speak to me, sister." Esper said. And then, tentatively, "Is it really you?"

"Of course it is her," said Trond, but he didn't sound sure. He took a step closer, squinting.

"Why are you silent?" asked Esper. "Are you angry with us? Why did you leave the village? Mother fears for you. *We* feared for you."

Katja took a rag from her pouch and wiped it carefully up and down the long blade until the clean steel shone brightly.

"What blade is that?" Trond asked. "That is fine godsteel. One of Jense's?"

Katja turned and walked away.

"Sister, wait!" cried Esper. "What have we done to anger you?"

"What will we tell Elke?" asked Trond. "Will you leave us at her mercy? You are not so cruel, sister. Not so cruel as that!"

Car-En approached Esper and gently touched his arm. Katja was already ten paces into the beech woods.

"I will follow her," Trond said.

"*We* will," said Esper.

"Wait," Car-En said. "There's something I need to tell you first."

PART TWO
THE CRUCIBLE

CHAPTER SEVENTEEN

Excerpt from 'The Four Phases of Earth Depopulation' by Lydia Heliosmith, age 17, written for *Terrestrial Anthropology 1*, 22.01.02719:

Phase 1: The Late Corporate Age

Phase 1 depopulation, from a peak of eleven billion in the late twenty-first century to just under seven billion at the end of the twenty-second, was gradual. The long droughts, devastating floods, and unpredictable storms of the Anthropocene resulted in suffering and some deaths, but the vast majority of the population drop was attributable to readily available birth control, near-universal literacy, and the high cost of raising children. Few nations made the choice to support parenting and child-rearing, thus creating economic disincentives for those who might have otherwise wanted to create and nurture new human beings.

A forty per cent drop in the number of human beings on planet Earth, over the course of a single century, devastated the global economy. Young people were overtaxed and overworked to support the growing burden of the old and entitled (with the latter, larger group always voting to preserve their entitlements). By 2180, half of all major cities (those less able to employ and entertain – and thereby retain – young people) went the way of the industrial metropolis Detroit (East America), with a hollowed-out city center, decaying infrastructure, trees pushing through the asphalt, and entire neighborhoods abandoned to weeds and feral animals.

A century of dismal economics brought a parallel psychological state. While the planet's greenhouse ecology was in a permanent state of summer, the minds of its inhabitants endured an endless winter. The human socioeconomic operating system, corporate capitalism, had revealed itself as deeply flawed (a growth-based system in a closed world), but also inescapable. Governments were neither by nor for the people, but rather puppeted regimes of the rarified elite. Localized attempts at revolution created chaos and disrupted the status quo, but failed to reorganize and fundamentally improve economic and social systems. Some nations revisited Marxist ideas and experimented with planned state economies. These proved unsustainable, as did the few religious fundamentalist movements that managed to leverage terrorism into full-scale national dominance (Kandaharistan, Islamic Emirate of Hausa). Going back to the past (be it the nineteenth century or the twelfth) didn't work.

Technology continued to advance, but failed to solve social, economic, or psychological problems. In the late twentieth and early twenty-first century, every job that could be performed by an algorithm or machine was so implemented, including many 'human' jobs in education, healthcare, transportation, agriculture, and the military. Every product that could be copied was replicated for free (not only works of information, but also physical objects, including complex electronics, that could easily be printed at home). This was the science-fiction utopia envisioned in earlier eras, but instead of living bright lives of leisure, citizens were left unemployed, broke, and depressed. Societies found themselves unable – or perhaps unwilling – to deliver the dividends of massive wealth creation to the average worker (for whom there was little work left to do).

Many nation states, with the bulk of their citizens impoverished and psychologically broken, deteriorated into tribalism and xenophobia. While floods and droughts created hundreds of thousands of refugees, religious and ethnic persecution created more. Some governments unofficially sanctioned the harassment, and while there were no repeats of the mass genocides of the twentieth century, many regimes flirted with fascism, indefinitely detaining, torturing, and often killing dissidents and minorities.

As with the first Dark Age, not everywhere was equally bad. Some nations upheld values of democracy, egalitarianism, and scientific inquiry. Others proved that it was possible to encourage commerce while still keeping a lid on wealth inequality, corporate malfeasance, and pointless consumerism. These nations were rewarded with happier, wealthier, better-educated citizens who possessed a sense of civic ownership and responsibility. From these bright spots (the steady Scandinavians, the stubborn New Zealanders, the exuberant Indians, and dozens of youngish post-colonial nations in Latin America and Africa) came the sparks of the Revival.

11.05.02727, the *Stanford*

Adrian Vanderplotz buttoned the top button of his shirt and admired his own reflection. A few years earlier, at the age of fifty-five, he'd indulged in a rejuv. Instead of avoiding mirrors, he now sought them out. Most of his wrinkles were gone; only tasteful crow's feet and faint smile lines remained. His skin was taut and smooth, his jawline straight, his pores barely visible, his gray hair reverted to black, his waist once again narrow, his arms and chest lean and muscular. Best decision of his life.

He was tall for a ringstation denizen – one hundred seventy-five centimeters – though he'd be dwarfed by the immense brutes of Happdal. He often imagined what it would be like to interact with the strange humans of the 'New Iron Age,' as some put it. A catchy but idiotic term. He had to give Townes credit for discovering the anomalous tribes in the first place, but to refer to them as anything besides Survivalists was ridiculous. Penelope Townes was trying to jumpstart her career on the basis of a single lucky observation. Her ambition had always outsized her talent. Townes was a second-rate scientist, and history would eventually forget her entirely. Her star was already dimming, as Adrian's successful election to Repop Council (which Townes had publicly opposed) had demonstrated.

The brutes of Happdal. It had a nice ring to it. For now, Adrian would have to keep the phrase to himself. Car-En's research project had a large fan base, bigger than any of the other field researchers, and many ringstation citizens had been following the project closely, reading and discussing each report as it was posted. People liked the Happdal villagers, even to the extent of idolizing them as larger-than-life characters (misplaced hero-worship of illiterate savages, in his own opinion). Car-En herself had no idea how popular her research had become. Her cult following included Academy members, thousands of citizens on the *Stanford*, and even a smattering among the other ringstations. Feed requests had come in from the *Liu Hui*, the *Alhazen*, even the *Hedonark*. Interest from the luxury space park concerned Adrian; it meant that Car-En's reports had entertainment appeal. Citizens were living vicariously through the research, and worse, were getting attached to the villagers.

This was problematic for a number of reasons.

The most pressing problem was that Car-En's reports had recently ceased, and the lack of information was generating controversy and attracting unwanted attention. He'd found a temporary solution, but it would only postpone the inevitable. Eventually it would become clear that the newest reports were incomplete, that key elements were missing. There would be questions.

Adrian left his apartment, deciding to walk the park tube to Council Hall instead of descending to Sub-1 to take a tram. He preferred walking. Not only would he avoid the midday rush on the trams, but he enjoyed the airy 0.95G of the upper levels. It was why he'd taken an upper-level apartment in the first place. More light and less gravity. Gradual bone loss be damned – the rejuv had given him density to spare.

The park tube was a semi-closed ecosystem, dimmer and moister than the open-air section of the main torus. The temperate rainforest atmosphere supported ferns, miniature redwoods, and spongy mosses, all tastefully landscaped to appear as wild as possible while still maintaining a clear pedestrian throughway. Adrian passed a young couple taking a stroll. An infant baby was strapped to the father. The mother smiled and said hello as they passed. Did he know her? No. He nodded and gave the woman a quick, tight-lipped smile. He hated friendly people, with their irritating leisurely niceties.

The second – and thornier – issue with the popularity of Car-En's research (and the Ringstation Coalition's fondness for the recently discovered Earthlings) was a fundamental incompatibility with Adrian's vision for Repop and the existence of illiterate, barbaric tribes roaming Eurasia. The first of the Earth settlers would need to focus their complete and undivided attention on sustenance, construction, and social organization. Worrying about the threat of invasion from sword-waving savages was not part of the plan. Europe had once endured three hundred years of Viking terror. That was quite enough.

The department's strict policy against Intervention was a bulwark against engagement. His pious colleagues took the sanctity of non-interference seriously, but Adrian couldn't care less about cultural contamination. To him, Non-Interventionism was purely utilitarian, useful in terms of preventing relationships and emotional attachments.

In ten or twenty years, the inevitable extinction of the dregs of the Remnant Age would be complete. Car-En's most valuable finding concerned natural attrition factors; some unknown radiation source was causing premature death among the villagers, and they were too stupid to relocate. This was excellent news. While Adrian didn't yet have enough data to calculate population growth or decline, it was possible that death from disease, combined with fatalities from skirmish raids (there was evidence of inter-village tension that could lead to warfare), might do Adrian's job for him.

Happdal and the nearby micro-settlements were not the only Survivalist groups to have endured the Remnant Age, but in terms of Adrian's vision for Repop, they were the most worrisome. Ideally, the villagers would do themselves in. If not, there were plenty of other ways to get the job done. An engineered virus would be the obvious choice, but risky. Crop interference would be safer, but slower, and starvation might inflame the sympathies of both the Interventionists and the general populace. Biologically and culturally, the Harz mountain villagers represented a dead end. Extinction was their destiny. Adrian would simply nudge the process along, as necessary.

Adrian Vanderplotz considered himself blessed in his

ability to both see the big picture, the long view, and also do whatever was necessary to steer humanity in the right direction. Most people were too vain, too obsessed with how others perceived them, to make the hard decisions. Progress, when it did happen, always happened the same way. It was a simple formula. Someone saw what needed to be done, they acquired power, then wielded that power to change the world. He'd always seen himself in that role. A doer of historic proportions. The fact that there would be a few casualties was unfortunate but inevitable.

He took a left turn onto a narrower trail that led to a glass exit portal. It slid open with a soft *whoosh* as he approached. The climate-control tube descended gently to the main level, where a second portal opened, depositing him in McLaren Park. From the exit pavilion he could see the arcing contours of Council Hall, and beyond that the gentle upward slope of the torus.

About half of the *Stanford*'s main level was dedicated to public use, including sprawling parks, government buildings with vast concourses, and the Academy campuses. Residences for the *Stanford*'s approximately eighteen thousand citizens, most of them in high-density apartment buildings, took up much of the remaining space. Aquaponic farms (which, unlike the meat-growing vats on Sub-2, required sunlight) took up the rest. Originally the ringstation had been designed for ten to fifteen thousand citizens, but a 2.05 fertility rate, ever-increasing longevity, and a stubborn refusal by the Over Council to adopt any mandatory number-of-children limit, had led to the current situation. By no means was the *Stanford* anywhere near its maximum capacity, but it was conceivable that within a few decades citizens might start to feel uncomfortably crowded, and perhaps even undergo the rationing of certain necessities (which would come as a rude shock after centuries of plentitude).

A surplus of ringstation citizens wasn't the only impetus for the repopulation of Earth. Repop was primarily a philosophical movement (or, depending on your perspective, a matter of biological determinism, a species-level Manifest Destiny). Only via bizarre turns of history had a reservoir of humanity ended up orbiting in space around the home planet. Human beings belonged on Earth. Via miraculous feats of engineering and unprecedented levels of co-operation, a number of hairless apes had made a good life for themselves in lofty, artificial worlds, but there was no reason to leave the mother planet empty. Not anymore. The insanity of the Remnant Age (and Regionalism, and the Corporate Age before that) was over. That particular branch of the species had played itself out, right down to the nasty endgame. The more enlightened representatives of humanity – who had built the ringstations in part to escape the insane asylum below – had won out. Earth would be their reward.

Adrian passed a few outdoor cafés and restaurants. It was a warm day, and more people were out than usual, sipping tall drinks, eating ice cream and sandwiches. Sunlight reflected in from the *Stanford*'s central mirror complex. The ringstation rotated on its axis in a position perpendicular to the Earth, in synchronous orbit. Adrian had watched, through Car-En's m'eye, the illuminated ring of his home against the night sky, stationary even as the distant constellations shifted. During the day, sunlight struck the mirror complex and was reflected ninety degrees to radiate circularly through the dual layers of ozone-enclosing semitransparent alumina that made up the inner ring of the torus. Looking up, the 'sky' was an even white with the faintest tint of yellow. One could climb the outward-facing side of the torus and view Sol directly through shielded ports. Those who were not prone to vertigo (this group did not include Adrian) could climb the Earthside of the torus and take in the stunning beauty of the home planet. From the *Stanford*'s current equatorial orbit, one could see Africa, lush and verdant, and the southern two-thirds of Europe, all the way up to the glacial line.

Some on the Repop Council favored direct and immediate contact with the European villagers, in the hopes that they could eventually integrate with future Repop settlements (or at least live side by side, peaceably, on the same continent). There were even some members of Adrian's own department who agreed with this idiotic tack; those individuals were completely ignorant of Earth history. One could not 'integrate' pre-literate (or, in the case of the villagers, devolved post-literate) groups with more advanced cultures adept at high-level conceptual thinking. The average ringstation citizen could read and write in multiple languages, was scientifically and mathematically literate, possessed cognitive sophistication and flexibility, was emotionally sensitive and self-possessed, and was socialized to understand and navigate complex institutions that simply did not exist at the lower levels of societal evolution. Earlier generations of anthropologists had naively elevated pre-literate cultures with notions of purity (the 'noble savage'). The truth, with very few exceptions, was that life in pre-literate societies was filled with ignorance, violence, and cruelty (in Hobbes's words, 'nasty, brutish, and short'). Life without a state, especially without a legal system and a means of tempered, even-handed justice, meant that each individual was their own judge and enforcer. In times of peace and plenty, anarchic, stateless societies could function reasonably well. But in times of resource scarcity or social upheaval, everything went to hell. Without letters, there could be no institutions of law. Without law, there was no order.

Integration would fail, and fail spectacularly. Adrian imagined a hypothetical case: a Repop settler would unwittingly violate some village taboo, and would then be subjected to the villagers' concept of just punishment. How would the gentle populace of the Ringstation Coalition react to seeing one of their own hanged, or beheaded? Adrian chuckled aloud. If that bothered them, how would they react to a Repop settler being drawn and quartered, or flayed alive? Just last night he had read about an ancient Viking method of torture and execution: the *rista orn* (blood eagle). The torturer would cut a deep incision on either side of the spine, reach in, crack off each rib at its base, then pull the victim's lungs out through the gaping wounds so that the organs of respiration were transformed into a pair of bloody wings. Finally, salt would be poured on the exposed lungs. The image both disgusted and excited him. Adrian wondered if the people of Happdal had somehow retained or resurrected this tradition.

The thought reminded him that he had lost access to direct observations of the villagers. He was furious with Car-En. Never had a student shown such insolence and poor judgment. He put the thought out of his mind; he couldn't afford to be upset right now. The Council meeting would require an even-keeled temperament. He would deal with Car-En later.

Adrian reached the concourse of the Council Hall, passing by elaborate artistic fountains, hollow bronze sculptures, carefully manicured trees, and other decorative elements that were constantly being updated and tweaked in accordance with current tastes and passing design fads. All a waste of time and resources, in his opinion. *The only thing that matters is Repop.* He passed through a wind wall into the main atrium. It was refreshingly cool inside, which helped him focus. There was just one thing that needed to happen at this meeting. With a little luck, he could pull it off.

His footsteps echoed in the large hall. A few people nodded at him. They all looked vaguely familiar. He was still newly elected, and generally bad with names and faces. But it didn't matter. What was important was that people knew *his* name, and that was more true than ever now that he finally held a seat on the Repop Council. He'd served as an advisor for years, but now he had real power, a vote. One vote wasn't much, but the Non-Interventionists were easy to manipulate. In effect, he already controlled a voting bloc.

He entered the Council Chamber. Along with a few other Council members, Penelope Townes was already seated. This annoyed him; he had hoped to arrive first (maybe he should have taken the tram after all). On the other hand, she looked tired and distracted, which was good.

"Hello, Adrian. Here you are again." Townes smiled wryly, unwilling to even pretend that she was happy to see him. Despite being a departmental colleague, she had stridently opposed his election campaign (though he had to admit her opposition had been on the up-and-up, no dirty tricks or character smears).

"Hello, Penny. Late night last night?" Her Academy nickname was too informal for this setting, especially considering her seniority on the Council. But he wanted to push her buttons.

Townes seemed unruffled. "Yes, in fact, we *were* out last night. Council member Troy and I" – she gestured to a timid-looking young man on her left – "closed out Vick's Lounge. Slope-4, Starside, have you been there? It's new." She continued without waiting for an answer. "We were brainstorming about the villagers, a long-term integration plan. Xenus has some excellent ideas, some of which we'll be discussing today." Xenus Troy smiled shyly at Adrian. Adrian pretended not to notice.

Townes was about sixty, and attractive, but looked her age. She didn't seem to mind having a few wrinkles, and had ribbed Adrian after his rejuv, calling him vain. She had an unkempt beauty, with highly symmetrical features, large, green eyes, and long, wavy gray hair, which she usually wore up in a bun. Most of the men in the anthropology department, including Adrian, had had a crush on her at one time or another; she was not only beautiful but also intelligent and charismatic. But her main characteristic was ambition. Her momentous discovery of living descendants of the Remnant Age was indisputably the most important finding in ringstation history. Even so, it had still taken some maneuvering for Townes to wrangle the Research Director position (Gupjay, the previous occupant, hadn't been quite ready to step down). On paper, as Department Head, Adrian was still her senior, but Townes had more influence. Or at least she *had*, before Adrian's election to Repop. Now they would see.

The remaining Council members had filtered in. The venerable Kardosh (well over one hundred years old) brought them to order. The first hour of the meeting consisted of design proposals for various aspects of settlement infrastructure, including temporary dome housing, water filtration systems, solar generators, waste composting soil-makers, and so forth. The main criterion for settlement-bound objects and devices was an unprecedented level of sturdiness and durability. Eventually Earth would once again house industrial production facilities equivalent to those on the *Stanford*'s Sub-2 level, including full-spectrum elemental printing of intricate machinery and computing devices, but first-gen settlers would have to make do with basic life-support machines, albeit rock-solid ones.

Kardosh cleared his throat and moved them on to the next item on the agenda. "Field research. Townes, what do the Kim brothers have to report?"

Harry and Bruce Kim were twins, anthropology field students who reported to Penny. The brothers had been observing what were believed to be the descendants of an ancient Israeli *kibbutz*, a communal agricultural society that had somehow endured the Remnant Age relatively intact (probably due to a combination of being extremely well-armed and having a vast supply of fruit and nut trees). Unlike the pseudo-Vikings that Car-En was studying, the *kibbutzniks* were literate, monotheistic, and all in all relatively civilized. The Kim brothers had even floated the possibility that the commune residents were *aware* of the existence of the ringstations; certainly they could not rule it out. While the descendants of the Israeli Jews were a technologically devolved culture (farming just above subsistence, using human and animal labor and simple wooden tools), they were culturally sophisticated, and had perhaps even retained some crude level of scientific literacy (at least in regards to food production techniques, medicine, and animal husbandry). In terms of metallurgy and modern materials, they had lost everything, but that, according to Townes, was irrelevant. The *kibbutzniks* were the best-known candidates for contact and possible integration.

Townes presented m'eye feeds from the Kims. Men and women in loose white shifts tended the orchards, which at first glance appeared to be planted chaotically, without rows and columns, but upon closer examination revealed a relaxed order structured around a vein-like irrigation system. The *kibbutz* agriculture was intensely polycultural: almond trees planted next to fig trees and apricot trees, legume vines winding along underneath, chickens everywhere, ducks paddling along in the irrigation canals, a few cows lounging in the shade.

"It looks messy," said Townes, "but in fact it's a sophisticated system, especially in terms of water conservation and nitrogen recycling. Some of the agricultural techniques we're seeing are consistent with high-yield, sustainable practices from the Revival Age. Though, to be fair, some of those techniques were pioneered by Late Corporate Age counterculturalists, in a spirit contrary to the zeitgeist of that time."

Spare us. Adrian bit his lip. He could tolerate only so much of Penny's pseudo-intellectual drivel. There was no single zeitgeist of the Late Corporate Age; Earth civilization had collapsed from its heady peak due to a plethora of warring philosophies, a mess of disparate visions that had ultimately resulted in massive non-action. Inertia had taken its course, and a complex global society radically unprepared for depopulation had crumbled (this, despite a century of warnings and predictions from demographers and statisticians).

"What protocols are the Kim brothers using to prevent detection?" asked Polanski. One of the younger members of the Council, Polanski was a prim rule-follower, and one of the staunchest Non-Interventionists. Adrian considered her part of his voting bloc. As long as a decision could be framed in terms of going 'by the book,' Polanski would vote for it.

"The feed is zoom-enhanced," Townes answered. "This one in particular came from Bruce Kim, cloaked and also hiding in dense foliage, from a two-hundred-meter distance." Polanski pursed her lips and nodded.

Kardosh cleared his throat. Having captured everyone's attention, he paused, twirling his mustache and staring at the projection image. Adrian could never tell if Kardosh's mannerisms were due to the eccentricities of an aged mind or if he was hamming it up for dramatic effect. Finally he spoke. "Could there be another reason for the...disorganized... planting schema?"

"What do you mean?" asked Townes.

"Well, at our last meeting you mentioned that the Kims had hypothesized the *kibbutzniks* might well be aware of *us*, the ringstations. What evidence did they present to that effect?"

"Bits of lore they had translated," Townes answered. "References to 'sky people.'"

"And what was the context of these mentions?" asked Kardosh sharply. Any whiff of elderliness had disappeared; Kardosh's interrogative tone put the chamber on high alert. Kardosh had earned authority not only from seniority; he was astute, a formidable analyst, and suffered no fools.

"I would have to review the data," Townes responded lamely.

"Please do. It occurs to me that this haphazard planting may serve an obfuscatory purpose, to render the settlement less visible from space. Had that occurred to you?"

"I had considered it," said Townes, in a way that made it clear that she hadn't. "In contrast, the mountain villages employ classical planting methods; that's part of what initially caught my attention and led to the initial discovery..."

That and the giant bonfires, thought Adrian, but he managed to hold his tongue. Kardosh was doing his work for him.

"...but the *kibbutz* was much harder to find," Townes continued. "Ultimately it was the herds of goats that gave them away."

"They should have no reason to fear us," said Kardosh, "but if there is evidence to indicate that they do, please make the Council aware."

"Of course," said Townes, slightly too loudly. Adrian suppressed a grin. What a blowhard, and Kardosh had taken her down two notches without Adrian having to open his mouth. But he could revel in schadenfreude later; the next bit was going to be tricky. He needed to focus.

Kardosh turned to a tall, pale, blond man, one who had yet to speak during the meeting. "Svilsson – do you have an intermediate report on the Sardinians?" Svilsson shook his head. At last week's meeting he'd presented feeds and written reports from the field researcher Han. Improbably – given their proximity to Campi Flegrei – a small community of gardeners and shepherds had escaped the immediate and total annihilation that had befallen Italy, Greece, Slovenia, and western Turkey. Wind patterns had spared the Mediterranean islanders the lethal torrents of burning ash. The Sardinians, a tough and stubbornly traditional people with a tight-knit communal lifestyle, had survived the ages with a way of life little changed since the late Neolithic. They had briefly embraced plumbing and electricity in the late twentieth and twenty-first centuries, but easily reverted to the old ways when those improvements proved unsustainable.

Svilsson, who abhorred talking, had presented Han's reports in written form, and the selected m'eye feeds were devoid of commentary. Adrian did not confuse silence for stupidity; he suspected Svilsson was perfectly capable of articulate speech when required. Which way would Svilsson lean? Townes and Svilsson had collaborated on projects in the past, so Adrian tentatively placed him in the enemy camp.

"What do you have for us, Vanderplotz?" asked Kardosh. "How is our dear Car-En? Her last biostat report gave us cause for alarm – as I recall she'd been eating nothing but nutrient bars and was running a severe caloric deficit. Has the situation been corrected? She is adequately equipped and trained to hunt the local fauna, is she not? Or at least procure edible plants? The prefabricated food supply was never intended to be anything but supplemental."

"Car-En is doing much better," Adrian said. He glanced at Penny, who was eyeing him suspiciously. He willed himself to ignore her. Using his m'eye, he directed the prerecorded feed to the main projector. The holographic image at the center of the conference table sprang back to life. This time, instead of farming *kibbutzniks*, the Council members were presented with a mountain vista, rocky terrain with scattered spruce trees, and a narrow, dark cave disappearing into the earth. A half-dozen burly, bearded men, together with a few lanky boys, labored, climbing in and out of the cave, filling up small carts with reddish chunks of rock.

"Miners," said Xenus Troy. It was a sharp observation, non-obvious, considering that no ringstation citizen had seen anything resembling this sort of mining. Ringstation minerals – and all other elements – were one hundred per cent recycled. In the rare instance when additional raw materials were required, they were extracted from near-Earth asteroids (or occasionally from the asteroid belt between Mars and Jupiter) by mining drones.

"Interesting!" exclaimed Kardosh, clearly delighted. "The source of the raw ore – a missing piece of the puzzle. Did they construct the mineshaft themselves?"

"There are dozens of ancient mines in the area, some from the Corporate Age, but many from much earlier," answered Adrian. "The Harz region is rich in silver, copper, lead, and iron. Some of these old mines they have repurposed and reinforced. All of the labor is done by hand, but their shovels and picks are fabricated from high-quality steel."

"Fabricated?" Kardosh raised a bushy eyebrow. "Don't you mean forged?"

"Yes, that would be more accurate," said Adrian, trying to hide his irritation. He glanced at Townes, who was – predictably – smirking. Townes still considered herself the preeminent expert on the Happdal villagers, and resented Adrian for taking over the project. It hadn't been hard. Adrian had persuaded Gupjay, as his final act as Research Director, to assign Happdal to Car-En Ganzorig, the department's star field student. Car-En's unswerving devotion to Adrian as her advisor and mentor thereby put Happdal firmly in his territory.

"What do they use for light?" Xenus Troy asked. "Oil lanterns? Is smoke a problem? Are there ventilation shafts?"

"We've seen them mine both with and without lanterns," answered Adrian. "Some of the villagers have wildstrain-enhanced vision."

"Is this a m'eye feed?" asked Townes. "It looks a little fuzzy, and the angle is high."

"A swarm feed," Adrian admitted. "After some close calls, Car-En has tightened her observation protocols. She's been using the drones for surveillance." The lie felt natural and easy, as it always did when Adrian felt justified in his motives.

"Split swarm?" asked Polanski. "She is maintaining a security perimeter at all times, yes?"

"Of course," Adrian said. He was relaxing into the presentation. This was going to work. He presented swarm feeds of mundane village activities for the next ten minutes, keeping his own commentary to a minimum. The Council members watched, enrapt, and Adrian remembered his own early fascination with watching the day-to-day routines of the villagers. It was like owning a time machine.

"Has Car-En made any progress in locating the carcinogenic radiation source?" asked Kardosh. "U-233, was it? That could be from a thorium fuel cycle." Kardosh was best known for his work as a historical biologist specializing in molecular evolution, but he was also medically trained, and knowledgeable in a number of scientific fields.

"Not yet," Adrian lied. "But she has narrowed down the search area via triangulation. It's possible the source is underground, contaminating the water supply." A little truth made the lie more plausible.

"We'd probably need an engineering group to contain it," Townes mused, "but if we locate the source, it's doable. A skeleton crew with the right gear could do it."

"We don't know that," said Kardosh. "We don't know what's leaking, we don't know how hot it is, and we don't know if we can do anything about it."

"It's got to be a homebrew reactor of some sort," Townes countered. "There are extensive containment protocols – the Japanese got really creative toward the end."

"I'm aware of the methods," said Kardosh.

"Wait a minute," Polanski blurted, "are we talking about Intervention?"

"The point of Non-Interventionism is to avoid cultural contamination," snapped Townes, "not to stand by and watch a tragedy unfold in slow motion. These are people, human beings like us. The Harz villages represent about one per cent of all human beings in existence. To not act would be a form of genocide. Slaughter through passivity and inaction."

That shut Polanski up. Adrian quickly checked the math in his head. The Ringstation Coalition was home to roughly six hundred thousand souls, spread out among the eleven ringstations and a number of smaller cylindrical and spherical vessels. Happdal was home to about three hundred; that number combined with the population of the nearby villages might just exceed one thousand. So the real number was about 0.16 per cent; Townes was off by a factor of six. Typical. He considered pointing out the error, decided against it, and glanced at Kardosh to see if the old man had caught the mistake. Kardosh was staring thoughtfully into space; he had missed it.

Adrian took a deep breath. Now was as good a time as any. Polanski, mortified, was staring at her hands, Townes was trying to compose herself, and the silence was getting uncomfortably long.

"That's all I have to present today, but if I might, I'd like to insert a proposal into the agenda."

"Today?" asked Kardosh, surprised.

"Yes, time permitting. Council members Townes and Troy, I'd like your permission to present my proposal before your own. The project is highly time-sensitive, and I'd like to secure the unanimous approval of this Council before taking even the first step."

He paused and faced Townes. He'd nailed it. All of them, even Townes and Troy, were burning with curiosity. And Townes had just come down too hard on Polanski, in effect accusing her of genocide. She would defer to Adrian in order to appear co-operative, to put the needs and wishes of the group over her own ambition.

"I don't see why you can't submit agenda items ahead of time, like everybody else," Townes snapped. He'd guessed wrong.

"Take it easy, Penelope," said Kardosh. "Is your proposal time-sensitive?"

"It could probably wait a week," Troy acceded, eliciting a glare from Townes.

"Very well, Vanderplotz," Kardosh said, "insert away."

With a single command he'd prepared ahead of time, Adrian modified the agenda and forwarded the lengthy document. He took a minute to savor their reactions as they reviewed the outlines of the project in their m'eyes. Kardosh was scowling (not necessarily a bad sign). Troy's mouth hung open slightly. Polanski knitted up her brow in worry. Townes clenched her jaw. The others looked confused, shocked, or dumbfounded. All in all, exactly what he had expected.

The document was entitled simply *Advance Field Station, Western Eurasia*. It outlined plans for a full life-support research camp (including energy generation and food production) at the base of the Italian Alps. The suggested location was approximately equidistant from the *kibbutz* settlement and the Harz villages. "Our field research program, as I'm sure you would all agree, has been a resounding success. This is the next logical step − ground support for the next wave of field researchers."

Kardosh spoke first. "This is a settlement. Repop, plain and simple. We're not there yet, Vanderplotz, and you know it."

Adrian was ready for this. "The research base is temporary, in no way a permanent settlement. You know my views on Repop. Slow, steady, and non-invasive. We're still in Research-1, this is part of that. Please review Section 12: 'Consolidation and Extraction.' The mission is clearly defined in Section 1. When the project achieves success according to the mission, there will no longer be any reason for the research station to exist." This, of course, was a lie. Once a human community had established itself on Earth, it would be inextricable. Adrian already had a nickname for the research station: Vander Camp. Which, over the years, might morph into Vandertown, or Vanderton.

"Adrian," said Townes, "we covered this option in Planning, and decided against it." Her eyes flicked as she checked something in her m'eye. "Unanimously decided, it says in the minutes. The field researchers already have all the support they need. They're in constant communication; they have bioskins; they have drone swarms. A great deal of effort went into making sure they were fully equipped, both in terms of safety *and* mission capability."

"Safety is relative," he answered. "Car-En has already had some close calls."

"We knew that going in, that there would be risks associated with each field position," said Townes. "Dangers specific to the particular location or community being observed. All the researchers were briefed and trained. We concluded, *unanimously*, that these risks were preferable to the risk of cultural contamination from a base camp."

"True," said Adrian, "for any research station within the proximity of the subject populations. But...the field station" – he'd almost slipped and called it Vander Camp – "is nowhere near any of the settlements. There is zero chance of accidental discovery."

"By the groups we're aware of," interjected Kardosh.

"We've been scouring Eurasia and Africa for settlement signs for the last five years. The Harz mountain villages, the *kibbutzniks*, and the Sardinians are the only ones we've turned up."

"Absence of evidence..." Kardosh started.

"Is not evidence of absence," finished Townes.

"Of course not," said Adrian, "but we're in the realm of diminishing probability. And location is only the first countermeasure against discovery. Please refer to Section 9...."

"Hold on a second," Xenus Troy said. "How do you envision this research station providing support, exactly, if it's hundreds of kilometers away from any of the researchers?"

And here it was, the moment he'd been waiting for. The argument had shifted from justifiability to viability, from credibility to logistics. And Xenus Troy, less timid than he had initially seemed, had provided the opening. Troy might be an ally of Townes, but he was unreliable in that respect. Adrian knew his type: above any political ties, Troy's loyalty was to science and discovery, to knowledge itself.

"Excellent question. Please see Section 2, Diagram 2.14. The schema describes a device I have co-designed specifically for this project. There is already a prototype. If you'd like a hands-on demonstration, just ask."

The room was silent while they looked.

"Hmph," Kardosh grunted, twitching his bushy eyebrows, one corner of his mouth turned slightly up.

CHAPTER EIGHTEEN

Katja found Henning bathing in one of the sulfurous pools. He beckoned for her to join him. "Come, the water is good even if you have no aches and pains to soothe." He sounded relaxed, with no trace of the fear she had heard in his voice in the library, near Raekae.

"Where is the hermit?" she asked. She had no intention of disrobing.

Henning stared pensively at the water. A minute later, he climbed out of the pool and stood before her, dripping and naked. "What do you want with her?" he asked, utterly unselfconscious. "Do you think she will show you a way out? If she knew one, I doubt she would still be here."

"Do you know for a fact that she *is* still here? How would you know if she left?" asked Katja, keeping her eyes fixed on his face.

"My apologies. One second." Henning took a robe from a nearby hook and donned it. "The modesty of youth left me long ago. I forget how young you are. You are not yet twenty?"

"Seventeen," Katja admitted.

Henning nodded. It was strange to think that he could be her ancestor.

"No dirk," he observed. "Did you attack Raekae? Ha! You do take after Mette. Did you draw blood?"

"A killing blow," she said, feeling proud even though she doubted Raekae was truly dead.

"Good for you. And yet, he lives. A few years ago I tried the same. Like you, I thought I had succeeded. That was the last time I saw my swords."

"Biter and Taker? I carry them now. With my true body. Raekae said that I fought with them, and killed."

"Ah…good. They are fine swords. Biter has the soul of a wolf, Taker the soul of a cruel man. Stian forged them, you know. Maybe one day he will tell you the story. The man was—"

"Where is the hermit?" she interrupted.

Henning smiled. "Go to the hut with the green door. But that will only be the beginning of finding her."

"What do you mean?"

"She is a world-builder. Raekae taught her. I have only spoken with her a few times, but I think she understands this place as well as he does. Maybe better."

"What is her name?"

"The crone's name is Zoë."

She stared at the man who purported to be her great-grandfather. His face did bear a resemblance to Esper's. "Well, goodbye," she said. "Thank you for helping me. I will not see you again." She was ready to forgive him for cutting her, and for his cowardice near Raekae. She sensed it was true that the terror was beyond his control.

He grinned. "You will see me again. So much that you will sicken of my face. Except that you will not, because life never gets tiring in this place. It is a great blessing."

★ ★ ★

The hut with the green door was easy to find; she had passed it before. There was no answer when she knocked. Her hand went to her hip but found only empty space where the pommel of her dirk should have been. It did not matter – she was not here to fight. Slowly, she turned the latch and pushed the door open.

She stood in the midst of a dense green rainforest. A cacophony of strange noises assaulted her ears. In the distance, rushing water, perhaps a large waterfall. Closer, a medley of birdcalls, all of them unfamiliar. Something howled exuberantly from a high treetop, answered by a more distant howl. The hair on Katja's neck stiffened. She recognized none of the sounds, none the plants or trees. Even the air was hotter and thicker than she was used to. A huge bright, yellow beetle landed on her arm. She brushed it off quickly, barely suppressing a scream.

"I want to go home," she said under her breath, to no one but herself.

She glanced behind her. The green door was there, and the hut, but once again she was on the *outside*.

She ignored the illusion. Nothing here was real. She followed a narrow path forward, weaving between thick fronds, passing beneath flowering vines. High above she glimpsed a sliver of bright blue sky through a narrow gap in the canopy.

"Zoë!" she called out. "My name is Katja – I need to speak with you! If you are an enemy of Raekae then I am your friend!" Her voice was quickly absorbed by the dense foliage. It was like yelling into an unshorn sheep.

She continued on. Something landed in her hair. Whatever it was flew off with a chattering sound when she batted it away. A sheen of sweat formed on her skin.

"Zoë," she said in a normal speaking voice. Yelling would not help – the hermit would show herself if and when she was ready. "Henning said you made this place. What do you call it? Why is the air so thick?" She did not trust the sensation. Air should not have a *feel* to it.

The path led to a clearing. In the center was a square pool lined with flat, polished stones. A woman with pale skin and shoulder-length black hair sat on a stone bench at the edge of the pool, watching Katja. She was older than Katja but still young, much younger than Elke. Except for her eyes, which were small and squinty, she was pretty. "What do you think?" the woman asked. "Costa Rica, Caribbean side, circa twenty-first century. I'm sure it looks much different now, but those are the databases I have to work with. It's all real, you know – everything is alive! This is a *real* ecosystem, complete with natural selection and evolutionary change. I've modeled over two million organisms. Not just flora and fauna, but bacteria and viruses, amoeba – the whole deal. The geology is accurate down to the mantle. Not just terrestrial, but also aquatic – if you hike a few miles in that direction you'll find a beach and an ocean. Fish, coral, squid, sea turtles...."

Something bit the back of Katja's neck. She slapped it, leaving a bloody smear on her hand.

"Sorry about that," said Zoë. "Like I said, accurate. Don't worry – you can't get sick here. You won't even have an immune response or allergic reaction. I'm working on a tropical paradise here, not a jungle torture chamber!" She laughed airily. "Oh, you must be so confused. Here, sit down." She patted the bench next to her. "Ask me some questions."

Katja warily took a few steps forward. Zoë did not seem dangerous, but neither had Henning, and he had sliced open her hand. Everyone in this place was insane and unpredictable.

"Where are we?" asked Katja, still standing.

"Costa Rica – I already told you. Oh…you mean where *are* we. We're in the Crucible. Or, more accurately, we're *of* the Crucible. And not *the* Crucible but rather *a* Crucible. Raekae's, one of eleven."

"And what—"

"What's the Crucible? Of course, how would you know? The Crucible has two parts. The quantum core – the egg – runs BioSim and GeoSim in a physics framework, using several billion qubits. The threading system is self-generating carbonwire that follows and mimics the host's nervous system, scanning and virtualizing until emulation is complete."

It was nonsense to Katja, even though the woman was speaking perfect Norse. (And how was that possible?) But Katja knew what a crucible was. She did not understand this woman's magic, but she would not be intimidated.

"The Crucible is the first secret of godsteel," she said loudly, as if giving a speech. "A container made from river clay, hardened by fire. The crucible is filled with iron ore, and also a handful of sand and a shard of broken glass to draw out the impurities."

The woman looked at her thoughtfully. "I didn't know about the sand and the glass," she said. "But yes, a crucible is a container in which you melt and meld metals. And in our case, a container in which you melt and meld minds."

"How do I get out?" Katja asked. There was no reason not be blunt.

"Please, sit," said the woman. "My name is Zoë, but I'm guessing you already knew that."

"Katja," said Katja, finally sitting down. If this woman attacked her, she guessed it would do no permanent damage. That seemed to be the way of this place. "They said you were an old crone."

"Ha!" Zoë exclaimed. "To them I am. To them, I look like this." Katja looked over to see a brown-skinned, hunched old woman, with a wide face, a broad, flat nose, and narrow black eyes. The crone wore a colorful woven garment that was half dress, half blanket. She smiled at Katja and spoke in a different voice, rougher and lower. "Or I could look like this." Suddenly Katja was sitting next to herself, and she was shocked to see how young she looked. She was still a girl. It was strange to see her own face so clearly, and also from a slightly different angle. Undoubtedly it was her, but was her nose really shaped that way? Not unattractive, but unfamiliar when viewed from the side.

Zoë changed back into her original form. "This is how I looked, more or less, the day I volunteered. That's what the Crucible was supposed to be: a volunteer program. It was never meant to be the prison that Raekae turned it into. And he's not the only Original to become a jailor." She looked thoughtful for a moment. "I wonder what the others are doing – the ones who didn't choose to be wardens. Even without hosts, the worlds continue on within the Crucibles. The threads can take energy from many sources: glucose, sunlight, decaying matter, almost anything."

"I need to go home," Katja said. "Is there a way to leave?"

"The original intent was to solve the Smooth Transition problem," said Zoë, ignoring Katja's question. "Create not only a brain-body backup, but also maintain the continuity of experience…prevent identity divergence."

Something enormous howled from the treetops, incredibly loud and much closer than before. Katja's shoulders tensed and she looked up, searching for the source of the racket.

"Howler monkey," said Zoë. "They're actually quite small,

and harmless." She cupped her hands to her mouth and skillfully answered the call. A few more responses echoed above. "You recognized yourself a moment ago. But did you think of that person as *you*, or as someone else?"

"As someone else," answered Katja truthfully. "Though it looked exactly like me. A twin."

"That's identity divergence. Or it would be, if I had made a complete copy of you instead of just mimicking your appearance. But that's not possible yet. You're not all-the-way mapped."

"Raekae said I was still using my own brain." Katja was not sure what that meant, but it seemed relevant.

"Yes," Zoë confirmed, as if she had said something that made sense. "That's right. And as long as that's true, there's a slim chance that you can get what you want."

"You mean I can leave?"

"Maybe. A very small chance. I've been working on something for a long time…. A project. Something wondrous and powerful and very dangerous. It's almost ready. If it works, there's a very good chance you'll die. But if you live, you can go home."

"I would rather die than live forever in this place," said Katja, feeling entirely sure of the words as they left her mouth.

Zoë stared at her, her eyes welling up with moisture. But the strange woman blinked back her tears and smiled.

"Me too, when it comes down to it."

CHAPTER NINETEEN

Excerpt from 'The Four Phases of Earth Depopulation' by Lydia Heliosmith, age 17, written for *Terrestrial Anthropology 1*, 22.01.02719:

Phase 2: The Revival (Part I – Messy Utopias)

Phase 2 depopulation, a gradual descent from seven billion down to five billion, was a brighter time for humanity. The Hundred-Year Recession came to an end (along with the Corporate Age itself) in the decades following Unified Europe's 'Second Reformation' of 2211 (not, this time, a schism within Christianity, but rather a massive do-over of the continental corporate charter). The key to sustainable shrinkage, it turned out, was to nurture and protect local markets. This necessitated a great clawing back of power from the massive blobs of private capital roving the globe willy-nilly, devouring and digesting local markets to feed their purposeless growth. The combination of capital controls and corporate charter reform finally tamed the persistent bubble-and-bust cycles of the Corporate Age, allowing regional governments to manage their economies with more foresight and less calamity.

Not every superpower transformed itself as effectively as Europe. Some disintegrated altogether (in the case of the American secessions) or awkwardly reorganized (China's slow, decidedly non-revolutionary Gõngpíng movement). Other nations merged to create heftier, more resource-diverse economies (the African Equatorial Alliance, the Arabian Emirates). The tipping of the global power scales from corporate to civic scrambled many borders, governing institutions, and international alliances. The world map, both literally and figuratively, was redrawn on a scale not seen since the end of the Second World War.

Shrinking economies could still be highly functional. Part of the solution was protecting local markets from predatory speculators.

Another factor turned out to be keeping old people healthy. Seniors who could still work and contribute, and who didn't overburden the healthcare system or their (generally fewer) descendants – these older citizens provided an economic buffer that saved nations from destitution. The Late Corporate Age, for all its excesses, did provide a number of medical gifts: vaccines that prevented heart attacks, most cancers, and dementia; bloodstream nanodrones to break up clots and destroy pathogens; pharma implants to enhance homeostasis on every level.

Many nation states followed Unified Europe's local wealth, local power mantra, and succeeded in maintaining quality of life in population-dense areas. Other territories were abandoned to the wild. Abandoned cities crumbled and yielded to grassland, forest, or jungle, while those that survived doubled down on infrastructure upgrades and beautification.

The end of reckless corporate profiteering was a boon for the human spirit. Despite retreating in numbers, humanity was once again advancing culturally. The dark age of the Hundred-Year Recession lifted, and the mid-twenty-third century came to be known, in the spirit of the French Renaissance, as the Revival.

Why not be hopeful? With the excesses of the Corporate Age reined in, life for most human beings was good. Climate change required some adjustments, but it was easy to grow delicious food on Greenhouse Earth. Industrial Age environmental conundrums (how to dispose of trash, how to generate cheap clean energy, how to limit toxic chemicals) had been solved over the decades; humans had finally learned to not crap where they ate. Even the oceans, reduced in large part to acidic, overwarm habitats for visible-from-space algal blooms and huge swarms of jellyfish, were beginning to show signs of recovery. In response to carbon sequestration from reforestation, a lack of acid rain, and a sharply reduced demand for seafood, coral reefs returned, and thought-to-be extinct species reappeared. Human beings had not irrevocably trashed the planet after all, and with this realization came the end of the psychological winter that had plagued humanity for a century.

As a means to sell more goods, the Corporate Age had promised the individual citizen limitless choice and freedom, but instead delivered 'option paralysis' and dopamine-driven consumeristic discontent. With less pressure from advertisements and a more civic-oriented zeitgeist, human beings rediscovered the joy of commitment (to family, to friends, to a place, to principles, to purpose), and though life on average was simpler, slower, and less extravagant, the angst and neuroticism of the Corporate Age faded. Consumerism was replaced by vocational, creative, intellectual, and spiritual pursuits. Even some religious practices and ceremonies were rediscovered and refashioned by the secular mainstream and scientifically literate, leaving mystical beliefs (Creation, Sin, Heaven and Hell, the Immortal Soul) as relics for theological historians to ponder and debate.

Culturally and philosophically, the Revival took a view of progress as not inevitable, but achievable, and citizens took to building 'messy utopias' with creative zeal. The Revival ethos emphasized practicality over perfection, empiricism over dogma, and working with existing realities instead of insisting on clean slates. The dreamers behind the new 'messy' utopias used whatever approaches worked, and viewed moral behavior as something to foster and encourage (not as a character prerequisite, nor as an ultimate goal).

With this new sense of global optimism, birth rates slightly increased, but did not reach replacement levels. Even with near-universal improvements in quality of life, there were fewer people every year, and ever-growing swaths of rewilded terrain.

14.05.02727, the *Stanford*

Adrian sipped an iced coffee while he waited for Xenus Troy. The coffee wasn't bad. Not as good as the imported stuff grown on the *Alhazen*, but drinkable. Still, he would have preferred a chilled Corsican mint if the vending machine had offered such an option. Hair Lab was *hot*. Literally hot, with lots of bodies and kinetic energy. Most of the engineers were young and ostensibly employed by the Academy, but few had any real responsibilities or well-defined job descriptions. The fab-labs were pure research and development. Engineers could either work on their own devs or volunteer for projects with specifications (Adrian had garnered a half-dozen eager recruits within an hour of posting his own project spec – contributing to a Repop Council project was worth a lot in terms of prestige and bragging rights).

Seeing Troy's close-shorn pate from across the hall, Adrian

stood and waved. The younger man joined him in the café area, smiling and extending his hand. Adrian shook it, greeting Troy warmly. He had misjudged Xenus Troy at first, mistaking the Council member's polite earnestness for weakness. What he had missed was Troy's ambition. It should have been obvious. Nobody ended up on Repop Council accidentally. All the positions were elected except for the appointed liaison to the Over Council (currently Kardosh).

"Thanks for meeting me here," said Troy. "Can you believe this is my first visit to Hair Lab? I've heard about it, of course…. Who hasn't? Why is it called that, anyway?"

"I have no idea," Adrian said. "Probably some inside joke. But who cares? Let's go look at the prototype."

Adrian led them to Bay-23. Two of the engineers, both men under thirty, were working on the craft. Nearby, two young women studied a wallscreen displaying a design schematic of the rotor-blade mechanism. Nobody noticed Adrian and Troy standing there until Troy spoke.

"Ah…I *suspected* you were going to show me a vehicle when you told me to meet you at Hair Lab. But a hovercraft…hmm…I suppose…. How fast can it go? It certainly is…"

"Small. And very light. But the payload is significant. Five hundred kilos."

The young developers finally noticed them. One of the women smiled and nodded at Adrian. As soon as the team realized it was a show-and-tell that didn't require their input, they went back to work. "Ignore us," said Adrian, formalizing what had already happened. Adrian briefly wondered if the hierarchy-free culture of the Engineering Department had gone too far. But the working group had certainly produced results, and quickly.

"How fast can it go?" Troy asked.

"About three hundred kilometers per hour, or two hundred with a full load," said Adrian proudly. "Mediterranean to the glacial line in two or three hours. It functions best between two and twenty meters above surface, over land or sea, and is stable in wind speeds of up to seventy kilometers per hour. Did I get that right?"

One of the engineers looked up. "Sorry, what did you say?"

"Never mind, back to work," said Adrian, forcing a smile.

"What's the maximum altitude?" asked Troy.

"Untested, for obvious reasons, but theoretically one hundred meters shouldn't be a problem, at least in calm weather."

"So it's really a flying vehicle. Is it safe? And how do you propose to get it down there?"

Adrian pointed to a nearby cargo cube. "Disassembled, the whole thing fits in a standard crate. We could mule down three at a time if we needed to. Assembly only takes a few hours once you learn how to do it. They won't let me touch the prototype yet, but I intend to learn the procedure myself."

Adrian was able to answer most of Troy's questions, and interrupted the developers only a few times (the devs were surprisingly unenthusiastic about showing off their creation – apparently all they wanted to do was work on it). How was it powered? (A high-voltage fuel cell, fed compost scraps or just about anything.) Could it be repaired from camp if it broke down? (Easily – and a backup crate of spare parts would be prepped for each unit.) What were the training requirements for operation? (Virtually nil – a small child could probably figure it out.)

Troy was obviously impressed, though he did his best to appear nonchalant. Certainly the young Council member was aware of the tension between Adrian and Townes; it could hurt Troy politically to be seen as cozying up to Adrian. But he was interested in the idea of an advance research station. Townes would vote against Vander Camp, but Troy was on the fence. Not for long, hopefully.

"You know," said Adrian, as if the idea had just occurred to him, "the station is going to need a Research Coordinator. The position would report to the Research Director – Penelope Townes – but the Research Coordinator would be more hands-on, and would have a great deal of say in prioritizing missions and determining investigative direction. Logistics too, of course, but not just that."

Troy was listening closely, but didn't say anything. No bite.

Adrian would have to be more explicit.

"I think you'd be ideal for the role."

Troy raised an eyebrow. "Don't you think it's premature to discuss that? Your proposal isn't even up for a vote."

"No, not yet. Maybe you're right. I'm just thinking out loud here. You'd be on my short list, that's all I meant to say."

"Wouldn't the position be elected, like the Research Director? Not appointed?"

"Of course! But I'd like to think a nomination by the Department Head would carry a little weight. No? You're by the book, Xenus, aren't you? That's good – I like that about you. A bit like Polanski." Troy grimaced at being compared to Polanski, as Adrian expected he would. The young man saw himself as independent, a pioneer. He was playing hard to get, but Adrian could tell he was interested.

Vander Camp. No matter who was appointed Research Coordinator, Adrian himself would be the visionary behind the project. He would be the chief cultural engineer, shaping and sculpting the first permanent Earth settlement composed of ringstation citizens. The first node was important. The values and cultural norms of that first settlement would ripple out through time, influencing the nature of society for centuries to come. What cities had thrived in the greater region? Damascus, Jericho, and Jerusalem in the Middle East; Argos, Athens, Thebes, Rome, and Byzantium in the Mediterranean; Lutetia (Paris) and Londinium farther north; they had all started as small settlements. Each had become a great city, thrived for millennia, and finally fallen, but their influence and legacies lived on among the ringstations. Vander Camp would be the same way, and Adrian would be the architect. The Founder.

"...food supplies. That could be problematic." Troy was speaking. Adrian's attention had wandered. "I wonder if there are herds of domesticatable fauna in the region? Maybe strains that have only recently rewilded, left over from Survivalist settlements. Would any of those animals have survived? Maybe wild goats?"

"Mmm...yes. Probably."

"And the soil – it must be fertile from the Campi Flegrei ash deposits. Productive gardens would only take a few months to establish. Crops within a year, fruit and nut trees within a few years."

Adrian suppressed a grin. Xenus Troy would be a poor poker player; his affirmative vote was all but counted.

"Xenus, I'm afraid I have another appointment. It's been a pleasure meeting with you. Would you like to schedule a follow-up meeting?"

"Yes, yes…of course. Just thinking out loud, as you say. If the research station…. Well, certainly I'll have some follow-up questions." Troy cleared his throat. Was he turning a little pink? Perhaps he was remembering his allegiance to Townes right now. "The craft…it's certainly well-designed. Your dev team is skilled. Kudos, engineers!" The devs, who had paid no attention to their conversation, returned Troy's awkward praise with tight smiles.

Adrian escorted Troy out of the lab and bid the younger man goodbye. Already he was thinking about the other Council members. Svilsson, the quiet one, was an enigma. There would also be a Station Director position; would Svilsson be interested? Adrian had considered volunteering for that spot himself. But without a majority vote, there would be no research station, no Vander Camp. What about Polanski? She would probably stay loyal to Adrian, unless she viewed the research base as a permanent settlement (and thus a violation of their established protocols). Was there a carrot he could dangle to secure her vote?

Adrian opened a line to Manning at SecondSkin. The consulting firm had designed the specialized bioskins worn by Car-En and the other field researchers. Manning was the lead tech and a contributing developer (he had personally designed a good chunk of the drone swarm interface). The technician didn't answer right away, but Adrian's m'eye indicated that Manning was at the SecondSkin office. Adrian took a walkway up to Sub-1 and patiently strolled through a shopping district, waiting for a response.

Finally Manning's unshaven face appeared in Adrian's m'eye.

"What is it?" He sounded irritable.

"Sorry for disturbing you, but it's important. I need another override for Car-En."

"Why?"

"She's been having some blood-sugar regulation issues. Her last biostat was totally out of whack. We're afraid her implants might be malfunctioning."

"What does that have to do with SecondSkin?" asked Manning. His brusqueness was bordering on rude. Adrian wondered if he would have to remind Manning that being respectful was still in his best interest.

"The bioskin kit talks to her pharma implant, doesn't it? If her blood sugar gets too low she could pass out, even slip into a coma. Normally we could rely on her implant to regulate, but with the technical problems...."

"Mmm," Manning grunted. "Just run a diagnostic on the implant. Or call *Stanford* Medical, talk to a technician."

"I already have," Adrian lied. "We need the override, in case of an emergency. Car-En is all alone down there. If she has a serious medical issue, she's days away from help – almost two hundred kilometers from the mule station. A kit override might be her only chance."

"I don't know. I mean, it's doable, but I'm not sure you should be talking to me. Let me put you through to Harriet."

"I'd rather you didn't. I like dealing with *you*, Manning. You know how to get things done. I'm almost done with your recommendation for SecSys on the *Liu Hui*. Personally, I think they'd be stupid not to take you."

Manning grunted again, looking down. Adrian had an advantage, being able to see Manning's face, while the tech could only hear Adrian's voice. He didn't want to be too heavy-handed, but he wasn't in the mood for patient cajoling.

"Look, I'll see what I can do. I might not be able to swing a full override."

"Access to the blood-sugar regulation subsystem is all we need."

"You need to be extremely cautious – you could really mess

her up if you don't know what you're doing. Why don't you just pull her in, get the implant fixed, and redeploy? Are you guys on some kind of schedule or something? A bad implant is serious. Let Medical deal with it."

"That's the plan, but remember she's on foot, days away from the mule station. Can you get me access, or do I need to speak with Harriet?"

A long pause. Manning stared at the recording dot, brow furrowed. "I'll see what I can do. Give me a day or two."

"The sooner the better. Thank you, Manning." Adrian closed the patch.

He checked his conscience, searching for misgivings or any pang of anticipatory guilt regarding what he planned to do. *All clear.* It made sense and it was justified. Beyond insubordination, Car-En had gone fully rogue. She was Intervening. And what was one life compared to the future of humanity? Without Car-En's interference, there was a good chance the Harz villagers would do themselves in. Adrian couldn't afford to have her mucking about in their business, aiding and assisting them.

Insulin was the perfect solution to the problem, and Adrian felt a renewed surge of pride for thinking of it in the first place. Car-En's death would appear to be accidental. With access to her implant, he could simply edit the algorithm that regulated her blood sugar. Her demise would be attributed to a programming error. There would be hell to pay at *Stanford* Medical. A full audit might reveal the code alterations, but Adrian would be sure to cover his tracks. And all that assumed an autopsy; a more likely scenario was that Car-En's body would never be recovered. The Happdal villagers would dispose of her, or her corpse would be consumed by wolves. Wolves weren't above scavenging dead meat, were they?

Adrian *did* have a conscience. He cared deeply about people, about humanity. He wasn't as empathetic as most; he was outside of Standard Edits norms (bordering on sociopathy, according to a private test he'd taken). Long ago he'd ceased to feel self-conscious about this difference. Society needed people like him to move forward. History would forgive him his harsher decisions – if they ever came to light – and remember only his contributions. It was the way of the world. Christopher Columbus had been a cheat, a kidnapper, a torturer, a slaver, and an accomplice to far worse crimes by his crew. And East America had named a holiday after him.

Adrian would accomplish far more, with far less death and destruction. Car-En's death would be painless. This was important to Adrian. Despite her stubbornness (maybe even because of it), he liked her. From the start she'd been bright, ambitious, precocious. He'd groomed her from her first days as a field student in the department. He would miss her. What would he say at her memorial service? He'd be able to share his true feelings, to speak honestly to her family, friends and colleagues. He respected and admired Car-En Ganzorig.

Didn't civilization ultimately *require* men like him, to progress? What good would it do to repopulate Earth with gentle *Homo sapiens melior*[2] if they would all eventually be slaughtered by sword-wielding brutes? Adrian cared for his species more than he cared for himself. He was dedicating his life to the greater good. Could Townes say as much?

Adrian passed an arcade, forcing a few teenagers to make way as he strode past. A girl glared at him sullenly through her augment lens, but looked away at the last minute when Adrian refused to break eye contact. The augment, wrapping halfway around her head, was probably for gaming. Adrian had no taste for holographic immersion himself. Life, unaltered, was interesting enough. One of his Academy friends had gotten involved in game culture and had stopped studying altogether. Adrian had redoubled his own academic efforts at that point, eventually graduating with honors and gaining the anthropology field position on the *Alhazen* that had launched his career. Now Adrian was an elected member of Repop Council, planning the repopulation of humanity's home planet. And what was his ex-friend doing? Probably still reliving ancient Greek sieges from millennia past....

Adrian took an elevator to Main, ending up on the outskirts of McLaren Park. He checked the time in his m'eye: 18:30. He was hungry. He briefly considered cooking, but there was no food in his apartment. He'd stop at a park café on the way home.

The Standard Edits made sense; they were for the benefit of humanity, even if Adrian himself didn't conform to them exactly. His amygdala might not function the same as everyone else's, but he was resistant to radiation, free of disease-causing traits, of small stature (compared to historical Earth norms), highly intelligent, and unlikely to succumb to any sort of degenerative disease as long he updated his nanodrones every decade or so. The social and personality traits emphasized by the Standard Edits were optimized for ringstation life (living in space, living inside of a closed loop – both literally and figuratively). The Edits favored genotypes associated with greater co-operation, greater empathy, less proclivity toward violence, cautiousness, conscientiousness, a high ability to defer gratification (low impulsivity), and a great propensity for advance planning. While any first-year psychology student could tell you that the greater part of moral behavior was condition-dependent (any person could be 'good' with a full belly, surrounded by supportive friends and family), genetics still mattered. Ringstation life provided optimized nature *and* nurture. The result was a smooth-running society, a vanishingly small crime rate, and extremely high levels of social trust. *A tube full of sheep* was the phrase that sometimes popped into Adrian's mind. It would be harder to get away with murder in a less trusting culture.

A line opened in his m'eye. He stopped in his tracks, giving the indicator his full attention. He hadn't been expecting this.

"Hello?"

"Hello, Adrian."

Her voice sounded different. Certainly colder – she didn't sound like she was calling to patch things up. But something else was different. Her accent, maybe.

"I know you don't approve of me helping the villagers," said Car-En. "I know you're completely against it, as is the Council. But something very strange has happened, and I need your help. Someone, or something, is *already* Intervening in their lives, and I think we should help them. Or at least find out what's going on."

It was surreal hearing her voice, as if she had risen from the dead. How quickly his mind had moved on.

"Adrian, can you hear me? Will you help us?"

Footnote 2. As distinct from *Homo sapiens populensis*, the taxonomical designation assigned to the bulk of human beings who had ever existed, products of the out-of-control population explosion of the mid-nineteenth to late twenty-first century. By contrast, *Homo sapiens melior* was the branch of (ringstation-dwelling) humanity that had subjected itself to the Standard Edits.

CHAPTER TWENTY

For sport, and to show that he could, Haakon fought two men at once. Olof, wielding an axe, circled, trying to flank him. Haakon, amused, kept most of his attention on Olaf – Olof's brother – who faced him, holding a blunted spear.

"What are you waiting for, Olaf? Two against one, and still you hesitate?"

Olaf took the bait and lunged. Haakon parried easily, deflecting the spear shaft with the flat of his blunted sword. A beat later, Olof attacked from the rear, swinging his axe in a wide arc. Haakon stepped forward, out of range, and in the same motion grabbed the shaft of Olaf's spear with his free hand. Pulling Olaf toward him, he sunk the point of his sparring sword into the padded armor of Olaf's armpit. The big man yowled in pain.

"Out!" yelled Haakon. "With sharpened steel that blow would have pierced your heart."

Olaf slunk away, chastised by the jeers of the onlookers. Haakon wheeled to face Olof. The villagers of Kaldbrek loved a good fight, even if it was only sport. Daily sparring was mandatory for all men of fighting age, resulting in frequent bruises, sprains, cuts, and the occasional broken bone. Egil had suggested Haakon's fighting force would be stronger if he gave them more rest. Haakon had laughed at that. It was important to know pain, to feel it often and to become numb to it. When the real fight came, his men would not faint at the sight of their own blood.

Olof fought with dulled axe and shield, while Haakon held only his sword. His left hand, clad in mail, sometimes gripped the hilt of his long-hafted sword, at other times stretched open like a claw. The strength of Haakon's grip was unmatched in the

Five Valleys. He could bend a steel rod into a perfect circle. Those who had wrestled the jarl said his grasp was like the bite of a bear.

Olof raised his axe and swung it down at Haakon's helmeted head. Haakon slashed at the long haft of Olof's axe, deflecting the blow and sending a chip of wood flying.

"A strong blow, Olof. I will give you this opportunity to yield."

"Yield?" bellowed Olof. "Do you mistake me for some Happdal cur? I will not yield."

Haakon grinned and feinted. Olof ignored the bluff. He was the brighter of the two brothers, and could not be tricked so easily. Olof swung his axe at Haakon's ankles, forcing the jarl to spring back. Haakon countered with a lunging thrust, which Olof blocked with his shield. The crowd jeered. There was a real bloodlust in Kaldbrek, a thirst for more than play-fighting. And there was hunger as well as thirst. Real hunger – the rye crop had failed, and belts were tight.

"Haakon! I need to speak with you." It was Egil. Haakon did not take his eyes off Olof, but the poet's voice was as distinctive as it was harsh.

"Begone, bard! I will hear you after I dispatch this oaf."

"You should hear me now."

Haakon stole a glance at Egil. The poet was tall and spindly, with long, black hair that looked greasy even when clean, and a black beard streaked with gray. Egil's countenance was serious.

An axehead swung inches from Haakon's nose. Olof had seized on his momentary lapse of attention. Haakon growled and took a two-handed swing. Olof raised his shield and blocked, but Haakon pressed forward, swinging again and again, relentless. Chips of wood flew off the sparring shield as Olof retreated toward the edge of the crowd. Two men pushed him back toward the jarl. Haakon grabbed the edge of Olof's shield, wrenched it away, and thrust the blunted tip of his sword into Olof's ribs.

"Oof!" Olof clutched his side. "I yield." Haakon laughed and slapped Olof's thigh with the flat of his sword. "Enough!" Olof shouted.

Haakon spat into the dirt. At some point during the fight he had bitten his own cheek, and now the salty, ferric taste of blood filled his mouth.

"What is it, Egil? Why must you interrupt my morning sport?"

Egil twirled the tips of his long beard, a habit that had neatly forked it in two, like the mane of a winter lynx. "The longhouse."

A private matter. Well, it had better be good.

Haakon drove everyone out of the longhouse except for Egil, his serving boy Svein, and Einar the Lame. Einar was triple cursed: stupid, crippled, and ugly. On top of that he was cruel and spiteful, but Haakon kept him around because of his unquestioning loyalty. Whatever Haakon asked, Einar would do without complaint. Haakon marveled at this faithfulness. Once, Haakon had passed a little girl clutching a small puppy, and as a lark (and also because he was hungry for tender meat) ordered Einar to take the pet, roast it, and serve it to Haakon for lunch. Einar had performed the task with great enthusiasm.

Once settled in the quiet longhouse, Egil shared his news. "Happdal spies on us, from the ridge. I saw smoke, and discovered their lookout. A boy watches down on our valley, through some Builder device."

"Builder magic!" squealed Einar excitedly.

"Shut up, fool," said Haakon, not bothering to raise his voice. "Did the boy see you?" he asked Egil.

"No, I stayed hidden."

"And did the watch change?"

"Not that I saw, but I crept away before an hour had passed."

Haakon nodded. It was wise of Happdal to post a watch, for Haakon did intend to march against them. Happdal had once been their sister hamlet, a good trading partner. Egil had advised against ending Summer Trade, but what choice had Haakon had, faced with Arik's arrogance and disrespect? Kaldbrek's villagers missed the bounty of the trade festival. Happdal made good cheese, and they had always had surplus grain to trade for Kaldbrek's iron ore and fresh mutton. Now the grain and cheese were eaten, and the flocks were thin. Haakon's window for marching against Arik was shrinking. If he waited too long, his men would be too thin and weak to fight.

"Bring me mead, boy. And quick." Svein scurried off at Haakon's command. The boy was fast and obedient. He could fight, too: still with a wooden sword, but his form was good. The boy's mother claimed that Svein was Haakon's son, and he could not rule out the possibility. He vaguely remembered having his way with the wench after a fit of drunken revelry.

"What will you do, master?" asked Einar. "If you capture the lookout, may I have him as a pet?"

Egil grimaced at this request, but Haakon laughed. "Perhaps you may, Einar."

"We have the advantage," said Egil, "for now. There are many ways we can use this knowledge."

"Are you counseling restraint?"

"There are reasons to wait, yes. Let them feel secure in their knowledge of our movements until the moment before we march. We will kill the lookout at the last minute and put our spears to their necks."

Egil's logic was sound. The poet was as wise as Einar was foolish. But something in Haakon's gut rebelled.

"I think not, bard. We pay the scout a visit tonight, at the coldest hour. You will show us the way, myself and loyal Einar here." Einar grinned at the compliment, scooting a little closer to Haakon. The boy Svein returned, clutching a brimming mug of mead, which he reverently handed to his master. "You will come as well." Haakon took a long draught and slapped the boy's cheek affectionately. It would be an opportunity to see what blood ran in his veins. If he was truly Haakon's, the boy would not flinch at the sight of blood or bone.

★   ★   ★

They climbed the ridge without torches or lanterns. The gibbous moon provided ample light. Egil led, followed by Einar and Svein, with Haakon bringing up the rear. The sound of a cracking branch brought them to a halt. Egil peered into the brush while the others listened.

"What is it?" asked Haakon.

"A lynx, I think. I saw a tail." The bard pointed with his oaken staff. Egil could see as well at night as by day.

"Three more cats and I will have enough for a cloak," Haakon said.

"That will be very handsome, master," said Einar. "My own cloak is made of rat."

"You have mentioned it many times," said Egil.

"I was not speaking to you," Einar hissed. "But I am sorry, Egil, that my simple stories bring no joy to your exalted ears."

"Shut up," growled Haakon. "How much farther?"

"We are close," Egil said. After they walked for a few minutes more, the tall poet stopped them again, and pointed. "See that flat rock ahead? That is the lookout."

Haakon grabbed young Svein by his collar. "Are you feeling brave, boy? I want you to go ahead. You are light of foot, yes? Scout ahead."

"I could go," said Egil. "My eyes are suited to the night."

"We know about your special eyes," Einar said. "I could go as well. I, too, am light of foot – not even a rat can hear me approach. The proof is in my cloak."

"The boy will go," said Haakon, settling the matter. He drew his long dirk and thrust the hilt at Svein. "Take this, but do not use it unless you must. Take a look and return here." The boy nodded and took the weapon. They watched him go.

"He is brave," Einar said. "Surely your son, as his mother says."

"Perhaps," said Haakon. "What do you think, Egil?"

"On this point I agree with Einar, though I do not know the boy well. He speaks very little."

"He is obedient," Einar said, "as he should be, toward his father and master."

Perhaps too obedient, thought Haakon, for he had noticed the same, and wondered if the boy was hiding a rebellious spirit, or simply had none.

A few minutes passed. "Look, he returns," Egil said.

"So soon," said Einar. "Has he lost his nerve? Or is he merely fleet?"

Svein stood before them, breathing quickly. He offered the

hilt of the dirk to Haakon, who took it. The blade was clean. "What did you see?" asked Haakon.

"One boy," answered Svein, "asleep next to dying embers. He carried no weapon that I could see."

"Go back," Haakon said, "and overpower him, but do not kill him. When you have succeeded, call out to us."

Svein's eyes shot to the dirk, but Haakon did not give it. The boy paled, but he turned and crept back toward the outcropping.

"You test the boy," said Egil. "A dangerous game. What if he fails? The lookout will flee to Happdal and our advantage will be lost."

"If he is my son, he will not fail."

The three men waited in silence. After some time they heard a distant cry. "Haakon!"

Svein had the Happdal boy in a chokehold. The lookout had put up a fight. A long scratch on Svein's cheek oozed fresh blood, and a patch of his brown hair had a grayish cast to it, as if his head had been ground into the dusty earth. But Svein had won the fight.

The lookout was blond and pudgy. Haakon would not have judged the Happdal boy a fighter. He gestured to Svein to release him. "What is your name, boy?"

The pudgy lookout coughed, then spat, moistening Haakon's boot. Egil laughed. Einar stepped forward and slapped the boy, hard, sending him to the dirt.

"Enough!" shouted Haakon. "Give him a chance to consider his situation. If he comes to his senses, he might escape with his skin still attached to his body."

At the mention of flaying, the boy blanched. "Stoke the fire," Haakon said to Svein, who was brushing the dirt from his clothes.

In the firelight, the boy looked younger, no older than thirteen by Haakon's guess. "Will you speak now? Who tasked you with spying on Kaldbrek?"

"Look, master," Einar said. The flat rock lay atop a giant boulder, forming a half-open cave. Einar was at the far end, pointing to a long, metal tube. The device was positioned at a gap between the rocks, aimed down into the valley, toward Kaldbrek. "The spying machine!"

"Do you know who I am?" Haakon asked. The Happdal boy nodded. "So you know to fear me. I will ask once more. *Who* told you to spy on us?"

The boy trembled but did not speak. Einar grinned, and came closer to watch. Egil looked away. Svein took a step back.

Haakon took the boy by the hand, almost gently. With a quick twist of his thumb, he folded the boy's little finger into a tight square, then cracked it. The boy screamed and clutched his hand. Tears streamed from his eyes, leaving streaks of clean skin where the dust had been washed away. Einar giggled, delighted.

"I already know the answer," said Haakon softly. "You will merely confirm it. Should I take your hand again? Or do you have something to say?"

The boy mumbled something. His voice had not yet dropped. Perhaps he was only eleven or twelve.

"What was that?" Einar shrieked, batting the boy's ear. "You need to speak up when Haakon asks you a question."

"Do not touch him!" snapped Haakon. "Let him speak."

"Elke," mumbled the boy.

"Arik's bitch," Egil said. The boy's eyes flashed toward the poet.

"Look, he is angry!" said Einar. "Is Elke his mother?"

"Elke's sons are grown," said Egil. "Esper and Trond. The latter is a smith, apprentice to Jense."

Haakon reached out and grabbed the boy by the top of his head, holding him still. The boy's eyes widened in alarm at the strength of Haakon's grip.

"You feel the vise," Einar said, "now tell us more. What preparations has Elke made against us?"

"None," said the boy, his voice quavering. "We merely watch you. To see if you march against us."

"He lies. He lies!" Einar shouted excitedly. "Crush his head like a gourd! No...wait...I want him as a slave."

"Why would Elke fear us?" asked Haakon. His voice was soft and languid, his eyes half-closed, but his arm was an iron bar holding the boy in place.

The boy trembled but said nothing.

"Does Arik regret insulting me?" Haakon asked, even more softly. "Does Elke fear my retribution?"

The boy grabbed Haakon's broad hand with his own, ineffectually.

Haakon slowly tightened his grip on the boy's skull. The bard watched him intently.

"Sing to save your life, boy!" said Egil. The lookout's eyes were scrunched closed, his mouth agape in pain. A moan escaped his throat.

"It is too late!" Einar cried. "Master does not see fit to grant me a slave."

Svein took a few steps backs. The lookout boy let out a long, animalistic cry.

"The end is near," said Einar excitedly. "So close now."

There was a dull cracking sound. The lookout boy convulsed and collapsed, his head misshapen and deformed. Blood leaked from his eyes.

"The bear's jaw," said Einar, somberly.

Haakon shook his hand out, loosening the joints. "Take the Builder toy," he said to Svein, pointing at the device. "Leave the boy where he lies," he told Einar. To Egil he gave a long look. "There is more than one kind of advantage."

Haakon led the way down the ridge, Einar at his heels. Egil lingered behind, gazing at the dead boy, twisting the ends of his forked beard.

CHAPTER TWENTY-ONE

Trond lagged behind his brother and the sky woman by a dozen paces. His brother's eyes were fixed on the ground. Esper had briefly lost their sister's trail, but had found it again. The sky woman watched Esper as they walked.

Trond felt stronger each day. The pain from his burns had ebbed to a dull ache. Esper had shot a deer, and now they carried venison, smoked and salted to preserve the meat.

His heart was full. He felt joy, absolute unfettered happiness, with his condition of being alive. He had accepted death, inhaling the smoke from his own burning beard, and yet now he lived. The Red Brother had spared him.

Mixed with his joy and gratitude, he felt a sense of wonder at the brown-skinned sky woman. It stretched his mind to imagine a race of people in the sky, descended from the Builders. If she were not there in front of him, he would be quick to disbelieve her existence. Yet there she was, walking in step with Esper.

And there was that. Why was it so easy for Esper to talk to women? Trond himself could barely look a pretty girl in the eye without blushing. He feared no man, yet even a young milkmaid could turn his tongue to jelly and his mind to mush.

Was he envious of Esper? Not exactly. He was not attracted to the sky woman. Her brown skin was strange, as was her silvery second skin. She was waifish, and gaunt – more like a wet rat than a woman. After a few good meals she no longer seemed close to death, but she was still insubstantial. He was surprised Esper had taken her as a lover. Her halting speech was unintelligible to Trond. She spoke first in her own tongue, then repeated her words in a garbled approximation of Norse. Esper seemed to understand, but Trond just smiled and nodded, completely confused.

Despite her strangeness, the sky woman seemed harmless.

Esper liked her, and her offer to help them find Katja seemed genuine. Had she really seen Katja, days earlier, being abducted from Happdal? Unlikely, but so was the sky woman's existence in the first place. Her story of the 'black egg' (that she believed had captured Katja's mind) was even less plausible.

Esper had stopped, and was examining the ground, brow furrowed. The sky woman crouched next to him, looking where Esper looked. They were in a thick spruce wood, heading north-east up a gradual slope. Ahead, Trond could see nothing but trees, but he knew the way. If they continued north-east they would eventually climb a steep ridge, then descend into the narrow valley that was home to Kaldbrek. Thinking of Kaldbrek made Trond think of Haakon, which made him think of Elke, which gave him a pang of homesickness.

Esper looked up. "What's the matter, brother?" he asked. "This morning you were joyous – why has your face gone dark?"

"We should be home, brother. Elke is not wrong to believe that Happdal needs defending."

"We will find our sister," said Esper, clenching his jaw and looking away. Esper was right – they could not return home yet. Trond's heart was pulled in two directions.

"What do you see?" asked Trond.

"Strange tracks," Esper said. "A small group passed through here." Trond looked and saw the signs for himself: trampled earth, torn moss, and snapped twigs.

"Could it be a group from Kaldbrek?" the sky woman asked. Esper had told her the story of the sister hamlets and how relations had soured under Haakon's rule.

"Maybe," said Esper. "Hunters, perhaps. We should be careful."

"Are these tracks older than Katja's?" asked Trond.

"No, newer. They could not be fresher," Esper said.

The sky woman stood with her head cocked, listening. She had proved her superior hearing days before, warning them of the giants' approach. "Anything?" asked Esper. The sky woman nodded and pointed west. Esper drew an arrow, nocked it, and led them single file through the trees.

Trond drew his sword and followed Esper and the sky woman. Stepping carefully, he was still the noisiest of the three. It seemed no fallen branch would support his weight. More than once Esper turned and glared.

They came to the edge of a small clearing. At the center lay a fallen buck, at least three days dead and starting to rot. Devouring the body with their hands and teeth were four filthy wretches. Caked in grime, clothes in tatters, they tore at the buck with mindless hunger. Two feasted on the entrails, pulling out the intestines with claw-like hands, chewing with dark, rotting teeth. One picked at the deer's head with long, filthy nails, leaving parts of the skull exposed. The last, the female, gnawed on the hind leg, but was having a difficult time of it, given the poor condition of her teeth.

"What horror is this?" whispered Trond.

The sky woman had turned green. She looked away and put her hands on her knees, trying not to retch.

"Mushroom men," Esper said quietly.

"I did not think they were real."

"Nor I," said Esper, "but what else could they be?"

One of the creatures turned and looked in their general direction, but did not seem to notice the three onlookers. His eyes were glassy and bloodshot, and part of his nose was missing, bitten or rotted off.

"He looks in poor shape," Trond whispered. The sky woman had pulled herself together and now huddled close to Esper.

"What...are them?" she said in Norse. With simple phrases she did not always speak in her own language first.

"There is a forest mushroom, white on the outside, reddish-brown in the middle, shaped like a saucer...." said Esper.

"Poisonous?"

"No," said Esper. "Delicious. But they are only safe to pick for a few days. As children we were warned to stay away from the larger ones, those that had lingered for too long on the forest floor. And we were told to hold our breath if we passed nearby."

"Why?" the sky woman asked.

"A disease that floats in the air. Not the mushroom itself, but something that grows on it. If you breathe it in, you become a mushroom man, always hungry, slow of body and mind."

The sky woman's eyes took on a faraway look. "*Ganoderma tsugae*," she muttered in her own tongue. "Ghastly reishi. Supporting some sort of parasitic spore...."

The half-nosed mushroom man looked again in their direction. He lurched upright and opened his mouth, emitting a low groan. A strip of deer intestine dangled from one hand.

"Perhaps we go now," the sky woman suggested.

"I think not," said Trond. Esper and the woman looked at him, surprised, as if they had forgotten he was there. "I have heard tales of mushroom men since I was a small boy. Yet I have never seen one until now. I will stay and take in my fill of this sight." Hearing the sound of his own voice encouraged Trond, and he decided to share another thought. He had said little over the course of the morning, deferring to his younger brother's superior tracking skills, and also wary of engaging the sky woman in conversation. But why not speak his mind? He was no wilting flower. He was Trond, full smith. No man in the Five Valleys could best him in a fight, and only Jense could forge a finer blade. "If mushroom men exist," he continued, no longer speaking in a whisper, "who knows what other creatures are real? Fairies, perhaps? Gnomes? Will-o'-the-wisps?" He did not mention the gast in his list.

A second mushroom man, who had been feasting on the buck's head, looked up. He was not as caked in filth as the half-nosed one, and a long scar ran across his left cheek. He pulled back his lips in a hideous grin, revealing long, brown teeth glistening with fresh blood.

"Keep your voice down, brother," Esper said in a fierce whisper. "You attract their attention."

"Can we go?" asked the woman, gripping Esper's arm tightly. Though he would not have been able to say why, this gesture of affection irritated Trond.

"Do not shush me, little brother. I speak as loudly as I please. Have you forgotten I am your elder? I do not fear these mushroom men. What can they do to us?"

Esper stood straighter. "You see bravery as a virtue, but

caution is just as important. It was *I* who rescued *you* from the giant's spit, myself and Car-En. You are reckless, brother, and trust too much in your strength."

Half-Nose lurched toward them, dropping the wet strand of deer gut and reaching out with his claw-like hands. A guttural cry escaped his throat. The sky woman screamed and hid behind Esper.

"Let's go!" she cried in Norse. *Hvata!*

"When I hung upside-down from the snare, I looked for help from my kin. Do you know what I saw? Your fleeing hindquarters. In my moment of need, you ran like a bunny. Do not recite the tale of my rescue as if you were some great hero. Yes, with the help of a woman, you were just barely able to pull me from the flames. I am grateful, brother, but truthfully you waited a bit long. I hope to never smell my burning beard again."

"Do not pretend to be grateful," said Esper. "You should also stop pretending that your beard can be rescued. Put your steel to good use and cut your chin clean. That thing on your face is a sorry mess. It pains me to look at it."

With this, the mushroom man pawed at Trond's meaty arm. Flecks of foamy spittle flew from its open maw. Trond gently shoved the creature in the chest, sending it hurling to the ground. Landing on its rump, it grunted and scowled at the smith.

"My own brother insults my beard?" Trond said, stroking the singed remains of his cheek hairs with his free hand, waving his sword recklessly with the other. "I held my tongue for years while you nurtured your soft fuzz, willing it to grow. Did you not go to Ilsa and beg her for a potion? Perhaps you should have paid her better, for the result is sorry."

Esper threw his bow to the ground. "Watch your tongue."

The mushroom man regained his footing and lunged at Trond, reaching out a filthy, blood-smeared claw toward the smith's face. Trond whipped his blade through the air, lopping off two of the mushroom man's fingers. Trond swung again, with more force, slicing deeply into the half-nosed man's neck. The poor wretch collapsed to the ground. Trond wrenched his sword out.

"They bleed red," observed Esper, somewhat calmed.

"They do," Trond agreed.

The female mushroom creature had not noticed the scuffle, and continued to gnaw on the deer's hind leg determinedly. But the other two, the head eater and the remaining eater of entrails, looked at Trond with interest, and – though it was difficult to read their emotions – a hint of concern.

"That one," said Esper, "he looks familiar." He pointed at the head eater, who was clutching the bloody deer skull tightly.

"You imagine things, brother," said Trond. There was still a shadow of anger in his voice. He cupped the remains of his beard protectively.

"No, look. See the long scar on his cheek? Was that not put there by Lars?"

Trond squinted at the mushroom man, who returned his gaze in a way that was not quite friendly, but was at least free of malice.

"It cannot be," Trond said.

"His eyes are the same, light brown like river pebbles," said Esper. "And though in poor shape, he is not old. Our age, perhaps, or just a little older."

"Per Anders!" Trond cried. "Is it you?" The mushroom man's eyes widened, briefly, yet he said nothing.

"It has been seven years since we saw you last, friend," said Esper. "I am Esper, of Happdal, son of Arik and Elke, brother of Trond, brother of Katja. Do you not remember me?"

"My brother was but a whelp when you last saw him," said Trond to the mushroom man. "It is *me* who you might remember. Trond Ariksson, full smith of Happdal."

The one who might once have been Per Anders looked back and forth between Esper and Trond. The other mushroom man, still holding a strand of intestine, gazed upon the fallen body of his half-nosed brethren. Some dim thought flickered in his damaged mind and he shambled off into the forest, looking furtively over his shoulder. The mushroom woman, still gnawing on the hind leg, remained oblivious to their existence.

"He recognizes us!" Trond exclaimed joyfully.

"Perhaps," said Esper, "but I fear he is too far gone."

"Is there no cure for breathing in the poison mushroom?" asked Trond. "We can bring him to Ilsa. She will know."

Esper turned to the sky woman. "Could your people help him? Is there Builder medicine that could cure him of this sickness?"

"I don't know," she said, with her laborious way of speaking twice. "If the parasite has ravaged his brain tissue, then probably not. But if the behavior is the result of some natural narcotic...." She made no more sense in Norse than she did in her own language, Trond thought.

Trond cleaned his sword on a mossy log and sheathed it. He took a few steps back from the clearing, into the woods, and beckoned the mushroom man to follow. "Come, Per Anders. Come with us, and we will help you." Esper retrieved his bow and followed Trond, as did the sky woman. Trond and Esper motioned and called to the mushroom man as they retreated. He did not follow, but stood, watching them, gripping the deer skull.

"Nothing of our friend remains," said Esper. "Should I end him? An arrow to the eye? It would be a quick and painless death." The woman said nothing, but her expression indicated agreement.

Trond shook his head. "No. If he will not follow, we leave him be. Who knows what goes through his mind? Perhaps he is happy, frolicking in the spruce wood, with no cares, eating fallen carrion."

Esper nodded. "That is wise, brother. We have no way of knowing what goes through his mind."

"Except for the grime," Trond said, "he looked better than the others. His mouth had many teeth left, and his eyes were clear."

"Look!" called out the sky woman, pointing. Per Anders was following. His gait was odd; his left leg dragged. His arms, mostly bare, were covered in old scars and new scratches, as if he had walked through brambles without care or caution. But standing upright, it was clearly Per Anders, now a grown man. He stopped a few paces away. He had dropped the deer skull, and stood with his arms hanging loosely at his sides.

"Yes!" cried Trond. "We are not yet going back to Happdal, Per Anders, but we will surely return there. First we must find Katja. Will you help us?"

Per Anders said nothing. His mouth hung loosely open, a rope of drool swinging from his lower lip. The sky woman looked doubtful.

"Be calm, sky woman," Trond said. "He carries no weapon, and has recently fed. What is there to fear? You and my brother shall lead the way, I will follow, and Per Anders here will bring up the rear. Always there will be two sons of Arik between you and the mushroom man. Will that satisfy you?" The sky woman nodded hesitantly. Esper looked grumpy – perhaps resentful that Trond had spoken to the sky woman in such a straightforward manner. Trond did not care. He was done being meek.

Esper led them back to where the mushroom men had crossed Katja's path. From there they continued north-east, pausing every so often while Esper examined the ground. Several times the trail went cold and they had to double back for a short distance, but Esper was sharp-eyed, and it had not been long since Katja had passed this way.

While they walked, Trond recited the recent history of Happdal to Per Anders. Now that he had found his tongue – and a willing listener – the words flowed easily. He told Per Anders about becoming full smith, about the godsteel swords he had forged (and also the sword he planned to forge, which he described at length: the shape of the blade, the materials he would use for hilt and pommel, even the design of the leather scabbard). He told Per Anders about Katja; she was as fierce as any man, and more skilled than most in battle. Did Per Anders remember Summer Trade with Kaldbrek? Well, that was no more. Haakon, 'the Rat,' who they had wrestled as boys, was jarl of Kaldbrek now, and the good relations between the villages had soured. Why? Well, Haakon hated Arik, had never forgiven him for the wooden axe contest during which Arik had bested Haakon not once but thrice, knocking out a tooth during the final bout. Haakon had nurtured his anger, fermenting it like *lutefisk*, and had finally lashed out with real steel, a season later, raiding Happdal, killing a man and stealing a giant wheel of cheese. Arik had turned the other cheek. The people of Kaldbrek had traded peacefully with Happdal for a hundred summers, had they not? But the raid did not soothe Haakon. Being ignored by Arik only stoked his rage. The next raid was more brutal. Haakon and his men killed and raped, and desecrated the longhouse. What did Per Anders think of that? Would Arik gather his men and march on Kaldbrek? Trond had been ready. But his mother had held them back. Was Arik a weak man, bowing to his wife's command? Per Anders should not be so quick to judge, Trond said, until he himself had stood up to Elke. Yes, he remembered now, had not Per Anders once stolen a baked loaf from Elke's kitchen? Had she not caught Per Anders, forced his confession, lectured him while he cowered, then told his mother, and also his father, and soon the whole village? For two years Per Anders had borne the nickname 'Loaf Lifter,' until Lars had come up with a cruder moniker. Trond laughed at his own story, and even Esper grinned, remembering it, but Per Anders himself seemed to have recovered from the shame, and did not even blush.

Though he did not notice at first, Trond's pace slowed while telling Happdal stories. Perhaps it was because he kept looking over his shoulder at Per Anders, or maybe to compensate for his old friend's slow, shambling gait. Esper and the sky woman moved farther ahead, and by dusk they were mostly out of sight. He could still catch a glimpse of his brother now and then through the sparser sections of the forest. Finally they caught up to the forward pair. The sky woman had lain down to rest. Esper looked worried.

"What is it, brother?" asked Trond.

"She is not well. She slowed, and her speech began to slur, and now...."

Trond bent over the woman and looked. Her eyes were glassy and rolled back. Her skin had gone from brown to nearly white, and had a sweaty sheen to it. Her breathing was shallow and rapid.

"She has fallen ill! And so quickly." Trond looked back at Per

Anders, who had stopped half a dozen paces behind, as if from politeness. "Could she have caught the mushroom disease?" he whispered to Esper. "Perhaps the sky people are more vulnerable."

Trond saw the lost, fearful expression on Esper's face, and all lingering traces of anger dissolved from his heart. He felt only love for his brother. "Do not worry," he said, "we have survived worse than this. Two of our friends are sick, but one can still walk. The sky woman weighs nothing – I will carry her."

Trond gently lifted Car-En, and looked to Esper, for Trond did not know in which direction they were going.

CHAPTER TWENTY-TWO

Katja and Zoë stood on the white sand beach. The midday sun was blistering hot, but Zoë had promised that Katja's pale skin would not burn. The other thing Zoë had promised – well, that was hard to believe. But anything was possible in this strange place.

"Come, it's safe," said Zoë, walking toward the water. They had left their clothes under a palm tree. Katja's leather breeches, boots, and woolen shirt made the larger pile; Zoë had been wearing only a light dress. Zoë was slighter than Katja, with small breasts, pale skin with a slight olive cast, and bony hips. Katja had felt self-conscious at first, but Zoë had matter-of-factly insisted on nudity, and showed little interest in Katja's naked form. The hot sun felt good on her bare skin.

Katja took a few steps into the water, wetting her feet and ankles. Zoë was already knee-deep, the gentle waves splashing against her thighs. The water was cooler than the air, but much warmer than the icy river Katja was used to.

"Nice, isn't it?" Zoë asked. Katja nodded. "C'mon – I want to show you something." Katja caught up to the hermit. Zoë took her hand, guiding her in. Soon the clear saltwater reached their midsections, and it became difficult to walk.

"Now this will be hard, but just trust me, okay? Crouch down, open your eyes and mouth, and breathe in."

Before Katja could protest, Zoë sunk beneath the water. Still holding Katja's hand, she gently tugged her down. Katja took a deep breath and bent her knees. She forced her eyes open, and while the salt briefly stung, the pain soon faded. Zoë was laughing with her mouth open. Katja let out half her breath, releasing a stream of bubbles to the surface. Zoë nodded encouragingly. Well, she could always stand up if she started to drown. She exhaled fully, then, against every instinct, inhaled. Her eyes went wide as the cool water filled her lungs. The sensation was strange and uncomfortable, but not painful. Her legs wanted to spring upward, but she willed herself to be still. Was she drowning? No. Somehow, her lungs were getting what they needed from the seawater. Katja opened her mouth and laughed silently, expelling water. Zoë grinned, squeezed her hand, and let go. Katja's long, blond hair drifted in front of her face, and when she moved it aside she saw that Zoë had shot off like a fish, away from the beach. Katja followed, swimming slowly and awkwardly.

Soon they left the cove, and though the water was still clear and shallow, here the ocean floor was populated by all sorts of strange creatures, some of which Zoë had described to Katja earlier. There were convoluted structures called coral: living rock formations swarming with colorful fish of all sizes. There were eels that shot back into their holes when approached, and creatures with five legs, and tiny blobs with many small tentacles, and oddities that Katja could not even begin to describe. Zoë pointed to a large green creature swimming above them. It had an oval shell and four flippers, and swam even more awkwardly than Katja.

Zoë had said this place was modeled on somewhere called Palau, one of her favorite places to explore before she'd volunteered for the Crucible program.

Zoë swam up to Katja, took her hand, and pointed down. Katja felt her feet moving together, and a ripple along her inner calves and thighs, and then an alarming sensation, as if her spine had suddenly descended all the way to her toes (except she could no longer *feel* her toes). Before her, the lower half of Zoë's body had taken on the form of a silvery blue fish. Katja looked down – her own body had changed in the same way. She gave an experimental swish of her tail, and shot upward with such force that she shouted, silently, in surprise.

Zoë led them to deeper water. Here, the ocean floor was still teeming with life, but more dimly lit. Katja quickly learned to use her fish's tail, and without any trace of awkwardness, swam here and there in short bursts, exhilarated. Zoë followed, nearby, until Katja deserted her with a burst of speed. Arms tightly at her sides, she used only her powerful tail, and found that even the smallest movements could propel her forward with great velocity. She stole a glance back – Zoë was far behind. The ocean floor looked sparser; the large coral reefs were all behind them. There was something dark ahead.

Katja looked down and was struck with vertigo. Below was a great black void; she had swum over some sheer cliff. Looking back she could see the wall, descending as steeply as any mountainside, from dimness, to darkness, to pure black. Terrified, she twisted about, and briefly lost her sense of up and down. Dark water, everywhere. Where was Zoë? She found the cliff again, and swam back to the edge. She was not falling, but felt as if she might. What lived in that blackness below? Her heart pounded. The heavy water in her lungs felt wrong.

Something tapped her shoulder. She spun around and clawed at the water, but relaxed at the sight of Zoë's calm expression. Her guide pointed back to the beach. Katja nodded, and they swam back to shore, languidly. As they neared the beach, Katja searched for ground with her tail, but instead touched the sand with her toes.

★　　★　　★

As the sun descended toward the ocean horizon, Katja helped Zoë gather wood and dried palm fronds. The hermit lit the fire with a match (another oddity to Katja), then ambled back down to the shore, where she speared a bright blue fish in the shallows. They sat on a driftwood log, bare feet in the warm sand, the fire contained by a circle of rocks. Zoë cleaned and gutted her catch efficiently, then carved out neat chunks of flesh with a short knife. "Sashimi," she said, offering a piece of the translucent meat to Katja. "It's good." Reluctantly, Katja tried a piece, and found the meat salty and tender. "How did you like being a mermaid?" asked Zoë.

"Is that what fish-women are called? Enjoyable, mostly." Katja took another piece of fish. "But it makes this meal traitorous."

Zoë laughed. "You changed the top half of my body as well," Katja said, more seriously.

Zoë nodded. "I made your breasts smaller and narrowed your shoulders a little, so you could swim faster."

"How? Can you control everything in this world?"

"There are some limitations, though they could probably be overcome with time and work. The mermaid is a 'form-only' invention. The musculature is real – or, rather, accurately simulated – and so are the various forms of tissue that make up the tail: the scales, the fin, and so on. But I haven't attempted to create a genetically accurate race of mer-people. Reproduction would be tricky – where would the sex organs go? And I wouldn't know where to begin in terms of creating a realistic culture for fantasy creatures. It's not enough to just simulate the genes for an intelligent brain. You need a society if you want to create a new intelligent being. Fish and insects are easier to simulate – they don't have much in the way of culture. But dealing with mammals, that's trickier. There's a pack of wild pigs in the jungle." She pointed back at the palms. "For the first generation, I had to program a whole behavioral level before they could start teaching their young. It's self-sustaining now, but I suspect somewhat stunted in terms of hog culture. They do pick up novel behaviors, so that's good. They're still learning, evolving culturally as well as genetically."

Katja understood little of this, but she thought she understood the main point. A baby would not grow into a man or a woman unless it was raised by people. If it was raised by wolves, it would become a wolf-creature, unable to speak in words, unable to understand village customs. Katja had heard of such a child.

"So no new people? Have you been lonely?" asked Katja.

"I prefer to be alone most of the time," said Zoë. "But yes, I've been lonely. I've modified my own neurophysiology so that I don't get depressed...." She laughed ruefully. "But I haven't found a cure for loneliness." She looked thoughtfully at Katja. "I know you don't want to stay, but you'd be welcome to, you know. There are so many things I could show you."

Zoë passed Katja another piece of fish. "You are like a god here," Katja said, after she had chewed and swallowed.

"In some ways. I prefer to think of myself as a biological artist. If I could make people, then maybe I'd be a god. I'm safe at least – Raekae can't touch me. I locked him out long ago. You know, when it comes down to it, he's a hack. An amateur. I have access to Crucible subsystems he doesn't even know about."

Zoë's boast seemed prideful, but Katja had no reason to doubt her. She had directly experienced the hermit's powers. "What about me?" she asked. "Am I safe?"

"For the moment, until you're virtualized, and your own brain tissue is remodeled in service of the Crucible."

"How long will that take?"

Zoë shrugged. "I don't know. The threads grow and learn quickly, but time passes more swiftly in the Crucible sim than in the real world, so that buys you a little time. A few days more – of subjective time – at least."

"You said you were working on something, a way that could…get me out. Get me home."

Zoë looked away and nodded.

"How would it work?" asked Katja, tentatively. Something in Zoë's manner made her feel as if she were treading on thin ice.

"It would work by destroying everything," said Zoë, gazing at the ocean. The sun was a glimmering orange orb, dipping into the reflective sea. Except that the sun was not real, any more than Katja had swum with a real fish's tail. But the light on the glassy water *looked* real, and the powerful tail had *felt* real. "Why don't you stay here with me?" Zoë asked.

Zoë stood and wandered to the water's edge. Katja followed and stood next to the hermit, a few paces away. She sensed that Zoë was distancing herself, but did not quite want to be alone.

"I could give you any form you wanted," said Zoë. "You could live as a bird, or a sea turtle, or even a mythical creature – a centaur or a dragon. You could live as a man or a woman." She glanced at Katja. "You're already beautiful, but you could be different if you wanted to. Like this." Zoë transformed, slowly and gradually, into a tall, beautiful, black-skinned woman, with close-shorn, bright green hair, wearing a long, shimmering dress, silk encrusted with thousands of tiny sapphires. "Or this," said the woman in a deep, sultry voice. The black woman crouched, and her face broadened, and fur emerged from her skin, and soon there was an enormous striped cat staring menacingly at her. Katja's heart raced and the hairs on her neck stiffened.

"Stop that," Katja said. "It disturbs me. I know you can take any form. I did enjoy swimming as a fish-woman, but I want my real body back, the one that bleeds. Your offer does not interest me. Can you make Raekae return what he has stolen? Or should I take it back myself?"

The great cat transformed back into Zoë. "Why do you want to go back? What waits for you there, in the real world? You're powerless there, you know. You could get sick and die within a week. Or be murdered, or raped. Or watch your family die. Those horrors don't exist here."

"I can take care of myself. And what waits for me? My brothers, Trond and Esper. My father and mother, Arik and Elke. My friend Jense. One day I will have a family of my own."

"I could give you a baby," said Zoë. "I could give you a handsome man to make love to – you could have your pick from thousands."

"A man, or a body? I met Raekae's father, you know. He was not a man – more like a ghost. Is that what you offer me? Could he be a father to my baby?"

"No," Zoë admitted, "but we could be mothers. It would be enough. You don't really need an entire society – just loving parents." This odd suggestion gave Katja pause for thought; for a moment, she gave her imagination to the possibility. What a strange family that would make. Two mothers, who could take any form (and maybe Katja would live as a man – she had often wondered what that might be like), and a baby who would grow up knowing only two people. None of them could be hurt, or die, and they would have endless worlds to explore.

But what if things soured between herself and the hermit? Zoë seemed pleasant and trustworthy; unlike Henning, there was no wildness or danger roiling beneath. But even so, they had just met.

On the other hand, at least Raekae did not control Zoë. Henning, Franz, and Stian – those three were puppets. Raekae could make them happy or fearful at will. He could probably annihilate them with a snap of his fingers.

And it would be the same between Zoë and Katja, if she stayed. Zoë might be a kinder master, but she held all the power. Katja would never be able to learn to create creatures and worlds the way the hermit could, even with Zoë as a willing teacher. Well, maybe she could, with years of study. But from where Katja stood, on the imaginary sand, it seemed impossible. She could not even read.

"What did you mean it would destroy everything?" asked Katja.

Zoë sighed. Katja let the question hang in the air. Finally, the hermit answered. "The algorithm – it can't run within BioSim or GeoSim, or even the underlying physics simulator. It's deeper than that. It's root level, bottom-layer – it can only interact directly with the Crucible's quantum core. Does that make any sense?"

Katja shook her head.

"Well, if I run the algorithm, it will erase and overwrite everything. All of this" – she gestured at the ocean, then back to the jungle – "will disappear. I will disappear. So will Raekae, and everything he has built, and Raekae's father. Erased."

"What about Henning? And Franz and Stian?" Katja asked.

"Gone. Extinguished."

"Killed?"

"Effectively, but they wouldn't experiencing dying." Zoë scratched her head. "Or would they? I don't really know. I suppose I would find out."

"And what about me?"

"If the threads haven't taken over your central nervous system, well…your brain would probably still be intact. It's the cold I'm worried about. Erasing data on a quantum system creates a huge amount of negative entropy. There would be an extreme cooling effect, starting at the core and radiating out through the threads, probably destroying them. I don't know if your body could survive it. You'd be in a coma; you'd be blind and deaf; you wouldn't be able to feel anything; you wouldn't have any motor skills. That's what the threading system prioritizes – input and output. Your autonomic system is probably still functioning, so hopefully you'd keep breathing."

Katja recoiled, horrified. "It sounds worse than death."

"You might recover," said Zoë. "For days, the cold would slow your physiology to a crawl. You'd be in deep freeze, essentially. Then, as the algorithm kicked in, the core would warm up. Your body might even expel the Crucible core – it doesn't go very deep. It lodges in the lining of the esophagus, growing the threads first back toward the spine, then up and down the spinal column. If you survived the cold phase and didn't die of exposure, then gradually your nerves might regenerate. The inactive threads would be gradually reabsorbed into your own tissues."

"Wherever my body is, I would lie there, helpless? Spring nights are cold – I would freeze to death. Or starve."

"Possibly. Though death by dehydration is much more likely. But if someone found you, and you received medical attention during the cooling period...well, like I said, you'd probably die. But with a bit of luck, there's a chance you'd survive."

Katja sat on the sand. The moon had risen; it was nearly full. She wondered what moon her brothers saw. The same? Zoë had said that time passed differently here.

"You give me a hard choice, hermit."

"I know," said Zoë, sympathetically. "I wish I had more to offer. But really, the choice isn't yours. It's mine."

"Then what will you decide? Will you kill us all? What would *you* gain?"

"Nothing, really. Except knowing that I'd created a universe from scratch. That's what the algorithm does. It creates a new universe. It will recreate *our* universe, in fact, with the starting values I use, the Planck constant and...well, it would begin much as our own universe began. I'd want to know it would be a place where matter was stable, a place where stars and planets would form, a place that could support life, and eventually consciousness. A few billion qubits isn't really enough – it may take hundreds of years in real time just for plasma cooling to occur. And as more complex interactive networks evolve – biology, and hopefully, consciousness, thoughts and feelings – the simulation will slow down further. But subjective time, if there are any beings to perceive it, will remain the same.

"For years I've wondered how to model the emergence of a new evolutionary layer. How does the molecular layer emerge from the atomic? How does the biological layer emerge from the molecular? And so on, up the Chain of Being, from biological to somatic, from somatic to social, from social to memetic, et cetera. I could tell you *precisely* how each layer emerges, in specific terms. The covalent bond – atoms sharing electron pairs – that enables the evolution of various molecules throughout the universe. Nucleotide sequences – RNA and DNA are the Terran forms – enable genetic evolution, the biological layer of reality. But how do you model the emergence of a new information layer – a new, higher-level network of agents – in *general* terms?

"Well, you can't. It's a trap, to think that way. You can't model separate layers of reality and then try to glue them together, or tell a story that connects them. NENT[3] attempts to do that, but it doesn't provide an algorithm. It's only descriptive.

"Everything is just one thing. From a ripple in the fabric of reality, you can initiate an unfolding that gradually generates multiple layers: space-time, from which energy-matter emerges, which eventually condenses into galaxies filled with star systems, and so forth. But you need to start at the bottom.

"Here's the deal. If I run the algorithm within the Crucible, I destroy all knowledge of the algorithm. I destroy my life's work. Not *this*." She gestured again, at everything around them. "These are just sketches. My *real* life's work – the algorithm itself. I want that knowledge to survive."

Zoë looked at Katja expectantly.

"What?"

"Will you learn it? I could teach it to you – it's not that complicated. You wouldn't need to understand it, just memorize it. Then, if you ever regain consciousness, you can write it down."

"What good would that do?" asked Katja.

Zoë sighed again. "Probably none. Just a long shot. But there'd be a chance — a very small chance — that my life's work would not be wasted."

Both women looked out to the ocean as the last glimmer of orange disappeared over the horizon. Zoë was a fine artist, Katja had to admit, though she did not understand the point of creating a new world when a perfectly good one already existed (most of it unknown and unexplored).

But she would help the strange hermit woman, if she could.

Footnote 3. Nested Evolving Network Theory (NENT)

A twenty-first century theoretical framework for modeling multilevel evolutionary simulations, with variable starting conditions/differing universal constants. NENT models evolutionary processes as layers of networked spaces, with each layer or 'level of reality' being completely dependent on structures and processes of all underlying layers for its existence. A network space emerges when an agent-level mutation results in a novel interaction class that facilitates a new level of information encoding and node type. Agents are considered to be nodes (irreducible, encoded structures, individuals) or supernodes (reducible, non-encoded structures, groups). In the Milky Way/Sol/Earth locality, nested networks or 'levels of reality' are commonly classified as follows, opposite.

Network Level	Encoding Mutation	Node type	Supernode types
Space-time	Superinflation	Particle-wave	Plasma density variations
Atomic	Big Bang cooling	Element	Stars, gaseous clouds, galaxies
Molecular	Covalent bonds	Molecule	Planets, solar systems
Biological	Nucleotide sequences	Prokaryote	Crude ecologies, atmospheres
Somatic	Tissue specialization	Plant, animal	Ecosystems
Social	Neocortex	Social animal	Tribes, kin groups, cliques
Memetic	Speech/song/poem	Person	Villages, towns, nomadic groups
Symbolic	Symbol systems/writing	Literate citizen	Nations, governments, institutions
Media	Printing/broadcast/ analog replication	World citizen	Corporations, superpowers
Programmatic	Programmable systems/ digital replication	Augmented citizen	Global/solar societies
Gensynth	Genetic manipulation, synthesized lifeforms	Enhanced citizen	Engineered climate, space habitats
Mindsynth	Quantum neural nets, replicable intelligences	Autonomous entity	Emergent/evolving sim. worlds

CHAPTER TWENTY-THREE

Excerpt from 'The Four Phases of Earth Depopulation' by Lydia Heliosmith, age 17, written for *Terrestrial Anthropology 1*, 22.01.02719:

Phase 2: The Revival (Part 2 – Extropian Fantasies)

By the mid-twenty-third century, despite shrinking workforces and contracting revenues, many governments found themselves in possession of budget surpluses. Lower military spending, lower healthcare costs, and an absence of banking bailouts (the private banking sector had been the corrupt lynchpin of the Corporate Age, and was no longer extant) resulted in fat coffers. What to do with the excess? East America, Canada, India, Australia, the Federation of Pacific Islands, Israel, Egypt, South Africa, Botswana, and all the Scandinavian countries lowered taxes, further stoking their economies, while the Pan American Union, West America, Unified Europe, the African Equatorial Alliance, Russia, China, United Korea, Japan, New Zealand, Indonesia, New Persia, and the Arabian Emirates launched scientific infrastructure projects on an unprecedented scale. Other nations and regions had negligible surpluses or continued indebtedness.

Technological progress had blossomed at the beginning of the Corporate Age (when companies had invested heavily in loosely supervised research and development labs), but petered out toward the end (when 'innovation' became synonymous with automating tasks for the purpose of replacing human jobs and chasing profits). During the Revival, ambitious R&D efforts came back in vogue (for both corporations and governments), and the individual inventor was empowered with access to polycompound, three-dimensional printing, laboratory and workshop co-operatives, cheap, rentable quantum computing power, and vast public libraries of research, code, schema, and art. Breakthroughs in materials science resulted in a smorgasbord of building blocks: stuff that was ultralight, ultrastrong, superconducting, superinsulating, light-bending, light-absorbing, energy-generating, megabendy, megabouncy, hydrophobic, self-cleaning, image-displaying, and/or intelligent.

The speculations of the Extropians (a late twentieth-century technology-evangelism cult espousing human enhancement and virtualization) proved prescient. Humans chose to self-modify and enhance, with effectiveness increasing and side effects decreasing as one climbed up through the social classes (which still existed, despite a more egalitarian world order). The power-up menu included cognition-enhancing and recreational drugs, sensory enhancements, epigenetic modulators (to stay lean and youthful, mostly), pharmaceutical implants, artistic body-sculpting and artificial skins, all the way up to full-brain backups. While indulgence in psychotropic compounds and basic medical enhancements transcended class boundaries, only the wealthiest could afford complete brain scans and neuronal virtualization into quantum cores.

In terms of achieving immortality through brain virtualization (another Extropian fantasy), the Smooth Transition problem was never solved. You could copy a brain, simulate its operation, and situate the quantum core in a grown clone or cyborg, but the resulting person had a different personality. Emotion and motivation, it turned out, were inextricably entwined with complicated neuronal wiring connecting the brain to the heart, gut, and endocrine system. The 'copy' had little sense of continuity with (or loyalty to) the 'original.' The outcome was usually total alienation from all previous friends and family. The core-clone or cyborg was a new person, one without social context or mooring. The results were messy and unsatisfactory.

A somewhat better approach, in terms of creating artificial people, was starting from scratch. An infant's brain and emotional circuitry could be modeled within a quantum core; the infant cyborg body could 'grow' via gradual part replacement as the mind developed. A number of synthanima were created this way, and lived for decades in human society with full citizens' rights, real families, and genuine emotional connections. These individuals were exceptional: they possessed magnificent cognitive abilities, could synthesize and utilize vast amounts of knowledge, and many made significant contributions in their profession or field of study. But these synthanima were not infallible. Their virtualized brains were modeled on human brains and were subject to the same developmental issues and complications (but with strange, difficult-to-understand differences attributable to the quantum core substrate). While not subject to dementia or other age-related brain problems, after a few decades they tended to veer toward one of a grab-bag of known psychological disorders (neuroticism, depression, catatonia, paranoia, psychotic hallucinations) or unfamiliar but equally dysfunctional conditions (related, in theory, to the inability of human brain architecture to handle the vast amounts of storage and processing power enabled by the quantum core substrate; the engine was too big for the frame). Nobody knew how to keep a synthanimus sane in the long-term. After a number of ugly incidents, most societies put an end to their creation.

Aside from these shortfalls in the realm of artificial people creation, the Revival was an era of invention and ambitious creativity. The space elevators and ringstations were built during this time, enabled by a multitude of novel materials and budget surpluses, fueled by a global lust for exploration and discovery. At least that was the official line. Historical hindsight showed that many world leaders saw the writing on the wall (in terms of Campi Flegrei) and orchestrated their own exit strategies under the guise of scientific progress. In all of human existence, world population had been reduced by more than half only once before, by the 'bottlenecking' Toba event seventy thousand years previous. Those who truly understood what was happening to the west of Naples were eager to get as far away as possible, safely encased in a completely independent and self-sufficient biosphere.

Ringstation culture was an extension of Revival culture, egalitarian and scientifically oriented, with a strong work ethic and emphasis on co-operation. Still, each of the huge space station projects had a unique origin, design, and distinct mission, and small cultural variations among these isolated systems quickly developed into larger differences over just a few generations. The tiny cylindrical Alhazen *was majority Muslim, designed primarily as a research oasis for astronomers and mathematicians. The* Stanford *was (and still is)* culturally pluralistic, mostly English-speaking, envisioning itself as a biological and cultural archive for humankind. The whimsically named Hedonark was a huge, wildly successful luxury space park, home to eighty thousand souls, until its unfortunate technical problems and population-culling disaster (attributed, by some, to a lack of P.M.C.[4]). The Michelangelo started out with an artistic focus, hosting a large number of great works (really an orbiting museum), but became increasingly isolated and paranoid over time, eventually retreating to the outer solar system and relying on an artificial fusion core in lieu of the sun for energy and warmth. The Liu Hui was the largest ringstation, similar in design to the Stanford but three times the size, a diverse metropolis with Mandarin as the lingua franca but with nearly fifty languages in use. It was the only ringstation with significant military capability, giving the others no choice but to trust in the good will and pragmatic tendencies of the Liu Hui leaders. After all, when it came down to it, the Liu Hui could blow them all to smithereens. Fortunately, their leadership had no militaristic ambitions. All they wanted to do was mine asteroids, and perhaps eventually build a wormhole drive capable of interstellar travel.

Life on Earth, and in space, was good, with only one caveat. Human population was still shrinking. The Revival was a time of hope, optimism, great public wealth, superior human health, and every possible kind of governmental support for fertility and child-rearing. Still, with greater human freedom and education came the universal desire to have slightly fewer children. The most religious countries, with the highest fertility rates, peaked at only 3.2 children per woman, while the global mean dropped to 1.8. By 2387 (the year Campi Flegrei unleashed its wrath), world population had already dropped to 4.8 billion (including the half-million or so in space). Two generations later, that number would be halved, and any notion of technological or cultural 'progress' (at least on Earth proper) would exist only in the history books.

19.05.02727, the Stanford

Adrian was regretting taking the stairs to Slope-4. The rejuv had restored some of his strength, but he would never be a young man again. His thighs were burning. Every few minutes he had to stop for a short rest.

He was meeting Townes for lunch. She hadn't given a reason for the meet-up. Usually he declined appointments if he didn't know the other party's agenda, but he was curious. He had to be careful around Penelope Townes. She was clever, ambitious, and she opposed Adrian at every opportunity. *Keep your enemies closer....*

During the day, the Starside ports provided the ringstation's only direct sunlight. Though 'direct' was a relative term. The light first passed through a layer of ionized plasma surrounding the ringstation (held in place by magnetic field generators situated along the eight main spokes), then penetrated two decimeter-thick, ozone-filled panes of transparent alumina. Even with these protections, cosmic and solar radiation levels were higher within the torus than on Earth. The Standard Edits mitigated the cumulative damage; nanodrones repaired the remainder.

Radiation was not the only danger in space. Hull breach was a constant threat, both from object impacts and rotational sheer forces. The outermost hull was protected from space junk and micrometeoroids by a thick layer of extremely low-density metallic microlattice. The nickel-based compound was not only ultralight and ultrastrong, but also flexible. The lattice functioned as a shock absorber, compressing to subsume collisions, then immediately rebounding to its original shape. Areas not covered by the microlattice (such as the viewing ports) were protected by auto-targeting lasers that incinerated any object approaching at high velocity. The targeting algorithms of these lasers were a constant point of debate; archeologists preferred to capture space junk with vast synthisilk nets and catalog the items, and considered the annihilation of orbiting wrenches lost during twentieth-century space missions to be a crime against humanity's collective cultural heritage.

He reached Slope-3 and checked the time; he was running ten minutes late. Good, let her wait. She'd arranged the lunch casually, as if it were a social engagement. He'd gone along with it. It wasn't as if he could *rule out* the possibility that she wanted to make peace. The power dynamic had changed – Adrian now had more of it – so why not?

The thought had occurred to him that this might even be a date. Nothing romantic – he knew Townes didn't like him – but why not casual sex? He was a handsome man (especially after the rejuv), and she knew that he had once been interested. She was older now – no doubt she had fewer suitors. Maybe she was interested in a fling? That *would* be a peace offering.

The last flight of stairs was easier (Slope-4 gravity declined all the way to 0.9G). There weren't any permanent residences this high; bone loss would be too severe. But for bars, clubs, sports venues, theaters, and restaurants, the centripetal reduction provided a 'lightness of being' that suited recreational establishments.

The slope levels were partial, wide shelves running along the center of the torus on both sides. Following the indicator in his m'eye, Adrian soon found himself in the midst of a vast sculpture garden. On one side, a long railing protected view-seekers from the steep drop to Slope-3. The lower slope levels extended farther out, with Slope-1 being the widest. The view of Main was stunning. From this height, everything within the long, shallow valley was a perfect miniature: colorful farms, steamy greenhouses, white buildings, verdant parks laced with curving walkways, shallow pools and tall fountains, transparent pedestrian tubes connecting habitation centers, and people everywhere, going about their lives.

On the other side of the sculpture garden, Vick's was tucked away, built right into the hull. The restaurant had no sign (an irritating pretense), but after walking the length of the windowless building he finally found a door hidden in an alcove.

Inside, Vick's Lounge was crowded, noisy, and brightly lit, with sunlight streaming in through a long hullside window that ran the length of the dining area. Adrian saw Townes immediately. She had already ordered a plate of grilled seafood and was sipping a pale orange cocktail from a martini glass. She waved him over.

"Adrian! You're late – that's not like you. Help yourself to the shrimp. Let's get you a drink. Corsican mint, right? Okay, I've just ordered it. Sit, sit."

He smiled and tried to match her casual, friendly manner. It was difficult; they'd been at odds for so long.

"It's brilliant at night," she said. "You can watch the shuttles dock at Central. The *Hedonark* has a new shuttle model, you know. It looks just like a cartoon rocket ship, like something out of *Tintin*."

Adrian smiled politely, waiting for her to get to the point. Why the *Tintin* reference? The twentieth-century Belgian comic books were a common historical reference point within the department, mostly as a post-colonial gestalt. The international adventures of the young reporter and his white dog perfectly captured the Eurocentric, racist views of the twentieth century; the accounts of Tintin's interactions with other cultures were a practical 'what *not* to do' anthropological guide.

"They've made a remarkable recovery, don't you think? The *Hedonark*? Svilsson consulted for them, during the rebuild. Cultural analysis of their engineering department. They wanted someone from another station. I heard he was very well-paid. Not from him, of course."

"He's very quiet," said Adrian.

"But when he speaks, people listen," said Townes. "Don't underestimate him." She locked eyes with Adrian. "How is Car-En?"

The sound of her name was jarring, and Adrian blinked. Hadn't that problem already been solved? Well, yes, it had been, but there was still work to be done. It took some effort to think about his former student. Car-En Ganzorig was part of the past.

"You know her as well as I do," Adrian said. "Absorbed in her work, and late on all her reports."

"When did you last speak with her?" asked Townes, poking at the shrimp with her fork.

"A few days ago," Adrian said truthfully.

It had made his decision easier, talking to Car-En. Not that he had been struggling with it, but her delusional state confirmed, in his own mind, the trueness of his course. What he had initially mistaken for poor decision-making and rebelliousness had actually been the first signs of a full psychotic break. Car-En's mental state had deteriorated to a point where she was hallucinating, talking about 'black eggs' that took over people's minds, requesting a medical intervention team. He *had* provided medical intervention, in a way.

"Why are you smiling?" asked Townes.

"The impudence of youth – just thinking about Car-En. She and I don't always see eye to eye on the specifics of her research protocols. She can be stubborn."

"What did you disagree on?"

A sudden pain arced between Adrian's shoulder blades. He grunted and shifted in his chair. This was not a casual line of questioning. Townes was homing in on something. He had to be careful. He found himself surprisingly disappointed to drop the sexual scenario. Still fantasizing, like a boy. He sighed.

"Are you all right?"

A young man brought him his Corsican mint. He waited to answer until the server had left. "Fine, yes. Just a muscle spasm."

"Did Car-En see a reason to Intervene? Was that it?" Townes had dropped any pretense that this was a casual social call. She was digging.

"All her reports are available for public viewing, Penny," he said icily. Penelope Townes was smart and ambitious, but she was incapable of being subtle. She'd have an easier time of things if she just admitted that to herself and played her cards straight.

Townes furrowed her brow, ate a shrimp, and slurped from her cocktail. "What's your opinion, Adrian, of Non-Interventionism during the Remnant Age?"

It was a non sequitur, and also an odd way to put the question. The isolationist policies of the ringstations during Earth's greatest crisis were commonly called *Watching*, and were universally regarded as the great moral failing of the Ringstation Coalition. This moral failing was not debated, it was *accepted*. There was a consensus among respected intellectuals. All but a few eccentrics and attention-seekers agreed that the highly organized, highly functional, resource-rich ringstation societies *should have done something* to prevent the total disintegration of Earth societies that followed Campi Flegrei.

But what could have been done? On this question, there was no consensus. What could half a million souls in orbit do to correct the problems of the billions below? There was not enough food to feed them. There was not enough military force to control them. And there was no moral authority to command or inspire them. To those left on Earth, ringstation citizens were considered elite cowards, even traitors. They had fled their home planet. They were *Others* now, aliens.

Modern intellectuals soothed their consciences by imagining *they* would have done things differently, acting more compassionately. But Adrian had no conscience to soothe; he saw things clearly. The ringstation governments of that era had acted correctly. They had remained above, aloof, in orbit, staying far away from the space elevator docks. In some cases, this precaution hadn't been necessary; vandals below had severed the lines, allowing the ultralight cables to whip across land and sea at great velocity, disintegrating anything with which they happened to collide.

But Penelope Townes knew exactly what Adrian thought. He had shared his opinions freely decades earlier, when he was a student, when it was more appropriate to openly explore taboo lines of thought. Why was she asking now?

"What are you getting at?"

"You know that eventually we're going to have to interact with them, right? And probably help them?"

"Who?" he asked.

She put down her drink and leaned forward. "The Harz villagers. They're dying. The *kibbutzniks* may need our help as well. Though they're better off, and they don't seem to want anything to do with us."

"You should share your views with the Council. I'm sure you'd start some lively debates."

"Non-Interventionism is a temporary measure," stated Townes. "It's appropriate for this phase of research, but it was never intended to be a permanent policy. We can't risk repeating the mistakes of the past."

"*Watching*, redux," said Adrian, smiling. "That's what you're scared of?"

"Look, you might be right about ringstation isolationism historically. Who knows? Everyone thinks that we should have done something...."

"Connolly's Eleven-Point Plan," offered Adrian.

"Right," Townes said. "Perfect policy in hindsight. It would never have worked." She ran her fingers through her long, silver hair, pushing it back. "But we have a chance to get it right this time. There are communities on Earth that could use our help."

"And you want me to get behind this," said Adrian.

He picked up a fork and speared a shrimp. It was tender and garlicky.

"A gradual policy change. We could start with fixing their cancer problem. Either help them relocate, or contain the radiation. We could even vaccinate them, for starters."

"That would make Car-En happy," Adrian said, allowing himself to imagine that she was still alive. "She really cares for them. You do too, don't you?"

She gave him a long look. She knew his emotions operated differently, and with her he didn't bother to maintain a pretense. They knew each other too well. So she didn't ask, *"Don't you?"*

But she didn't really know what he thought, or she wouldn't be asking for his help. Pre-literates could not (and would never be able to) integrate with more advanced cultures. Nothing good had ever come of any attempt to do so. The Harz villagers should be allowed to die off. Or be killed off, if necessary.

"Honestly, Penelope, I think it's too soon to revisit Non-Interventionism. We're just beginning to understand these new cultures. We have no idea how they might react to us – to space aliens, essentially."

She drained her orange drink, then unfocused her eyes, ordering another with her m'eye.

"I called Car-En," she said.

"And...." he said, keeping his face open and relaxed.

"Her fans are going nuts. It's been weeks since her last update."

"I know that better than anybody. Believe me, I've been nagging her – it doesn't do any good. What am I going to do, go down there?"

"Maybe," she said. "Maybe you should. What if she's in trouble? She didn't respond to my patch – she could really be out of air. When did you say you last spoke with her?"

"A few days ago."

"Would you mind forwarding me the conversation?"

The server delivered her drink. Adrian took advantage of the pause to collect his thoughts. "Actually, I *would* mind. She shared some things that were confidential."

"Then just send me the metadata."

Pushy. "Why?" he said. He could push back.

She answered with a question. "Why didn't you use any of her m'eye feeds during your last report?"

"Because she locked me out," he said. That much was true. "I think she's hiding some things from me. I'm not sure what."

"You should have included that in your report. It's a big deal. Is she competent?"

"I wanted to give her the benefit of the doubt. If I shared something like that with Repop, or even Academic Conduct, she'd be immediately recalled. So I'm giving her some time."

Townes leaned back and gazed at him. He locked eyes with her and pretended, for a moment, that she was seducing him instead of interrogating him.

"If I get behind your research camp proposal," she said, "it passes. It's that simple. And I'm not necessarily opposed to it. Especially if Xenus is Research Coordinator."

So she'd spoken with Troy. And she still considered him to be *her* ally.

"I'm pleased to hear that," he said. "I think Troy would be an excellent choice. The obvious choice, really."

"So if Xenus and I introduce a policy change on Non-Interventionism, will you get behind it?"

Was this the same proposal they had tried to introduce at the last Council meeting? They really were pushing forward.

"Have you read his thesis?" she asked. "He makes a persuasive argument that the existing human settlements should really be classified as Phase 1 Repop, as opposed to late Survivalist tribes. All the groups are culturally distinct, not only from each other, from but the prevailing norms of the Remnant Age. In his model, our own settlements would constitute Phase 2, with Phase 3 being a gradual integration, facilitated and assisted by the Ringstation Coalition."

Adrian smiled. Penelope Townes was old, but not wise. She was as naïve and blindly optimistic as a first-year field student, thinking the villagers would be peaceably inclined toward modern humans. *Rista orn*, was all he could think. The blood eagle.

"I'm sorry, Penny, I just don't agree. Non-Interventionism is the right policy for now. We shouldn't open that can of worms."

She looked away, visibly angry. Fine, let her be. He held the cards now.

"I don't get you, Adrian," she said. "I never have and I never will. I thought I was doing it your way, you know? Making a deal?"

He reached for another shrimp. They were good; buttery and perfectly salted. The sauce was mostly parsley, maybe a touch of sweet basil, some garlic but not too much. Vick's Lounge – he'd have to come back for dinner sometime.

"I'm going to keep calling Car-En. She'll talk to me eventually."

No, she won't.

Townes got up. "The shrimp and the drinks are on me. It's your last freebie – enjoy it."

She left. Adrian ordered another Corsican mint and basked in the warm, natural sunlight streaming in through the long viewing port.

Footnote 4. *Paranoid Maintenance Culture (P.M.C.)*

A term describing the obsessive nature of ringstation citizens (especially technicians) with regards to double- and triple-checking safety systems, backup systems, and various layers of redundant life-support systems. Life in space is hostile, and borderline OCD is adaptive in environments where miscalculations and maintenance failures lead to death (as in the *Hedonark* catastrophe).

CHAPTER TWENTY-FOUR

Scowling, the old woman handed Elke a small bundle wrapped in worn leather.

"Do you have something to say, Ilsa?" Elke asked.

The crone looked away and shuffled down the hall. "You will only need a small amount," she muttered, over her shoulder.

Elke tucked the bundle into her sleeve and left the old woman's house. Outside, she breathed in the fresh spring air with relief. The smell of the sickhouse overwhelmed her.

She walked in the direction of the smithy, nodding at Farrel as she passed by. He sat on his stump, smoking, and, more importantly, watching. At dusk he would stop by Elke's house, fill his tankard with Arik's öl, and tell Elke the day's tales. Always there was something worth hearing. Every so often her husband complained at how quickly his cask seemed to drain, but he complained softly. Not a week went by when Arik did not come to Elke for advice, asking for insight into the thoughts and feelings of the villagers. If Happdal ever had a mood, Elke knew it. And Farrel was not her only pair of eyes and ears.

She passed the smithy. The bellows station stood empty; the forge was cold. Trond was gone, and she had sent Jense to find him. Had that been wrong? Who would she send to find Jense, if *he* did not return? Would she send the whole village into the forest, one by one, until only she remained, alone in her empty house?

Most of all, she missed Esper. She loved both boys, but the sight of Trond still filled her with shame. Arik knew, and had forgiven her long ago, accepting Trond as his son. Most others guessed. It was not hard, when one looked at Jense, then at Trond. The boy himself had no idea, and no one was brave enough to tell him. Not even Esper. Or perhaps Esper was too kind.

Elke loved her daughter too, if not as fiercely as she loved her sons. Katja was willful, impatient, and slovenly. Trond and Esper obeyed Elke (usually) and respected her, but Katja thought only of herself. The girl was well-loved in Happdal; others did not seem to notice or mind her selfishness. They admired her beauty (which Elke did not see) and her strength (this, Elke acknowledged) and found her charming (a quality lost on Elke entirely). Arik loved Katja; she was his shining jewel. And Trond and Esper would do anything to protect their beloved sister.

Bile rose in her throat. Would she lose the best two in the search for the third? Had they *both* needed to go? She suspected it had been Esper's idea. Her anger cooled a little, and she smiled, remembering the look of horror on Esper's face as Trond had lifted her, moving her aside so they could pass.

Esper, her middle child, was her favorite. He had her wit and her will, but he was also kind and gentle like his father. Esper would take Arik's place one day. Secretly, she dreamed he would unite the Five Valleys. Why not? Who would not follow strong, wise Esper?

First, though Haakon had to be dealt with. Until yesterday she'd been content to wait and prepare, to be ready to defend Happdal. No longer. She had not told Arik of her grim discovery. Her husband was a patient man, but this news would force him to act, bringing grave danger to himself and to the village. Her way was better.

She smelled the cows long before she reached Harald's barn. The cheesemaker had recruited some of the bellows boys to help with spring milk. They had agreed to help without too much protest; Harald's daughter was pretty and buxom. The wench still could not look Elke in the eye (on account of her indiscretion with Arik), and when Elke was near she found somewhere else to be. Perhaps that would be the case today. It made no matter, her business was with neither Harald nor his prize heifer.

She found the boys working over a long wooden trough, pouring the clotted milk through fine cloth, collecting the curds. The clear whey they poured into ceramic jugs; it would later be delivered to the baker to make rich bread and dense cakes. Grundar, the blond one, wore his usual scowl. The tall, lanky one, Karl, bore a stoic expression, though he had more of a right to be miserable. His mother Buried, his father slaughtered, his sisters raped (and one killed), and yet Hinrik's son pushed on, accepting the foul dish life had served him.

Now Elke would add more bitterness to his plate. Though maybe also something sweet.

"Do you miss my son, boys? Pumping the bellows is hard work, but it might turn your twigs into arms. Making cheese looks too easy. Perhaps you should be churning butter instead."

"Women's work," said Grundar.

"Could you best a milkmaid in a fight, Grundar? Her shoulders are strong from the yoke, and her arms are like iron from turning the paddle. Instead of water she drinks whey, which makes her stronger still. Shall I find a milkmaid and arrange a contest?"

Grundar blushed and looked away. Karl grinned – he seemed happy to see her.

"And you, Karl, do you miss my son, and the bellows? Did you think when Harald gave you work that you would gaze upon his daughter while you labored? That the hours would pass quickly? That she would smile at you, and tease you, and offer you cream and honey? Yet I see no trace of her."

It was Karl's turn to blush. "She was just here!" Grundar protested.

Elke laughed. "Perhaps she heard me coming. Or someone saw me coming up the road, and warned her." She went to Karl and pulled on his sleeve. "Come with me – the cheese can wait a few minutes." Karl nodded. Grundar shrugged, and collapsed into a nearby pile of hay.

She took Karl to a quiet corner of the barn and sat him down on a bale. She noticed a tear in his trousers, a smear of dried blood beneath. "What happened to your leg?" she asked.

He looked down at the injury as if noticing it for the first time. "Make sure to clean that wound. You know as much – even a small cut might fester if not washed. If it becomes infected, go see Ilsa." The boy nodded, avoiding her gaze.

"Brace yourself, young one – I have foul news. I went to check on Jesper, and found him dead."

Karl paled, but said nothing.

"His head was crushed, as if squeezed in a vise. There were no blade wounds on him."

"Haakon?" asked Karl softly. The strength of the jarl's grip was known throughout the Five Valleys.

Elke nodded. "Others were with him. Egil the Bard, I think, for I saw marks in the dirt from the stick he carries. I made out tracks for three, maybe four others." She did not tell Karl that she had smelled the scent of three men she knew (Haakon, Egil, and Einar the Lame), and one more whose scent she did not recognize.

"I remember Egil from Summer Trade," said Karl. "His voice is not sweet, but I remember his poems."

"Do you wish to avenge your friend?" she asked. The boy nodded. "Speak!" she snapped. "Do you want me to give you this task?"

"I wish to avenge him. And my father and my sisters too."

"And what will you do?"

The boy had no color in his face, but his jaw was set. "I will kill Haakon," he said. Elke nodded, satisfied. His voice was low – she saw a boy but heard a man. More importantly, she heard truth in his timbre.

"Good. Then I will help you. Here, take this." First looking to make sure no eyes were on them, she took the bundle from her sleeve and gave it to Karl. He took the object wrapped in soft leather and regarded it solemnly.

"Put it away," she said. "Look at it later. You will go to Kaldbrek – you know the way, yes? Go there and deliver it to Haakon. In the dead of night would be best, while he sleeps. Then run back to Happdal as fast as your feet will carry you. If your lungs burn, keep running. Do you understand?"

She liked the boy, and did not wish to see him flayed.

She patted Karl on his head, feeling sad. Why was it her job to send men into danger? Karl tucked the bundle away and went to rouse Grundar.

From outside she heard a commotion, yelling and shouting. She ran to the road and looked. Was she too late? Had Haakon come raiding so soon? She was not ready. The lookout post was empty. She cursed herself. Of course the raiders came now, after discovering they were being watched, and slaughtering the boy. The men of Happdal had armor, leather boiled until it was stiff and hard, but they would not wear it while they worked; it impeded movement too much. They had spears, probably leaning up against walls, inside their homes, while they labored elsewhere. They were not ready. All Elke's work, and fear, and worry – for nothing. Where was Arik?

She ran toward the noise. A crowd had gathered in the road. It made no sense. Haakon's raiders would come down through the High Pass, from the opposite direction. Had they found another way?

She pushed through the crowd. She saw smiling faces, and some with open mouths, confusion or shock. "Let me through!" she cried, shoving people aside. Everyone jostled forward to get a better look.

Finally she broke through to the front rank, and gasped. Her son Trond stood before her in the mud. He looked different, not as broad and mighty as when he had left, and his face was roughly shaved. But it was him, looking like the beardless, unwashed boy she remembered so well.

Trond carried a small woman. She hung loosely in his arms. She was brown-skinned, but most of her body was covered by silvery cloth. The shiny material reflected light like the scales of a wet fish. It was the woman who had come before, who called herself Car-En. Did she live? Her arm twitched – she was not dead. Elke had warned her not to return unless accompanied by Elke's children. It looked as if the strange woman had made good on that deal, even if she was the worse for wear for it.

Next to Trond stood Esper, tall and proud. She rushed forward to embrace him. "Esper! Trond! My sons have returned!" She looked around, hopefully, but they had not brought Katja home.

CHAPTER TWENTY-FIVE

Jense sat on a flat rock and ate the last of his brown bread, stale but still good. He thanked his hunger for that; an empty stomach turned the meanest scraps into delicious morsels. He had finished the last of the cheese yesterday. He checked his food sack – what was left? A few dried apples, three small smoked fish, a single strip of dried goat meat. Enough to make it home, if he turned back now.

But he could not go home yet. Not until he found Katja, or her brothers.

First he had taken the northern trail, passing the Three Stones. Elke thought that Trond and Esper had taken the Silver Trail west, along the Nyr Begna, so Jense had taken a different direction. He had seen nothing. This did not mean there was nothing to see; he was no expert tracker. But the woods felt empty. It was easy to imagine he was the only man left in the world. One day he would die, and there would only be birds, and boar, and a few lynx. And bugs, of course. There would always be bugs.

On the first day he took the northern trail all the way to Skrova, the smallest village of the Five Valleys. The people there were friendly, and he saw faces that looked familiar from years past. Boys had grown into young men, full-grown men now had gray in the beards. Had they seen Katja? They had not. What of Kaldbrek? They feared Haakon, and kept their distance. They gave Jense food and drink, and a place to sleep. The next morning, he went on his way.

First he traveled west along Skrova's wide valley until it rose and narrowed, finally reaching the headwaters of the Nyr Begna. He followed the river south for a day, stepping carefully and making slow progress. When he reached the High Pass trail, he took it west, climbing the high mountain range that separated Skrova and Happdal from Kaldbrek. The trail was steep. He did not want to go to Kaldbrek, but where else was there to look? Haakon had raided Happdal before – perhaps the Kaldbrek jarl had taken Katja.

He loved the girl. She was too young for him, and she was half-sister to his son, so he kept his love to himself. But she knew. She must. Even Trond seemed to know. With nowhere else to put it, Jense had poured his love into Katja's blade. He would finish it, and give it to her when she returned to Happdal.

Did Elke know of his love for her daughter? He had once loved the mother. Fierce, beautiful Elke. He still respected her, and feared her a little, but long ago he had pulled his heart away. Elke was cruel and hard. It had taken him years to learn that. She hid her ruthlessness beneath her beauty and persuasiveness. If he ever touched Katja, and Elke found out, she might murder him.

Did Elke love her daughter protectively, or was she jealous of her? Maybe both. His real mission, Jense knew, was to find Elke's sons. For Elke, finding Katja was an afterthought. No, that was cruel. Elke cared for her daughter. But whatever the woman's feelings, Jense knew his own. He would find Katja first.

He swallowed the last of his bread, gathered his things, slung his greatsword, Bár, over his shoulder, and continued his trek. He would reach the top of the ridge within the hour.

Bár was a soulsword containing the spirit of a mighty brown bear. Jense had resolved that upon his return he would teach the final secret of godsteel to Trond. The time was right, and he was sick of secrets. The other secret he would take to his grave – that much he had sworn to Elke – but there was no reason to jealously guard his craft. His son was full smith and had earned the right of knowledge.

Jense had learned the Five Secrets from his father, Baldr, who had learned them from the swordsmith Kai, who had learned them from Jakob the Bold, who had learned them from Happdal's first smith, the great Stian. What if Jense had waited too long, and now Trond was dead? Who would carry on the knowledge then? One of the bellows boys? Grundar was too impatient, but Karl showed promise. Hinrik's son was stoic and a quick learner. On the downside, the boy was thin-limbed and prone to injuring himself. Was Karl immune to pain, as his father had been? Hinrik had lost several fingers and received many burns because of it. To feel no pain sounded like a blessing, but pain kept you whole. Especially in the smithy.

Harald the cheesemaker had asked Jense if he could borrow the bellows boys while the forge was cold, and Jense had given him Grundar and Karl. The other two, Jalmar and Gregers, he had sent to the mines. For years Jense had relied on trade with Kaldbrek to obtain iron ore, but Summer Trade was no more, and now a crew of Happdal men worked in open pits, digging red rock from the earth and hauling it back to the forge. It was hard work, and Jalmar and Gregers had complained. Did they want to become apprentices or not? They had bowed to his threats, though in truth neither was bright enough to become a full smith. Jalmar was the least dull of the two. Maybe one day, with hard work, Jalmar might learn to make a decent mudsteel plow.

Ultimately, Trond would choose his own apprentice. Deep down, Jense did not fear for his son. Trond would not die easily. Perhaps one day Trond would lose his shyness around women and find a wife, and the Red Brother would bless them with a son. The baby would have arms like fat sausages and would grow into a beast of a man, like his father and grandfather. Jense grinned at the thought and picked up his pace.

The first secret was the Crucible. To make godsteel, first go to the riverbank. There, collect clay, and from that fresh clay construct the vessel. The size and construction was important; too large and it might crack, too thick and it would not get hot enough, too small and it would not hold enough ore to make a weapon. A conical shape was ideal.

Once fired, fill the crucible with iron ore and a small amount of black charcoal dust to add strength to the steel. Last, add a handful of river sand, and a shard of broken glass, to draw the impurities from the metal.

The next step in the process – the *true* second secret – was the one that Jense had hidden from Trond. It was not necessary to make godsteel, but it was the only way to make a soulsword.

Before sealing the crucible, add a bit of burned bone. To make Bár, Jense had used a fragment of the jawbone of a great brown bear, one he had slain himself with a half-dozen arrows over the course of a three-day hunt. You could make a soulsword with any piece of bone, as long as the soul had not already been captured (or, in the case of a warrior, ascended to Valhalla). But if you killed the man or beast yourself, the soulsword would be loyal to you. The weapon was enslaved to the killer of the soul it contained. This secret was named the Captured Soul.

War was coming to Happdal. It was time Trond learned the secret of the soulsword. Jense had been reluctant to give it up. Had he been guarding the knowledge jealously? Maybe, but he had also wanted to protect his son. A soulsword was a powerful weapon, but also a dangerous one, for the trapped soul was angry. When you held the blade, the rage of the enslaved soul coursed through the hilt, into your hand, up your arm, and lodged in your heart. Heart thus blackened, a man could fight with great ferocity. But could he lay down the sword when the fight was done? Would he be able to distinguish friend from foe? One could only hope, and pray to the Red Brother.

The third secret: the Sealed Oven. Construct the oven from brick and clay, adding vents on the sides. Gently place the crucible inside, and seal the top with river clay. The heat from the charcoal fire thus contained, the crucible within would be fiercely heated, as if by hellfire. This required constant, tireless stoking from the bellows, but that was what the bellows boys were for.

The fourth secret was the Gentle Shaping. Break off the top of the crucible, pour the molten metal into the mold, then allow it to cool. The resulting godsteel ingot could not be brutally smashed and sparked like a chunk of mudsteel. With godsteel there were few sparks; the metal had already been purified from the heat and the sand and the glass. You struck it gently, and for longer, slowly shaping the ingot into a rod, and from a rod into a sword, constantly reheating the metal to keep it supple. Too hard or too fast and the steel might crack.

If shaping mudsteel was like lying with a married woman, then shaping godsteel was like lying with a virgin. A married woman with children might not mind if you held her roughly; a little pain did not scare her. She had already known the agony of childbirth and emerged whole. But you had to be gentle with a virgin. Later, she would become strong, but she was vulnerable while you lay with her the first time. If Elke was mudsteel, then Katja was godsteel.

He grunted, relieved that nobody could hear him think. He supposed only smiths had such thoughts.

The last secret: the Flaming Sword. Quench the hot blade in oil, not water, to cool it more slowly. Demand silence, and listen, and hold your breath, and pray to the Red Brother. If there was no ping, no high sound of cracking steel, then the blade was sound. As you raise the sword, the oil burns off, the sword is alight, and it looks magical. And some *were* filled with magic, with angry souls.

Then, the sword could be etched and sharpened and polished like any blade. After a final heating to add strength, construct the hilt around the tang, using the finest materials: hardwood and bone, thin strips of softened leather, perhaps a gemstone in the pommel. Craft the scabbard in wood, and line it with fur to keep the blade oiled.

The godsteel blade was a fearsome weapon. It could slice a foe in two. In battle, the blade was strong and flexible and pointed; it could whip around a man's shield and slip into his body in a single motion. A godsteel sword could shatter a mudsteel blade. It could slice through the haft of an axe. It could pierce mail. There was no higher form of weaponry.

Jense had almost reached the top of the ridge. Something caught his eye – a blur of orange fur, fifty paces up the slope. A fox. He climbed, and cleared the tree line. The fox was long gone, but he saw what had attracted the animal in the first place: the blood-soaked carcass of a bear. The beast had been hacked apart, partially eaten, and abandoned. Jense knelt and touched the thick, brown fur. The carcass was cold but still fresh. There was no smell of rot, and while the ants had begun their work, the flies had not yet discovered the feast. There were clear blade wounds; a man (or woman) had killed the animal. Some of the meat had been cut away, but most had been left for the forest scavengers. It was a wasteful scene, and Jense felt ashamed. He too had once killed a bear, but every bit of it had been eaten, or used for tools or clothing. He touched Bár's hilt and felt the soulsword's rage.

Jense searched the area carefully. There were no signs of a campfire or bedding. Whoever had killed the bear had not stayed here long. Faint tracks headed south along the ridge. He followed them, and continued south even after he lost the trail, walking until the sun was low in the sky. He would soon need to find a place to camp.

Kaldbrek was west from here, down into the valley. If he rushed down the mountainside, he could make it there in less than an hour. But that would be foolish. Jogging down a steep slope in the dark was a sure way to turn an ankle, or worse. And even if he made it to Kaldbrek whole, what would he find there? Katja, as a prisoner? Even if he found her, what then? Sneak in, kill her guards, and take her away? Jense was not light-footed; a stealthy approach was unlikely to be successful. How many men could he kill before they felled him? Dying bravely would not help Katja, even if he slaughtered half of Kaldbrek before he was overcome.

In the dusk light he saw something move, far ahead. Perhaps a lynx or a marten, or the fox he had caught sight of earlier. When he made his way to the spot, he found nothing. He stood still among the tough grasses and rocky ground of the high ridge, and let his mind go blank. The Red Brother would show him the way, if he waited long enough and listened. For a long time he remained still, until the mountain air cooled his limbs and face, and only his innards remained warm. A thought came to him. He took a deep breath and cried out as loud as he could: "Kaaatjaaaaaaaaaaaa!"

He waited, then he called her name again. And again, holding the last syllable in a long, mournful cry.

"Kaaatjaaaaaaaaaaaaaaaaaaaaaaaaaa!"

Jense was quiet for a long time, listening for a response. There was nothing, except for the wind and the distant, high-pitched chattering of siskins from the tree line below. Jense shivered, missing the warmth of his forge.

"I will make a fire," he said to the siskins, and slapped his body and legs with his hands to warm himself, and also to drive out his self-pity.

When he looked up, he noticed a figure, watching him, not twenty paces away. A woman, clearly – but it was too dark to make out her face.

"Hello! I did not hear you approach. I am Jense, from Happdal."

He stepped closer, slowly, holding up his hands to show that he meant no harm. At ten paces, he saw that she was thin and ashen-skinned. Her long hair was in braids that had come partially undone, tangled and beginning to mat. Her bare arms were smeared with dirt, or blood, or both. At first, Jense did not believe his own eyes.

Finally, he muttered, "Katja," and took a step back. Something was wrong.

She stared at him, dead-eyed. Who had mistreated her so? He would find the person responsible and cut them down. Or perhaps devise a harsher punishment. A smith's tools could be used for more than just shaping metal....

Two crossed longswords were slung across her back. In a single motion she drew both, silently, from their fur-lined scabbards. He had never seen her wield two swords. She preferred a single blade, or a two-handed sword (like the one he had almost finished, to gift her), or a spear.

She spun each blade in the air, lazily. Her motions were fluid, devoid of any beginner's awkwardness. Somehow she had learned to fight in this style.

"Katja!" he yelled. "Do you not recognize me? It is your friend, Jense. Elke sent me to find you, and now I have." He had imagined that he would feel a sense of jubilant relief when he found her, but he felt nothing of the sort. Instead, dread filled his heart. What had become of her?

She approached, circling. He drew Bár, turning to face her.

He could feel the bear's hunger in his hands and shoulders and heart. "Careful, woman," he said, "this sword has not fed for many years." He did not use her name, for he was no longer sure it was his friend he faced.

She tested his defenses with a lazy thrust. He reacted with a single step back, keeping his sword raised defensively. She would have to do more than that to make him move his metal. Her face was dead, unsmiling. He had sparred with Katja many times, and was used to seeing a glint in her eye and a smirk on her face while she fought. She loved to play with steel, and fought joyfully. There was no sign of that joy now, or any other emotion for that matter.

She swung at his head, with full force, and an instant later thrust the other blade at his belly. He parried the first blow easily, the second with difficulty. These were no playful blows; she meant to gut him.

"Whoever you are, release my friend! What has she done to hurt you? Take me instead, if you need a body to play with." There was no other explanation; Katja was possessed.

She swung a blade downward, as if to split his head like a log. He blocked, holding his steel upward at an angle. Her sword slid down the length of his blade and caught against the hilt. He noticed a mark on her weapon, one he recognized. Stian's mark. He had one of the founding smith's blades in his collection, and had studied it often for inspiration.

Next to Stian's mark was the etched outline of a tooth. He recalled a legend, twin blades made by Stian: Biter, holding the soul of a wolf, and Taker, with the bound soul of a cruel man. A man from Kaldbrek.

Jense twisted away as the other blade came in, but not soon enough, and the point pierced his leather shirt and dug into his belly. He grunted – a shallow wound, but it hurt.

Who had ended up with those blades? Elke's grandfather. Morfar Henning, who had disappeared into the forest, never to be seen again. But some had sworn they *had* seen him, years later, still lurking in the woods.

As soon as the pieces fit together in his mind, he let out a great shout. "I know who you are! Release this body, gast, and return to your spirit world!" With this proclamation, he swung Bár. He did not know if there was a remedy for possession, but maybe the forest sprite would flee its host if he could make the body bleed. It was worth a try. If that did not work, maybe he could knock Katja out and carry her back to Happdal. The crone Ilsa might have a cure.

The gast stepped back fluidly, easily avoiding the blow. *That* motion he recognized. Katja could judge distance like no other, and make a man look foolish, staying just out of reach while her opponent swung at empty air. So, somehow, she was still in there. That, or the gast had stolen her fighting style, and added to it. He had heard legends of Henning's speed and skill with two swords (godsteel soulswords, crafted by a master, no less), and now he felt genuine fear. The gast was only playing with him. The real fight had not yet begun.

Confirming his suspicions, she leapt at him, swords whirling. The blades moved too fast for his eyes to follow, and he retreated, parrying desperately, relying on instinct to guide Bár. His ankle collided with a sharp rock on a backward step, and he stumbled, crying out in pain.

He had not seen the blow, but now he bled from his arm, as well as his belly. Still, her ashen face betrayed no feeling. Behind those cold eyes, did the gast laugh delightedly?

He yelled and thrust his sword, holding nothing back. Jense's arms were powerful and also long, and the length of Bár nearly matched his own height. The gast tried to dodge the blow, stepping back and to the side, but the tip caught Katja's body in the bicep, and drew blood.

He studied the gast's face, searching for any glimmer of Katja's soul. There was nothing. He noticed, for the first time, a web of thin black lines beneath her pale, translucent skin. The observation sickened him. Was she beyond saving? Would it be kinder to end her, if he could? He screamed in anguish and charged, swinging his sword in wild arcs. She retreated, blocking his blows with strong, precise motions, as if biding her time. He paused and stood before her, breathing hard. She watched him.

Was there a glint of curiosity in those eyes? He could not tell. But the gast let him rest for a moment, whatever the reason.

"Why did you choose my friend?" he asked between gasps. "She is no great warrior, like Henning. She is merely a girl. When you took Henning, he had a wife and children. He had already lived a full life. But Katja had none of that. She had not even known a man, one of life's simple pleasures." Of the last point he was not quite sure (and, truthfully, did not really care). It was possible that Katja had done more than kiss the village boys (if she had, none would dare boast). But still it seemed a good point, if the gast could be convinced.

The gast said nothing, and gave no indication that his words had been understood. For the moment, it held both blades loosely, level with the ground. For the first time, Jense noticed a third weapon, a sheathed dagger, tucked into Katja's belt. It was an unusual make. What smith had forged it? Perhaps Völund, from Kaldbrek? That smith had been busy, according to Elke's spies. Kaldbrek's armory was well-stocked. But no – Völund was a skilled smith, but his designs were stubbornly traditional. Maybe Orvar, who served as both blacksmith and fletcher to Skrova, had made the dagger. Certainly Orvar loved strange designs. But Jense had just been to Skrova, and spoken with Orvar, and the man had sworn he had not seen Katja.

A single crow landed between them, squawking rudely. Did it want them to hurry, and finish the fight, so it could feast on the eyeballs of the vanquished?

"Katja, if you can hear me, there is something I need to say. I love you, and have always loved you. First I loved you as one cherishes family. Though we share no blood, still you called me Farbror Jense, and you delighted in playing in my smithy while your brother toiled. Your eldest brother is my son – had you guessed?

"As you grew into a woman, my love for you changed. But I pushed my desire aside. What was I to do? I did not wish to incur Elke's wrath, and I had no way of knowing if you felt the same. I could not ask."

The crow pecked at a shiny black pebble, then flew off. The gast spun the soulsword Taker in a single, graceful circle.

"So, I've said it. If you can hear me, now you know the truth of my heart. And to you, gast, I say this: drop the blades and come with me willingly to Happdal. Let Ilsa drive you from this body. Heed my words, or I will cut you down."

The gast leaned forward and lifted both blades. First a slow step, then a quicker one, steel held high.

Jense set his foot against the same rock he had stumbled on earlier, and braced himself, pointing his sword at Katja's heart. She swung Biter to knock his blade away, but he had anticipated this, and let his blade drop. She ran into it, and Bár's tip pierced her belly, low and deep. She stopped short, gutted.

He wrenched his blade out and watched the blood seep from the wound. He had not meant to cut so deep. He studied Katja's face for any hint of her soul, but saw none.

"I am sorry!" cried Jense. "Forgive me!"

Katja dropped the swords, bending over and coughing. A stream of dark blood ran from her mouth. She fell to her knees and clutched the earth, pale fingers digging into the dirt.

"Let me help you," Jense said, setting Bár down. "Gast or friend, let me help you. What can I do?"

He touched her arm, just above the bite his sword had taken. Her flesh had gone from gray to grayish-blue, and was cold to the touch. "Get out, gast, get out! Leave her!" Jense could not see through his tears. He wiped his eyes and blinked.

She coughed and retched, convulsing. Blood streamed from her mouth and dripped from her abdomen. He had killed her.

Then something emerged from her mouth – a shiny, black lump. It lay in the dirt and seemed to move a little before settling. A nearby weed turned white, as if frostbitten. Katja collapsed onto her back. Her body convulsed in one final, slow twist, and she was still.

Jense recognized the color of her skin and the stiffness of her flesh. He had seen the same, one cold autumn morning, when he and Arik had searched the woods for Mette, Elke's mother. After much searching, they had found the old woman, frozen stiff, and dead as could be.

Jense knelt over her, clutching her cold corpse, wishing that their places were reversed. What good was his life now? His tears had dried. All that remained was a tightness in his throat and dread in his heart.

He noticed, out of the corner of his eye, that the dark lump was egg-shaped, and coated in a shiny carapace of frozen blood. All the ground nearby had frosted over, as if in the dead of winter.

Jense stood, and with all his strength drove the heel of his boot down on the black egg, smashing it into the frozen earth.

CHAPTER TWENTY-SIX

"Bring me real food!" yelled Haakon, hurling the tray aside. The bread had a moldy taste to it, the cheese was green and foul-smelling, and the roasted fish was small and bony. The wasted food scattered across the longhouse floor.

The serving girl cowered. "The bakery has nothing today. Emma says she can make no bread without flour."

Einar the Lame limped forward and slapped the girl. "Watch your tongue, wench," he shouted. "Do you forget who you speak to?" The girl screamed, clutching her head defensively.

"Leave her be!" Egil snapped. The bard slouched in a low chair to Haakon's right. "No fault of hers, that we have no flour." Egil looked at Haakon accusingly.

"Go," muttered Haakon. The girl scurried off, leaving the spilled food. "Clean that up," he said to Einar. The cripple scowled, but obeyed, eating the soiled food from the ground.

Haakon turned his gaze to Egil. "What exactly do you propose?" he asked the bard. He would no longer let such comments slide. His advisor should advise him, not needle him to death. From now on, he would make the poet earn his keep.

"I have told you. Renew Summer Trade. Send messengers to Skrova, Silfrdal, Vaggabœr, and Happdal today, with peace offerings. They will gladly trade with us – they need our ore. We have wool, too. And of food, our neighbors have surpluses."

"And I have told *you* that is not an option. Do you have only one idea, bard?"

Egil did not back down. "Our valley is small and narrow. Our farmers cannot scrape a living from it. Mining is our strength, and we have always relied on trade." The bard punctuated this statement by rapping his oaken staff against his chair.

"Not always," said Haakon. He was thinking of his own ancestor,

Tyr the Lusty, who had raped a Happdal girl who had been visiting her cousin in Kaldbrek. The girl turned out to be important – the jarl's niece – and Summer Trade had been canceled for four years while the young towns feuded. The matter had finally been settled when Happdal's smith, Stian, had hacked off Tyr's head. The legend said that Stian boiled Tyr's head until the skull was clean, removed the jawbone, charred it over an open fire, then used a burned fragment of the smith's jaw to forge a soulsword.

"Are you thinking of the Rib Years?" Egil asked, interrupting Haakon's dark reverie. "We did not fare well during those times, according to my grandfather."

Haakon gripped the arm of his chair. The throne was made of solid oak, but he felt the wood give a little under his crushing grip. He relaxed his hand – he liked his chair and did not wish to wreck it on account of Egil's insolence. Perhaps he would crush Egil instead.

A commotion from outside saved the bard. Two of Haakon's guards entered the longhouse, holding a man between them. As they walked him forward, Haakon saw that the prisoner was merely a boy. The lad was tall and spindly, his face unlined and beardless. But he held Haakon's gaze, refusing to cower.

"He says he is from Happdal," said one of the guards. "He came unarmed."

"Let him go," commanded Haakon. "He can speak for himself." This could be interesting. At least it would be a break from Egil's sour advice. "Well?" he said to the boy.

"I am Karl Hinriksson," the boy said in a deep, strong voice. He straightened himself as the guards stepped away, and stared at Haakon boldly. The young man was tall and slender, with a well-formed face, but his skin had a greenish pallor, and he swayed slightly when the guards released him. "I bring you a gift from Happdal."

"Karl, son of Hinrik. Should I know that name?"

"You killed my father and raped my sisters. One of them died from her injuries."

A long silence fell in the longhouse, until Haakon laughed. "If that is true, then I cannot wait to see the gift you have brought for me. This day has been truly dull. But now you have arrived, with your gift and your sad tale, and my interest is piqued. What is your gift, young Karl Hinriksson?"

"You also killed my friend Jesper," said Karl, ignoring Haakon's question. When the boy spoke, Haakon saw that his teeth were stained brown. Did they not know how to clean their teeth in Happdal?

"All this killing," Haakon said. "I cannot keep it straight. Do you know who he speaks of, Egil?"

"Perhaps he speaks of the lookout," said the bard.

"The chubby one," Einar chimed in. "The one who spat on your boot. You crushed his head like a pumpkin."

"Oh, him," said Haakon. "Elke's spy. Is this Arik's official response? He sends a boy with a gift? Arik loves his peace. I raid Happdal, and he ignores me. I rape and kill, and he ignores me. I kill again, and he sends the son of a victim, with a gift.

"For I remember your father and your sisters now, boy. Your sisters were sweet. Though in truth I had only two of them. The one who died, well, we may blame that on Einar. He may be crippled and ugly, but in one area the Red Brother has seen fit to gift him. Within his trousers lies a great snake. And he is too stupid to use it gently."

"I remember!" Einar squealed. "I remember her!"

The boy turned deathly pale at Haakon's speech, but stood his ground. Haakon noticed Svein had slipped into the longhouse, and stood in the shadows, near Egil, observing. This riled Haakon for some reason; whenever Svein was in his sight he found himself wanting to impress the boy. Haakon sat up straighter in his chair and spoke loudly. "What is your gift? I tire of waiting."

"Elke said I should deliver the gift in the dead of night, but I choose to give it to you in the light of day, so I can see your face as you appreciate its meaning."

"*What* meaning? You madden me, Karl Hinriksson. My patience has a limit, you know. Shall we just have you flayed and be done with it? That would be a gift as well…a fine sight. Entertainment for all of Kaldbrek."

The boy slowly reached into his sleeve and drew out a tiny packet. He unwrapped the soft leather covering, revealing a small, rusted knife.

"A knife? You bring me a tiny, dirty knife? What kind of gift is that?" asked Haakon. Einar stepped forward and peered at the small blade. Even Egil sat up and looked, cautiously.

"It is a special knife," Karl said. "It is coated with venom from a long-nosed viper." It was eerie, hearing a man's deep voice come from a boy's face.

Haakon heard the soft sound of metal against leather. The guards had drawn their swords. He held up his hand, holding them at bay.

"And how do you propose to give me this gift, Karl Hinriksson?" he asked.

"I will stab you with it, and take pleasure in your death throes," said Karl. The guards looked to Haakon, eager to cut the boy down, but the jarl shook his head. He would do his own killing.

"Well said, boy. How many times have you practiced that line in your head? Perhaps you consider yourself a poet? You have a strong voice, you know, and something of a way with words. I do have a bard, right here, but he brings me no joy. Instead of poems and songs he offers me only bland advice. Perhaps, if I let you live, you can take his place." Of course he would not let the boy live. He *could* not, after such a threat. But it was refreshing to think of replacing Egil, who was as amusing as a sack of wet grain.

"Do you not fear for your own life, boy?" Egil asked. The bard had stood, and regarded Karl curiously, as if he were some strange animal as yet unseen in the Five Valleys.

"You cannot hurt me," said Karl. "None of you can hurt me."

At this, Einar shrieked with laughter. So long and hard did stupid Einar laugh that Haakon's guards began to chuckle, until Haakon scowled and lifted his hand, silencing them all.

"Very well," said Haakon. "Give me your gift."

Haakon remained seated as the boy approached. Karl's gaze was steady, but his hand trembled, and his face had no blood in it.

"Come, Karl Hinriksson, give me the gift."

The boy lashed out, quicker than Haakon had expected. But not quick enough. Haakon caught the boy's wrist in a viselike grip. He squeezed a little, until the bones cracked. The boy did not cry out, but his hand opened, and the knife fell to the ground. It was over.

"There, you have done your best," Haakon said gently. "Your

father would be proud, for you tried to avenge him, and your sisters. I admit you are courageous, and you bear pain well. How do you wish to die? Right here, in the longhouse, by my hand? Or shall we find a tree and hang you? The choice is yours, brave child."

In response the boy growled and pulled his wrist away with such force that Haakon stood, and found his arm extended out. Hinrik's son had strength in those twig arms! A second surprise: the boy was biting his arm. Haakon yelled in pain and rage, and released his grip. Still, the boy clung to his arm like a crazed marten, digging his stained teeth into Haakon's muscular forearm.

"Get him off!" he yelled to his guards. His men leapt forward and grabbed Karl, yanking him back. Still, the boy would not unclench his jaw, and ground his teeth into Haakon's wound.

Einar jumped about excitedly. "He bites! He bites! The Happdal boy is a rabid dog!"

Egil joined the fray, swinging his heavy oaken staff. Whatever his intent, he only managed to hit Einar, smacking him in the head. The result was a wet cracking sound, not unlike the splitting of a pumpkin, and Einar collapsed to the floor.

Finally the guards wrenched Karl away, holding him fast. Haakon examined the damage to his arm. Blood poured from the wound and dripped into his palm.

"I retract my earlier statement. *I* shall choose your death. You will die by *rista orn*."

The longhouse fell silent. Haakon watched his blood pool on the ground, slowly seeping into the packed earth. His arm hurt fiercely, and a great heat was growing in the wound.

Egil clutched his staff and stared at fallen Einar with wide eyes. "Was that an accidental blow, or did you mean to fell the cripple?" asked Haakon. Egil did not answer, but instead shifted his gaze to Haakon's arm, then to the boy.

"What trick have you played?" the bard asked. The boy smiled.

Haakon sat back down in his chair, feeling woozy. Somehow, he missed, and tumbled to the ground. The pain in his arm had faded a little, but the limb was swelling up, and his neck felt stiff. *What have you done to me?* He meant to say it, but his throat produced only a feeble croak.

Young Svein leapt forward and hit Karl in the gut, over and over again, while the guards held the Happdal spy. Each blow stained the cloth of the boy's shirt with a dark spot; each spot bloomed into a splotch, until his entire front was drenched. Svein held the fallen knife, and was stabbing Karl. Strangely, it was not enough to wipe the grin from the boy's face, even as he slumped in the grip of the guards.

Haakon spasmed, then discovered that he could no longer move his head, or even breathe. Einar's ugly face filled his field of vision, which was narrowing, darkening at the edges. Einar looked quite dead.

"Enough, Svein. Karl Hinriksson is slain." It was Egil who spoke. There was a long pause, then the bard's rich, rough voice rang out once more. It seemed Haakon would hear one final poem before he departed Midgard. For Haakon had finally realized the truth, that the clever boy had poisoned him.

Blood gushes from the jarl's wound
His smiling killer wears a shirt of red
The killer is a good son, who avenged his father's death
He became a man today, before he died

The same is true for Svein, the chieftain's son
Who also avenges his father
Who also becomes a man today

Young Svein Haakonsson
Will you take your father's chair?
Will you rule with a cruel grip, and lead us to ruin?
Or will you find a better way?

CHAPTER TWENTY-SEVEN

Katja worked alone, in the highest room of the monastery tower, afternoon light streaming in through the stained-glass windows. On the left side of her heavy wooden desk was a large stack of handmade paper, covered in her own writing. To her right was a pot of tea, now cool, delivered by a monk several hours earlier.

Zoë had brought her to the monastery only a few days ago, but it felt like much longer. Time passed slowly when you were working alone.

Katja put down the pen and flexed her hand. Zoë said that she clenched it too tightly. When she concentrated on her grip, she could manage it, but when her attention shifted to the material (she wrote out the algorithm, over and over again), her grip tightened, leaving her hand cramped and exhausted.

"Can you change my hand so that it will not tire?" she had asked Zoë. "It is not a real hand, after all."

"I could," Zoë had answered, "but writing is a good skill. You might as well learn it correctly. It might come in handy afterwards."

Afterwards. That's how Zoë referred to the time when she would initiate the algorithm within the Crucible, destroying herself and all her constructed worlds in the process. Katja would probably die as well. She would likely freeze to death immediately, unless the Crucible ejected itself from her body in time. If she managed to survive that process, there was still the question of the threads. Had they already taken over her vital functions, like breathing? If they had, she would die within minutes. And even if her body could still function on its own, she would be deaf and blind, probably unconscious, and completely helpless. Unless someone found her and helped her, she would die of exposure.

Still, they said *afterwards*, as if they were planning for real events that would really take place. For now, they were ignoring the certain fact of Zoë's end, and the almost certain fact of Katja's.

She stood and stretched, then descended the spiraling stone staircase to the bottom of the tower. On the ground floor, she passed a monk sweeping the floor.

"More tea, Lady Katja?" he asked, in Norse. He was young, bald, clean-shaven, and wore a thick, gray robe.

"No," said Katja, before quickly leaving the tower. She found it awkward to converse with the monks. Were they real or not? Zoë had said that their conversational skills were limited. They had no feelings or thoughts. But they *seemed* real; their speech seemed fluid and natural. *She* was the one limiting the conversations; she did not want to interact with them at all. She felt guilty for leaving quickly, for being rude when the monk had been polite. But the monk himself – at least according to Zoë – felt nothing.

Zoë was working in the garden, pulling weeds from between the carrots. Zoë had designed the weeds to be 'biologically accurate,' and now she dirtied her hands pulling them from the earth. She had also created the dirt itself; it teemed with worms and 'microbes' (extremely tiny creatures, too small to see, which did something good for the soil). Katja did not pretend to understand Zoë's obsession with creating things that already existed, but she was beginning to accept the trait. Her new friend was an artist, or at least a crafter. Zoë reveled in making things that worked, things that looked and acted *real*.

"I am done," said Katja. Zoë looked up and pushed her hair aside, leaving a smear of dirt across her forehead.

"You know it? You can write it?"

"Forward and backward," Katja answered. It was true. She had memorized the algorithm. She even knew what some of the symbols meant. Zoë had taught her the numerals zero through nine, and even how to write larger numbers using those numerals. She had learned the entire Greek alphabet as well. Most of the mathematical symbols still meant nothing to her, but she at least knew some of their names (and the ones she did not know, she could still draw the shapes).

Zoë stood and brushed her hands on her pants. "Show me," she said.

They returned to the tower, where Katja demonstrated that she could correctly transcribe the algorithm from memory. Zoë was pleased.

Later, at dinner (which they shared with a dozen or so monks), Zoë conversed and laughed with the men in a language Katja did not understand. "What tongue is that?" she asked.

"Latin," said Zoë. "And some Italian – the jokes at least. I didn't program that bit, how they switch up their language use. It's interesting. It makes me want to spend more time with them."

Zoë had said that the grounds and the monks were based on an eleventh-century monastery in Italy (a place directly south of Happdal, but quite far – perhaps half a year's march). The real monks had kept important scientific and historical knowledge alive during the 'Middle Ages,' copying manuscripts by hand. Katja had had to learn a great deal of Builder history just to understand what the Middle Ages were. As she studied the various historical eras, characterized by types of materials (ceramics, bronze, iron, steel, plastics), centers of power (warlords, kingdoms, dynasties, churches, corporations), and forms of communication (speech and song, writing, printing, invisible messages sent through the air), she began to see herself as part of a larger continuum. 'Builder' history was really *her* history. Human history. In any case, the monastery was an appropriate setting for Katja's work: the memorization of Zoë's algorithm.

"Pass the roast beef," said Zoë. Katja did so, but not before helping herself to a large pink slab.

After dinner, they relaxed in a small courtyard illuminated only by a crescent moon, starlight, and a few torches flickering in their sconces. The monks smoked long pipes, burning a floral, damp tobacco. They had offered a pipe to Katja, which she had turned down, but now she regretted that choice. The smoke had a delicious, seductive smell. She accepted the drink they offered, *grappa*, but regretted that as well; it burned her mouth and tasted foul. Zoë seemed to like it, and drank enough so that her speech began to slur.

"Maybe I'll delay the algorithm," Zoë mused. "Will you stay a little longer, if I do? This is nice here, isn't it?"

"The longer I stay, the less chance I have of living," said Katja. "Is that not right? You told me the threads would take over my breathing, my heartbeat – all the things my body should do on its own."

"Yesh," said Zoë, disappointed at having been reminded of the obvious.

"Or do you think my real body is already beyond saving? If so, you should just tell me."

Zoë shook her head. "No, you're right. We should do it as soon as possible. There's still a chance you'll live."

"What if I could get Raekae to make my body go to Happdal? Then, once I am there, you could start the algorithm. My real body would be among my friends and family...they could help me."

Zoë stared at the ground as if she had not heard. "How?" she finally asked.

"Perhaps I could convince him somehow."

Zoë shrugged. "It's worth a try, I guess. You should be careful. I can't protect you when you're with him. Here, in the worlds I've built, he's locked out. But he knows you're here."

"What can he do to me?" asked Katja. She noticed that the monks' conversation had paused. With her, they spoke Norse, so potentially they could understand her conversation with Zoë. Except that they were not capable of understanding. Maybe they had just run out of things to talk about.

"Raekae can manipulate your perceptions – he can change anything about your environment. Depending on how deep the threads have gotten, he can inflict pain." Zoë took another large sip of grappa. "Or invoke fear."

"Henning was scared, when we paid Raekae a visit. But I was not."

"That was days ago. The threads hadn't yet gotten to your amygdala. That might be different now."

Katja stood, feeling restless. "I can control my emotions. I am not weak-minded, like Henning. I will go to Raekae, and trick him into taking my body to Happdal. Even clever men can be tricked." Katja strode over to the young monk who had greeted her earlier in the tower and took the pipe from his hand. The other monks laughed. She put the stem to her lips and pulled the sweet smoke into her mouth. It tasted as good as it smelled.

"And another thing I wish to do – warn the others. Franz and Stian were kind to me. I like Stian especially. If they are to die, they should have some warning. Perhaps one of them would have me take a message to their descendants, should I survive. If I can learn your strange symbols, then I can also remember a line or two for each of them. I might even extend the offer to Henning."

"Whatever you tell them, that knowledge may make its way back to Raekae." Zoë seemed sober now, almost instantly. Perhaps she had simply decided to no longer be drunk.

"Henning may be traitorous, but I trust the other two."

"It's not a matter of trust. Raekae can peer into their minds at will. He can *become* them, merging his own consciousness with theirs. He controls the metamind."

Katja handed the pipe back to the young monk. "I heard Raekae mention the same word."

"It's a software layer within the operating system of the Crucible. Practically, it allows one mind within the Crucible to gain information from the others, or build a bridge between two minds. Telepathy, of sorts, but not always in both directions."

Katja knew about mind-reading. Ilsa – the healer crone – often it seemed as if she could read thoughts. The same was true of her own mother. "I heard voices in my head, before I was transported to this place. I remember hearing Franz's voice in particular, telling me about the rings in the sky. He said people lived on them." She looked up at the night sky above the monastery and saw thousands of stars, and the bright crescent moon, but no rings.

"That was Raekae using the metamind, building a bridge between your mind and the others. The threads had probably just begun to penetrate your auditory nervous system."

"Raekae seemed worried that someone could take over the metamind. He said Haakon – Kaldbrek's jarl – might try, if he were to use him as a host."

Zoë nodded. "I could have taken it over. Raekae would have been relegated to a mere mind, the same as Henning and Stian and Franz."

"What stopped you?" asked Katja. The monks had fallen silent again.

Zoë took a long moment to answer. One of the torches popped loudly. Finally she spoke. "I didn't want to be a jailor. And I didn't want to die, either. So I just locked him out, and started to build my own worlds."

It seemed a fair answer. Soon after, Katja asked Zoë how to return to the hut with the green door, to Raekae's world. Zoë told her. Katja bid her goodnight. She thought that it might be goodbye as well – depending on what happened when she confronted Raekae – but saying goodbye seemed too difficult.

★   ★   ★

She made her way through the jungle again, swatting aside both plants and insects, and finally found Zoë's hut. She passed through the door, and once again found herself disoriented. She was still *outside* of the structure. But now she stood on a well-manicured path, surrounded by landscaped gardens, breathing cool, dry air. The look of the place was different: the colors were less vibrant, details less vivid. Zoë was the better world-maker, she decided.

She found Stian first, sitting on a bench, a book on his lap. Once again the big smith reminded her of Jense, and she felt a pang of loneliness. Stian looked up and grinned at the sight of her. "What is it about?" she asked, motioning to the book. She still could not read, but the idea of reading a book for pleasure no longer seemed odd.

"Vikings," he said. "A Builder people. They seem similar to our kind – the people of the Five Valleys – but I do not know why."

"You will injure your mind if you think too hard," she advised.

Stian stood and embraced her awkwardly. She allowed it, but did not move her arms from her sides. "I have missed you," he said. "How was your journey? Did you find the hermit? Henning said you left to seek her out."

"I did. She is powerful – more powerful even than Raekae. More god than woman."

Stian raised an eyebrow but did not contradict her. "My memories of her are dim," he said. "I knew her before I learned to read, and my impressions were colored by my ignorance. But even then I thought she was keen-witted."

"Where are the others?" asked Katja. "I have grave news – you should all hear it together."

Katja told them to meet in her own hut. Henning came last, looking wary. "Sit," she told them, and they did so: Stian and Henning at the small table, Franz cross-legged on the floor. She remained standing, and looked at each of them in turn, letting the silence linger heavily. Franz adjusted his spectacles. Stian fiddled with his beard. Henning, reclining in his chair, wore his usual smirk. She would watch his face while she delivered the news, and see if she could wipe his smile away.

"I have found the hermit. As I told Stian, she is godlike in her powers. She intends to destroy this world, and all the worlds she has created, to begin anew. You will all die when this happens. It may be soon."

No one said anything at first. Franz looked out the window thoughtfully. Stian scowled. Henning looked incredulous. "She is bluffing," he said. "Why do you think she has such power?"

"I saw her change the world at will. Raekae has no power over her. She knows what this place is – she calls it the Crucible – and she knows how to control it."

"I do not believe you," said Henning. "If there is a god here, it is Raekae. He can reach into our hearts and fill them with fear."

Stian nodded. "This is Raekae's place – we are mere guests here."

"You are prisoners, not guests!" Katja thundered, slapping the table with her palm. "I should cut off your beard, smith. You talk like a frightened boy, not a man."

Stian shrugged. "What can we do? We have tried to fight him. He cannot be killed."

"Zoë can kill him," she said. "She will, too. This place is ending. All of it." She put her hand on Stian's broad shoulder, and continued more calmly. "All of you will die. But as the host, I might survive. A slim chance, but a chance nonetheless. If I live, is there anything... is there a message you would have me take back? I could remember words from each of you, and deliver them."

There was a long silence, which Franz finally broke. "Everyone I know is dead," he said, matter-of-factly. "I have no message."

"The same is true for me," said Stian, "but if there is a smith in

Happdal, send him my greetings." Katja smiled at this. Both Jense and her brother would delight in a greeting from Stian, if she ever had a chance to give it.

"What about you, ancestor?" she said to Henning. She had no love for him, but her dislike was tinged with pity. If he had words for someone, she would take them back if she could. But he merely stared at her coldly.

"I didn't believe in an afterlife," said Franz, from his floor seat, "but I found myself here. Maybe I will live again in another world."

"Perhaps I will finally see Valhalla," Stian said. "I am cheerful enough in this place, but deep down I tire of it. I tire of you two especially," he said, looking to Franz and Henning in turn.

Franz nodded. "The feeling is mutual," he said without rancor. "And I don't fear death – at least not yet. It will be a change at least, even if only to oblivion."

Henning said nothing throughout this, but Katja was satisfied to see that his smirk was gone. "Why so sad, Henning?" she teased cruelly.

To her surprise, he answered honestly, with tears forming in his eyes. "I am sad for my wife. If she still lived, I would ask you to bring her greetings from me, and to tell her that I missed her fiercely for many years, and to say that I am sorry. She never knew why I left, and I could never tell her. Now she is dead, and my children are dead."

Katja had nothing more to say after this, and soon after Franz and Henning left. Stian lingered, which she did not mind, and they spoke of Happdal. But after a stretch of silence fell between them, the smith also bid her farewell.

Two days later, while Katja was walking alone in the woods, she felt a cold pain in her gut, and doubled over. She clutched her stomach and rolled onto her back. It was noon, but the sky itself dimmed, and the trees around her froze in place, as if they were mere paintings. "What is happening?" she said to no one, and no one answered. Her last thought, as her vision dimmed, was of the emerald ocean, and swimming with Zoë, with the tail of a fish.

CHAPTER TWENTY-EIGHT

Ilsa's house had not been so full in years, not since her children and their many friends had roamed the halls and warmed the beds. She remembered young Arik, her sister's boy, leading the pack even then. Her own children and the rest of their little tribe had followed Arik because of his fairness and thoughtfulness. His temperament had stayed steady over the years; Happdal was lucky to have such a jarl. They had prospered because of it. Men and women devoted their energies to growing and building things, instead of fighting and raiding.

Their friends in Kaldbrek were not so lucky. Ilsa wondered, as she mixed the tonic, what Karl's fate might be. Ilsa was no fool – she knew how Elke used the village boys as instruments in her own plots. Karl, filled with righteous anger – he was the one she would send with Haakon's gift.

The gift: a paste made from viper venom, extract of spotted hemlock, crushed thornapple fruit, and a powder of green death cap. If Karl had delivered it to Haakon, then Kaldbrek's future had changed. Would it be a brighter one? It was impossible to say. But murdering Haakon could not be a bad thing. At least that is what Ilsa told herself, and hoped was true.

Now she made the opposite, a mixture that would heal – or so she hoped. First she ground the ingredients into a paste: crystallized honey, crushed garlic, dried sage, fresh mint, a dash of red rock powder. Then she stirred in mead until the concoction was of a drinkable consistency. In truth, she had no idea if the tonic would help. All three of her wards were in dire shape. But the medicine was unlikely to cause harm. Watching Esper as he tended to the small brown woman, Ilsa knew she had to try something. Elke's boy was in love.

She went to them first. The brown woman lay still, though

earlier Ilsa had seen her thrash about, yelling incoherently. Esper sat next to the bed on a wooden stool, holding the woman's hand. He had not left her side since their return earlier that day. The brown woman had looked limp and lifeless in Trond's arms, but there was still some fight in her. "Hold her head up," instructed Ilsa, and Esper did so gently. The woman's eyes fluttered. "Hold her mouth open," said Ilsa.

Esper complied. "Her name is Car-En," he said.

She poured a little of the mixture into Car-En's mouth, but the woman spat it out. She stared at Ilsa, disoriented but angry, the brown fluid running down her chin and dripping onto her silvery, skin-like garment. "She is not herself," said Esper.

"I know," said Ilsa. Elke's boy wanted more than healing. He wanted acceptance: for the sky woman, and for his own choice in bringing her to Happdal. "We will help her," she said. "Hold her mouth open again." With some persistence, they got some of the sweet tonic inside of the strange woman.

In the other room, Katja lay in a single bed, with Jense sitting on the floor beside her. In the corner, the lost boy – now fully grown, but sick – sat in a chair, staring mutely at the wall. Trond had wanted to stay with them, but Ilsa had sent him off; the room was too small to house both giant smiths. The lost boy seemed placid, not dangerous, and if there was any protecting to do, Jense could do it.

She recognized the lost boy, faintly. Per Anders. He had disappeared years ago, a long walk that had lasted seven summers. He had returned fully grown, but not quite a man. Poisoned by the mushrooms, Per Anders was a shadow of his former self. He seemed to understand very little, and stared dumbly at whatever was before him, unless he hungered. His appetite had not left him; he preferred raw meat, and consumed it readily (despite a few missing teeth). Ilsa had washed him, and put ointment on his many scratches, but his mind was damaged. She did not know if she could help him.

Ilsa poured half of the remaining tonic into a ceramic mug and handed it to Per Anders. He gazed at it but did not move to take it. "Drink!" she commanded. He took the cup. "Drink it," she said more softly. Still, he just stared. She moved his hand, and the mug with it, to his lips, and as soon as the sweet mixture touched his tongue, he remembered how to drink from a vessel, and drained it.

"We will see if that helps him," said Ilsa. "I do not think it will."

"What about Katja?" Jense asked.

Ilsa stood over the bed and looked at Elke's daughter. Even so thin and pale, the girl was beautiful, not so different than Elke in her youth. Thin, black lines formed a spiderweb beneath her translucent skin. Jense said that Katja had been possessed by a spirit – the gast – but that he had driven it from her body.

Ilsa placed her hand on the girl's chest. Her heartbeat was slow, but steady. Though her face had no color, she was breathing well enough. Ilsa had no idea how to cure her, but perhaps she could keep her alive. "Where is Elke?" asked Ilsa. Jense shrugged. Katja's mother had visited earlier. She had stared down at her daughter impassively, not touching her, saying nothing.

"Elke is cold-hearted," said Jense. "She cares only for herself." Ilsa knew neither statement was true, but she let the words stand. Jense's heart and mind would always be clouded when it came to Elke. That was his own fault – no one had made him bed the jarl's wife. But at least one good thing had come out of that mess. Trond was a fine man, and who could hold a grudge against Jense and Elke for producing such a fine human being? Even cuckolded Arik had eventually forgiven them, and accepted Trond as a full son. Someday someone would have to tell the boy himself, for while he was not stupid, to this one fact he seemed blind.

Ilsa handed Jense the jug that held the remainder of the tonic. She dipped a clean cloth into the fluid, gently opened Katja's mouth, and squeezed a few drops of the fragrant mixture onto her tongue. "Very slowly," she instructed. "Too fast and she might choke. Keep her head up – two pillows." Jense nodded. She trusted the smith, both his hands and his heart. No one loved Katja more. Whether that love was wise – that was another question. But for now, Jense's dedication would keep the girl alive. She handed him the wet cloth.

Her hands now free, she lifted the girl's shirt and checked the wound. Jense's sword had bitten deep. The blade had nicked her bladder; Ilsa had seen blood in the girl's urine. Ilsa feared the blade might have gone deeper, piercing Katja's womb, but she had no way of knowing.

At least the cut was not wide. Ilsa had closed it with a short length of thread. She had spread a thick coat of honey over her work, which was now mixed with blood, but there was no pus that Ilsa could see. She put her face close to Katja's belly and sniffed. Honey, the girl's own musky scent, and a strange, sharp odor Ilsa could not name. But no rot; the wound was clean.

"Ilsa! Come!"

It was Esper's voice. Ilsa was not so old that she could not run from room to room. A moment later she stood in the other doorway, witness to an odd sight.

The brown-skinned woman was ripping off the silver suit, or trying to. The material was both flexible and strong, and the woman was no less clothed for her struggles. "Let me help," said Esper. He pulled on something, and the suit split down the side, as if he were skinning a beast. The woman yielded to Esper's touch, and soon she stood naked before them. She kicked the silvery skin into the corner.

Her body was scrawny and undernourished, but aside from her skin color, her appearance was normal: small breasts that had not held milk, a light covering of hair on her pubic mound, a flat belly never stretched by a full womb.

"*Brenna*," she said. Her accent was strange; it took a moment for Ilsa to understand. She was pointing at the silvery garment. *Burn it.*

"Can you find her some clothes?" asked Esper. Ilsa nodded and left the room, hiding her smile. She smiled in part because of Esper's love; the feeling echoed in her own heart. But mostly she was happy that her medicine had somehow helped the girl. At least one of her wards would live.

CHAPTER TWENTY-NINE

Trond and Arik led the men – and a few boys as well – up the High Pass toward the ridge. Trondfist, the great warhammer, was slung over Trond's back, along with the soulsword Taker, and a pack stuffed with provisions. Behind them marched Jansen, and Jansen's eldest son, who was thick-armed from farm work. Both father and son carried spears and wore hardened leather armor. The next ranks were made up of eager boys hefting makeshift weapons. Jalmar and Gregers, pulled from the mines, had their picks. Grim-faced Grundar wore his usual scowl and carried a sickle. Grundar's younger brother, just as blond but more cheerful than his sibling, proudly gripped a small knife. Behind them walked Lars, who was always eager to swing his sword, and Karina, Hinrik's middle daughter and sister to Karl, who had insisted on coming. Farrel and Gustav (the latter armed with a rusty mudsteel blade) brought up the rear. Trond had offered to forge the cobbler a new weapon, but Gustav had politely refused, insisting that the sword (gifted to him by his farfar) could cut as well as any.

"Karl is dead, or captured," Elke had told them. She had confessed her plot to her husband and sons after the homecoming feast. It angered Trond to hear that his mother had sent a boy to his almost certain death, but as usual Arik forgave his wife.

"She only wishes to protect us," his father had later said. "And besides, it was Karl's right to avenge his father's death. At least to try."

"Perhaps," Trond had answered, "but he should not have gone alone. We all have business with Haakon."

"And so we march, tomorrow. Time to end this feud." Arik had not said 'one way or another,' but Trond heard the words in his mind nonetheless, and wondered if he could best Haakon in a fight. He thought that he probably could, but in truth the incident with the giants (being hunted and captured and nearly eaten) had shaken him. Perhaps he was not so strong and mighty as others thought.

They were a small group – no war party – for Arik hoped it would not come to war. What if Karl had succeeded and Kaldbrek had a new leader? Why not make peace? Trond could see no sense in his father's thinking. Why would they be warmly greeted if a Happdal boy had slain the Kaldbrek jarl? Still, he obeyed his father, and stuffed his pack with peace offerings: wheels of cheese from Harald, tiny boxes of herbal ointments from Ilsa, jars of pickles from Elke. Others carried sacks of grain, whole honeycombs, dried fishes, and fermented fish paste.

Trond's heavy load – the two great weapons and several large wheels of cheese – was a welcome relief. The pain in his legs served to distract him from his own thoughts. There was much to dwell on. Jense, soon after returning to Happdal with Katja in his arms, had insisted on meeting Trond in the smithy. There, with the heavy oaken door closed, cloth pulled over the windows, and the furnace filled with cold ash, Jense had confessed to Trond that there was a *fifth* secret of godsteel, and that he, Jense, had been wrong to keep it from Trond for so long. Jense told him the story of the twin soulswords, Biter and Taker, and how to trap the soul of a man in a blade, using a bit of burned bone. He showed Trond the actual blades, which had been in Katja's possession, and also a strange knife, the makings of which were a mystery to Jense. Trond thought he might know the story of the knife, but he said nothing, for his mind was already racing, and he found the act of speech to be difficult under such circumstances.

The godsteel secret was a revelation (though Trond doubted he would use the technique – it sounded dangerous), but mostly Trond dwelled on his sister, who seemed in poor shape. At least the sky woman was well again; Ilsa had cured her quickly. As for Per Anders.... Well, he was home, and in good hands, and no longer wandering lost in the woods.

As they crested the ridge, they saw a tall man stumbling toward them. His face was smeared with blood, both eyes were bruised, and his black hair was hacked short (by a dull blade from the looks of it). He limped, relying heavily on a long staff, and did not notice their group until Arik hailed him.

"Greetings, wanderer!" called Arik. The man lifted his gaze from the ground and examined their party dubiously, as if trying to decide if they were real or illusory. "We come from Happdal, on our way to Kaldbrek," said Arik. "Who are you, and what is your destination?"

"Do not go to Kaldbrek," the man said. "You will be slaughtered."

Trond's impulse was to contradict this statement, but he held his tongue. Perhaps he *could* be killed. He remembered the large hands of the giantess, spreading rancid grease over his body, preparing him for the roast. What if Esper and the sky woman had not rescued him? If that were the case, he would now exist only as giant spoor. Certainly no man was stronger than Trond, but strength did not grant one immunity against death.

"I know you," said Arik. "Egil the Bard, advisor to Haakon. What has happened to you?"

Egil shrugged. "Haakon is dead. Your boy killed him. The new master has no love for me – I am exiled." The bard's voice was harsh and gravelly, impossible to ignore.

"Does the boy Karl live?" Trond asked.

Egil snorted and spat; a yellow glob streaked with red landed in the dirt. "No," said Egil. "The new jarl killed him, though truthfully I think he would have died from the poison. He coated his own teeth with the stuff, and bit Haakon."

Arik raised his eyebrows. "Indeed."

"Clever," said Egil, "and ruthless. The boy thirsted for vengeance."

Karina pushed through to the front. "I am glad Haakon is dead," said Hinrik's daughter. "I hope his death was painful, and filled with shame."

"It was," Egil admitted. "And many share your sentiment. Truthfully, I count myself in that group, for Haakon was cruel and unwise. But the death of a cruel man does not necessarily lead to good things. The new master is worse."

"Who?" asked Arik.

"Svein, son of Haakon."

"We come to Kaldbrek in peace," said Arik. "Will this Svein Haakonsson not accept our gifts and begin anew?"

"Look at my face," Egil said. "Does this look like the work of a reasonable man? Svein is crazy with rage and drunk with power. Karl killed his father, whom he hated, but his father's death brings him no peace – only fury and discontentment. The boy's heart is closed to forgiveness, his mind unmoored from reason."

"A fine leader, then," said Arik. Egil smiled darkly.

"What will you do?" Trond asked.

"Wander the mountain trails until I starve? I do not know. I had thought to come to your village and surrender myself to you, Arik. Will you grant me food and shelter? In return I can tell you sour tales, and sing you sad songs."

Arik thought on this for a long moment, and Trond wondered if he was considering how Elke might react. But Arik turned to Karina. "Was this man among those who killed your father and your sister, who attacked you and Kristin?"

Karina shook her head. "No."

"I am many things," said Egil, "but I am no raper, nor a murderer of innocents."

"Very well," said Arik. "Go to Elke," he said to Egil, "and tell her I said not to flay you. That is the most I can offer."

Egil nodded and shuffled along. As he passed, Trond offered the bard his waterskin. Egil drank from it deeply and handed it back without thanks. The bard continued on his way and did not look back.

"Well, what do you think? On to Kaldbrek?" asked Arik. He spoke to Trond directly, as an equal, and Trond was forced to quench his pride so that he could consider the actual question.

"That seems unwise," interjected Farrel, who had come forward from the back. "This new jarl will not welcome us. Kaldbrek is in flux...should we not wait?"

"Flux is good," said Trond. "Before the metal has cooled – that is the time to shape it. We should continue on."

Arik patted Trond on the shoulder. "Well said, my son. We will do as you advise." Arik led the way along the ridge trail, and the others followed.

★   ★   ★

Trond's spirits rose as they descended into the lush valley. In the distance, they saw a few sheep grazing on the steep, verdant hills. Perhaps Arik was right; maybe Svein could be reasoned with. Maybe Trond had not seen his last Summer Trade.

They walked into Kaldbrek unchecked. The villagers gave them dark looks but only a mangy dog approached, smelling the food in their packs. Trond shooed it away. The men and women looked thin, tired, and sour; the children walked when they should have been running. Despite the sheep and green hills, there was hunger here.

Six men wielding spears stopped them as they neared the longhouse. The tallest stepped forward to challenge them, but Arik spoke first. "I am Arik, jarl of Happdal. Take us to Svein Haakonsson!" Trond was impressed by the strength of his father's voice, which had taken on a commanding, irresistible tone. The Kaldbrek guard stepped back as if slapped.

"I will see if the jarl will grant you an audience," he muttered.

"Do that," said Arik.

One of the younger guards scurried off, and soon returned. "Arik may enter the longhouse, and one other," he said breathlessly.

"Bring Farrel," Trond said. "I will stay with the others."

"No," said Arik, "I would rather have you by my side." Farrel was wise, and no doubt loyal, but Arik disliked him. The old man spent too much time with Arik's wife, and drank too much of his *öl*.

"We will be fine," Lars said quietly. "These men are too weak from hunger to cause trouble."

"Very well," said Trond, touching the pommel of his dirk. His father was already leading the way, flanked by guards on either side. "Follow us to the longhouse," Trond said to Lars, "and bring the food."

At the entrance to the longhouse, the guards asked for their weapons.

"We come to make peace," said Arik. "So I will give you my sword for safekeeping. My dirk I will keep."

"I will hand over Trondfist, if you are strong enough to lift it.

The sword is a gift for young Svein. I will also keep my dirk."

"I will carry the sword for you," the tall guard said. Trond gave him the longsword Taker, and put Trondfist on the ground. Two of the Kaldbrek men were able to lift the warhammer together and carry it awkwardly to the side of the longhouse, where they leaned it against the wall. His load lightened, Trond took the provisions from the others: sacks of grain, honeycomb wrapped in paper, jars of preserved fruit, dried beef, and a sack filled with fresh loaves. Arik entered the longhouse. Trond followed, carrying the many gifts.

The interior was dim and smoky. The young jarl sat in his chair, surrounded by guards and servants. The room smelled foul: too many bodies, acrid smoke, and a hint of rot.

"What brings you to my village, Arik?" asked Svein. The boy had dark hair, narrow blue eyes, and a weak chin. A long scar ran along his right cheek.

"Is it *your* village?" Arik asked. "What happened to Haakon?"

"My father is dead. I am jarl now. You know as much – you sent his assassin. I should thank you, for you have done Kaldbrek a great service. Haakon was a terrible leader, and much hated."

Trond coughed; the bad air irritated his lungs. He counted the spearheads in the room. Seven, that he could see. And no doubt twice as many hidden knives.

"Yes. It was we who sent Karl to kill Haakon," said Arik. "Haakon murdered his father Hinrik, and raped his three sisters, killing one. It was his right to exact vengeance."

"It was cowardly to send a boy. You should have come yourself, to accuse us," said Svein. His mouth writhed as he spoke, as if he did not entirely control his own face.

"In truth he was sent without my knowledge, but I take responsibility," Arik said. "Has there not been enough death? Can we now make peace between Kaldbrek and Happdal?"

Svein leaned forward, making a tent with his fingers. "Have you come to apologize for causing my father's death?"

"I owe you no apology," said Arik. "Haakon deserved to die. And as I heard it, you have already exacted your revenge upon poor Karl. The score is even."

The dim light from the fire pit reflected off the steel heads of the long spears. The weapons rippled like tall grass in the wind after Arik spoke.

"Perhaps children are not taught proper counting in Happdal," said Svein. "Your tally is wrong. Happdal trickery has felled but one man – my father – while Haakon and his brutes killed a man and his daughter, as well as the lookout boy. And the assassin you sent – I killed him myself. That makes four. Even if you count the death of poor Einar, who died in the fray, and the loss of Egil, who I have forced into exile on account of his disobedience, you are still down one. How can I trust you under such circumstances? Perhaps you *can* count, and have come to even the score."

Trond furrowed his brow. What was Svein up to? Could he not accept peace when it was offered to him? "Give him the sword," said Trond to the guard. At that moment he was glad the guard had taken the weapon from him, for he had no free hand to hold it himself. He wished to place the many sacks and packages of food down on the ground, but Arik had not yet made any mention of gifts, so he continued to hold them in his arms.

"What is this?" Svein asked, when the longsword was handed to him. "A gift?"

"No," said Trond, "it is a man. A soulsword, binding the captured soul of Tyr the Lusty, of Kaldbrek. Your ancestor, if you are truly the son of Haakon. Tyr was slain by the smith Stian, who then chopped off his head, boiled off the flesh, roasted the skull, and forged a godsteel weapon with black from the jawbone. The sword is named Taker, for Tyr took what he wanted when he lived. The sword is your fourth man. The score is even."

Svein drew the sword from its sheath, and the room fell silent while they all gazed upon the weapon. The steel was old and tarnished, but unblemished, and the blade was long and beautifully shaped. Svein inhaled deeply. "You are a fool to gift me this weapon. I feel a bloodlust when I hold it."

"Then sheathe it," said Arik, "for we want no war with you. Enough blood has been spilled. Look, we have brought trade goods. Would you not share in our bounty and let us share in yours? Your sheep produce fine wool, which we could sorely use when winter comes."

At his father's cue, Trond laid out the provisions (a relief – his arms had begun to ache), as well as the cheeses, ointments, and pickles from his own pack. Arik produced dried fishes and fermented fish paste. "There is much more," Arik said, "but these goods are yours to keep."

An appreciative murmur rose from Svein's servants and guards, but the young jarl scowled. "You Happdal folk overvalue your own cheese. To my taste it is overly salted and aged too long. I prefer our own fresh sheep's cheese."

"But is there enough of it?" said Trond. "I have yet to see a fat man in Kaldbrek."

"We are not so fat as you Happdal folk, but there is food here. And there will be more. I have only been jarl for a few days – do not be so quick to judge."

The room fell silent while Svein's servants gazed hungrily upon the laid-out food.

"Let us meet for Summer Trade," Arik said in a gentle voice. "High solstice approaches. We will host this year, next year we will come to Kaldbrek, the third year we will go to Skrova, if they will have us."

Svein shook his head. "No. We will not march into Happdal to be slaughtered. Or roasted alive, should we fall ill."

"Only the Afflicted are Burned, and they choose it," Trond said angrily.

"Do they?" said Svein. "Not even one decides to live out their natural life?"

"Then host at Kaldbrek this year, and Happdal the next," said Arik, ignoring the jibe. "We will come to you."

Svein looked away. "I have heard enough. Escort them out." Trond gripped the pommel of his dirk, furious at this display of disrespect toward his father, but Arik shook his head and turned his back on Svein. Trond followed Arik to the door.

"I bid you goodbye," said Arik, calling over his shoulder, "but our offer stands."

"Yes, scurry off!" Svein shouted. "You are not welcome here. Do not return!"

Arik turned at the door and pointed at Svein. "If you hunger during the winter, do not be tempted to raid us. Taker has a sister blade, with the soul of a wolf. If you raise a hand against us, I will use it to bite off your head."

Svein stood. "Threatening words from the peace-loving jarl. You do not scare me. Off with you! Or should I have you split open, and your lungs pulled out of your back?" The young jarl's face twisted into a ghastly grimace and spittle ran down his chin.

"Enjoy the cheese," said Trond, and pulled his father out of the longhouse.

Outside, Trond retrieved Trondfist from its place against the wall, and a guard handed Arik's sheathed sword back to him, avoiding eye contact. They rejoined the others, who had passed the time unbothered. Together they left Kaldbrek, hastily.

They walked in silence for the better part of an hour, eager to put distance between them and the mad jarl. With empty packs, their pace was quick. Trond found himself invigorated, and soon he and Arik were ahead of the others. Stopping to let the group catch up, Trond asked his father for a swig of water. His own skin was empty.

"Perhaps it was unwise to visit Kaldbrek," said Arik. "I was warned – both by you and by the exiled bard. Svein Haakonsson is not a sane man."

"No man at all," said Trond, "just a scared boy."

"Whatever he is, I fear that Happdal is not yet safe."

"At least we know," Trond said. "And it was good of you to try for peace."

"I failed," said Arik. Trond shrugged, but he saw that the burden of leadership weighed heavily on his father. Trond noticed the lines on his face, and his eyes looked tired. Arik would not be jarl forever. Would Trond take his place, in time? He was the eldest son, but in truth he hoped that Esper would be jarl. His brother was the wise one. Trond was happiest with a hammer in one hand and a rod of hot steel in the other.

"You did what you could," Trond said. "I am proud to have you as my father, and my jarl." Arik gave him a strange look, and opened his mouth to speak, but Trond interrupted: "Look – the slowpokes have caught up with us! With any luck we will make it home before nightfall. I hope that Mother has saved us some stew."

CHAPTER THIRTY

Excerpt from 'The Four Phases of Earth Depopulation' by Lydia Heliosmith, age 17, written for *Terrestrial Anthropology 1*, 22.01.02719:

Phase 3: Campi Flegrei

Campi Flegrei, also known as the Phlegraean Fields, was a geographical region of Italy, west of Naples, famous for its wine, wildlife preserves, military history, underwater cities, historical tombs, and mythological significance (the crater Solfatara being home to Vulcan, the Roman god of fire, and Lake Avernus/Lago Averno being the entrance to the underworld, as described by Virgil).

The region was also home to Italy's largest supervolcano, a vast cauldron containing more than twenty craters formed by previous eruptions. Prior to 2387 there had been no major eruption for over twelve thousand years (the most recent occurring toward the end of the Epigravettian period of the Upper Paleolithic, and coinciding with a massive megafauna die-off and the subsequent migration of surviving human populations to the coastal regions). An even earlier eruption, approximately 37,500 years earlier, played a role in the transition from the Middle Paleolithic (Neanderthal-dominated) to the Upper Paleolithic (Homo sapiens-dominated).

Prior to the 2387 eruption (predicted decades earlier), there were three basic modes of preparedness. The first was to ignore the impending disaster, instead relying on supernatural intervention or good luck. A small, stubborn cohort of Italians and southern Europeans chose this option; all of them were annihilated. Those who were not immediately incinerated were suffocated; those who survived suffocation starved in the following months. The sky was too dark to grow food locally, and the airborne ash dimmed the entire stratosphere, reducing crop yields on every continent and gutting international food aid.

More sensible residents evacuated. North of the Alps was relatively safe; the Mistral protected central France, and northerly blowing winds protected most of Africa. Evacuees moved to those areas, or beyond. Despite the welcoming official immigration policies of many nations, actual immigration proved difficult. Thousands of towns and cities doubled in size over the course of a few months. Most communities lacked the infrastructure and goodwill to handle the influx of refugees. Crime rose, as did xenophobia and nationalism.

The third mode of preparedness was Earth emigration. The Campi Flegrei eruption had been predicted for decades; those with the means and foresight had plenty of time to wrangle passage onto a ringstation. There were many ways to emigrate into orbit. Many professions were actively recruited: scientists and engineers, teachers and professors, medical professionals, farmers and biodynamicists, artists and musicians, city planners and public health experts. The next wave bought their way on with money or influence: entrepreneurs, celebrities, politicians and their families. Some ascended the elevators on temporary work visas and found ways to stay. Others found ways to sneak on. The ringstation populace was not an even slice of humanity; the qualities that gained individuals their initial ascension were overrepresented.

Who controlled the ringstations? While most began as joint ventures between nations and corporations (or in some cases extremely wealthy individuals), without exception they declared independence within a decade or two. Each ringstation was a sovereign entity. Who would say differently? No nation had the military capability to touch an orbiting ringstation, especially one that decided to undock from a space elevator and enter asynchronous orbit, or even traverse the solar system (as did the Michelangelo*).* China *protested when the* Liu Hui *defected, but had no space-faring military force to back up their threats.*

As the ash clouds spread throughout the lower atmosphere, choking off the planet from its main source of warmth and energy, not all nations and peoples fared the same. Smaller, more sparsely populated countries endured the hunger with fewer fatalities, as did nations with higher levels of social trust and co-operation. But few countries remained intact. Most balkanized into regional territories, organized around agricultural areas and fresh water sources, each region declaring militia-backed independence. Many nations tried to suppress secession movements with military force.

The typical result was mass defection from the military; soldiers were too hungry and demoralized to care about national borders.

When the troops didn't defect, the results were worse. The East American Boston Massacre of 2399 dwarfed the carnage of the original event of the same name. Stormtroopers fired on thousands of men and women, young and old, without discrimination. In hindsight, it was the dying gasp of the old system. No longer did any major nation state hold the slightest shred of moral authority.

The end of the powerful nation state also meant the end of globalism. International trade routes, vulnerable to piracy at sea and banditry over land, dissolved. Passports became meaningless; regional borders could now only be crossed stealthily, or via barter and bribe. Without international trade, industrial manufacturing died. Regional companies focused on producing what people needed to live: food, clothing, shelter, batteries, generators, and weapons. It was the beginning of technological devolution. Major internet cables were severed, never to be repaired. Wireless transmitter hubs were sabotaged. Satellites fell out of the sky. The world became disconnected. Technology reversed its 'inevitable' march forward.

Some nations maintained the facade of 'civilization' far longer than others. The stalwart Norwegians, the stolid Canadians, the even-tempered Japanese: these countries maintained order and national identity long after their southern neighbors descended into regionalism or chaos. Climate had something to do with it; it seemed that in cooler countries, cooler emotions prevailed. But the eruption of Campi Flegrei provided a climactic twist. The ashen sky immediately erased any lingering Anthropocenic temperature gains. Global cooling was immediate and persistent. Greenhouse gas emissions had been falling (in lockstep with human population) for over three centuries, but 2387 proved to be the last year of the Holocene, a warming epoch that had stretched twelve thousand years (the entire course of human history), an 'interglacial' respite from the Quaternary Ice Age. The ash eventually cleared from the sky, but industrial manufacturing never recovered, and even the return of burning wood and coal for fuel could not produce enough carbon dioxide to offset the absence of cars and trucks on the roads, planes in the sky, and ships on the sea. Global temperature dropped seven degrees Celsius. Glaciers that had once retreated now advanced, farther south than had ever been observed in human history, and over the next few hundred years the 'lucky' northern countries were essentially erased by kilometers-high walls of moving ice.

So why did Earth continue to depopulate? While the actual eruption killed hundreds of thousands, and millions more starved to death in the years that followed, it was ultimately human choice that led to fewer human beings on Earth. Humans lost many advanced technologies, but birth control was not one of them. More women than ever before chose not to become mothers. They would live out their own days as best they could, but why bring a helpless baby into such a cruel, dark world? While hope and optimism reigned on the ringstations, despair was the mood below. By 2400, mean global birthrate had fallen to 1.2, far less than replacement. By 2450 (the beginning of the Remnant Age), world population had fallen to under a billion.

Two hundred years later, that number would be under ten thousand, with the majority of Earth inhabitants descended from unbroken lines of hunter-gatherer cultures (those who had clung to their traditional ways, never adopting modern technology).

The vast majority of human beings would live in space.

11.06.02727, Earth

Adrian drove as they sped east along the Mediterranean coast. As promised, the hovershuttle was easy to operate. It was fast, too, though the ride was smoother if they stayed close to the ground. The shuttle had a number of built-in safety features: stabilizers and speed checks and collision avoidance systems, all of which Adrian was thankful for. It wasn't as if they were riding a rocket, but it was new tech, and relatively untested.

The hardest part had been unpacking the thing from its cargo cube at the mule station. There was a light crew there to help them, but even so it was more strenuous work than Adrian was used to. Once they got the parts laid out, the hovershuttle mostly self-assembled, but by that time Adrian was sweaty and disheveled. Troy, on the other hand, reveled in the process, and kept pointing out design and construction details that highlighted the brilliance of the engineers. Adrian kept looking out the window nervously. It was his first time on Earth, and while the gravity was the same, the open sky was disconcerting. The horizon looked wrong too, flat and endless, with no gentle upward slope.

Now, breathing the ocean air and feeling the salt spray on his face, Adrian felt more relaxed. The coastal route was a detour, but they had time to spare. Their mission was simple: scout several possible locations for Vander Camp. They were racing toward Adrian's destiny.

Xenus Troy was proving to be a tolerable traveling companion, a good conversationalist but not too chatty. He was a good pick for Research Coordinator. With both Adrian and Penelope backing him, he'd been elected nearly unanimously, with only Svilsson abstaining. Perhaps the quiet man had wanted the position for himself (but since he said nothing, it was impossible to know). It was more likely that Svilsson was abstaining on principle, considering that he had voted against the research station itself. In the end only Svilsson and Kardosh had voted against it. Polanski had stayed loyal to Adrian. Troy had taken the bait and approved the proposal, eager to lead the terrestrial research effort. And in the end he had cut a deal with Townes. He hadn't wanted to, but she'd made him an offer he couldn't refuse.

Adrian himself would be Station Director. Troy had nominated him, and nobody else wanted the job. Repop Council had acknowledged, implicitly, that the research station was his brainchild. He was the visionary. Vander Camp. He still hadn't said the name out loud, but in time he would. Maybe first as a joke. Was there a way to make a joke of it, and make it sound self-deprecating? How did one make self-deprecating humor? You had to highlight one of your weaknesses. Did he have any weaknesses?

"Look," said Troy, pointing out toward the sea. A pod of dolphins swam parallel to the hovershuttle, less than fifty meters away. Every so often they leapt from the water, propelling themselves with powerful flukes, flying through the air in shallow arcs. "Did you know this sea is filled with coral reefs? The ocean floor was completely barren during the Corporate Age, but it's recovered now. It must be a regular fish buffet out there."

"They do look well-fed," Adrian said. He had to admit the animals were graceful and impressive, even though they didn't really interest him. But the cetaceans and other wildlife would interest others; there would be no shortage of zoologists and biologists who would want residency at Vander Camp. He would welcome them, and encourage them to set up research facilities. It would all create inertia toward a permanent settlement. In time, Vander Camp would become Vandertown.

Adrian would resign his position as the head of the anthropology department – that was part of his deal with Townes. He would be busy enough serving on Repop, as well as Station Director. It was time to move on. Penelope Townes would be the shoo-in for Department Head; he would then be reporting to her. But he could live with that. After all, he'd be on Earth, she'd be in space. There was only so much she could do from orbit to control his actions. He'd learned that the hard way with Car-En.

"What's the matter?" asked Troy.

"Nothing, just a little nausea. I'll slow down a bit."

"We can take a break if you want. Put our feet in the sand." They passed a pile of rubble, perhaps once an oceanside resort. The salt air had long ago rusted away any steel, plaster had been washed away by rain, and valuables had been pillaged over the course of the Remnant Age. Only rock remained.

"Let's push on," Adrian said. "I'm eager to see the first site."

Townes might be trouble. They had a deal now, but would she honor it? He'd have to watch her closely. As for Manning, well...eventually Adrian would repay the bioskin tech for his betrayal. Manning had gotten the position at SecSys without Adrian's recommendation. No doubt he thought he was safe on the *Liu Hui*, but Adrian would find a way to get to him. Nobody crossed Adrian Vanderplotz and got away with it.

As for the bioskin, he wished he'd gotten a final reading confirming that Car-En was deceased. Her last biostat report had indicated perilously low blood sugar and unconsciousness. She'd had hours left to live, unless she'd gotten help. Though even if she'd found allies among the Harz villagers, what could they do to help her? As skillful as they were at forging steel, their practice of medicine was crude, completely devolved into superstitious folk remedies and useless ointments. Car-En was dead – he should stop worrying about it.

"Life on Earth," said Troy. "It will be an adjustment. But I could get used to this." He swept his hand in a broad gesture, taking in the sea, the sand, the inland salt marshes.

"It could be dangerous," Adrian said, gripping the steering stick more tightly.

"Really? I don't think so. We'll have a full medical team. And Campi Flegrei is sleeping. If she starts to wake up again, we'll have plenty of time to leave."

Adrian grunted, keeping his eyes ahead. It was a clear day, and he could see hills and the faint outlines of mountains beyond.

"Or do you mean animals?" said Troy. "There are probably some bears in the region, but I don't think they'll bother us, as long as we don't feed them. Poisonous snakes maybe…adders and vipers. But we'll have their genomes on file, and there should be a venom database somewhere. We'll be able to synthesize antidotes easily enough."

"I don't mean that," said Adrian. "I mean the villagers. They don't think the same way as we do. I'm not sure you understand that."

"But we're so far away…." Troy said.

"For now," said Adrian. He twisted the accelerator. The hovershuttle hummed loudly, speeding up. He was eager to reach the coordinates and explore the site of his new home.

CHAPTER THIRTY-ONE

Trond was happy to see a fire in the furnace. It had been cool for too long. He had warned Grundar, Jalmar, and Gregers that they would be back working the bellows soon. A younger boy, Pieter, would also be joining them. Jansen's youngest son had been lurking about the smithy since Trond had returned. When Trond had asked him if he would be willing to pump the bellows until his hands bled, Pieter had nodded eagerly. The boy had only nine fingers, but that would be enough to hold the bellows handles (or even a hammer, one day, if he stuck around). Trond liked him – Pieter was bright and sharp-eyed. It was he who had seen the gast steal Katja, on the night of Bjorn's Burning.

Trond's sister was home, and alive. Katja was still unconscious, lying in a cot in Ilsa's house. It pained Trond to see her, but Jense stayed by her side day and night, feeding her Ilsa's tonic. Jense swore that Katja was no longer possessed by the gast; he had seen its foul soul leave her body. The older smith pointed out that Katja's color was improving. Her cheeks were pinker, and the web of black lines beneath her skin was fading. Still, she slept, and Ilsa could not say when – or even if – she would awaken. At least the deep bite from Bár, Jense's sword, was healing.

Trond examined his worktable, considering where to start. Requests had piled up in his absence. Happdal needed nails, hammers, hinges, kitchen knives, and lengths of chain. There would be no godsteel forged today. That suited Trond well enough. In truth, he was a little tired. Too much excitement in the previous weeks. He was glad to be back in the smithy, and for the moment, glad to be alone. He picked up one of the smaller hammers, testing its weight. With his free hand he stroked his chin. His beard was still short, but growing in nicely.

He heard a knock, and opened the door. It was the sky woman, looking scrawny, dressed in baggy trousers and a loose blouse. Katja's clothes, perhaps – too large for her small frame.

Where was Esper? He did not know how to talk to Car-En without his brother around.

"May I entering?" she asked. Her Norse was halting but comprehensible, and she no longer spoke first in her own language. Trond stepped aside, holding the door open. Car-En looked around, her face illuminated by a shaft of sunlight lancing through a gap in the ceiling beams. Her eyes were light brown with a hint of green. Had they always been that color? Trond remembered them a shade darker.

"You have many tool," said the woman. She was carrying a small cloth bundle.

"Yes," Trond said, "and much work to do." He felt uncomfortable being alone with his brother's lover, despite the fact that he felt nothing toward her. Well, that was not quite true. He felt deeply uneasy in her presence.

"I am sorry to disrupt," she said. "I have request." She unwrapped the cloth bundle, revealing her silver suit, neatly folded. "Can you burn this? Needs a hot fire. Very hot."

Trond nodded. "Yes. I can do that. Next time I forge godsteel. Soon."

"The soonest the better," said the sky woman, looking at him intently. Yes, her eyes had definitely changed color. She rewrapped the bundle and thrust it toward him. "Thank you. It may make bad smell – do not breathe smoke."

She turned to leave, which relieved Trond, but as she opened the door he found himself asking a question. "Will you stay? In Happdal? You are welcome here, you know."

She looked down contemplatively. "Welcome by most. Not your mother."

Trond laughed. Perhaps the sky woman was not so strange after all. "Do not worry about Elke," he said. "She likes nobody, except for Esper – she barely tolerates her own husband and her other children. Just stay out of her way."

Car-En smiled, looking unconvinced, and left, closing the oaken door behind her. Trond carefully placed the bundle on his worktable and, in doing so, noticed something. He grabbed the object and ran to the door, flinging it wide open.

"Wait! Car-En! I have something that belongs to you!"

CHAPTER THIRTY-TWO

Car-En walked through the familiar beech wood, not far from the clearing where the Happdal villagers prepared for High Solstice. It was a good time to be alone. Even Esper was occupied with the Midsummer tasks: raising the maypole, building the bonfire, positioning tables and benches, setting out vast amounts of food. There would also be a Burning, but not (Car-En was relieved to learn) of a real person. An effigy of the gast, if Car-En had gotten the meaning right.

Life without her m'eye, and her kit, was difficult. She felt stupid – not sometimes, but *all* the time – and she didn't like feeling stupid. The villagers were patient with her (except for Elke, who mostly just ignored her), but she could tell they didn't think much of her. Except for Esper. He understood. He loved her, as much as she could tell. Certainly she'd given him her own heart, recklessly and perhaps unwisely. It all went together: loving Esper, burning her bioskin, deactivating her implant, removing her m'eye lenses, and vowing never to return to the *Stanford*. She was no longer an augmented cybernetic human being. She was just a woman, plain flesh and blood. She would live out the rest of her days, few or many, on Earth.

Car-En was slowly acclimating to daily life in the village. In the mornings she worked in the gardens alongside a group of older women who tolerated her inexperience. She was already making herself useful with simple jobs, like weeding and picking, and in time she'd learn the seasonal intricacies of planting and tending. In the afternoons she helped out wherever there was a job that needed doing: grinding rye kernels into flour at the watermill, milking cows at the dairy, even taking a turn pumping the bellows (though Trond didn't approve of this). She ended each day sore and tired, but she was gaining a reputation as a willing and cheerful – if somewhat inept – worker.

Now she walked alone in the woods, with a purpose. She intentionally made noise as she walked, stepping on dry branches, kicking rocks. They were out there, camouflaged in the foliage, watching her. She knew their tricks; she'd *been* one of them. But she wouldn't make a fool of herself, running around the forest yelling. They'd contact her when they were ready.

A tall, broad-shouldered woman stepped into the path, twenty meters ahead of her. Her bioskin shifted color, from muted greens and browns to its default shimmering silver. At ten meters, Car-En recognized her. Long, gray hair, green eyes. Penelope Townes.

"You should be careful with skins," said Car-En. "They can kill you."

"SecondSkin is in a world of trouble, believe me."

"The company?" Car-En asked. "Why?"

"We got a tip-off from an ex-employee. Vanderplotz got illegal access to your pharma implant via your bioskin kit."

"He nearly killed me," said Car-En. "I was in full insulin shock. I'm lucky to be alive."

"I know," said Penelope, furrowing her brow. "Do you want to prosecute? We don't have much of a case against him unless we can pull the data from your kit."

Car-En shook her head. "Too late for that. Besides, I don't care what happens to him. I'm not going back. But you should know that Adrian is a psychopath."

"Believe me, I know. And he knows that I know, which means that to some extent I can control him now. We didn't go public with the SecondSkin business—"

"You mean the *attempted murder*," Car-En interrupted.

"Yes. We went to Adrian directly. He's agreed to resign as Department Head, and he approved something on the Repop Council – something that needed his vote to pass."

"What's that?" asked Car-En, scanning the trees. She wondered suddenly if Penelope would try to *take* her back to the *Stanford*. As far as she knew, no one had defected to Earth from a ringstation, ever. Car-En touched the handle of her carbonlattice blade, which was tucked into a broad, deer-leather belt. Stolen by the white-haired man, the blade had made its way to Katja, then to Jense, then to Trond, and finally back to her.

"It's just me," Penelope said, glancing at the knife. "The proposal…. We sent a cleanup team to contain the radiation leak. Vanderplotz gave us the coordinates – you contacted him from near the cave. From there—"

"You already found it?"

"And contained it. It's done. We used lead foam, mostly, then several layers of aluminum foam over that – considering lead poisoning isn't really preferable to radiation poisoning. It's not a permanent fix, but it should last at least a hundred years. There's hardly any seismic activity in this area, so maybe longer. Anyway, the river water is now safe to drink. Safe for them, at least. Your own gut biome might have some adjusting to do."

"I'm pretty well-adjusted," said Car-En. She checked over her shoulder to see if anyone from the village had followed her, or had happened to take a walk along the same trail. "Look," she said, "I should get back. Is there anything else you wanted to tell me? Or ask me? I'm staying here – I'm sure of that."

"Your friends and family will miss you. And so will your fans. You know you had thousands of followers who were tracking your research? And I'm sure they're still interested. It's not too late to go public, you know. We may not be able to prosecute Adrian, but we can let the world know you're alive. It would mean burning a bridge with Vanderplotz, but I don't care about that."

"I appreciate that. But no – let's keep things the way they are. I don't want Adrian to know I'm alive."

"Fair enough," Penelope said. Her bioskin shimmered, shifting back to green and brown tones.

"Wait," said Car-En. "Tell my parents that I'm alive. Tell them I'm fine, and that I miss them. And tell Lydia the same. Do you know her?"

"Lydia Heliosmith? Yes."

"Tell them that I'm okay – but to keep it a secret. Will you do that?"

Penelope nodded.

"Hey, how did you get here? Did you walk from the mule station? That's a long way."

"Hovershuttle," said Penelope. "New tech out of Hair Lab, commissioned by Vanderplotz. Want to see it? It's parked behind those big rocks." Penelope pointed to a cluster of three giant granite blocks. Esper called them the Three Stones. Car-En hadn't realized how far she'd come along the trail.

"Can it carry more than one?" Car-En asked.

"Sure. Have you changed your mind?"

"No, but there's an interesting medical case here. Well, there are two, in fact." She considered trying to explain the white-haired man to Penelope, and the black egg-thing that had emerged from its mouth and somehow taken over Katja's body. Esper had a simple explanation: possession by the gast. But that obviously wasn't true. Maybe *Stanford* Medical could figure it out. Except that Elke would never let any of her children leave Happdal again. "There's a girl – Katja – who needs medical attention, but I don't think her family is going to let her out of their sight. But there's also a young man – his name is Per Anders – maybe you could take him back to the *Stanford*. I think he needs antifungal treatment, but it's a strange infection – nothing my kit could diagnose."

"Is he dangerous?" asked Penelope. "The radiation team has already gone home. I wasn't kidding when I said I was alone here."

"Not very. Not if you keep him fed."

"Does he speak the same dialect as the others?"

"He doesn't speak at all, at the moment. But I get the sense it's because of localized cognitive inhibition, not brain damage."

"From a fungus, you say." Penelope Townes looked worried.

"I'm pretty sure it's not contagious. You don't have to take him…but there's medical knowledge to be gained. And if he recovers…well, you'll have your own villager to study."

"Hmm," said Penelope. The older woman looked off into the trees, making some mental calculation. "Fine," she said. "Can you get him here tomorrow morning? This same spot? I can camp here tonight."

"I think so," said Car-En. "I'll try. If not, well, *bon voyage*. Have a safe trip home."

Car-En half walked, half ran back to Happdal. The Midsummer festivities had no doubt already started. Esper had also referred to the night as *Jonsok* – the festival had many names. She thought about Penelope, and Lydia, and Adrian, as she hopped along the trail toward home. Those three, and so many others, had loomed so large in her mind. Now they seemed like ghosts – even Penelope, whom she had just seen.

After a while, her thoughts drifted to a different topic: the feast. There would be fresh bread, and aged cheeses, and roasted fish, and sweet cream. And *öl*. Maybe she would get drunk and try to have a conversation with Elke. She laughed, imagining the scene. She was not entirely sure Elke would not have her killed in the coming weeks; the mother was not pleased with her son's choice of lover. Maybe Esper would protect her. Maybe she would die. At the moment, she didn't care. All she wanted was to get to the festival, and see the maypole dance, and hear the Midsummer hymn, and kiss Esper.

EPILOGUE

The crow pecked at the ground, tasting a flake of dried blood. The men had fought here; two of them, with their shiny sharp sticks. The crow had thought it might feast that day, but after the fight the larger man had carried the smaller one away, apparently to eat it. Selfish men, always stealing from crows.

What was this? Something had changed since the crow's last visit. Why were the trees black with webs? The crow looked for spiders, for they were good to eat, but saw none.

Were they webs? The black stuff came from a central source, a black mass that formed a small hillock, emanating warmth. It was alive, then. But what kind of thing? Black branches grew from the hillock, and climbed the nearby trees. Some of the black branches plunged into the ground, like roots. When the crow looked closer, it saw that each black branch was covered in smaller filaments. Definitely not a spider web, but not a plant either. Plants were not warm.

Was it edible? If so, the crow would feast, for there was a great deal of the stuff. It pecked at a narrow black filament, breaking it off. It tasted foul. No feast.

After eating a few more flakes of dried blood, the crow flew off. There was nothing of interest here.

In Ilsa's house, in the small sickroom, Katja opened her eyes.

ACKNOWLEDGMENTS

The following were helpful in writing this book: *The Long Ships* by Frans G. Bengtsson, a brilliant fictional account of Viking adventure; NOVA's *Secrets of the Viking Sword*, which provided inspiration for the Five Secrets of Godsteel; *The Last Apocalypse, Europe at the Year 1000AD* by James Reston, for Viking history and names; and Adrian (imprecisely) quotes C.S. Lewis's *The Last Battle*: 'By mixing a little truth with it they had made their lie far stronger.'

Without the encouragement of Kia Simon (my wife and first reader) and my daughter Tesla Rose, this book wouldn't exist. And the same is true of my parents, the two people in the world I most want to impress, even though they've always given their love and praise freely. I also owe thanks to other early readers, including Jason Kleidosty, Jason Wohlstadter, and Rob English. And thank you to Don D'Auria for taking a chance on this book, and to Josie Mitchell and everyone at Flame Tree who meticulously polished this manuscript (and indulged my desire to include a map).

FLAME TREE PRESS
FICTION WITHOUT FRONTIERS
Award-Winning Authors & Original Voices

Flame Tree Press is the trade fiction imprint of Flame Tree Publishing, focusing on excellent writing in horror and the supernatural, crime and mystery, science fiction and fantasy. Our aim is to explore beyond the boundaries of the everyday, with tales from both award-winners and original voices.

•

Other titles available include:

•

Join our mailing list for free short stories, new release details, news about our authors and special promotions:

flametreepress.com